For Bryan,
and Solo

Glory & Promise

Also by Kim Murphy

Promise & Honor
Honor & Glory

Glory & Promise

Kim Murphy

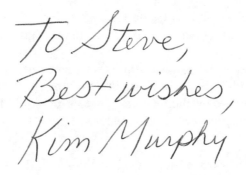

To Steve,
Best wishes,
Kim Murphy

Published by Coachlight Press

Published by Coachlight Press September 2005

Coachlight Press, LLC
1704 Craig's Store Road
Afton, Virginia 22920
http://www.coachlightpress.com

Printed in the United States of America
Cover design by Mayapriya Long, Bookwrights Design

This is a work of fiction. Names, characters, places, and incidents either are the product of the author's imagination or are used fictitiously, and any resemblance to any actual persons, living or dead, events, or locales is entirely coincidental.

Library of Congress Cataloging-in-Publication Data

Murphy, Kim.
  Glory & promise / Kim Murphy.
      p. cm.
  ISBN-13: 978-0-9716790-8-5
  ISBN-10: 0-9716790-8-8
  1. Reconstruction (U.S. history, 1865-1877)–Fiction. 2.
Fredericksburg (Va.)–Fiction. I. Title: Glory and promise. II. Title.
  PS3613.U745G58 2005
  813'.6–dc22

                           2005010620

Chapter One

Near Fredericksburg, Virginia
June 1865

*T*HE RAPPAHANNOCK RIVER CHURNED to rapids, and the waters kept rising. A woman shouted. Wil Jackson shielded his eyes from the lashing downpour. Trapped in the middle of the ford, a mulatto woman slapped a whip across the thighs of a mud-drenched horse. The horse strained in its harness, but the cart behind it failed to budge. Hysterical, she lashed the poor animal again. Eyes bulging, the horse only grew more nervous.

Damn—she'd likely drown if he didn't go to her aid. Gritting his teeth, he plunged into the chilly water. The water wasn't just cold, but downright bone-chilling. Already waist deep, he slogged toward the cart. The woman whipped the horse again. With the rising water and increasing current, he struggled to keep from being swept under. Wil reached the cart and pushed from behind as the horse pulled. The cart rocked forward, then back again, but remained mired in the mud.

No use. His feet slid from under him. Sucked under the water, he grasped the edge of the cart and righted himself. He extended a hand to help the woman from the cart.

Her eyes wide with fear, Lily thought he was a ghost. "Miss Amanda say dat you dead."

"I assure you I'm not, but if we don't get to the bank . . ." His hands were nearly frozen, and he barely managed to release the horse before it broke free of its own accord.

"I cain't swim, Mr. Wil."

She panicked with pounding punches and shrieks. With one arm securely wrapped around her waist, Wil suffered the blows. Only his grip on the horse's mane kept him from going under. The horse towed them toward the bank. Lily stopped fighting him, and he boosted her onto the horse's back. She leaned low against the animal's neck. The bank got closer. A swell hit Wil and tugged him under. He swallowed a mouthful of water. A hand gripped his forearm and helped him pull his head above the surface. Sputtering and coughing, he fought for breath.

Near the bank, the water seemed less deep. *An illusion.* An undercurrent tugged at his feet. His firm grip on the horse's mane kept him from being sucked under. They reached the slope of the bank, and the horse skidded in the mud, falling to its knees.

Lily sailed over the horse's head. Then nothing. A crosscurrent caught him, and only water surrounded him. Unable to breathe, he struggled to shove his head above water as the river swept him downstream. Although ordinarily a capable swimmer, he had never felt water this cold or swift running. He resisted the temptation to fight the current. He wasn't strong enough and went with the flow. On and on . . . His muscles ached and he choked and sputtered, fighting for each breath.

Stupid bastard—survive four years of war, only to die like this.

His lungs were exploding, and his mind went numb. A net of branches swept over him. His hands were frozen, but somehow he managed to curl his fingers around a swaying limb and latch on. Swirling water tugged on his body, nearly dragging him underwater again. Clinging to the branches, Wil pulled himself toward the bank. Progress was slow. His hands bled, but there was no pain from the brambles slicing into his skin—only the cold. He reached a pitch black pool and tumbled in head first.

At least he was out of the river current, but his arms grew heavier and heavier. He struggled to reach the surface. His shoulders ached. *Not much strength left.* He clutched a tree branch and hoisted his head and shoulders above water, gasping for air. Still clinging to the branch, he hauled himself to the shallow edge and wedged his body between tree limbs and rocks. Then he laughed.

No one would ever find him here. Why had he bothered? The instinct for self-preservation was often stronger than made sense. He only laughed harder at the irony.

Somewhere a fish splashed, and a hawk floated overhead. Buzzards would soon appear. He should have let go. It would have been easier that way. All sensation in his hands was gone, and his feet were numb. His mind drifted, and he thought of *her*. Wil regretted few things in life, except for burning the letter to her that had revealed his feelings. All he had left was to die.

Not dead yet. He reminded himself that Lily would have gone for help. He tried to stay awake, but his thoughts continued to wander. The hawk—he could almost imagine it lifting him toward the sky. Once he was airborne, the passage of time had little meaning. Voices whispered in the wind, and he heard someone call his name while he soared with the hawk.

"Wil . . ." It was *her*, and she sounded frantic. "Wil, please answer."

Another voice—a man's—called for the woman. "Alice?"

The hawk vanished, and Wil blinked, returning to earth. It wasn't *her*, but . . . "Alice . . ."

"Wil? Sam, fetch Ezra! Wil, where are you?"

Still sluggish, he breathed her name as Alice came into his view. "Thought I was dreaming."

"Wil . . ." Tears streaked her cheeks. She grasped his arm and tugged. With her help, he was able to drag himself from the murky pool, but he fell into the slosh of the bottomland. She wrapped her cloak around him and cradled him in her arms. "Sam's gone for help. Everything shall be all right now."

"Alice . . ."

She hushed him. "Save your strength."

But he had a rare need to talk. Four years of war, and nothing had been gained by it. Bad times weren't over yet. The South would likely be punished for the war. Then he spoke about the fall of Petersburg and his journey home. Black—she was wearing black. He clutched her skirt, and her green eyes met his. "Alice, why are you wearing black?"

With a laugh, Alice brushed away her tears. "There's plenty of time to explain."

His hand fell away and made a splash as it hit the muck. Her fingers stroked through his hair, and he closed his eyes. She hugged him tighter and whispered her love. Drawn to her warmth, he drifted until he heard voices. He recognized Sam and the elderly Negro servant, Ezra. Another man was with them—a tall blond-haired man. "Brigadier Jackson, I wish we could have met under better circumstances."

His mind was muddled. One of his men? Wil attempted to offer a hand, but it refused to move. He forced a laugh. "I'd shake your hand, but nothing seems to work right now."

"Don't worry, sir. I'm honored that I can help."

With a groan, the men lifted him from the muck and settled him on a blanket. Alice was beside him once more, gripping his hand. "Everything is going to be fine now," she said with firm conviction.

He couldn't feel her touch—not even her warmth. As the blanket was hoisted, he slipped into dreams of flying with the hawk.

Wagon wheels rolled up the tree-lined lane. Afraid of what she might discover, Amanda stepped onto the porch and placed a hand to her rounding belly. The baby kicked wildly, matching the anxious rhythm of her heartbeat. A blond-haired man sporting a moustache and riding a black thoroughbred accompanied the search party. Faces remained tense as she watched for any sign of hope. The men withdrew a blanket from the bed of the wagon. She gasped. It was weighted down with a body. *They had found Wil—dead.*

With a tear-streaked face, her sister joined the procession along with their servant, Lily, as if it were some sort of funeral march. Amanda clutched the porch rail to keep from falling until her knuckles turned white.

Then came the sound of excited women's voices. Drenched from head to toe, Alice was shouting at her, smiling and laughing. Her tears were from joy, not grief. "He's alive, Amanda. Wil's alive."

Had she heard right? Overwhelmed by the news, Amanda maintained her tight grip on the rail as the men carried the blanket inside. "Alice, you had best get out of those wet clothes."

Her sister frowned. "But Amanda . . ."

Amanda squeezed her arm. "Go, you won't be of much help to him if you catch your death of pneumonia. Lily and I will see to him. Besides, you have a fussy baby who needs to be fed."

Alice sent a fretful glance at the men proceeding to the back of the house. Resigned, she agreed and scooted from the parlor.

By the back bedroom door, Amanda met Sam and the blond-haired man, who had accompanied the search party, as they were leaving. "He was in the water for several hours," Sam whispered. "Sometimes, he makes sense, other times . . ."

Amanda nodded that she understood.

"I'll fetch a doctor."

"Take my mare," the blond-haired man offered. "She's fast."

"That's very generous of you, Mr. Chandler," Sam replied. "But I'm more comfortable riding my own horse. Thank you for your help."

Chandler? The name sounded familiar, but Amanda couldn't place where she had heard it. She'd fret about that later. "Make yourself at home, Mr. Chandler. I'll thank you properly after I see how Wil is faring."

He smiled in understanding, and Amanda stepped inside the bedroom. Shivering uncontrollably, Wil sat on the edge of the bed with disheveled hair and the blanket wrapped around him, while the servants, Lily and Ezra, towelled him off.

"Lily, if you could fetch extra blankets and some dry clothing—something of Sam's . . ."

"Straight away, Miss Amanda." Lily dashed from the room.

"As long . . . ," Wil said with a shudder, ". . . as it's not blue."

"Wil," Amanda snapped. "You're in no condition to be choosey." She approached the bed. "What have you gone done now?"

His teeth chattered. "Took an unexpected dip in the river." He held out ghostly pale, water-wrinkled hands.

She closed her hands over his and cringed. They were like blocks of ice. Repressing a shudder of her own, Amanda continued holding them, hoping to warm them. "Can you move your fingers?" He shook his head. After Sam's warning, she was relieved that he seemed lucid. "Can you feel anything?"

"No."

Definitely not a good sign. "You've got to stop this habit of rescuing damsels," she said, trying to make light of the situation.

"You're aware of my weaknesses."

"Do you know how worried Alice was?"

"Only Alice?" he asked, trembling.

"All right. I'll admit it, you had me fretting something fierce too. Lily came rushing in here . . ." She checked his pulse—slow and erratic. "Let's get you out of those wet clothes."

A devilish spark lit up in his dark eyes. "I thought you'd never ask, Amanda."

Leave it to Wil to say what was on his mind—no matter how close he might be to death's door. "Wil, please . . . be serious."

His gaze met hers. "I am."

At one time, his insinuation would have embarrassed her, but she dismissed the remark to his plunge into icy water. "Ezra . . ." The servant helped her as she tugged off Wil's drenched jacket and shirt. Aware the Nez Percé medicine pouch tied by a deerskin cord around his neck was a relic of his guardian spirit the mountain lion, she left it alone. A scar on his chest reminded her of the bullet that had nearly claimed his life during a battle in the Wilderness.

Lily returned with blankets and a bundle of clothing. Amanda reached for his trousers, then hesitated before turning away, leaving the task for the servants to finish. She chastised herself. Helping Wil change was not unlike the duties she had performed in the hospital during the war. But it *was* different with Wil. She had once cared for him—maybe deep down, she still did. Pretending to busy herself with gathering up the wet clothing in a neat pile, she chided herself once again for even thinking such a thing. He was married to Alice now.

When she turned around, Wil was wrapped in a pile of blankets. Beneath the woolen mound, his shivers remained visible. Amanda drew the rocking chair nearer to the bed. "Lily, if you can warm some broth, I'll wait here until Alice returns."

The servants left the room. Until the search party's return, she hadn't seen Wil since the previous Christmas in Petersburg. Using the same techniques she had learned early in the war, she had smuggled food to him and Alice in the war-starved city. Then after the city's fall, word had been sent by messenger that he had died as a prisoner in a Yankee hospital. Alice had resorted to wearing black, and not until Lily met him at the ford in the river had they discovered the truth. His prominent cheekbones were more pronounced than usual, and he seemed weary—like he had been through hell.

"Are you feeling any better?" Shivers were the only answer. She patted him on the shoulder, and the door creaked behind her.

"Amanda, how is he?"

She glanced over her shoulder at Alice, looking on with a worried frown. "Quiet."

"I'll sit with him now."

"Of course." Amanda got to her feet and wandered into the parlor. Seated in the green-velvet wing chair, Mr. Chandler stood as she entered. Because of his boyish-looking face, she guessed that he was in his mid-twenties, but his moustache with tipped up ends made him look years older. "I apologize, Mr. Chandler. I don't usually run out on guests like that. I'll fetch some tea now."

"Perfectly understandable under the circumstances, Mrs. Prescott, and there's no need. Your servant said that she would tend to the tea. I do admit that it's been quite sometime since partaking in such a delightful luxury."

Sam supplied her with most of her household goods, and she had forgotten that most Southerners would find such items unavailable to them. "Then I'm glad you can join us. We appreciate your help."

Taking her hand, he bowed and kissed it. "I was only too glad that I could be of service."

His accent was definitely Virginian. Relieved to be away from the bedroom, Amanda sat on the tapestry sofa. "Your name sounds familiar..."

"Douglas Chandler," he said, reseating himself in the wing chair. "My family is from Culpeper County. Perhaps you've heard of them?"

A memory triggered. "I recall meeting an Estelle Chandler before the war."

He gave a dazzling smile. "That charming woman is my sister."

"Then you're on your way home from the war?"

"No," he replied with a shake of his head. "My family home was burned to the ground by *Yankees*."

The way he said Yankees made her uneasy. "I'm sorry."

His sky-blue eyes grew fixed. "As am I."

"Where is your family now?"

He blinked. "Estelle is the only one left. She's staying with friends. I was on my way to see her when I happened by your husband and servant attempting to rescue Brigadier Jackson from the river. One of my boys would be most interested in meeting the general."

The general? And she had a feeling Wil wasn't the sort to make the transition to civilian life easily. "We're very fortunate that you chose this path today."

"A pleasure to be of service, ma'am." He stood. "But I should be leaving."

Amanda got to her feet. "Your tea . . ."

"I thank you for your generosity, but Estelle frets."

"I understand."

With a bow, he kissed her hand. His blue eyes sparkled, and Amanda accompanied him to the door, bidding him a good day. At the end of the brick walk, he untied the black mare from the rail and mounted. She thought it odd that a Southerner could afford such a flashy horse these days. She shrugged, and he galloped off in a trail of dust.

Neatly-pinned auburn hair had long since given way to stray locks. For a week, worry frowns had been evident on Alice's face as she kept her day-and-night vigil seated in the rocking chair beside the bed, holding Wil's hand.

"You need rest, Alice," Amanda insisted.

Her sister shook her head. "I can't leave. Not now."

"You're not going to do him one bit of good if you drop over from exhaustion. Let me sit with him for a while."

Alice looked in her direction but continued to clutch Wil's hand.

"I'll let you know if there's any change."

Reluctantly, Alice got to her feet and kissed Wil on the cheek. "I should check on Emma." She wrapped her arms around Amanda in a tired hug. "Thank you, Amanda."

As Alice left the room, Amanda seated herself in the freshly vacated rocking chair. Barely had Doctor Gordon pronounced that Wil would most likely be fine when pneumonia had set in. He had been bled and mustard plasters were applied to no avail. She wished her servant, Frieda, were still alive. The old Negro woman's medicinal knowledge had been well known throughout Stafford and Spotsylvania Counties. "Wil, it may not be one of Frieda's medicines, but if you drink the willow bark tea I've made, it'll help the pain."

Pillows were propped behind his back to help him breathe, but with each breath, he struggled.

She placed the cup to his lips and helped him drink. He laid his head to the feather pillow and closed his eyes. Relieved that he was resting, Amanda settled back in the rocking chair, but before long, she heard him stir.

"Amanda . . . I knew you'd come."

His eyes were glazed, and she pressed a hand to his forehead. "You're feverish."

"I was afraid."

Wil Jackson admitting to fear? "You've been through quite an ordeal. It's a perfectly natural reaction."

With an intoxicated-looking smile, he shook his head. "I meant the letter. You were right. I was afraid to mail it, so I burned it."

She swallowed hard—the letter where he had admitted his feelings for her. But that was before she had married Sam. "It's not proper to think of such things."

"The present doesn't change the past."

"That may be, but . . ."

"*You're* afraid."

"I am most definitely not afraid," she protested louder than she had meant. She lowered her voice. "Wil, nothing good can come from dredging up old memories."

"I beg forgiveness. I didn't mean to embarrass you . . ."

Amanda . . . Even though he hadn't said her name, she heard it all the same. Why had she been sharp? The rude comment had been his fever speaking. Something pressed her. She *had* to know what he had written in the letter. "Wil . . ." She cleared her throat, but the question wouldn't come. "We shouldn't even be having this conversation."

"Whatever you say . . ." With a throaty cough, he sat up and a hand flew to his chest.

"You need to take it easy."

"Can't." Gasping for breath, he latched onto the bedpost and stood. "Got to inspect the line."

"Wil, you're not well enough to be up and about." Amanda grasped his elbow.

He stared at her as if not really seeing her, then he blinked. He stroked her cheek. "I knew you'd come."

She tightened the grip on his arm and guided him back to bed. Thankful that he offered no resistance, she watched him as he closed his eyes. *What would life have been like if she had chosen . . .* Amanda reached for his hand, halted in midair, then thought better of touching him, and sat in the rocking chair.

Folding her hands on her lap, she began a mindless back and forth motion. *Regret?* She chastised herself for thinking such a thing. But if Wil had mailed the letter. . . *If*—he hadn't, and she had nearly taken advantage of his feverish state. She was better off not knowing the contents.

Another week passed. Though Alice spent most of her waking hours by Wil's side, Amanda continued to relieve her sister from time to time. His fever had finally broken the day before. At last, the worst was behind them, and Alice agreed to get a good night's sleep. On the sultry late-June morning, Amanda brought a breakfast tray to the back bedroom.

Propped with pillows behind his back, Wil sat up. His coal black eyes were clear but remained bloodshot. He breathed easier, and hopefully, he would regain some weight on his lean frame.

"You're looking a mite better today." She set the tray on the bed beside him. "Now you need to get your strength back. Eat something."

With a forced grin, he saluted. "Yes, ma'am. You always were good at giving orders. Amanda . . ." He picked up a piece of dry toast, stared at it as if solid food might be less than agreeable, then took a hesitant bite. "If I said anything to embarrass you, you have my apology. I was confused."

So he remembered mentioning the letter. "I understand. Apology accepted," she replied weakly. To ease her discomfort, she parted the lace curtain and opened the window wide to rid the room of its stuffiness. "We may actually get some rain today. Lord knows that we can use it." She turned.

He eyed her quizzically.

"If there's something that would be more to your liking, I can fetch it."

Amanda collected the tray, but Wil grasped her forearm. His gaze met hers. "You're sorry that I returned."

She glanced at his hand wrapped around her arm, then at him. He let go. "Don't be foolish. When I thought you were dead . . ."

"Amanda, I sincerely meant my apology. I wouldn't do anything to jeopardize our friendship."

She believed him. So why did she get that gnawing feeling when he was near? "We've been friends a long time," Amanda agreed. "And I hate to admit it, but you probably know me better than any of my women friends."

A devilish spark entered his eyes. "Or Sam?"

It was just like Wil to say one thing one minute, then the exact opposite the next. He must be feeling better. Amanda gritted her teeth. "I suppose that depends on what you mean by *knowing*."

"Fine, now if you don't leave the room, we shall become more familiar than I think you care to."

"Wil . . ."

He latched onto a bedpost and stood. "Can't help it. I need to use . . ." Slightly unsteady on his feet, he gestured to the chamber pot.

"Oh . . ." She felt warmth rise in her cheeks. He was *definitely* feeling better. His wicked little grin warned her that he was enjoying her discomfort. "Are you well enough . . . I mean, if you need . . . assistance . . ."

He laughed. "As much as I relish the idea of your assistance, I think I can manage on my own."

"I meant that I would fetch Ezra," she stated firmly.

He only laughed harder. "You're not an innocent maiden, Amanda. Your *enceinte* state is proof of that."

She raised her hands in disgust, but before she could turn, he lowered his head and clutched the bedpost. He *did* need help, and she had never thought of Wil as the modest sort. "I wish you would stop pretending that you're all right when you're clearly not."

"A habit of mine, but I am capable of tending to necessities. Now if you don't wish to be flustered further, I suggest that you leave." He reached for the buttons of his trousers.

Definitely not modesty. In frustration Amanda yanked the door shut on her way out.

"Amanda, what's wrong?" At the end of the hall Alice stood with clasped hands and a worried frown.

"Your husband—that's what's wrong," Amanda grumbled. "He's insufferable, and I don't know whatever possessed you to marry him."

Alice's face brightened. "Wil must be feeling better."

"Smirk if you like, Alice, but . . ." Doubting that Wil had ever told her sister about the letter, Amanda fell silent. Some things were best left unsaid. "Never mind, it wasn't important. Why don't you go in and see him? He's feeling better this morning."

"Thank you for your help."

Suddenly uneasy, Amanda nodded. "It's the least I could do."

"Amanda, are *you* all right?"

"Just a little tired." She patted Alice on the back of her hands. "Now go see Wil." Why wouldn't the ache go away? The war was over, and now she'd have to see them together—strolling arm in arm. Wil had been right. She deplored the feeling and hated the way it gnawed at her inside, but she *was* sorry that he had returned.

After nearly a month of fighting off his bout of pneumonia, Wil slowly began to regain his strength. Though he was still weak, Alice had returned to sharing his bed, and they had made up for the four-month separation. A lot had happened in that time—his wounding during the fall of Petersburg, his stay in a Yankee hospital, his survival of the end of the war, only to nearly reach his destination and almost drown in the Rappahannock River. For the time being, he had decided to move his family back across the river to Alice's home before the war.

On the porch, Alice hugged Amanda and her mother goodbye.

Impatient that farewells were taking longer than he had anticipated, Wil checked the only possession left to his name—his pocket watch. "You're only going to Fredericksburg."

As he went down the steps, three horses trotted into the farmyard. Flanked by two other soldiers in blue, Sam dismounted and tied his red horse to the rail. While Sam's habits had been to return home to Amanda every few days, the fact that he was accompanied by a couple of his men led Wil to believe he was making an official call. *They were coming to arrest him.* "Sam . . . ," Wil said evenly.

"Jackson." Definitely not a social call, or Sam would have used his given name.

Alice stepped between them. "Please Sam. You were friends before the war."

Wil grasped her arm and gently drew her aside. "I won't hide behind a woman's skirt. What is it you want, Prescott?"

Sam's forehead wrinkled as he withdrew an official-looking paper from his frock coat. "Lieutenant Greer was carrying the order," Sam said, indicating the red-haired officer with a drooping moustache to his left, "but I thought it would be easier if I delivered it personally."

The paper wasn't an arrest warrant, but the Oath of Loyalty, swearing allegiance to the United States. Wil studied the document.

"Well?"

Watching Wil closely, Greer rested a hand on the butt of his pistol, his fingers twitching nervously.

"I'm unarmed, Lieutenant."

Sam gave his officer a hard stare. "At ease, Greer. The general won't give us any trouble."

At the mention of Wil's former rank, Greer sent him a harsh glare but complied with the order.

"I'll sign it."

Breathing out in relief, Sam gestured in the direction of the house. "Shall we go inside?"

Sam and the lieutenant followed him to the study, while the women lingered outside the door. Wil never thought there would be so much interest that he signed a piece of paper. He dipped the pen and scrawled his signature at the bottom. "What about a pardon?"

"The government isn't in any hurry to hand out pardons to former generals, but . . ." After tucking the paper in a pocket, Sam closed the door to keep the women from eavesdropping. "I can put in a good word, which may help."

Suddenly curious, Wil leaned back in the chair with amusement. "In exchange for?"

"For the most part, the area has been peaceable since the surrender—a few barroom brawls, petty thievery, only a few scuffles between Negroes and whites. I'd like to keep it that way."

"What exactly are you asking me to do?"

"Wil, you could still be tried for treason."

The comment brought satisfaction to Greer's face, and Wil had a fair idea what the red-haired lieutenant thought would be appropriate justice for former Confederate officers. "I'm aware of that. Get to your point."

Sam ordered the lieutenant to leave them in privacy. He watched the subordinate officer exit, then continued, "If you see or hear anything out of the ordinary, report it."

"And what would you regard as out of the ordinary? You Yanks have taken everything. I wouldn't know what is customary anymore."

"You will when you hear or see it."

Straightening in the chair, Wil laughed. "You're asking me to spy. Sorry, Prescott, the fact that the war is over doesn't change who I am, and I won't become a turncoat for the likes of you or anyone else."

As if expecting the answer, Sam nodded. "Then you should take Alice's advice and head for Canada."

A number of former Confederate officers and politicians had already fled the country. "I won't run."

Sam's brow furrowed. "Suit yourself, but if we're given orders to arrest Confederate officers . . ."

Wil stood. "I won't cause any trouble, Sam."

The worry lines faded from Sam's face. "I wasn't fretting about that, Captain."

Captain—his rank before the war, when they had served together in the New Mexico territory. There had always been respect between them. He gave Sam a salute. "Lieutenant . . ." But New Mexico had been a long time ago, and his military career had faded with the Confederacy.

Chapter Two

*W*ITH SOME TREPIDATION, Alice returned to the house she had shared with Mama in Fredericksburg. Fortunately, Mama had stayed behind with Amanda. As things stood, she had no idea how they were going to feed themselves without Amanda's help, but with Wil regaining his health, the time had come to move from under her sister's protective wing. At least Wil had relented and allowed Amanda to pack a few provisions as well as accept the loan of a horse and a rickety buggy.

As they traveled through the streets of charred houses and buildings reduced to rubble, Alice noticed that little had changed since she had evacuated the city, except for the men in blue uniforms. She had come to welcome Sam into the family, but seeing so many Yankees wandering through her hometown made her uneasy.

Among those clad in blue were men in tattered gray or filthy butternut. One man in bare feet swept the steps of a shop, while another sat outside with a vacant stare. On the far corner, a former Confederate captain wore a shabby yellow sash. When two Yankees approached the officer on horseback, Wil narrowed his eyes and slowed the buggy.

Alice hooked her arm through Wil's. The Yankees dismounted and in an overly loud voice one said to the officer, "Perhaps, you haven't heard . . ." He produced a pair of shears. *Snip*—a button popped from the man's uniform. Then another, and another.

She felt Wil's muscles tense, ready to spring into action. "No, Wil. Those are the regulations now. There's nothing we can do."

Refusing to be humiliated by the Yankees actions, the captain retained his straight, dignified stance. The buggy rounded the corner, and Wil's muscles gradually relaxed. Thankful that he hadn't tried to intervene, Alice blew out a breath. She was even more grateful that he no longer possessed any Confederate insignia for he'd be fool enough to wear it in public for the Yankees to see, and she doubted he would take their actions quietly.

They traveled another few blocks before Wil halted the buggy outside the boarded-up, red brick house. Two and a half years had passed since Yankees had looted the house. What they hadn't vandalized had been ravaged during the battle. At least on this homecoming, she had Wil with her. He tied the horse and helped her from the buggy, then took their sleeping seven-month-old daughter, Emma, out of her basket and held her in his arms.

As they went up the walk, Alice gripped Wil's arm. Beneath their feet, the steps creaked. She held her breath when Wil opened the door and followed him inside. The house was vacant of furnishings. Wallpaper peeled, and plaster cracked from the walls in places. Still, this return to Fredericksburg was less traumatic than after the battle, when she had discovered a dead Yankee on the back porch.

"I'll bring things inside." Wil placed Emma in her arms.

"Wil, it may not be much, but it's ours."

"If we can pay the back taxes," he reminded her and vanished through the door.

The entire trip from Amanda's had been traveled in near silence. She suspected the burden of the loss of his career and how he would support them weighed on his mind. A squeak and rustling sound came from within the walls. *Rats.* She shivered. Would they be reduced to eating rodents as Sam had in Libby prison?

"Well, Miss Emma, should we set about to making this place liveable again?" she said, attempting to sound cheerful.

For the next three days, she did nothing but clean and scour. Like the time when the Yankees had pillaged her home, she stuffed a burlap bag with straw for a bed. Wil made some service-able furniture from odds and ends. Their makeshifts would suffice until they could afford better. Still, she needed cloth for mending, and the food supply was already getting low.

Wil searched for employment, but the answer was the same wherever he went—no money to pay wages. Alice quickly learned not to ask him how things went. Despair reflected in his eyes, and he'd retreat to the study, where he'd sit in the darkness for hours at a time.

After a week of the same pattern, she followed him and lit the tallow candle that sat on the boards he used for a desk. "Wil, I know you don't like the idea, but during the war, I darned socks and mended uniforms to make ends meet. I could also sew shirts and trousers."

"How would that solve anything?" he replied evenly. "No one has the money to pay you."

"The Yankees do."

His black eyes seethed. "I'll not have my wife playing servant to those scoundrels."

"Do you regard Sam in the same light?"

The question only infuriated him further, and he stormed from the room. The front door slammed on his way out. Resolved to give her idea a try, Alice decided that she would borrow enough money from Amanda to buy some cloth. Wil would eventually come around, when he found an occupation to replace his military career.

His lungs were exploding, and his mind went numb. Branches swept over him, and he managed to latch on. He pulled himself toward the bank. Wil didn't recall reaching the pitch black pool, but he had wedged himself between the tree limbs and rocks. There he had waited for help that he never expected to arrive. But Alice had discovered him half dead in the muck. To what end? If he were ten years younger, he'd head west and start over again. Instead, he had taken to spending his days in the tavern, sometimes playing a few hands of poker. Right now, it was the only source of income he had, but he had forbidden Alice from taking money from the Yankees. Why should he excuse himself?

"Sir . . . Brigadier Jackson?"

The voice intruded on his thoughts, and he refocused on the chatter and laughter of drunken voices in the tavern. A gruff-looking young man with stubble on his chin stood beside the table. The boy's patched jacket and threadbare trousers reminded him of Confederate soldiers wearing rags in the field. "Were you in my command?" Wil asked.

"No, sir. Lieutenant Chandler said that I might find you here. Do you mind if I join you?"

Wil motioned for him to be seated, and the bartender brought the young man a beer. After taking a swig from the mug, he introduced himself, "Jesse Morgan."

Unfamiliar with the name, Wil shook his head. "Should I know you?"

Jesse gulped down the beer and wiped foam from his wispy moustache. "I believe you knew my mother, sir." He slid a daguerreotype across the table.

The photograph must have been the boy's family—three adolescent boys, one being Jesse and the oldest, a girl in pigtails, and a woman in her thirties. Though she wasn't the stunning belle he remembered from the summer while on leave from West Point, she had maintained an elegant beauty. *Caroline* . . . "Your mother is Caroline Holmes of Charleston?"

"She *was* my mother. She died two months before the surrender."

"I'm sorry to hear that. She was a fine woman."

"That she was." Jesse's gaze met his. "If I'm not mistaken, you once courted her."

"I did," Wil admitted, "but that was over twenty years ago."

The boy's fixed stare failed to waver. "I was born in May of '45, sir."

The date meant nothing, then it dawned on Wil—the summer he had courted Caroline was 1844. "What *are* you trying to insinuate, Morgan?"

"Nothing." But Jesse kept glaring.

Wil's mind was trying to make sense of the jumbled mess going through his head. To celebrate his time home as a cadet, there had been many parties and dances. Even now, he recalled Caroline's flirtatious smile while playing the pianoforte. Then came the evenings when she would slip away from the ever-watchful eyes of her parents, only for him to feel the sting of her hand when he got too forward. Before the summer was over the lash of her hand came less and less often. But the summer ended all too soon, and he had returned to the Point. Wil sucked in his breath. "Why . . ." Swallowing hard, he clenched his right hand. This boy—*this man*—couldn't be his son. "If what you're suggesting is true, then why didn't she ever tell me?"

Unsympathetic, Jesse remained unyielding. "At least you don't deny the disposition of your courtship. My mother was afraid that you'd be dismissed from the Point, *sir*."

Behavior unbecoming of an officer and a gentleman would have been grounds for certain dismissal. He should have guessed Caroline had been unselfishly thinking of his well-being. If only he had taken the time to do the same for her.

"She knew you were commanding a South Carolina brigade."

Wil closed his eyes. *All these years . . .* She had kept track of him, and he had given her little thought. He reopened his eyes. "If you have come for money, the war has taken nearly everything."

"Money," Jesse grumbled. Standing, he shoved the chair back and drew a pistol. "Actually, I've been debating whether or not I should kill you."

Several patrons shrieked, and Wil got to his feet. "Jesse, if what you claim is true, then you are within your right to correct the disgrace that I've brought to your mother's name. By all means— shoot."

The pistol wavered slightly. "A mighty slick bastard, aren't you?"

"Considering the circumstances, your choice of words seems inappropriate."

Jesse's finger hovered over the trigger, but he lowered the gun. "Chandler told me you'd be unafraid." Turning, he shook his head. "I can't. This isn't the battlefield."

As always, Wil's initial reaction was to turn his back from the

problem and let Jesse walk away. *What if he spoke the truth?*
"Jesse . . ." The boy faced him once more, and Wil stumbled over
his words. "Your mother—she deserved more than I could have
ever given her."

"She didn't feel that way."

The last thing he wanted was forgiveness from Caroline. "Your
mind must be full of questions. I know mine is. Let's discuss this
in a reasonable manner." As Jesse reseated himself at the table,
Wil did the same.

"Jesse . . ." A yellow-haired man joined them at the table with
a painted whore draped from his arm. "I bet the boys that you
didn't have the grit to shoot him." He flashed a toothy grin and
shoved out a hand. "It's an honor, Brigadier Jackson. Our previous
meeting was less than ideal. Lieutenant Chandler at your service."

Previous meeting? It dawned on him. Chandler had been in the
rescue party fishing him from the river. A feeling stopped Wil cold.
The war's aftermath was far from over.

A pounding on the front door woke her in the middle of the night.
Alice rubbed away the sleep but was unable to see through the
darkness. As the hammering grew louder, she lit a lamp. Wil's face
was squashed in a sound sleep against the pillow. As had been his
pattern for the past fortnight, he had returned home in the early
morning hours, smelling of liquor and cigars.

She shook him. "Wil . . . there's someone at the door."

Massaging his head with a groan, Wil squinted his eyes.

"Never mind," Alice grumbled. She grabbed a cotton robe and
rushed downstairs. Before the door, she hesitated. What if it was
Wil's drinking buddy, Mr. Chandler? Though the blond-haired
man was always dashing and polite, something didn't set quite
right about his charming smile. Taking a deep breath to calm herself, she opened the door to a bucktooth Negro boy.

Nostrils flaring, he gasped for breath and fidgeted with a straw
hat. "Miss Amanda gonna have her baby."

Alice pressed a hand to her chest. "But she's not due for another two months."

"Don't matter none," he wheezed. "She havin' it now."

"What are you doing dallying around here? Amanda and the baby are at risk. Fetch Doctor Gordon."

The boy shook his head. "Da doctor out on a call. Cain't find him."

"Oh no . . . you return to the doctor's and wait for him. I'll go to Amanda."

"Yes'm."

Alice closed the door and turned. Though he was fully dressed, Wil leaned against the bannister on the stairs as if he might retch. "While you change," he said, clearing his throat, "I'll hitch the buggy. It's not safe for a woman to travel alone at night." He swayed as he descended the stairs and nearly stumbled at the bottom.

"You're as drunk as a fiddler's bitch. I'll manage on my own, thank you."

She strode past him, but he grasped her arm with his fingers digging in. "I'll accompany you."

Amanda needed her, and this was no time to quarrel. "Suit yourself." She jerked free of his grip and rushed to the bedroom. After changing, she bundled up her black-haired daughter for the cool fall air and went outside.

Walking in less of a stagger than before, Wil led the horse and buggy from the barn. After securing Emma's basket, he helped Alice into the buggy. He climbed in beside her, and cued the horse to a fast trot. "Faster . . . " Alice insisted.

"It's not safe."

"I'm worried about Amanda." She crossed her arms and sat back. As the lights of Fredericksburg vanished into the background, only a lantern broke through the darkness. Amanda needed her, and at this slow-paced clip, it would take forever to reach her. "Can't you send the horse a little faster?"

"No." His tone sent a final warning.

Hopefully, a Yankee patrol wouldn't cross their paths and arrest them for some trumped-up violation. Then again, they'd likely be understanding, since Amanda was the colonel's wife, and by the time they arrived, she would be holding a spry new baby in her arms. "Wil, tell me what's going on?"

"Except for Amanda having a baby, I didn't know anything was going on."

Alice raised her voice as they traveled along the deserted road. "You stay out until the wee hours, and return home smelling like the tavern. Even during the war, I could guess where your mind was at, but now . . . I'm at a loss." He grunted but offered no explanation. She hesitated before asking the next question. "Is there another woman?"

His answer was a long time in coming. "No."

She let out a relieved breath. "Then it's because of the loss of your military career." His head shook. "Then what?"

"I can't answer that—not now."

So there *was* something that he was keeping from her. "Wil . . ."

He rubbed his temple as if his head ached as a result of his intemperance. "Alice, I said—not now."

Again his tone had been final. The night passed, and the red glow of morning arrived before they reached the farm. Wil brought the buggy to a halt outside a whitewashed house. Alice clambered from the buggy before he could help her down. "Wil, can you bring Emma?" He nodded and she dashed along the brick walk and up the stairs to the door.

A stout nut-brown midwife named Bess answered Alice's knock. "Thank goodness you here, Miss Alice. Miss Amanda ain't had the baby yet. She be callin' for you." The hefty woman gave the disheveled Wil an appraising glance, then stepped aside and allowed them to enter.

Inside, Sam paced the parlor floor. The stubble on his chin and bloodshot eyes warned Alice that he had been crisscrossing the floorboards most of the night. "I can't lose another," he muttered.

Whether he meant another child or wife, she was uncertain. During the war, he and Amanda had lost their son to scarlet fever, and four years earlier, his first wife had died in childbirth. Since Wil had suffered similar losses before marrying her, Alice hoped he was lucid enough to be of some comfort to Sam. As she climbed the stairs to the bedroom, she overheard the men talking—not about Amanda or fatherhood, but she thought she heard the name of Douglas Chandler.

"Amanda . . ." Alice crossed the floor and grasped her sister's hand.

An exhausted smile appeared on Amanda's face. "I'm going to die, Alice."

"Nonsense," Alice said, putting on a brave front.

Amanda's eyes rolled up, and she laid her head to the feather pillow with a groan. Bess grasped a cloth, wetted it from the porcelain pitcher, and placed it on Amanda's sweaty forehead. "Miss Alice," Bess said, in a low voice so Amanda wouldn't overhear, "your hands smaller dan mine. Maybe you can shift da baby so it can come out. We lose both of dem if da baby ain't born soon."

Lose Amanda? How often had she counted on her sister being there for her? *Stop thinking of yourself.* Alice lifted Amanda's stained nightdress. Between her sister's legs, blood and feces caked her pubic hair and covered her thighs. Transfixed by the tiny leg poking from the birth canal, Alice froze. A breech birth.

Amanda's birthing pain ended, and she let out a weary breath. "Alice . . . , " Amanda whispered.

In the hospitals, Alice had witnessed more than her fair share of maimed men. She shouldn't find the sight of blood so unsettling. *But this was her sister*. She had to do something to help but was unable to move.

"Alice . . ." At the sound of Amanda's weak voice, she blinked. The baby had made no progress. "Will you care for Rebecca?"

Sam's daughter from his first marriage—but she wasn't about to let Amanda die. "Amanda, how long have you been trying to have the baby?"

"Already a day, ma'am," Bess answered.

A day. Like when she had tended Wil after he had been wounded in the Wilderness, her duty was to remain brave. She had to do something. *But what?* Bess had suggested that she might be able to shift the baby. She knelt and wrapped a hand around the baby's leg. With Amanda's next birthing pain, Alice tugged gently. Her brow furrowed, and Amanda whimpered, but the baby made no headway. Bess sponged away Amanda's sweat. As Alice watched the pudgy hands make soothing, circling strokes, she examined her own hands—calloused but slender.

Alice followed the tiny leg. Inside the warm birth canal, another leg was tucked underneath. She gently straightened it, and with Amanda's next birthing pain, most of the baby popped out. A boy. His head came next. He wasn't breathing. *Don't panic.* Neither was Amanda's first son when she had helped deliver him. But this baby was so tiny, he easily fit in her hand. She grabbed a clean linen and swabbed out his nostrils, then rubbed him, trying to warm him. Nothing. He didn't move.

"My baby . . ."

Unwilling to give up, Alice continued massaging his blue arms and legs. *Breathe* . . . She heard Amanda wail. *He wasn't dead.* She massaged harder, but the baby's flesh remained cold.

Bess gathered up the baby and placed him in Amanda's waiting arms. Cradling the limp form, she put him to her breast and tried to get him to suckle. Alice sank to the floor. Bess grasped her arm and helped her to a chair. She dissolved into tears. "You done everthin' you could, Miss Alice. He born too soon an' you save Miss Amanda."

But she wasn't crying for Amanda's loss. Ashamed of her weakness, Alice was afraid for herself. With the end of the war, they had anticipated a new beginning. Her whole world was disintegrating, and she feared for herself.

The nip of October was in the air. Along with the passage of seasons, Wil was no closer to learning whether Jesse Morgan's insinuations were the truth. Across the road from the tavern, he checked his pocket watch. In approximately ten minutes, Douglas Chandler would arrive for another night of drinking and gambling against the Yankees. He took a deep breath and strode for the tavern.

Before he reached it, a frantic mulatto woman tugged on his arm. "Mr. Wil . . ."

But the rest of Lily's jumbled words were lost to her overwrought state, and he thought of when he had nearly drowned in the river.

"Miss Amanda . . ."

"Amanda." He grasped Lily's arm.

"She in da shanty village. A white woman ain't got no business dere. She goin' to get hurt."

As Chandler entered the tavern, he nodded to Lily. "I'll fetch my horse."

After retrieving his horse, he followed Lily to the shanty village. South of Fredericksburg, makeshift cabins and mud huts covered the countryside. Nearly two years before the same location had been the winter quarters for the Army of Northern Virginia. Here—he had brought Alice to sing and dance, helping everyone escape the ravages of war for a little while.

Outside a wood hut with gaping holes between the boards, he recognized a familiar red stallion. At the back of the buggy, dressed in black, Amanda ladled soup and passed out bread. Though many of the Negroes gathered around sent suspicious stares, women with small children took advantage of her assistance. Like the time during the war when she had smuggled blockaded medical supplies for sick and wounded soldiers, she was helping those in need. Dismounting his horse, Wil approached her.

She glanced around. "Wil, what are you doing here?"

"Lily was worried."

"Fiddlesticks." Continuing to scoop out soup, she forced a smile. "There are hungry people to feed, and I have food to give. I've got some cloth in the buggy for mending and next time, I'll bring books for schools."

Wary faces pressed closer. Wil grasped her elbow, and she dropped the ladle to the pot. "Amanda, it'll be dark soon. It's not safe here for a woman."

"Wil . . . I need to be useful."

"Then come back during the day. I'll escort you."

This argument seemed to sway her. She nodded. Even Lily sighed in relief. Wil helped her gather her supplies together and loaded it in the buggy. After tying his dapple-gray mare to the back, he climbed in beside her and cued Amanda's red stallion to a trot. Tense men stepped out of their way, and Amanda sat back in silence.

"Amanda..."

"Please, no lecture."

"All right, no lecture. You knew exactly what you were doing just as you did when you smuggled supplies for me during the war."

"Thank you for understanding." She fell silent again and a mile passed before she resumed speaking, "Alice says you're having difficulty with the transition to civilian life."

He slowed the stallion to a walk. "Did she put it that politely?"

"No," Amanda admitted. "But I also don't believe that you've suddenly resorted to gambling as a way of life."

"Then you don't know me as well as you think you do."

"Stop it, Wil! Don't lie to me!"

She knew him better than—anyone—including Alice. But it wasn't something he could openly admit. "What else is someone with my military experience and suddenly no career left *supposed* to do?"

"You were trained as an engineer at West Point," she suggested.

"And nearly failed. Why do you think I was assigned to the infantry?"

"Wil, you were almost dismissed the first year due to demerits. John took some on your behalf to keep that from happening, but you did *not* nearly fail."

He should have known that her first husband had told her about their experiences at the Point. Over the years, they had come to know each other *too* well. By nightfall, they reached Fredericksburg. Moonlight illuminated dreary chimneys and buildings still shattered by war. He halted the buggy out front of the brick house that he shared with Alice. After climbing down, he helped Amanda. For a brief moment, she was in his arms. She felt good. But he had to keep those thoughts to himself. So many secrets—he could no longer keep track of them.

As they went up the walk, Alice stepped onto the porch. "Amanda..."

"I was at the shanty village. Wil was kind enough to escort me here."

Alice looked in his direction. "How did you know she was there?"

"Lily told me."

"And Lily found you—let me guess . . ." Tapping an impatient foot, Alice crossed her arms. "At the tavern."

"Alice," Amanda interrupted, "some tea would be lovely right now."

"Of course, Amanda."

As Alice turned, Wil sent Amanda a thankful glance for intervening. And true to her word, Amanda made the trek from her farm to the shanty town twice a week. The residents grew less suspicious, and her mood brightened from helping those in need. Alice accompanied them on a couple of occasions, but with an upcoming dance, women had requested new dresses, and her sewing duties required her to answer constant demands from customers.

On a fine Indian summer day, two weeks later, the shanty village faded into the background. "Wil, stop the buggy," Amanda said with a smile.

Wil hadn't seen her smile since losing her baby. He clambered from the buggy, then helped her down. As he secured the stallion to a sycamore tree, she strolled along the edge of the river. Removing his hat, he joined her on the rocks near the bank.

She lifted her face to the sun, seeming to relish in the warmth. "I thought all of our problems would be over when the war ended."

"In many ways, it was only the beginning."

Raising her black skirt, Amanda scrambled over the rocks to a sandy edge by the river. She stumbled and skidded in the dirt, but he grasped her elbow and kept her from falling. "I was naive."

He glanced out to the river. Unlike the day that he had nearly drowned, the Rappahannock waters were peaceful. "Naive?"

"You heard me correctly. Not only was I naive, I was a fool. The war made us delay any thoughts for tomorrow, but if we didn't resolve issues back then, we're left facing them now."

It was uncharacteristic for her to speak in riddles. Totally perplexed, he met her gaze and asked, "What issues?"

Suddenly red faced, she shook her head. "Forgive me for bringing the subject up. It wasn't proper."

"Proper? Amanda, we've been friends for years." But there was one topic they could never broach. *The letter...* If only he had mailed it, she would have never married Sam. So close, yet so far away. He nodded in understanding.

"Wil, I think it's best if you don't accompany me anymore, unless Alice is along." Her skirts rustled, and tears streaked her cheeks as she dashed past him to the buggy.

So he wasn't the only one who felt the tension. The Rappahannock waters churned, carrying him under. Sputtering and gasping for breath, he managed to put his head above water. At the end of the murky tunnel, Wil saw Amanda. It had always been Amanda, and no one else.

Chapter Three

*T*HE ACRID SCENT OF SMOKE assaulted his nostrils, and canister whistled. Men screamed, and he heard that godawful Rebel yell. Saturated in sweat, Sam Prescott woke with his heart racing. *Only a dream...* The war had ended over six months before. Relieved that it was nothing more than a dream, he snuggled next to Amanda's sleeping form, relishing her warmth. With tearstained goodbyes behind them forever, they had behaved more like newlyweds—until the loss of the baby.

Her eyelids fluttered and Amanda stretched, enhancing the curves of her breasts beneath the fabric of her cotton nightdress. Like a stiff shot of whiskey, she was intoxicating. He pressed against her, but she turned away, closing her eyes. "Amanda..."

Her voice quavered. "I'm sorry, Sam."

He let out a frustrated breath. "I should be more patient."

She faced him and grasped his hand. "I haven't been fair to you over the last couple of months."

"I understand," he whispered. "Really, I do." He squeezed her hand in reassurance, and she let go.

As Sam rolled to the side, he smelled smoke. It hadn't been a dream. The stench grew stronger. Unable to determine where the smell came from, he fumbled through the dark, tugging on his trousers and boots. He looked out the window. Smoke billowed from the barn. *The horses...* Half-dressed, Sam stumbled down the stairs with Amanda, clad only in her nightdress, on his heels.

He rushed outside into the nippy night air. From inside the barn, he heard frightened nickers and the stamping of restless hooves.

As he threw the door open, smoke poured out, instantly blinding him. He raised an arm to protect his face and stepped inside. Sputtering and gagging, he staggered through the cloud of smoke to the nearest stall. Eyes bulging, the gelding danced nervously and landed a shod hoof directly on Sam's foot. Muttering a string of choice curses, he struggled with the taut rope. Finally, he worked the rope free. The gelding was loose. Another horse had broken free of its own accord and raced half-crazed up and down the aisle. Outside the stall, Amanda grasped the gelding's lead line.

Thankful for the helping hand, Sam sought Amanda's prized stallion, Red. Dizzy from the smoke, he limped to the horse's stall. A human effigy with a rope around its neck swung from a narrow beam. In its scarecrow hands spread a banner. YANKEE GO HOME! *Don't think about it now—only rescuing the horse.* But the stall was empty.

The stallion must have been the horse that had worked its way free. He moved to the next stall. With a nervous whinny, the mare snorted and pranced. Barely had Sam worked the horse's line free when he heard a whoosh and felt intense heat. A blazing wood beam struck him square in the back. Gasping for breath, he dropped to his hands and knees as the the rope tore through his hands. Someone tugged on his left arm, then his right. Amanda on one side and Ezra on the other were leading him to safety. In the cold fresh air, he could breathe again.

Sam heard a scream. One of the horses remained trapped inside. He moved toward the sound, but hands held him back. At the sound of panic-stricken wails, tears streaked down Amanda's cheeks. The wind fanned the flames, and embers danced and swirled upward into the night sky.

Alice rocked her drowsy daughter in the cradle, humming a lullaby. With her black hair and coppery skin, Emma resembled Wil. Only the baby's green eyes were more like her own. Alice stopped rocking and checked her daughter. Certain Emma was asleep, she tiptoed from the room. At the bottom of the stairs, she checked the time. It was after eight, and Wil wasn't home. *She was losing him.* For so long, he had been her stoic warrior, but she was all too aware of the mask he often hid behind.

Instead of brooding and spending needless time fretting, she pinned a dress for one of her customers. With the upcoming dance, she had more orders for new dresses than she could possibly sew and had been forced to turn some women away. Even then, times were still tough, and she feared that a number of customers would be unable to pay. While Wil brought home his gambling winnings, they were inconsistent, and sometimes the losses were the greater share. She had hoped Amanda would be able to talk some sense into him, but their outings to the shanty village had stopped as suddenly as they had begun. Still, on the nights he didn't go out gambling, he was often the familiar person whom she had always loved and she held hope of mending the growing distance.

At ten, she heard a key in the door and prayed that Wil hadn't brought Mr. Chandler with him. He looked in on her. Thankfully, he was alone, and she breathed a little easier. "Supper," he grumbled.

"It got cold. I put it away hours ago, but you're welcome to help yourself."

He gave her a look, warning her that if she didn't comply, a quarrel was in the making. She dropped her pins. As she passed him on her way to the kitchen, she got a whiff of alcohol. Once there, she dutifully reheated supper and placed it on the table. Without comment, he devoured the meal as if he hadn't eaten in a week. He barely finished before he grasped her hand and led her upstairs to the bedroom. Treating her with the same brusqueness as the meal, he satisfied his physical need, then rolled over and fell asleep.

Even during the siege, he had made time for a tender touch. She pressed her face to her pillow and sobbed. What a fool she was. From the beginning, she had known that Wil wasn't the sort of man to settle down with a wife and children. Yet, she had hoped he would change. Determined not to fall into a trap, she dried her tears and gathered her courage, rising up on her elbow. "Wil, we need to talk."

"About what?"

Shocked that he hadn't been sleeping, she managed to keep her resolve. She sat up and lit a lamp. "Your recent behavior." Though he said nothing, his eyes grew harsh. "I'm trying to understand what you must be going through, but you keep pushing me away. I want to help."

Without responding, he continued to stare. Self-conscious by her state of undress, she pulled the quilt to her chin.

He began to laugh. "You still think things can be fixed, just like that..." He snapped his fingers.

"Wil, I know you must be hurting, but a lot of Confederate officers lost their careers. I just hope you haven't set your sights on a pardon that may never come. No matter what happens, we don't need to let it affect us."

"How can we not be affected?" He gathered his clothes together and started to dress. "I won't weary you with my presence any longer."

When he suffered the moods, there had to be somewhere within him that she could still reach. "Wil, don't go—not like this." She shoved the quilt away from her to reveal her naked body.

Bitterness faded from his eyes, and for a minute, she spotted a familiar sparkle. "Are you trying to seduce me, Mrs. Jackson?"

Good—his eyes were taking every inch of her in as they had done in the past. "I've tried everything else." She forced a laugh. "I don't know why I didn't think of this sooner."

"Alice..." He sat on the edge of the straw mattress and his hand went to her face, caressing it. "I have been a bit of a bastard."

"You won't get any quarrel from me."

The mask returned suddenly, and he strode from the room. "I wish I could explain, but you wouldn't understand."

"Wil..." She barely got her dressing gown on before a rap came at the front door. Thinking of Douglas Chandler, she shivered. Why did she have the feeling that all of their current troubles were linked to him? The door thumped, then she overheard nasal voices in the foyer. Unsettled further, she rushed to the top of the stairs. "Wil?"

"You had best come here, Alice."

Disquieted by the edge in his voice, she caught her breath and dashed downstairs. In the foyer, four Yankee soldiers gathered around Wil. One was Lieutenant Greer, who had accompanied Sam on the day Wil had signed the Oath. A sergeant with a moustache drooping like a horseshoe locked shackles around Wil's wrists. Her heart thumped. When did the foolishness end? The war was over. "How dare you come into our house . . ."

Wil shook his head. "Alice . . ."

She bit her lip to keep silent. Aware that he could eventually be arrested for treason, she had maintained they should flee to Canada for safety. But Wil wasn't the sort to consider such advice. "Why are you . . ." As chains went around his ankles, her voice cracked.

The lieutenant lowered his hat. "Your husband is under arrest for suspicion of arson and being in cohorts with guerrillas, ma'am."

Arson? Guerrillas? "That can't be." Wil shot her a glance, and a sudden sick feeling churned in the pit of her stomach.

"Colonel Prescott had a barn fire last evening," Lieutenant Greer explained.

Her hands covered her mouth in disbelief. "Sam and Amanda? Was anyone hurt?"

"The only casualty was a horse, ma'am."

"I won't give you any trouble," Wil said to the soldiers. "If you would allow me a moment . . ." The soldiers stepped aside, so he could speak to her. In his usual, calm tone, he continued, "I'm certain you're appalled by what must be going through your head right now, but there is an explanation."

So—the lieutenant spoke the truth. Her mouth dropped open, and Alice blinked back her disbelief. "Explanation? You risk being accused of arson or shot as a guerrilla and claim there's an explanation. After what happened to Sam and Amanda . . ." How could she have been so wrong about his recent changes? His eyes met hers, but it was like seeing a stranger. "Are the chains necessary?" she asked the lieutenant. "He gave you his word."

"We aim that he keeps it." The lieutenant shoved his hat on his head. "Ma'am . . ."

"Wil?" Her throat constricted.

"Don't fret. I've fared worse." Wil turned. As the soldiers led him away, the chains clanked. Wishing she could shut out the sound, she closed her eyes. The door closed behind them, and she slumped against it. *Calm down and think.* She must fetch Sam. As a respected Yankee colonel, he would resolve the matter in short order.

Collecting her courage, Alice rushed up the stairs, changed, and bundled Emma for the chilly evening. After leaving the baby in the care of a neighbor, she saddled Wil's horse. A sorry looking piece of horseflesh, the bony, dapple-gray mare had been the prize in a poker game. Mounting up, she kicked the mare in the side. The horse groaned but charged off at a gallop. After a mile, she brought the gray to a trot, then a walk. Best to conserve stamina. It would be the middle of the night before she arrived at Amanda's farm.

Another mile passed. Alice pressed the mare to a brisk canter until coming to the sound of rushing water. Night crossings on the Rappahannock were often dangerous. She didn't care. Wil's life might be at stake. Slapping leather reins on the gray's shoulder, Alice clucked her tongue. Water splashed as they made their way across the river. Near the middle, waves lapped at her feet and ankles. Thankfully, the water level was low, and she said a silent prayer for small blessings. They reached the other side.

Once on dry ground, she squeezed the mare for speed. Heavily lathered, the gray gave everything she had. Hooves pounded against the dirt lane. With an intimate knowledge of the roads since childhood, she continued the mad pace. Finally, they entered the lane and dashed into the farmyard. Alice slid from the saddle. Her knees weakened from the frantic ride, and she fell to the dirt. Up and running again, she reached the porch and pounded on the door with both fists. "Amanda! Sam!"

The door opened and Amanda, clad only in a cotton nightdress, rubbed sleepy eyes. "Alice?"

Alice burst through the door. "I need Sam's help. The Yankees have arrested Wil."

A hand went to Amanda's mouth. "I'll fetch him."

"Thank you, Amanda."

As Amanda's footsteps retreated up the stairs, Alice tossed kindling on the dampened embers in the fireplace and stirred them. Flames burst, and she held her hands out to warm them.

"Alice . . ." At the sound of Sam's voice, she turned. With bare feet and his shirt rumpled, he looked as if he had rushed to make a semblance of a respectable appearance. Beside him stood Amanda. "Amanda tells me that Wil's been arrested. There are no orders to arrest . . ."

"Orders," she grumbled. Her eyes narrowed, and Alice's hands curled to fists. "I don't give a damn . . ."

"Alice, I'll remind you to watch your mouth."

Always acting as the older sister, Amanda often chastised her for swearing. Alice stamped a foot and threw her hands in the air. "Amanda, how can you fret about swearing at a time like this? The Yankees told me your barn burned down last night, and they have arrested Wil because of it. No matter what he's done recently, I can't believe he'd be involved in such a thing."

"Alice, calm yourself." Sam grasped her arm and led her to the tapestry sofa. As if he had ordered her to do so, she sat. "Now tell me what's happened."

His voice had a calming effect, and she took a deep breath. After relaying the harrowing events of the evening, Alice struggled to control the quaver in her voice. "You don't think they'll hang him, do you?"

Sam sat beside her and squeezed her hand. "They won't hang him. You have my word as an officer and a gentleman."

With her dress soiled from the frenzied night ride, Alice straightened the folds and whisked her hand over blotchy red stains. The nervous gesture had been fruitless. It took more than a wave of a hand to remove stubborn Virginia clay. "It seems we're indebted to you yet again, and I'm sorry for not showing appropriate concern for your troubles."

He patted the back of her hand. "The two of you saved my ass . . ."

"Sam," Amanda hissed.

He laughed and got to his feet. "Let me finish dressing, and I'll see what I can do."

As he disappeared from the parlor, Amanda sat next to her. Alice forced a laugh. "I foolishly thought with the war over that all this endless waiting would also cease."

"He'll be fine, Alice. Sam doesn't make promises lightly."

Promises—during the war they were such a fleeting thing. And the way things were now, little had changed for the better.

After persuading Alice that his job would go more efficiently if she remained behind, Sam rode to Fredericksburg headquarters. He didn't like leaving Amanda alone so soon after the fire. The creak of an iron door made him shudder. *So little food—rats were a delicacy.* He blinked back the memory of Libby Prison and lowered his hat. Inside the cell, Wil sat on a cot. Though his wrists and ankles were shackled, he appeared none the worse for his ordeal. "You certainly took your time getting here," Wil grumbled.

Sam raised an index finger. "You're lucky I came at all, Jackson. In fact, if you weren't married to Amanda's sister . . ."

The remark only made Wil laugh as he stood to greet him. Chains clanked as he raised his forearms. "Do you mind? I'm getting too old for this sort of thing."

"Remove the chains," Sam ordered the guard. "Leave us."

Chains rattled as they fell to the dirt floor. The guard scooped up the chains and left the cell with a hurried salute on his way out. Wil rubbed his wrists.

"Who made the arrest?"

"Your lieutenant."

"Greer?"

Wil nodded. "I get the distinct impression that he doesn't care for me very much."

"What are the charges?"

"Suspicion of arson and colluding with guerrillas."

Sam shoved his hands behind his back. "Are they true?"

"That doesn't even dignify an answer."

Sam exhaled a weary breath. "Wil, I know you've been having a difficult time."

"I haven't taken up arson," Wil replied in annoyance.

"And your friends?"

"Like many former Confederates, they're down on their luck and short on cash."

"Chandler rode with partisans during the war. Men like that don't suddenly change."

"So we're nothing but a bunch of bushwhackers. Then arrest us all. I thought you were one Yank we could trust." The irritation in Wil's voice was unmistakable.

"You can, but I need to know what's going on, Captain."

Wil's gaze softened with the mention of his former rank. "As far as I know, none of them were involved in the fire, or any other illegal activities."

In the New Mexico territory before the war, Sam had accused Wil Jackson of many things, but being a liar was not among them. Yet his gut warned him that he wasn't hearing the whole story either. "Wil," Sam continued, "would you tell me if you discovered they had been involved?"

"Depends."

"On what?"

"Various factors."

He obviously wasn't going to receive a straight answer, which unsettled him further. Sam decided not to press the issue. "I'll see what I can do about getting you out of here."

"Much obliged."

Shoving on his hat, Sam called for the guard. What was he going to tell Alice? With a key in hand, the guard unlocked the door. The iron creaked as the door swung open. No matter how hard he tried, he couldn't suppress the shudder. Wil had helped him escape Libby, and he was repaying him by keeping him—locked up. *Only temporarily*, he reminded himself. So why did that thought not comfort him?

As much as she despised the woman, Alice measured and pinned the hem of Holly's taffeta ball gown in the spare upstairs bedroom where she did most of her sewing. The deep emerald color accented her almost black hair. As always, she looked fetching and would turn men's heads. "What will you be wearing, Alice?"

If she attended the dance at all. It was mostly a Yankee affair, but she had promised Amanda that she would attend for her benefit. Yet, with Wil in jail that prospect grew slimmer each passing day. Holly knew this and undoubtedly delighted in seeing her squirm. Determined not to let Holly get the best of her, Alice replied, "I haven't decided yet."

"Such a pity that Wil doesn't see how hard you work."

He had, and even forbade her to make Holly's dress. Fully aware that Holly was merely flaunting the wealth of her new carpetbagger husband, Alice had been unable to decline the extra income. As she straightened, a rap came at the door. "Oh dear, I think you had best do something about that."

"What?" Holly twisted from side to side, examining her reflection in the mirror.

"That . . ." Alice covered her mouth as if gasping in astonishment. "You have a gray hair." Another rap. Alice kept her mouth covered to keep from snickering as she rushed down the stairs to answer the door.

About to rap again, a gruff-looking young man with stubble on his chin lowered his arm. "Ma'am . . . ," he said with a slight bow. "I wish to speak with Brigadier Jackson."

Obviously he was a former Confederate—or someone connected to Douglas Chandler. No one besides Mr. Chandler had called Wil by his military title in months. "My husband isn't here. May I leave a message that you called, Mr. . . ."

"Jesse Morgan."

"I'll let him know that you called, Mr. Morgan."

He smiled slightly, but the dark eyes flickered in a penetrating way. He must be connected with Chandler, and she definitely didn't trust him. He tipped his hat. "Much obliged, ma'am."

As he turned and retreated down the steps, she shivered and closed the door, only to find Holly peering out the window beside the door. The ragged curtain fell from Holly's hand. "Who was that?"

Alice took a quick glance herself. "I don't have any notion," she replied.

With a growing grin, Holly smirked. "Delightful, isn't he?"

Disgusted, Alice threw her hands in the air. "Do your wedding vows mean nothing?"

"What *are* you insinuating? There's nothing I take more seriously." Miffed, Holly scuttled up the stairs to the second floor.

Resisting the temptation to hurl a biting remark, Alice held her tongue. Holly's first marriage had been to Sam's brother. During that time, it was a well-known fact that she was also Wil's mistress. It made no sense why such happenings from before he had courted her angered her—especially of late. But with Holly's elegant face and curvaceous figure, she attracted men like worker bees to a hive and flaunted it. Alice bet she performed lavish entertainment in the way men liked beneath the sheets as well. It was best not to think of such things. Wil had married her, not Holly. But then, didn't men often wed women vastly different from the type they bedded?

By the time Alice reached the sewing room, Holly pirouetted in front of the mirror. Annoyed with the primping and fussing, she dashed over and helped Holly unfasten the back of the gown. "I have another appointment. Lily will be here soon to mind Emma. Now if you don't mind, I must hurry."

Casting a glance over her shoulder, Holly regarded her quizzically and raised her eyebrows in delight. "Going to see Wil?"

Damn her. Alice met her gaze. "Not that it is any of your business, but yes."

"Honestly Alice. I meant nothing by it."

Alice took a step back and crossed her arms while Holly struggled to remove the gown. Let her get stuck by a pin or two. After a couple of "drats" and "ouches," Alice went over to aid her. "Here, let me assist you."

The gown was off, and Alice gathered it in her arms. Holly's gaze smoldered. "Still jealous, I see."

A hand went to her chest. "Jealous? Why would I be jealous?" She knew her voice was far from convincing.

"You needn't be."

For once, Alice thought she detected sincerity.

"He never cared for me the way he does you."

Regret? Alice was certain she had heard it. "That's reassuring."

Holly reached for her day dress draped over the back of a chair. "Besides—Wil is a has-been, and I don't need anyone reminding me of my dear, departed first husband."

"But Charles . . ."

"Was loving and dedicated—an incredible bore."

Alice heard regret in Holly's voice once more. "You tried to nurse him back to health."

"As my husband, I owed him that much."

As Holly finished dressing, Alice thought she saw a tear in the woman's eye. Holly wasn't as cold and callous as she led everyone to believe. She had loved Charles. Alice suspected she had cared for Wil too. "And Mr. Whyte?"

The tear was replaced by a growing grin. "Frank has the money to keep me entertained in the manner to which I'm accustomed." Snatching the gown from Alice's arms, Holly waved her from the room. "Now hurry or you shall be late for your appointment."

"I need to wait for Lily," Alice reminded her.

"I'll mind the little one until the servant arrives." Uncertain, Alice hesitated. Holly shooed her one more time. "Please, Alice. Emma will be fine with me—honest."

Alice nodded and left the sewing room. In the kitchen, she collected some leftover soup in a bowl that she had kept simmering over the hearth and stored it in her basket. More often than not, Wil was famished from the meager Yankee rations and found her cooking a welcome relief. After three days, she wondered how much longer such excursions would be necessary. Not that she would complain too much. Ironically, he seemed more like his old self in jail. But his health had never fully recovered since taking the bullet in the Wilderness, and she fretted the ever-growing nippy evenings that he spent in a jail cell might damage his well-being further.

On the path to town, a man joined her—Jesse Morgan. Clad in tattered trousers, he appeared like so many of the Confederate soldiers before the war's end. He lowered his hat. "Mr. Morgan," Alice acknowledged.

"You could have been forthright, Mrs. Jackson."

She arched her brow at his blatant brashness. "About what?"

"That the general remains jailed."

"I didn't think it was appropriate."

"Ma'am, I mean no harm."

Alice stopped walking and faced him. Before now, she hadn't realized just how youthful his face was. With his wispy whiskers, he couldn't be more than twenty, but his expression carried a weariness beyond his years. It was the same fatigue she had spotted in far too many returning soldiers. "Did you serve under my husband?" He shook his head. "Then you must keep company with that despicable Mr. Chandler. Good day to you, Mr. Morgan." Turning away, she quickened her pace.

The lanky legs easily caught up with her. "While I admit that I'm acquainted with Lieutenant Chandler, I assure you that my intent is honorable."

Annoyed with his badgering, she halted once more. "Then who are you, Mr. Morgan?"

"Jesse Morgan. For seventeen years I lived on a North Carolina farm. After I was conscripted into the Confederate army, I did my share of fighting and spent nearly a year in Yankee prison. I have a letter that I thought your husband might appreciate reading. Does that answer your question satisfactorily, ma'am?"

Her irritation changed to sympathy. Yankee prisons had fared little better than Confederate. Sam had nearly died in Libby, and barely out of his boyhood, Jesse Morgan held a frightening void lurking within his almond eyes. "I already said that I will let him know you called, and I shall."

"Thank you, Mrs. Jackson. It was a pleasure meeting you."

With a bow, he returned his hat to his head. Then he vanished as quickly as he had appeared. Alice shrugged at the strange encounter and continued the last few blocks to the end of town. Even though the late-autumn afternoon remained warm, she shivered. As she stepped inside the jail, two Yankees and Wil sat at a table. Engrossed with cards spread in their hands, they either hadn't heard her enter or didn't care. "Here I am on an errand of mercy, fretting whether you're being treated proper, and you're playing poker," she said in disappointment.

Wil held up a hand for her to wait. Bets were placed and raised. Ignorant of the rules by choice, she watched as Wil tugged on his moustache. A nervous gesture—he must be losing. Finally he tossed his cards on the table and stood to greet her. One of the Yankee guards whooped. "My apologies, Alice," Wil said.

At least in jail, he wouldn't have been drinking. Furious that he would risk their hard-earned income to gambling yet again, she wasn't going to allow him to resort to his smooth-talking style. "How much did you lose?"

He grasped her arm and led her to the dingy cell in the back. "Five dollars."

"Five? Wil, do you realize how far I can stretch five dollars . . . "

He pulled a wad of bills from his pocket and pressed them into her hand. She set the basket on the floor and counted—over thirty dollars. "Unlike Chandler, the Yankees are lousy poker players. I believe we have cause to celebrate." He tugged on her arm.

With her body molded to his, his mouth met hers, and he touched her in the ways she liked. Appalled that he would even think of having relations in such a filthy environment, she shoved away from his embrace.

"Alice, it's been a while since you've been shy about such things."

"Wil Jackson, I don't care how long we've been married." She wagged a finger at him. "I still expect some respect, and what if the guards walked in?"

He laughed. "They've agreed to leave us to our privacy."

Her jaw dropped. "You actually asked them? Never mind, don't answer that." Even while courting, she knew he was no gentleman. That fact would never change. She let out an exasperated breath. Sometimes she wondered why, but she loved him anyway. "I brought you some supper." He only laughed harder when she retrieved the bowl of soup from the basket. "Eat." He took the bowl from her hands. "Wil, how much longer are they going to hold you here?"

He sat on the cot and gulped down the soup. "Ask your dear brother-in-law. He said that he'd get me out of here."

So much for Yankee hospitality—he *was* famished. Thankful that his attention had diverted to the meal, she said, "I brought some cornbread too." He nodded his appreciation. After bringing him up to date on the latest events, she found she had been right: he wasn't pleased about her continuing to make Holly's gown for the upcoming dance. She thought it best to change the subject. "A Mr. Morgan called."

Wil's black eyes grew piercing. "What did he want?"

"He said he has a letter that he would like to show you."

"That's it?"

"Yes. Wil, what's going on? First, Mr. Chandler and now, Mr. Morgan . . ."

He set the empty bowl aside. "All in good time."

That bothersome chill returned, and a sick feeling rose in her stomach. She nearly dashed for the chamber pot to retch. The last time she felt this way was in Petersburg, when Wil left every morning to inspect ever-thinning Confederate lines. Each day she expected a courier bearing the news that she had become a widow. "You're trying to protect me from something. Wil, after all we've been through . . ." But she already knew her plea fell on deaf ears.

Chapter Four

*T*HE HUT WITH HOLES BETWEEN the planks was hardly a suitable school building. As the days grew shorter and chillier, Amanda felt the piercing wind and gathered her cloak around her. She had no cause to complain. The Negroes had to live in the run-down village. She had brought a handful of books for reading, and six former slaves shared one slate for practicing their letters. Each session often brought a new student. If their numbers continued to increase, the shack would burst its seams with attentive bodies, and she would have nowhere to hold her classes.

In their enthusiasm for learning to read and write, a couple of students had kept her late. The fading sunlight cast long shadows. Not relishing the idea of driving home in the dark, Amanda clicked her tongue and tapped the whip to the horse's rump. As the shanty village faded into the background, she heard hoofbeats behind her. She cast a glance over her shoulder but saw no one.

Clip clop. There it was again. Amanda guided the horse to Sam's headquarters. As she climbed from the buggy, Lieutenant Greer drew his horse to a halt beside her and dismounted. "Is my husband here?"

"I don't know, ma'am," he replied, lowering his hat. "I'm returning from patrol myself. Why don't you step inside, and we'll see."

The lieutenant escorted her into the war-torn, crumbling brick building. Sam had responded to a report of a barroom brawl over an hour ago. Amanda glanced to the door that led to the jail cells. "Has Mr. Jackson been released?"

"No, ma'am. Would you care to see him?"

Debating what she should do, she hesitated. Ever since the loss of her baby and the barn fire, her nerves had been getting the best of her. So what could Wil do to help from jail? She had to learn to stop depending on him and shook her head. "Thank you, but I should be getting home now. Please tell my husband that I stopped by."

"I will, Mrs. Prescott. Good evening, ma'am."

"Good evening." With a shiver, she walked outside to the darkening sky.

His head ached. A little lightheaded, Sam felt something warm running in his right eye and wiped the blood from his brow. He paced in front of the lined row of five men standing at full attention. Three former Confederates stood on the opposite side of the room under full guard. Chandler had that look in his eye, reminiscent of men in the war ready to kill. Even the barmaids sent glares of hatred.

Sam met his gaze. "Who threw the first punch?"

Chandler's scowl only grew harsher, and Sam glanced at Morgan. "Not us, sir."

At least the boy was more compliant and didn't seem to share Chandler's hatred. "I don't believe you."

"Then arrest us. It seems the only crime one needs to commit around here is being a former Confederate."

Sam winced at the accusation and stopped pacing. He looked to his own men. "Well?" Silence, but no denials. "Sergeant, who threw the first punch?"

"They insulted us, sir."

His own boys. Morgan spoke the truth. His own boys started the goddamn brawl. "It must have been quite an insult."

"It was, sir. They called you a tyrant and compared you to Attila the Hun."

Though he couldn't officially condone their actions, Sam
puffed with pride that they would defend his name. "I get the idea,
and after they said all that, you threw the first punch?"

"No, sir. We contained ourselves. You told us to stay out of
trouble."

"I did," Sam agreed, his self-esteem deflating. "What was it
they said?"

The sergeant gestured to the Confederates. "They denied they
were cheating at poker."

Chandler shouted, continuing to deny the accusation. Thank
goodness for the guards, or the brawl would have resumed. "Attention," Sam bellowed. His men returned to their stiff, upright
stance. "Return to headquarters. I'll deal with you five in the
morning. Dismissed." His boys filed from the bar. "Chandler, you
have my apology. However, if I discover that you have been cheating, I'll close the goddamn bar down to keep the peace. I'll also
start having my boys enforce the rule of no gatherings of three or
more Confederates. Understood?"

No response. Satisfied that his message was heard, Sam ordered the guards to let the men go. He left the bar. After a quick
trip to headquarters, he got a report from Lieutenant Greer that
he had missed Amanda by about fifteen minutes. On the chance
that she had stopped by to see Alice, he reined his horse to a halt
outside the red brick house.

As he made his way to the door, he heard a baby crying inside.
He knocked.

"Sam . . ." Alice rocked the baby in her arms. Now quiet, Emma
smiled. "What are you doing here?"

He lowered his hat.

"You've been hurt." She tugged on his arm and drew him inside.

"It's nothing. My head got in the way of a flying bottle is all. I
merely wondered if Amanda was here."

"Amanda? Why would she be here?"

"She stopped by headquarters. I thought she might have come
here before heading home."

Alice shook her head. "No, but I'd feel better if you would let me take a look at your head. It looks like you got a nasty gash."

He no longer resisted, and she showed him to the kitchen, motioning for him to take a seat at the table. The chair rocked on uneven legs when he sat, but he supposed people made do with what they had. Alice placed the baby on the floor to play while she collected a tin basin, water, and a clean cloth.

"The fuss really isn't necessary," he assured her, setting his hat on the table.

She sat beside him. "It's no fuss." Alice dipped the cloth in water and dabbed it to his forehead.

Pain. He jerked his head back.

"I know it hurts, but you need to hold still."

He gritted his teeth and managed to keep from jiggling as she cleaned the wound.

"Sam, how much longer are you going to keep Wil in jail?"

How much should he reveal? "I had hoped he would give me some leads as to who was responsible for the fire."

With a worried frown, Alice withdrew the bloody cloth from his forehead. "Then you think he knows more than he's telling?"

"I'm not sure. I only know the company that he's been keeping of late is less than desirable."

"Mr. Chandler and company." She dipped the cloth in the water basin and returned to cleaning his forehead. "If Wil knew something, I think he'd inform you."

"Why do you say that?"

She sucked on her lip. "Because Amanda might be in danger if he didn't."

So she had noticed the close relationship between them, too. Spending too much time at headquarters and general peacekeeping, Sam blamed himself. Maybe he should give up his commission, and do what? Become a farmer? After the war's end, he had volunteered for the position in Fredericksburg, so he could be near Amanda.

"Sam . . ." Alice's hand came to rest on his arm. "She loves you. Just give her a little more time to recover from the loss of the baby. Amanda's tougher than nails. You'll see her usual self return." She began bandaging his forehead. "And I need my husband back. Lord knows why sometimes, but if for no other reason than the fact that Emma misses her papa."

"Alice, you should learn to listen to your own advice."

She finished winding the bandage around his head, then pinned it. "You're right," she said with a contemplative smile. "You'll be good as new in a few days."

Sam collected his hat and stood. "Thank you. I'll make certain that Wil's released tonight." Alice's smile widened, and she threw her arms around his neck with a kiss to his cheek. After freeing Wil, he would make the ten-mile trip home to Amanda.

Although she had been married to Sam for nearly three years, Amanda continued to feel like an outcast attending gatherings hosted by Yankees. Carpetbaggers mingled with soldiers, and the Southern wound remained raw. In a brilliant emerald gown, Holly glided across the dance floor in the arms of a blond gentleman with a moustache. Mr. Chandler was most definitely not a Northerner, nor Holly's husband. The balding Franklin Whyte had retreated to the smoking room with several other men to discuss politics. Ready for a good debate, Sam had followed suit.

Amanda joined a chestnut-haired woman wearing a flowery calico dress at the food table. "Mae, you haven't been by to see me . . ."

"I've been busy." Mae waved her fingers at another guest across the room. "Amanda, if you'll excuse me."

Ever since marrying Sam, she frequently received a cold reception from friends she had known all of her life. The indifference had grown worse since she had begun to teach former slaves. Amanda spied Alice chatting with three local women. Unlike her, her sister never had difficulty putting on appearances in a social setting, even if the majority of the women were the wives of Yankees. But what of Wil? As a former Confederate officer and further humiliated by his recent stay in jail, he certainly wouldn't be discussing politics with Yankee soldiers and carpetbaggers.

An aged black servant poured her a glass of punch, and a baritone voice with a distinct Charleston accent came from behind her. "I find it surprising that a man would leave such a lovely lady to fend for herself."

She looked over to familiar dark eyes, flickering at her in amusement. "Wil," she acknowledged, delighted for the company, "I was wondering where you had vanished to."

"I had some business that required my attention."

"Another card game?"

"You'll be happy to know that I've acquired a real occupation again. I took your advice to heart and have returned to my engineering roots. Of course, it will entail some travel."

"That is good news."

Both stared at the other as if not knowing what to say. She had never known him at a loss for words, but after their excursions to the shanty village, she had forced a wedge between them. For some reason, even after all of these months she still expected to see him clad in a gray uniform with brass buttons and gold embroidery on the sleeves. Now he wore a threadbare waistcoat and a several-times-patched sack coat. Yet, his beard was neatly trimmed, and the waves in his hair matched the black depths of his eyes. He had always been quite dashing, and it was wrong for her to take notice.

Finally, he broke the silence. "Would you care to dance, Amanda?"

Dance? Surely one dance wouldn't hurt. "I'd love to." She set her glass on the table and took his hand.

As they reached the dance floor, the strains of gay fiddle music reduced to that of a slow waltz. When he drew her close, she instantly regretted her decision to dance with him. Quickly deciding that she was reading more into his unspoken words than he intended, she relaxed. What happened between them had been a long time ago, and before Alice had entered his life, she reminded herself. Her feisty little sister had been the one to tame him, and he showed no signs of impropriety. But she remembered after her first husband's death, Wil's strong arms around her, consoling her. At the time, she had needed his strength.

The dance ended all too soon, and Amanda curtsied a thank you. His moustache tickled as he kissed the back of her hand. "How have you been?" she asked.

With a mischievous grin, he met her gaze. "Since my ordeal with the Yankees?"

Hoping no one had overheard him, Amanda glanced from side to side. "Wil, would you please keep your voice down?"

"For propriety's sake? Amanda, you should know me better than that, but I am pleased to see that you're no longer wearing black."

She spread the folds of her russet-colored gown. "Sam insisted on it."

"Indeed, Amanda . . ." On the arm of Mr. Chandler, Holly sidled between them. "You should know *Mr.* Jackson better. Besides you, I don't think he's ever cared what anyone thinks." Wil's smoldering gaze fixed on Holly. "Good gracious, where are my manners?" Pressing a hand to her chest, she gave an insincere laugh. "Y'all," she said in mocking tone, "remember Mr. Chandler? Wil, I believe he helped save your life."

As Douglas Chandler took Amanda's hand and kissed it, the anger faded in Wil's eyes and changed to a wicked dance. "Tell me, Chandler," Wil said in an equally sly voice, "have you noticed that she tends to be self-conscious about the scar on her . . ." He glanced in Amanda's direction, then cleared his throat. "Ask her how she got it."

Fanning herself, Holly sent Wil a scorching look, and Amanda clapped a hand to her mouth to keep from snickering. "I knew I should have shot you when I had the chance," Holly said, fuming.

Wil grasped Amanda's elbow and led her over to the food table. "Wil," Amanda chastised in mock anger, "you should be ashamed of yourself."

"My apologies, Amanda."

She struggled to hold the giggles in, but was unable to contain them. "You're not sorry, and you know it. You meant to embarrass Holly in front of her . . . *friend.*"

Indifferent to the accusation, he shrugged. "I suppose I haven't changed."

She lowered her arm. "But you have."

His expression grew distant, and he shook his head. "Appearances can be deceiving."

"Wil . . . " Her hand went to his arm. "I know you're going through a difficult time, but Sam says a pardon will eventually come through."

"Pardon?" With a drink in one hand and Holly draped from his other arm, Mr. Chandler joined them. "Did I hear the lady correctly in saying that you have signed the Yankee Oath, *sir?*"

Wil met Chandler's gaze—in a challenge. "You did," he answered evenly.

Left with the impression that she had said something she shouldn't have, Amanda swallowed hard, but Mr. Chandler smiled pleasantly. Amanda breathed out in relief.

"Wil . . ." Holly again. "Do you usually let your wife dance with poor white trash?" His eyes narrowed, but Holly motioned for him to look behind him. On the dance floor, Alice waltzed with a young man whose suit bagged two sizes too large and needed mending in several places. While the gentleman appeared less than refined, he looked more down on his luck rather than what most folks regarded as "white trash."

Wil sprinted over to the dancing couple and seized Alice's arm. As he stepped between the pair, Amanda overheard heated voices. She looked to Holly's escort to intervene, but his eager grin suggested he was itching for a fight. Detecting trouble brewing, Amanda lifted her skirts and dashed to the smoke-filled parlor. She raised on her tiptoes and craned her neck to locate Sam. There he was—in the corner.

"Sam . . ." She latched onto his arm and tugged for him to come along.

By the time they returned, Alice stood alone—dumbfounded, and the men were gone. "They've decided to settle it outside." Sam headed for the door, and Alice dabbed her eyes with a lace handkerchief. "I've never been so humiliated, Amanda. What am I to do?"

A crowd of onlookers stared at them, and Amanda squeezed her sister's arm. "I've never known Wil to be the jealous sort," she whispered.

With a condescending grin, Holly joined them. She covered her mouth, so only they would hear. "I'm betting on Jesse Morgan. After all, Wil is forty."

Ignoring the gawking faces, Alice grasped Amanda's elbow and led her outside. To her relief, Sam had tempered Wil's fury before blows had been exchanged. Though she couldn't overhear their words, the men were speaking—calmly and rationally. The young man, whom Holly had referred to as Jesse Morgan, left the group and vanished on the dark street.

As Wil strode toward them, Alice shook a clenched hand. "How could you, Wil? You've shamed me in front of everyone. I won't be able to show my face in public again."

His gaze fixed on Alice, and he regarded her a moment before saying anything. "Many of them are nothing more than Yankee soldiers who have raped the South and taken everything to our name. Do you seriously believe I give a damn what the lot of them think?" Grumbling, he turned and stalked off in the opposite direction Mr. Morgan had taken.

Alice shoved the handkerchief to her face and took panting breaths. Amanda patted her sister's arm. "Who is this Mr. Morgan?" The question only brought more exaggerated breaths.

"I think," Sam said, answering for Alice, "he and Chandler may have had something to do with the fire."

The fire . . . Then Wil's motive hadn't been jealousy. Amanda wished she could pretend that night was nothing more than a bad dream. She forced back the all-too-vivid memory of discovering her mare's blackened body in the debris and her stallion among the missing.

"Let's get Alice home," Amanda suggested. Sam nodded.

The street was quiet, except for the occasional couple strolling to and from the party. As they walked past charred ruins, Alice spoke about the unusual circumstances of meeting Jesse Morgan.

Amanda sent Sam a questioning glance. "You knew about this, didn't you?"

A carriage with drunken patrons singing rolled past on the street.

With your ring umma ding umma da
Whack for the daddy 'ol
Whack for the daddy 'ol
There's whiskey in the jar

Sam jingled the change in his pocket. "Chandler, Morgan, and a couple of others have been involved in some petty activities. I think they're involved in more but can't prove it. I had asked Wil for his cooperation to find out, but he refused to give it."

Wringing the handkerchief, Alice stopped walking, and Amanda was uncertain whether her sister was about to laugh or cry. Instead, she cursed. "I feel like such a fool for fretting about my humiliation. Wil's jail sentence suddenly makes sense," Alice said in an accusing tone.

"Alice . . ."

"No, Amanda, let me finish. I thought all of this hatred would end with the war, but your husband seems to think that anyone who is a former Confederate is involved in criminal activities."

Amanda raised her voice. "Alice . . ."

"She's partly right," Sam intervened, frowning. "I didn't arrest Wil, but I allowed him to stay in jail longer than necessary. If it makes you feel any better, Alice, I don't believe he had any part in the fire, but I had hoped he would help me find out who was responsible. Because of his rank during the war, he still carries respect among former Confederates."

Now Amanda felt like the fool. "I may have said something I shouldn't have. I mentioned a pardon to Wil, and Mr. Chandler overheard me. Wil admitted to signing the Oath."

In silence, Alice started walking again. Outside the house, Sam caught Amanda's hand as they went up the steps. "Stay with her, Amanda. With their latest disruptions, I have enough evidence to arrest Jesse Morgan and the band he keeps company with. No one would think twice if I ordered all of them shot."

Amanda shivered. Alice was right. When did the hatred end? Sam gave her a goodnight kiss, and she followed Alice inside. Lily had left a lamp burning to see by. "After I visit the necessary, I shall sit with you."

"Thank you, Amanda."

By the time she returned, she overheard a masculine voice in the parlor. Wil had returned home. At least his whereabouts no longer weighed on her mind. Though his anger had faded, to her disappointment he hadn't seen Sam. Now she'd be fretting about Sam's safety.

As Alice brought in a platter with a teapot, Wil watched her. Amanda recalled the time when his gazes were meant for her. Had she chosen another path, would he have been as devoted?

"Amanda, would you care to join us in some tea?" Alice asked, pouring from the teapot.

"That would be lovely, thank you." Amanda made herself comfortable on the sofa.

Alice handed Amanda a steaming stoneware cup and said, "Wil, you could have warned us about Jesse Morgan."

"I'm not certain how involved he is with Chandler."

"In any case, Mr. Chandler is a former partisan," Amanda reminded him, taking a sip of the hot liquid, which was a blend of herbs rather than real tea.

Narrowing, his eyes came to rest on her. "That doesn't mean all Confederate veterans are bushwhackers and horse thieves."

She hadn't meant to insult him. "I'm aware of that and you have my apology. I only meant that I know how difficult it has been for the two of you. I can understand how someone even less fortunate might turn to ways they wouldn't ordinarily, and from what Alice tells me, Mr. Morgan spent a year in Yankee prison."

"Elmira," Wil responded.

Dubbed as Helmira by the prisoners, it was equal in the number of deaths and atrocities to any Confederate prison, including Libby, where Sam had been imprisoned. Recalling Sam's emaciated body, Amanda closed her eyes. "Mr. Morgan has my sympathy."

"Amanda, I truly don't know the depth of his involvement." Wil took a deep breath. "He claims . . . to be my son."

Alice's expression paled. "It appears there has been nothing here of late except secrets." She fled from the parlor.

"Go after her, Wil."

He shook his head. "I'll give her a few minutes."

"Then Jesse Morgan is telling the truth?"

Wil held out a letter. "He gave me this."

While she was aware that he had associated with some less than desirable women in the past, the letter was addressed to Wil from a young woman in love. The crumpled, yellowed paper suggested that the letter was indeed twenty years old.

"I never received it, Amanda."

Like the letter that had been meant for her. Suddenly uncomfortable, Amanda set her teacup on the platter. "If you don't mind, I think I'll retire."

"Still afraid?"

She didn't like the way he saw through her. They had been friends far too long for either to fool. "This is between you and Alice. But if Mr. Morgan speaks the truth, I suggest that you contact Sam. He was ready to order Jesse Morgan shot for his disruptive activities."

"Sam won't take any drastic action without just cause. I'll offer my assistance in the morning."

Since Sam wasn't in any immediate danger, she'd be able to sleep easier. So much like during the war, she could delay her fears. "Then I'll bid you goodnight."

He gave her a slight bow, whispering "goodnight." Any other time, he would have also kissed her hand, but his eyes met hers in familiar recognition, almost a longing. She knew the look, and her heart skipped a beat. Amanda turned.

On the stairs, she met Lily. The servant girl also bid her goodnight. The door on Amanda's right was partly ajar, and Alice poked her head out. "Amanda, it's you. I thought it might be Wil."

"Alice, give him a chance to explain. He didn't know about Jesse either. You knew when you married him there had been other..." Amanda couldn't think of a way to phrase it delicately. "...women."

Alice giggled. "You have often accused me of being naive, but I'm not shocked by Jesse's claim." In a more serious tone, she added, "The secret I was talking about is why *my* husband decided to inform you first."

Amanda's throat constricted. "There is nothing . . ."

"I know," Alice said, clasping her hands to prominently display the gold wedding band on her finger. "You've both said that you have never been anything more than friends. I don't know what happened between the two of you, but Wil married me. Life only recently has begun returning to normal. Face the truth, Amanda."

"What truth?"

"You're still in love."

"Love? You're my sister, and I would never do anything to hurt you."

"You already have." With that, Alice ducked back into her room.

Debating whether to follow her sister, Amanda struggled with indecision. True, she cared for Wil—like a brother. But love him? Amanda went into the guest room and readied for bed. She climbed beneath ragged sheets onto a lumpy straw mattress. She tossed and turned. Unable to sleep, she decided to return to her sister's room.

Amanda cracked the door open and saw Wil on the stairs. Immediately changing her mind, she closed the door and returned to bed. Straw poked her in the side, and she struggled to find a comfortable position. Flat on her back, she heard Alice's laughter filter from the adjacent room. At least her sister and Wil must have made up.

Straw dug into her spine, and Amanda pounded it back into the burlap covering. Then, she heard a throaty moan. They had more than made up. She and Sam had only shared a restrained and awkward encounter since the loss of the baby.

Amanda thought of Sam, running his fingers through her hair and kissing her breasts. Bare arms and legs were intertwined in rhythmic unison. Hands and mouths touching and fondling. Lord forgive her, but Alice had been right. She wasn't thinking of Sam at all.

Lieutenant Greer's summons were marked urgent. The tavern girl's naked body had been discovered on the banks of the Rappahannock. "She was still warm when we found her, sir."

Sam lifted the blanket. Bruises were prominent around her neck.

"She was a favorite of Douglas Chandler's."

Sam recalled the barmaid being among those at the brawl. Weary from hearing Chandler's name, he rubbed tired eyes and ordered the formation of a search party.

"Sir, I'll have the boys together at first light. Why don't you get a few hours rest before then?"

"A splendid idea, Lieutenant. Thank you."

The lieutenant saluted. Instead of heading for the bunk Sam normally used at headquarters, he decided to check that Amanda had arrived safely at Alice's. Due to the late hour, the brick house was dark. He reconsidered waking the entire household, but Amanda's safety was a priority. He pounded on the door. No answer. Another knock.

The door opened, and he found himself staring down a pistol barrel. "If that's you, Jackson. It's just me."

The pistol lowered, and Wil's shirtless form stepped into the dim light. "With all of the recent happenings, one can't be too careful these days."

"Understood, but I don't think it would speak well for a potential pardon if you shot the commanding officer." Wil remained silent. "That was meant to be a joke, Captain."

"Forgive me if I don't see the humor when you could just as easily be carrying an arrest warrant."

"A poor attempt," Sam agreed. "I wanted to make certain Amanda had arrived safely."

Wil motioned for him to step inside. "Now that everyone is awake, why don't you see for yourself? She's in the spare room upstairs."

Sam apologized for the intrusion and tiptoed up the stairs. In the darkness, he nearly tripped but groped through the hall and successfully found the room. With the increasing chill of the autumn nights, there was a nip in the air. "Amanda," he whispered.

"Sam, it is you. I was so worried. Can you stay?"

"Till morning. I'll have one of the boys escort you home."

With a kiss to his lips, Amanda placed her arms around him. Suddenly anxious, she touched him everywhere. His fatigue faded. Reminiscent of their life before the loss of the baby, he undressed and joined her on the straw mattress. Whatever had brought about the change in her pleased him. He had denied the ache of her indifference for too long and unable to contain himself, he shoved her nightdress above her thighs. Her desire grew to a feverish intensity, and he entered her in his own frenzied eagerness. After both were satisfied, Sam collapsed in exhaustion.

When he woke, Amanda lay snuggled in his arms, and the first remnants of dawn shown through the window. "Damn. I'm late." He dressed quickly and gave Amanda a goodbye kiss. "Don't leave until I send your escort."

She assured him that she would wait. Another kiss, and they parted. At least their separations were no longer for months on end.

In the kitchen, the household had already stirred to life. Wil held Emma, while Alice hovered in front of the fireplace, cooking breakfast. If anyone had told him while stationed in New Mexico that his former commander would take up a domestic routine with a wife and child, Sam would have never believed them. But Wil appeared entirely at ease with his daughter and accepted a tug on his moustache good naturedly. A twinge of envy spread through Sam. Due to the war, he had missed a large portion of Rebecca's life, but thankfully, even before they were married, Amanda had always been there for her.

"Coffee?" Wil offered.

Aware the household could ill afford feeding extra mouths, Sam declined the offer with his appreciation. "I need to get back to headquarters. I was hoping that you would join the search party as liaison."

"I'm not certain anything I say will make a difference, but if it'll decrease the chance for bloodshed, I'll try my best."

"That's all I can ask for. Thank you, Captain." Wil nodded. Sam checked his pocket watch. "Then meet me at headquarters in half an hour."

When Sam reached headquarters, Greer saluted. "There's a Mrs. Whyte waiting to see you in your office, sir."

Holly? What could she want? "Thank you, Lieutenant." Sam grabbed a cup of coffee and went inside. Holly sat in the chair near his desk, straightening the folds in her dress. "Make it quick, Holly. I don't have much time."

"Frank informed me about the barmaid this morning."

Curious, Sam took a sip of coffee and sat in the chair behind the desk. "How did your husband find out?"

"Sam, Fredericksburg isn't that large. The word has already spread throughout the community."

After blowing on the hot liquid, he took another sip. "So why does the news bring you to my office at seven in the morning?"

"Because I know you're going to blame Doug Chandler for her murder."

"So?"

Holly swallowed noticeably. "Must I spell it out, Sam? Doug was with me at the time the girl was murdered."

"I see." Sam rubbed his chin, then shook his head with laughter. "Holly, I swear . . . some of the men you get involved with."

"Like your brother?"

He sobered. "Leave Charles out of this. He's been dead nearly three years now."

She smirked. "Then perhaps you'd rather discuss Wil Jackson. Married life certainly hasn't changed him. Or didn't you notice the way he and Amanda danced and carried on at the party?"

So the intimate friendship between Amanda and Wil had caught the attention of non-family members as well. Shoving the disquieting thought from his head, Sam took a deep breath. "Leave Amanda out of this too. Are you willing to testify on Chandler's behalf?" She hedged. "I thought not. Then if you don't mind, I intend on bringing him and his little band in for questioning. Do you know where he is?"

"No."

"If I discover you're lying . . ."

"I'm not," she insisted.

She appeared sincere, but with Holly, he could never be certain. He stood. "I have a job to do." With a troubled frown, she rose. "Holly, I won't take any drastic action unless I'm forced to."

"That's reassuring."

She *was* worried. "I will bear in mind that Chandler has an alibi."

"Thank you, Sam."

He nodded, and for the first time that he could recall, Holly left his office without being in a huff.

Chapter Five

WITHIN AN HOUR, LIEUTENANT GREER headed up twenty men, and Sam led another group. Their first stop was the tavern that Chandler frequented. Greer had questioned the bar owner the previous evening but had met with resistance in receiving answers to his questions. Sam hoped that Wil's presence might loosen a few tongues.

After twenty minutes of waiting outside, he grew restless.

"With all due respect, sir," stated Sergeant Stanley, "I'm concerned that you place your faith in the word of a Reb."

Sam gave the balding sergeant a piercing look. "That *Reb* helped me escape from Libby. Any other questions, Sergeant?"

"No, sir." Stanley saluted.

Another ten minutes passed before Wil returned. A private spat near Wil's foot. Wil's eyes narrowed with contempt.

Intervening before the displays escalated, Sam held up a hand. He turned to the private. "If you so much as show any Southern citizen disrespect again without cause, I'll have you in stocks. Is that clear?"

"Yes, sir."

"Mount up."

The private obeyed.

"Sorry, Wil," said Sam.

"I get that a lot these days."

Even Amanda had complained about rude soldiers, and Sam suspected she was treated with higher regard than most citizens.

He wished for a way to ease tensions. "Did you learn anything?"

"Not much. People know you're here and are reluctant to talk. A friend of the dead barmaid said she left early to meet someone, but the friend had no idea whom."

Definitely not much to go on. "That's it?"

"A patron said that Chandler had visited the Wallace farm a couple of days ago."

Wallace? Sam checked the map. There were a couple of Wallace farms across the river. "I don't suppose the patron said which one?"

"No."

"That's better than no lead at all. I hope you'll accompany us." Wil nodded that he would.

"I appreciate your help. I realize that it can't be easy for you."

"I have my reasons."

"Care to enlighten me?"

"Not really, but I'm certain Amanda will tell you when she has the chance. Jesse Morgan claims to be my son."

Which meant that Wil was helping him as a result of a personal stake, not because they had served together before the war. "I see. Let's check out the Wallaces in the area." He ordered his men to mount up.

The closest farm turned out to be an abandoned house, crumbling to ruins. When they approached the second, Sam feared the same fate. While keeping his men out of sight, he let Wil go in alone. He positioned himself on a nearby ridge where he could keep watch through his field glasses. An elderly woman attired in black stepped onto the porch. As Wil spoke with her, a motion toward the back of the cabin caught his eye. Nearly ready to sound the alarm, Sam caught himself.

Another woman, also dressed in black, seemed to float across the yard, then sat on the porch steps. Wil was returning. He reined his horse to a halt. "At first, she refused to talk to any Yankees, but she has agreed to talk with you—just you—in exchange for food."

So many, black and white, were starving. The government handed out supplies, but it was never enough. "I'll have one of the boys bring up some rations." He ordered a private to fetch them. "Did you see the other woman?"

"No, but I heard her calling for a child."

Odd, but he hadn't seen any children. The private brought a bag, containing salt pork, dried vegetables, and a little coffee. Not much, but if it could tide a family over until their next meal . . . Accompanied by Wil, Sam reined his horse in the direction of the cabin. Once outside, he dismounted and lowered his hat. "Ma'am." He handed the woman the canvas bag.

A withered hand reached out, accepting his offering. Sunken eyes inspected the bag. "Much obliged, Colonel."

"We're looking for Douglas Chandler."

"Brigadier Jackson has already informed me who you are looking for. I fear that I have never made the gentleman's acquaintance. Now if you'll excuse me, I grow ill around *Yankees*. I have lost two grandsons to your kind."

Sam glanced to Wil for guidance. He stepped forward. "Mrs. Wallace . . ."

"And you're the worst kind of traitor, *Mr.* Jackson." She sent Wil a smoldering look. "A former Confederate general, aiding the Yankees. You should be shamed." She hustled to the cabin and slammed the door behind her.

Wil hurled his hat to the ground and mounted his horse.

"Wil, remember you're helping to save bloodshed—on both sides." The argument seemed to temper Wil's fury. Sam leaned down for the hat and gave it to Wil. "Let's see if the woman around back is more cooperative."

"You're risking a shotgun in the face."

"If you're afraid of a little granny, I can always summon some of my boys."

"Prescott . . . ," Wil grumbled under his breath. But the words had the desired effect. He dismounted. "Maybe grannies from the backwoods of Maine don't carry shotguns, but down here, they do. And they know how to use them."

Rounding the corner of the cabin, Sam laughed. "I'm from the coast, not the backwoods, but I'll heed your warning." Around back, the woman in black remained on the steps. Like Amanda, her hair was blonde, and she was almost as pretty. On her hands, she wore black lace gloves. Staring into empty space, her eyes held a vacant look. Once a few feet away from her, he lowered his hat. "Ma'am . . ."

Her gaze lifted, and she looked at him as if not really seeing him.

"We're looking for Douglas Chandler."

Her eyes widened with fear.

"There's nothing to worry about if you . . ."

Her lip curled, revealing glistening white teeth. Before Sam could react, she sprang at him, screaming and with her fists flailing. The impact of her body against his sent him sprawling. He attempted to grasp her wrists, but her moves were lightning fast. He suffered the blows of her pounding hands, then he felt her weight being drawn off him.

The woman tussled with Wil, but he had a firm grip on her arms. Finally, her fight faded, but she continued to scream. "He killed Faith!"

As Sam stood, a bullet whirred over his head. "I told the two of you to get." On the steps, the old woman held a rifle. Even without Wil's warning, he had no doubt that she knew how to use it. "You, Mr. Yankee Colonel. I said that we don't know Mr. Chandler. Isn't it enough that you've killed our kin and taken everything we got?"

Sam retrieved his hat from the ground. "We're going." Wil joined him as he went around to the front where the horses were tied.

A couple of his men galloped up the lane and halted before him. "We heard a shot, sir," said Sergeant Stanley.

"Everything is under control."

Sam didn't like the way Stanley scowled at Wil. Weren't they a reunited country again? Why couldn't that fact be accepted without bitterness? Because, he could very well have been the cause of the loss of the women's kin.

For two days, they followed empty leads. Chandler hadn't returned to the tavern and was apparently aware the Yankees were looking for him. After the second day of searching, a bar patron, who had consistently lost to Chandler's hands of poker, gave Wil a solid clue. As in wartime, some of the local citizens aided the partisans. On the turnpike, rotting knapsacks and battered canteens were ugly reminders of the battles that had been fought in the area.

Suddenly, there was a flurry of activity with couriers and scouts dashing here and there. Accustomed to being in charge instead of sitting idly by, Wil fidgeted in the saddle. A mustachioed scout brought his lathered horse to a halt and gave Sam a salute. "We got 'em, sir. They're holed up in a shack about half a mile ahead."

Sam jotted down a note and handed it to the scout. "See that Lieutenant Greer receives this. I want his men to join us." Another salute, and the scout galloped off. Sam shouted for his men to fall in line. "Hold your fire unless I order otherwise." He finally glanced in Wil's direction. "What?"

Wil shook his head. "I didn't say anything."

"You didn't have to. We easily outnumber them. If they try to run, they don't have a chance."

"Just like a Yank to think like that."

Sam grimaced, then relaxed with a wry smile. "What's your esteemed advice, Captain?"

More than four years had passed since they had served in the New Mexico territory before the war. Wil finally accepted the honorary title. "They're desperate men, and if necessary, will fight with everything they have for their lives."

"Are you suggesting that I let them go?"

"No, but if you end up shooting them as horse thieves, you'll never know the truth about the fire or barmaid's murder."

"True, but . . . What do you have in mind?"

"You asked me to be a liaison; let me go in alone. I might be able to talk to them."

Sam shook his head. "Too risky." He ordered the scouting party forward.

"Sam," Wil tried again. "Remember, I have a personal stake in this. Let me try."

"All right," Sam said, breathing out in reluctance, "but let me get my boys stationed, just in case I need to send them in."

To this, Wil agreed. After riding a half mile, he got a feeling in his gut that the scout's report was incomplete. The log shack nestled in a pine grove ahead, and the woods had grown mighty quiet. Sam motioned for his men to assume strategic locations around the dilapidated building. Once they were in position, he signaled for them to hold their fire.

"It's your turn. Just don't go do anything stupid like getting your fool head blown off, or I'll have hell to pay."

Dismounting, Wil laughed. "Always looking out for yourself, Prescott." He unbuckled his gun belt and handed it to Sam.

"You sure as hell don't think I'm fretting a lick about you." Sam grasped the gun belt, then signaled once more for his soldiers to hold their fire. "Wil, be careful."

Taking a deep breath, Wil nodded. "I'm unarmed," he shouted in the direction of the shack. He raised his hands, keeping them in plain sight, and stepped into the open. No gunfire. That much was a good sign. As he moved toward the hovel, he saw no evidence of guns aimed at him from the windows. Without missing a beat, he kept walking until he reached the door.

The place seemed unusually quiet—too quiet for comfort. He turned the knob and went inside. Nothing. The one-room cabin with a loft appeared deserted. Four tin plates sat atop a flimsy table. Wil held his hand over the nearest plate. The eggs were still warm. Someone had hightailed it out of the hovel in a mighty big hurry.

He looked to the loft and thought he saw movement. "I'm unarmed. I've come to talk." No response. If someone hid up there, all they had to do was fire, and in a flash, Alice became a widow. Shrugging the thought away, he reached for the ladder. It wasn't the first time he had stared down the wrong end of a gun barrel.

Wil began climbing. Halfway up, he felt the ladder sway. A crouched figure stood near the top and gave the ladder a shove. Before he could grasp onto a support beam, the ladder swung backward. As he smacked to the dirt floor, he heard a wild shriek, and a cold blade ripped through his sleeve.

The knife sliced through the air. Slightly dazed from the fall, Wil managed to grasp a flailing arm before the blade plunged down once more. He flipped the assailant, kicking and scream-ing, to his back and pinned his shoulders. He blinked. His as-sailant was a woman. Not just any woman, but Alice's servant, Lily. Bulging bruises covered her arms and face. Her right eye was nearly swollen shut, and her dress torn and bloodied. Furious that she had been beaten and possibly raped, he kept his rage in check for Lily's sake.

"Lily," he said, releasing his grip.

As he got to his feet, she curled her body into the shape of a cocoon. The blade thumped to the dirt, and she began rocking.

"Lily, what happened?"

"After I leave da house da other night, dey wait outside," she responded in a monotone voice.

"Who?"

She shook her head and kept rocking. "If I say anythin', dey kill me da next time."

He knelt down. "If you remain silent, they won't be brought to justice."

Her dark eyes met his, and tears formed in them. "Da law ain't changed with da Yankees. White men can do whate'er dey like to a nigger." She pressed her hands to her face and cried into them.

Fighting the urge to withdraw, Wil held his ground. He put his arms around her, and she sobbed on his shoulder. With a tear-streaked face, she looked up at him in a silent thank you. As he helped her to her feet, Sam entered the shack with a few of his boys and their guns drawn. Lily shrieked.

Sam lowered his pistol and ordered a couple of the men to search the place. "Who's responsible?"

Wil shook his head. "She won't say."

"Lily . . . ," Sam said, gently.

"It might be best if Alice talks to her," Wil suggested.

Sam motioned for one of his men to accompany Lily. "Take her back to town and contact Mrs. Jackson."

When the private grasped her elbow, she recoiled from his touch. Lily looked to Wil for guidance. "I'll escort you," he assured her.

Nodding in relief, she trudged from the shack.

"Wil," Sam said, "I don't think it's coincidence they abducted your wife's servant."

Not a coincidence at all, and the message was all too clear. It could have been Alice. He felt anger rising once more. *Let Sam investigate.* The Yanks wouldn't appreciate any interference on his part. Wil turned away. Outside the shack, three Yankees sat astride their mounts. As usual, Sergeant Stanley glared at him as he strode to his horse where Lily waited for him. When he took his gun belt from his saddle, a private spat. Instead of narrowly missing, this time he hit Wil's boot. *Ignore them.* He buckled the gun belt about his waist.

"George, you know what the colonel said about treating Southern citizens," came Stanley's nasally voice.

"I do," the private responded. "But as I recall, no one's pardoned any Reb generals. They *ain't* citizens. Sarge, shouldn't we do our duty and make him swear the Oath?"

Wil met the gaze of the scraggly bearded private, and the sergeant snickered. "I have already taken the Oath," Wil responded.

"None of us heard it." The private eyed Lily with suspicion and snorted a laugh. "As I see it, you still got your nigger gal. I've heard yellow gals are a good fuck, but the Oath says you got to pay her now for her services."

Wil's muscles strained. Ready to punch the Yank's face in, he moved toward the private. Lily locked onto his arm. "No, Mr. Wil. Dey ain't worth it."

The sergeant leapt from the back of his horse and landed beside him. "The Oath. We're waiting to hear you say it."

"I've taken your goddamned Oath once. I don't intend on repeating it."

Several horses approached the hovel with Lieutenant Greer in the lead. He gave Wil a a look of disdain, then shifted his gaze to the sergeant. "What's going on here?"

"Nothing, sir," the sergeant responded. "Just following the colonel's orders and being friendly to the Southern *citizens.*"

Taking Lily's advice, Wil touched his hat in a good day gesture, then mounted the dappled mare. He helped Lily on behind him. Although he didn't particularly like Greer, his appearance had defused the situation. With the sergeant's mouth left agape, Wil reined the mare around and squeezed her to a trot.

Once on the turnpike, he spotted a red-tailed hawk soaring in the sky, reminding him of the day he had nearly drowned in the river. Until seeing the noble bird, he had been ready to let go. *Had he made the right choice?*

During the siege of Petersburg, Alice and Lily had huddled together in a flooded bombproof of icy water, exchanging their dreams for the future. Illusions now shattered, Alice winced at the nasty bruises and scrapes covering Lily's body. After sponging her off and helping her change into a clean nightdress, Alice showed her to the spare bedroom.

Finally, Lily stopped crying. "When Nathan return, he go after dem."

Lily's husband hadn't returned from the war yet, and Alice suspected that he never would. Fighting her own tears, she grasped Lily's hand and squeezed it. "He won't need to," she reassured her. "The Yankees will go after whoever did this."

Lily shook her head. "Miss Alice, you live in a dream world. Darkies ain't no better off wi' da Yankees. Dese men will go unpunished for what dey do, an' when my Nathan go after dem, which one do you think da Yankees punish?"

"Colonel Prescott isn't like that. These men—you haven't said if they've done more than..." During the war, a Yankee lieutenant had attempted to rape her. One shot, using Wil's pistol, had stopped him. Unable to say the word, Alice tugged on her collar. "...hurt you. They're guilty of other crimes. Sam will see that they're brought to justice."

Lily's eyelashes fluttered, and she sounded distant when she spoke. Alice thought she might start crying again, but Lily maintained her poise. "Dey do a lot of drinkin' an' make me dance wi' dem. Said dey was just funnin'."

"How many?"

"Three, but dey don't hurt me, not until... A man wi' a moustache arrive..." Her hand made a sweeping gesture above her lip, indicating a moustache.

Douglas Chandler instantly popped into Alice's mind.

"One of dem carry a flag wi' bullet holes in his saddlebags."

Alice shivered. "A flag?"

Lily wrung her hands. "One dey carry in battle."

"Confederate?"

With a nod, Lily continued, "He call me a nigger wench an' tear my dress." She dug her nails into her palm and moaned like a wounded animal. "He take me to da loft . . . an' make me lay down on da flag and do things."

Alice sucked in her breath. "What sort of things?"

"Touch him in ways dat I only touch Nathan. He let me know dat if I talk, he'd expect more da next time." Her arms went around Alice's neck and she was crying again.

Lily poured out her grief on Alice's shoulder. Finally, when Lily's tears were cried out, Alice sat with her until she fell into a restless sleep. Tiptoeing to the door, she carefully closed it behind her.

Once outside the study, she waited. Slatted boards covering windows had yet to be replaced with glass and cut a pattern of broken light. A shadowy figure sat behind the desk. While it was an improvement over the board Wil had used initially, it wasn't much more than a camp desk, but it served the purpose until they could replace more important furnishings first. She wandered into the room, and he watched her as she lit a lamp. "Lily's finally asleep."

Steepling his fingers, Wil leaned back in the chair. "Did she tell you anything?"

"A man fitting the description of Douglas Chandler . . . He beat her, then threatened her. She also said he had a Confederate flag."

"Was she raped?"

He said the word so easily. Alice swallowed hard. "No, but he forced her to do things that should only happen between people who care about one another."

Wil thumped a fist to the desk. "I'll see to Chandler." He collected his gun belt and got to his feet.

As he strapped the belt around his waist, she grasped his arm. "No, Wil. Let Sam handle this."

He strode for the door. With a shiver, Alice called after him, but it was no use. She heard the outside door shut, and like so many other evenings, he vanished into the mist.

Light flickered through the window as overly loud, drunken voices chattered from the tavern. Wil stepped inside and scanned over the patrons. No sign of Chandler. Odd that he hadn't been seen in days, unless he *was* guilty of abducting Lily—he usually spent half the night playing poker. Wil lit a cigar and ordered a whiskey from the bar. He made several inquiries, but heads shook in answer to Chandler's whereabouts. Even more peculiar. Then it dawned on him. At the dance Holly and Chandler kept to each other's company. No doubt existed as to whom her latest lover was. Sam had mentioned questioning Holly on a couple of occasions, but Wil doubted the Yankees would search the house of a prominent carpetbagger.

Wil snuffed the cigar. After collecting his horse, he rode to the west end of town. Only the Kenmore plantation had a larger house than Frank Whyte's columned mansion in all of Fredericksburg. He tethered the mare to the hitching post out front, then climbed the massive staircase. He pounded on the door. A diminutive, chocolate-brown girl answered. "Mrs. Whyte," he grumbled to her.

"Dis highly improper, sir."

"I don't give a damn about propriety." Wil shoved past the girl into the foyer. "Mrs. Whyte! Where is she?"

The servant girl latched onto his arm, attempting to herd him back to the door. "You cain't just come bargin' in here."

Lugging the girl still attached to his arm along with him, he glanced in the parlor. The table was set for tea service with fine silver, but no Holly. Disgusted by the carpetbaggers who preyed on innocent Southern citizens, he bellowed, "Holly, get your god-damned ass out here!"

"Wil Jackson!" Eyes blazing, Holly appeared at the top of the stairs and descended the sweeping staircase.

"I sorry, Miss Holly. He jus' barge in here hollerin' an' screamin'."

"That's all right, Sally. *Mr.* Jackson has always been known for his lack of manners." Clad in a silk dressing gown, she reached the bottom step. "How dare you, Wil. If Frank were here, he would have shot you for trespassing and deservedly so."

"To hell with *Frank*. Where's Chandler?"

Her eyes widened in disbelief. "I have no idea what you could be talking about. Though you certainly made a spectacle of yourself the other night; I merely danced with the man."

"A sixty-year old man keeps you sufficiently entertained? With your carnal appetite, I find that difficult to believe." She yelped when he seized her arms and nearly hoisted her off her feet. "Where's Chandler?"

She pressed her hips against him in a provocative manner. His body reacted and she smiled sweetly. "Why Wil, I wasn't aware that you still cared."

Uttering a curse, he let her go. "You always were a cockteaser."

She threw her head back and laughed, then narrowed her eyes in contempt. "What gives you the right to come storming in here making demands? Just think how awkward Sam would feel if I pressed charges, and he found it necessary to arrest you."

Awkward? The tipped corners of her lips suggested that she relished the prospect. Wil lowered his hat. "If I behaved rashly . . ."

"I'm certain that's the closest I'll ever get to an apology. I accept." Holly laced her arm through his and showed him to the parlor. "When you barged in, I was in the midst of dressing for supper. As is usually the case, Frank is late, but then he works so dreadfully hard—unlike others around here."

Ignoring the innuendo, Wil decided that he would get more information from her if he controlled his temper.

Her smile changed to a gracious one. "Would you care to join me in some tea and tell me what has you all fired up?"

The hostess image was a sham. Wil grasped her hand and tugged her to him. His mouth met hers, and her arms went around his neck. He reached inside her dressing gown. As he had guessed, she wasn't wearing a stitch underneath. He felt soft skin and the curve of a bare breast. Like a black widow, she was drawing him into her web for the kill.

Weary of her incessant games, he stepped back and drew his pistol. Holly shrieked. Retreating from the parlor, he charged up the stairs and into the hall. Which room? He stood to the side while cautiously opening the first door. The room was empty. A thud of hurried footsteps came from the next room. Wil booted in the door. The linens on the bed were rumpled and an autumn breeze swirled the curtains to the open window. Too late— Chandler had already made his retreat and there was no sign of anyone on the street below.

From across the room, Holly hailed him. "Wil . . ." He turned. Her silk dressing gown fell open, revealing her pale-white body, and firm, ripe breasts. In her slender hands she held a pearl-handled derringer.

Before he could react, Wil went reeling to the floor. A blinding pain radiated through his head. Something warm ran in his eye.

Holly stood over him. "Damn you, Wil Jackson. Have you gone loony? Why couldn't you leave well enough alone?"

Drifting, he fought through layers of fog, and her face remained a blur. He heard her shout for the servant, when the fog sucked him under, and his head thumped back.

She lifted his head, and a cup went to his lips. Water trickled down his throat. "Wil . . ."

He blinked, and her face shimmered in and out of focus. Wil tried sitting up, but the pain intensified.

"Take it easy. You've been shot."

He laid his head back to the floor. "No thanks . . . to you."

"What did you expect when you came in here raging like a mad bull?" He felt a cool, wet cloth press against the side of his head. "I think it's only a graze. Why are you so intent on finding Doug?"

"He . . ." Her face blurred again.

"Never mind. Sally is fetching the doctor. Hopefully, we can get you out of here and the blood cleaned up before Frank gets home."

"And if you can't?"

"I refuse to try and explain this to him. I shall press charges, *Mr.* Jackson."

In spite of the pain, Wil laughed. She would never change.

Chapter Six

*F*LOORBOARDS CREAKED AS ALICE WANDERED the length of the parlor. *Where was Wil?* He had left the house hours ago. If he had gone after Douglas Chandler, then he could be lying on some deserted street—dead. She nibbled her fingernails to the quick—something she hadn't done since they had helped Sam escape from Libby prison.

A key rattled in the door, and she breathed out in relief. She dashed into the foyer. It wasn't Wil, but Jesse Morgan. She choked back a cry. "Mr. Morgan, I'll thank you to leave. My husband..."

"Is right here," Jesse groaned as he struggled through the door.

"Wil—is with you?"

"I could use some help, ma'am. He's been hit."

Her heart thumped, and she rushed to the door. "Hit? Is he hurt bad?"

"It's a graze, but it was to the head."

Alice fought a gasp as Wil leaned against Jesse for support. His head was swathed in a crimson bandage and his sack coat was streaked with blood. "Wil, what happened?"

"I think... my head greeted a bullet."

Always a joke. "Wil, for once in your life, be serious." To Jesse, she said, "Let's get him into the other room." She drew his free arm over her shoulder, and they helped him to the parlor. After easing him to the sofa, Alice plumped a cushion behind his head. "How bad is it?"

"There might be a minor head injury, but the doc doesn't think it's serious," Jesse responded. "He prescribed laudanum and rest."

Her heart finally settled from its galloping rhythm. "Mr. Morgan, I have some laudanum in the kitchen—in the cupboard near the wash basin. Could you please fetch it?"

"If you would call me, Jesse, ma'am."

"Of course—Jesse." As the boy left the parlor, she turned her attention to Wil. "The next obvious question is, who did this?"

Wil's eyes seemed to have difficulty focusing on her. "One of your patrons . . . Mrs. Whyte."

"Holly shot you? Why would she do that?"

"To protect her lover."

Douglas Chandler. A good sign—at least Wil's answers seemed coherent and lucid. "I bet you have a walloping headache."

"I didn't think you were a betting woman, Alice."

More jokes. "Hush up, Wil. I don't think you realize just how lucky you are. Why," she said, shaking her head in astonishment, "you must possess nine lives. And the fact that you didn't answer my question only confirms I would have won the bet."

Jesse returned with the laudanum in a teacup. She helped Wil drink. He must be hurting if he didn't protest. "So how did you happen on Holly and Mr. Chandler?"

"A gut feeling." His eyes grew fixed.

"Wil . . ." She snapped her fingers in front of his face. He blinked, but she had witnessed enough head injuries in the hospitals during the war to be familiar with the symptoms. "Are you feeling dizzy?"

"A little."

The laudanum wouldn't have had time to take effect yet, and if he was making an admission, she knew that it was just cause to fret. "Jesse, did the doctor say he might become disoriented?"

"He did and said not to worry unless the symptoms become severe."

At least that much was a relief, but she detected bewilderment in Wil's eyes. Then he glanced around the room and familiarity returned to them. "Are you all right?" she asked. He nodded. Shaky on his feet, he stood, and she offered him a steadying hand. "What do you think you're doing?"

Wil put a hand to his head. "I'm not certain."

"Jesse, let's get him upstairs. I think he'll rest easier there." With Jesse's aid, she helped Wil to their room. After half an hour, he was finally resting comfortably. Jesse waited at the bottom of the stairs. "We're indebted to you for your help, Mr. Morgan."

"Jesse," he reminded her.

Feeling awkward in Jesse's presence, Alice twisted her handkerchief. A long past affair in itself hadn't surprised her, and Wil had been young and foolish at the time. Happenings from over twenty years ago shouldn't bother her, but the fact that Jesse might be his son did. "How did you happen by my husband this evening?"

Jesse blew out a breath. "I saw him at the tavern, so I followed him."

"Did you follow him out of concern for his well being or as an informant for Mr. Chandler?"

He ran a nervous hand through his whiskers.

"Wil has informed me about your claim."

"Ma'am, I didn't come here to cause trouble."

Angered by such a blatant lie, she raised an accusing finger. "Then why are you here?"

"Because . . ." He cleared his throat. "I don't expect to be greeted with open arms, but the general is the only kin I have left."

Her anger faded, but confusion remained. "Then why are you mixing with the likes of Douglas Chandler?"

He shifted uneasily on his feet. "I met him after the war. I was aware he had been a partisan, but had no place to go. By the time I found out that he hadn't left the war behind, it was too late."

She feared his statement was an attempt to get sympathy. "Were you involved in hurting Lily?"

He shook his head. "No, ma'am."

For some reason, she believed him. Any remaining anger was replaced with sympathy. "All right, I believe you. Jesse . . ." Before she could finish her question, a rap came at the door. A little nervous as to who might come calling at such an early hour, she cracked the door open. With his hat in hand, Sam stood outside and she widened the door. "Sam, come in."

"This isn't a social call, Alice." Sam eyed Jesse as he stepped into the foyer. "You're under arrest. I hope you'll take into account there is a lady present and come along peaceably."

Jesse nodded.

"My men are waiting outside."

Jesse lowered his head and stepped outside.

"Sam, is this really necessary?"

"I have a warrant for his arrest." He fidgeted with his hat. "Alice, I need to speak with Wil."

She should have guessed as much and sighed. "Are you going to arrest him too?"

"No, but if Holly decides to press charges, I won't be left with a choice."

"Holly shot *him!*"

"That may be," Sam agreed, "but he forced his way into her home. She was well within her right to defend herself."

"Sam, I can't believe we're having this conversation. You would have died in Libby if Wil hadn't pulled you out."

"I'm aware of that," he said gently, "but I must uphold the law . . ."

"Yankee law," she hissed.

He blew out a breath in frustration. "Fine. Have it your way, but tell Wil that I want him in my office tomorrow morning at eight o'clock. If he's not there, I'll return for him with a warrant in hand."

As Sam strode for the door, Alice's head reeled. "Damnyankee. We should have left you in that hell hole to rot."

Without turning around, Sam halted by the door. "And do you think another commander would have been as lenient as I have been? Good day, Mrs. Jackson."

Alice bit her lip to keep from hurling more curses, and Sam stepped outside, closing the door behind him.

When Wil woke, his head pounded. He recalled taking laudanum for the pain, and now he was groggy. A woman sat on the edge of the straw mattress, but her face remained out of focus. "Alice . . ."

"I'm here," she whispered. He clutched her skirt with his head coming to rest in her lap. Her fingers stroked through his hair. Freshly scrubbed, she smelled like lilacs. Caught up in her scent and wishing she were naked, he squeezed her buttocks through the padded petticoat layers. "I don't think that's what the doctor meant by rest," Alice giggled, "but it's good to know you're feeling better."

After taking a bullet in the Wilderness, Alice had tended him day and night while he hovered between life and death. One morning he had woken to her beside him. He wanted to ask her to join him, but the laudanum euphoria held him captive.

"Wil, I believe Jesse is telling the truth."

"About what?"

"His claim. You admit to *knowing* his mother."

Suddenly less groggy, Wil sat up. "And one indiscretion automatically makes him my bastard son? Alice, given my past, I can guess what you must be thinking, but Caroline was a lady. Even though I was at West Point, she would have said something, rather than face the wrath of her parents."

"Men," she grumbled, "you always see things so clearly, whether it's the way things are or not. Would you have married her?"

This wasn't the sort of conversation that a man tended to have with his wife, and he wasn't about to start now. Would he have married Caroline? The answer—he didn't know, but he doubted either family would have allowed him to return to Charleston if he hadn't. And that's precisely why he had difficulty believing Jesse was his son. Someone—somewhere would have said something.

"Don't bother answering," Alice continued. "It's none of my business really. I only want you to be honest with yourself. It may not be logical to you, but she may have had a reason for keeping quiet." She fell silent for a long while before speaking again, and he almost drifted off to sleep. "Wil, he needs your help."

"Who?"

"Jesse. Sam took him into custody. Whether he's your son or not, he could use someone on his side. Besides, Sam insisted on seeing you this morning."

"I can hazard a guess as to why." Wil struggled to his feet. When he swayed, Alice latched onto his arm to help steady him. With her help, he dressed and made his way downstairs.

Between the bumpy axles and the washboard road, the buggy ride of half a mile to military headquarters was less than ideal. Exhausted from the trip and with his head hurting like hell, Wil was escorted to Sam's office by a sergeant. When he shuffled in, Sam remained seated behind his desk. Like an inquisitor, Lieutenant Greer stood by his side.

Sam pounded a fist on the desk and stood. "What in the hell did you think you were doing last night, Jackson?"

"Attempting to discover Chandler's whereabouts."

"I'm handling things around here. Is that clear?"

"It is," Wil agreed.

Relief spread across Sam's face, and he reseated himself. "Besides, you foolish bastard, you should know better than to rile Holly. You could have got yourself killed."

Wil shook his head. "She'd have difficulty explaining the body to Frank."

Sam laughed. "And he is precisely the reason why she's not pressing charges, but if she changes her mind . . ."

Wil nodded that he understood. "May I see Jesse now?"

"He hasn't been very cooperative."

"If you'll permit me, I'll see if I can get him to talk to you."

Sam agreed. For a change, Greer didn't scowl at him like he was some sort of vermin and showed him to the back. Wil insisted on seeing the boy alone. The lieutenant grumbled but left them to their privacy. He gripped the jail cell's bars to keep from falling. Jesse Morgan stood at attention like a soldier greeting an officer. Wil motioned for him to remain at ease. "We're not in the military anymore."

"Old habits die hard. Sir . . ." Jesse gestured for him to have a seat on the cot.

"Enough of the sirs, but much obliged." Though dizzy, Wil made it over to the cot and eased himself onto it. "Colonel Prescott says you haven't been very cooperative."

Clasping his hands together, Jesse licked his lips. "I reckon not."

"Who are you afraid of?"

Jesse unclasped his hands. "No one."

Wil met the boy's gaze. "I don't believe that." Still he was met with silence. "I can't help you if you don't tell me everything."

"Help me?"

"My word might carry some weight with Colonel Prescott. At least it would have before last night."

"There's nothing you can do, General. I wasn't involved in the fire or the incident with your wife's servant, but I have been stealing horses and livestock and selling them."

A hanging offense, right there. Wil sighed. "Is there anything else I should know?" Jesse opened his mouth as if about to say something further but closed it again. He shook his head. Detecting the boy was holding back, Wil stood. That wasn't such a good idea. His head throbbed, but he somehow made it to the door and called for the guard. "The guard plays a lousy hand of poker."

"I'll remember that," Jesse responded with a laugh. "Sir . . . why are you helping me?"

"Because I owe Caroline that much."

For a minute, Wil thought Jesse might break down and cry, but his eyes remained dry.

"When you were my age . . . ?" Jesse inquired.

"I was shipped off to Mexico."

The guard entered the holding area. "After West Point?" Jesse asked.

As the guard unlocked the door, Wil nodded and turned. Although his military record was fairly common knowledge, he wondered why the boy would be curious unless his claim happened to be true. There were still many unanswered questions.

November had arrived. Either Douglas Chandler had been lying low for more than a fortnight, or he had vanished from Fredericksburg, leaving Jesse to suffer the consequences. Some normalcy had returned to life, and Wil had reported for an engineering position with the railroad. Unfortunately, it required him to be where they were relaying war-torn tracks and rebuilding burned bridges, which at the moment was the primary line in Petersburg.

Alice had taken ill during the night. Bent over the chamber pot and retching her guts out, she feared by the symptoms that either she had the influenza making the rounds or she might be with child again. She relished that aspect of married life which created babies, but wished they weren't such a frequent consequence. Even fastidious use of a sponge was no guarantee, but more reliable methods were in short supply or exorbitantly expensive. She prayed that her current sickness was due to the flu.

Her conscience chastised her. Instead of feeling sorry for herself, she should be rejoicing if she were in a family way. After all, Emma was nearly a year old, and a second baby wouldn't be brought into the world during the midst of a war. Unlike during the siege, food would eventually be plentiful again. Though money was tight, they'd find a way to manage.

Alice rinsed her mouth and got dressed. She barely had time to dress Emma before Lily arrived. The servant remained despondent from her abduction but performed her duties satisfactorily.

Noon arrived before she had all of her chores finished around the house. Gathering up her basket, she traced the path to town, barely noticing the broken brick walls and weed-infested foundations. At least every other day, she stopped by the jail to see how Jesse Morgan was faring. On a couple of occasions she had brought Emma along. The young man was surprisingly gentle with her daughter, and he always asked about Wil.

As she stepped into the headquarters, she was relieved to be out of the ever-increasing fall chill. Sam was on patrol, but she had apologized for calling him a "damnyankee" the day before. The guards smiled and one left his post to escort her to the jail cell. Apparently, Jesse didn't possess Wil's finesse. At least she never caught him playing poker with the guards.

When she entered the cell, Jesse stood to greet her. She retrieved a warm plate from her basket. The smell of the greasy stewing hen and weevil-infested flour made her queasy. "I have brought chicken and biscuits."

His almond eyes brightened. "Much obliged, ma'am."

"I wish you would learn to call me by my name."

"Yes, ma'am . . . I mean Alice." Grasping the plate, he returned to the cot and hungrily forked the biscuits to his mouth. "Your cooking reminds me of my ma's. Pardon me, I shouldn't have mentioned her."

Like many Southerners, he had no home to return to. Was it really so surprising he had found himself on the wrong side of the law? "I take no offense in you mentioning your mother. When was the last time you saw her?"

"Three years ago."

And now she was dead, and the Yankees thought hanging Jesse would be justice served. "You miss her, don't you?"

"Miss a lot of folks these days, but then I'm sure you know someone who didn't make it back."

Nodding that she understood, she remembered holding many men in her arms when they had died. "I nearly lost Wil."

"The general was wounded?"

"In the Wilderness."

Jesse momentarily stopped chewing.

"Don't let him fool you. He wants you to think he's in peak health, but he's never fully recovered. That's why I can never thank you enough for your help."

"It's the least I could do. After all, the general . . ." He shook his head that it wasn't important and returned to his meal.

Once he was finished, Alice placed the empty plate into her basket. Jesse Morgan was such a strange, sad young man. She guessed she'd never fully understand him, but the war had done the same to a lot of Southerners. Yet, his accent and manners suggested a former prominent status. More perplexed than when she had arrived, she left the cell and tended to her marketing before returning home.

As she neared the house, a buggy with a perfectly matched pair of bays waited out front. Scrambling up the steps, she had difficulty believing Holly's audacity for calling on her. With her arms crossed, Holly waited inside, tapping an impatient foot. "What kept you? I have numerous calls to make."

"Exactly what *are* you doing here?"

"Our appointment . . . Don't tell me that you've forgotten?"

"Forgotten. How dare you for even showing your face around here. Or are you going to shoot me too?"

"Alice, I never meant to shoot Wil. As he's so fond of saying, if I had meant to kill him, he would be dead."

Infuriated, Alice doubled her fists. "Leave, Holly. Before I throw you out."

Holly's bracelets clattered as she threw her hands in the air. "I'm going."

Suddenly queasy, Alice thought she was going to be sick again. Covering her mouth, she dashed up the stairs for the nearest chamber pot. Barely reaching the brass pot in time, she leaned over it and retched. Someone patted her on the back as she threw up again. Expecting to see Lily, she turned and found Holly standing behind her.

"I certainly hope it isn't catching."

If what she feared might be true, definitely not. "I don't think so."

"Alice, I'll pay you a bonus of ten dollars if you finish my dress."

Ten dollars? She could certainly use the money. "Holly, how can you continue to bribe me after what's happened?"

"I told you, it was an accident. All right, if you insist—fifteen."

"I don't care if it's a hundred . . ."

"Then what can I do to prove to you that it was nothing more than an accident? Wil and I have had our share of differences, but remember, I tended him, so he could return to you."

At the end of the war, Holly had indeed helped Wil. Alice's anger faded. She motioned for Holly to follow her down the hall to the sewing room. She grasped a dress from the back of the chair. "Here, try it on, then I'll finish pinning it."

As Holly reached for the dress, Alice suddenly felt faint. Her hand went to her head. "You really are sick," Holly said, her agitation fading.

"It's nothing."

Holly helped her to a chair and stared at her in disbelief. "If you don't have the influenza going around town, then you're going to have another baby." Her own fear, but she couldn't admit as much to Holly. When she failed to respond, Holly arched an amused eyebrow. "Babies are dreadful on the waistline. Thank God, I've never had the annoyance. Not for lack of Frank trying, but I doubt he could get that puny beanpole . . ."

Alice raised a hand. "Holly, please spare me the details."

"Right." A patronizing smile appeared on Holly's face. "You certainly don't have that problem with Wil."

Why did she put up with this woman? Alice gritted her teeth, reminding herself of the income.

"Alice . . ." Holly's voice had turned gentle. "Is another child what you want?"

"Want it? Holly, I'm not even certain that I am in a family way. I'm hoping that it is nothing more than the flu."

"Then you don't want it," Holly stated with certainty.

"Holly!"

"I'm just trying to be helpful. There are ways of ridding yourself of such parasites before they're born. If you haven't told Wil what you suspect, he doesn't need to know."

Alice finally understood how a woman like Holly with so many lovers never had any babies. "I'm telling Wil that it's influenza."

"That's good." Holly patted her hand. "That way if you are in a family way, you never need to tell him."

"Holly, if I discover that I'm in a family way, I'll tell him at that time." Holly breathed out in disgust, but said nothing further. Alice worried more about Amanda. After the loss of two babies, her sister would find it difficult to accept if she were indeed in a family way.

Chapter Seven

*A*S THE GUARD CREAKED THE JAIL CELL door open, Sam thought of Libby. No matter how hard he tried to suppress it, he could not control the shiver that crawled along his spine. Jesse stood to greet him. "I've been authorized to release you, but first, you must agree to cooperate."

"You have that, sir."

Sam held up his hand. "It's under my recognizance. If it wasn't for..." He had nearly said captain. "Mr. Jackson's deposition requesting that you receive another chance, I wouldn't put my neck on the line for the likes of you. You will do exactly as I say when I tell you, or you'll find yourself right back here facing trial faster than you believed possible. Is that clear?"

"Yes, Colonel."

"Now do you have any prospect of gaining legitimate employment?"

Jesse shook his head.

"My wife could use an extra hand on the farm."

"Sir?"

"You originally came from a farm in North Carolina, didn't you?"

"Yes, sir."

"Then you'll work for my wife on the farm. Ezra is getting on in years, and she needs someone who can see to the heavy work and come spring the plowing and planting. It'll be long hours, six days a week, and the pay won't be much, but if you stay out of trouble and pay back what you owe folks, I should be able to get the charges against you dismissed."

"Much obliged, sir."

Sam showed Jesse to the outer office, where the young man collected his belongings. Immediately confiscating the pistol, Sam watched as Jesse gathered up a hat, a pocket knife, and a photograph of a family. The daguerreotype had three adolescent boys, one being Jesse and the oldest, a girl, and an older woman who he guessed to be in her late thirties. "Your family?"

Jesse merely nodded.

Suddenly feeling sorry for the boy, Sam decided he was glad they were taking a chance on him. Once outside, he said, "First, we need to get you some new work clothes."

Jesse turned his ragged pockets inside out. "I don't have the money . . ."

"You'll repay us."

"Yes, sir."

After collecting supplies at the general store for Amanda, Sam climbed into the wagon and motioned Jesse to the other side. The boy clambered aboard, and Sam clicked his tongue for the team to move forward. As horses' hooves pounded against the dirt road, axles creaked.

Several miles passed in silence. "Got a sweetheart back home, Jesse?" He shook his head. "What about kin?"

"A brother and a sister. Another brother died during the war."

Comprehending Jesse's grief, Sam thought of the picture, and his own brother who had died at the Battle of Fredericksburg. "So why didn't you return home?"

"Couldn't."

But Jesse failed to elaborate. Sam tried breaking the ice by telling boyhood tales of growing up in Maine. Stubbornly, Jesse refused to open up. It was evening by the time he turned the wagon up the tree-lined lane. Halting it outside the farmhouse, he set the brake and jumped down. Amanda stepped onto the porch. Once she recognized him, she dashed down the steps to greet him. "Sam . . ."

As soon as she was in his arms, she stiffened. Except for the night of the dance, she continued to grieve for the baby. He longed for something to do or say that would ease her mourning. He gave her a kiss, and she stepped back. "You already know Jesse," he said.

"Of course. Jesse . . ."

"He's going to be helping on the farm."

"Sam . . ." She grasped his elbow and drew him aside. "Is that wise? Will he work with Negroes?"

"I didn't stop to ask, but I reckon he will. His choices are rather limited. If he doesn't help on the farm, he could be facing a hangman's noose. I'll have him bunk in the cabin next to Ezra."

"All right," Amanda agreed. "Have him come up to the house for supper."

With a nod, Sam waved for Jesse to follow him. "After I show you where you'll be staying, you can see to the team." Sam escorted the boy to the cabins in the walnut grove. At least Jesse didn't balk at the sight of the former slave quarters. Outside one hut, the old Negro servant, Ezra, sat smoking a corncob pipe. "Ezra, this is Jesse. He's going to be helping us on the farm."

Jesse eyed the servant but didn't say anything.

Showing him inside to the one-room cabin, Sam thought of another time. After the Battle of Fredericksburg, he had met Amanda secretly here. They had made love on the cot. "It's not much, but it's a place to hang your hat."

"I've lived in worse."

"Yes, I reckon you have." Sam turned to leave. "After you tend to the horses, you're welcome to come up to the house for supper. You'll take most of your meals out here, but tonight, we'd like you to join us as our guest."

"Much obliged, sir."

Sam spoke briefly with Ezra before returning to the house. The scent of freshly baked apple pie drifted his way. Though his stomach rumbled, he had best not disturb Amanda while she was cooking. She'd only shoo him from the kitchen. He joined his daughter from his first marriage in the parlor. At five years old, Rebecca had curly dark brown hair that reminded him of her mother,

Kate. She threw her arms around his neck in a welcoming embrace. "Papa..."

Gone for months at a time during the war, he had often been a stranger in the household. Those trying times were behind them now. He stretched out, getting comfortable on the sofa, while Rebecca cradled the rag doll Amanda had made for her. Pretending to feed its button mouth, she rattled on about proper baby care. He played with Rebecca until a rap came on the door.

Striding over to answer it, Sam noted that Jesse had taken the time to wash up and change into his new clothes. Even the grime from under the boy's nails was clean. He suspected the Morgans had been a fairly prominent family. Sam waved the way into the parlor, showing Jesse to the velvet wing chair.

A pale Alice carried in a silver platter with a teapot. Jesse stood. "Mrs. Jackson, I didn't expect to see you here."

As she started to pour, she smiled. "I got tired of that big house and being alone with Emma while Wil is away." She handed Jesse a cup of tea, and he muttered his thanks. "I'm pleased to see that you're out of jail, but I thought we had agreed to less formality."

"We had . . . Alice."

Undecided what to make of Jesse, Sam once again got comfortable on the sofa. Amanda and her mother joined them. They made small talk about the weather and farm operations, which continued throughout supper. As the women put the children to bed, Sam offered Jesse a cigar. The boy declined. Sam struck a match to his and leaned back. "So Jesse, what do you know about the fire?"

The boy nodded as if he had been expecting the question all evening. "Very little."

Suspicious, Sam blew out a puff of smoke. "I wouldn't take your answer as being cooperative."

"Sir, if I knew more . . ."

"Then it wasn't started by that gang of horse thieves you hang out with?"

"I suspect they had something to do with it, but . . ."

Sam snuffed his cigar in an ashtray. "But what?"

"Sam . . ." Amanda stood on the stairs. "That's no way to treat a guest."

"Dammit Amanda, we lost a valuable horse in that fire. Another is missing, probably sold for a pretty penny."

She joined them in the parlor. "I'm well aware of that, but if Jesse says he doesn't know . . ."

Sam raised his voice. "And you believe him? Or are you protecting him because he's Jackson's bastard?"

"Sam!"

Alice rejoined them, pretending that she hadn't overheard.

"Alice, I'm sorry." Sam returned his attention to Jesse, and the boy got to his feet. "Jesse, I want to believe you, but your record hasn't been the best. After serving time at Elmira, you probably have cause to hate all Yankees . . ."

"Sir, as I understand, you spent time in Libby."

Sam shuddered. "True, what's that . . ."

"Do you hate all former Confederates?"

Nodding in understanding, Sam realized they had more in common than probably either of them had ever guessed. He held out his hand.

Jesse hesitated but shook it. "Thank you, sir."

"Now if y'all don't mind . . ." Only with Amanda's giggle did Sam realize what he had said. Jesse glanced from face to face as if he had missed part of the conversation.

"Best be careful, Sam," Alice said with a taunting squeal. "We'll make a Southerner of you yet, and the accent will stick."

Now comprehending, Jesse joined the women's laughter. No doubt about it. With each passing day, Sam was becoming more like a Virginian. Relieved the worst was behind them, Sam drew Amanda in his arms. With her near, he no longer cared if he ever returned to Maine.

But Amanda shoved away from him and dashed upstairs. As time passed, he thought her blue moods would get better. Sam excused himself and followed her upstairs. He entered the bedroom. Amanda was curled on the bed, sobbing. "Amanda . . ."

"Sam, I'm sorry." She sat up and sniffed back her tears. "It's Alice."

He dabbed a handkerchief to her streaked face. "What's wrong with Alice?"

Amanda grasped the handkerchief and twisted it in her hands. "She says it's the flu, but I can tell she's hiding what she really thinks."

"What does she think?"

"That she might be in a family way."

Although everyone had asked about Amanda's health since the loss of the baby, Sam felt a tug of emotion. He struggled to keep a strong appearance for her sake. "You can have another baby," he suggested.

Tears renewed. "I can't lose another."

Two sons rested on the hill behind the house—one to scarlet fever and the other born too soon. "Amanda, I want to do what's right for you."

Through her tears, she forced a smile. "I have Rebecca, and I love her as if I had birthed her myself."

And Kate had died giving birth to Rebecca. "I know. Rebecca does too, but I think I understand a woman's need to have her own baby."

"It's selfish," she insisted.

"Amanda, you of all people are far from selfish. I can't think of a more loving and caring woman." Drawing her close, he hugged her tight. He needed her. Reminiscent of times past, she kissed him full on the mouth. He touched and fondled her. Tears again, but she didn't pull away.

For nearly a week, Alice had perched on the knoll in the pasture— watching and listening. At the war's end, she had waited here for Wil's return. For some reason, when he was away, she felt closer to him here than anywhere else. Near dusk, a raccoon skittered by in its quest for food. An animal that hid behind a mask. Was the raccoon her guardian spirit? She closed her eyes and concentrated on the animal's attributes.

"Alice . . ."

Startled by Amanda's arrival, Alice leaped to her feet. "Amanda, I didn't hear you."

"What on earth are you doing? You've been coming out here for days."

"I'm attempting to discover my totem."

"Wil certainly has filled your head full of fanciful daydreams."

Amanda's voice sounded peculiar. Disgust? No, her sister was the racoon hiding behind a mask. "The animal spirits are real. If you take the time to listen."

"Then perhaps you'll listen to the spirit telling you that your daughter is hungry." Amanda lifted her skirts and started down the hill.

"Amanda . . ." Alice dashed after her and caught her sister's elbow. "What happened?"

Her sister's brows knitted together in confusion.

"Between you and Wil."

"Alice." Amanda clamped a hand to her mouth as if she had been struck by sheer terror. "Dredging up ancient history does no good. I married Sam, and you married Wil. Nothing else matters."

"There's more. Both Sam and I see it in the two of you. I don't mean to cause you discomfort, but only by confronting the past can we embrace the present and future."

Her shock fading, Amanda slowly lowered her arm. "This is my little tomboy sister speaking, who always acted so impulsively? I think I had best study those animal spirits."

"Here, sit with me." Alice took her sister's hand.

"What about Emma?" Amanda gestured in the direction of the house.

"It'll only be a few minutes." With Amanda beside her, Alice reseated herself on the knoll. "Please, tell me."

"We were only friends, and sometimes even that relationship was strained."

Why had she expected an honest response for a change? "Are you trying to fool me or yourself?"

"I'm not trying to fool anyone," Amanda insisted, jumping to her feet. Her voice raised as she started to meander along the knoll. "At the beginning of the war, I helped Wil smuggle medical supplies, and that's all. Wil was keeping company with Holly, and who knows how many others like her. But then, you know all about that, don't you? As I recall, you were one of many flirting with him."

Amanda had warned her against Wil, and she hadn't realized the rift with her sister went back so far. "Thank you for reminding me, but why were you jealous of me then?"

"Jealous?" Amanda shook her head. "I wasn't jealous. I have always loved Sam."

"I believe you," Alice stated with sincerity.

Suspicious, Amanda continued, "Then why all of the questions?"

"Because you're afraid to openly admit that you loved both of them."

Amanda's voice suddenly wavered. "What good could come from such an admission? It would only hurt you and Sam."

"We're already hurting. If you admit it to yourself, then you can accept how things turned out and let Wil go."

"Let him go? But I have no hold over him."

"Amanda, I'm well aware which one of us he would have chosen."

"Alice . . ." Amanda cleared her throat. "When you gave me the news that Wil was missing after the battle at Sharpsburg, I was certain he was dead. By the time I found out he was alive, I already . . ." Her voice broke. She breathed deeply, then continued, "I already carried Sam's child."

Suddenly lightheaded, Alice swayed on her feet. "So if you hadn't been with child, you would have chosen . . ."

Amanda gripped Alice's arm to help steady her. "I don't know. Alice, I'm telling you the truth when I say that I simply don't know. Wil said that he had written a letter, but I never received it. And I was never allowed to resolve my feelings before the decision was forced upon me." Tears formed in Amanda's eyes. "I told you nothing good could come from this." Amanda gathered her skirts together and dashed down the hill.

The raccoon had finally lowered her mask.

* * *

Winter rains halted the acquisition of supplies for the railroad. After being absent for nearly a month, Wil had returned to Fredericksburg only to discover Alice had gone to Amanda's earlier in the week. By the time he arrived at the farm, it was nightfall. During supper, strained looks and clipped words passed between the sisters. Alice and Amanda's mother, Jean, kept the conversation going by asking him about his time away. Around ten, they retired for the evening, and after an intense reunion of frolicking in bed, Alice nestled in the crook of his arm. A hint of a contented smile tugged at the corners of her mouth. He laid his head to the feather pillow and dozed off. "Damn you, Wil," she cursed under her breath.

Only half awake, he opened his eyes to narrow slits. "May I inquire as to what I've done now?"

Her smile had vanished. "You come in here and make love to me, yet you never acknowledged the letter where I feared that I might be with child again."

"I got your letter. I also received the next one a week later, informing me that your monthly had started. What else do you want me to say?"

As she sat up, the bedclothes fell away, exposing her breast. Unable to resist, he cupped it in his hands and kissed it. Before he got too carried away, she yanked the quilt to her neck. "That's just it. You didn't bother to let me know that you had received either letter."

Tugging the quilt from her naked body, he drew her in his arms. "So what are you asking me now?"

"I had hoped you would share my concern, is all." She twisted free of his grip. "It would have been the wrong time to have a baby."

"The right time is during a siege?"

With a soft laugh, Alice clutched the medicine pouch around his neck. His first wife, a Nez Percé, had given it to him for luck. She was afraid. He untied the deerskin cord and placed the pouch in her hand. Her fingers curled around it. "You're right," she agreed. "Emma didn't exactly put in an appearance at the best time, but . . ."

He hadn't helped calm her fear. "But what? It didn't come to pass."

She shook her head. "I think it's because of what Amanda's been through. It scared me."

He brushed her hair away from her cheek. "If it will help, I promise if you get with child again, I shall attend the birth."

"The last thing I need is a ham-handed husband in attendance," she grumbled lightheartedly. "Men have no business in the birthing room." She returned the medicine pouch to his hand. "Besides, this is the essence of the mountain lion. I want to discover my own totem."

"I hadn't realized that you actually believed."

"I do. I sat outside for days, but it hasn't come to me."

"It will. Give it time." Her bare breasts and right thigh pressed against him. In tired satisfaction, he drifted. Wil felt her quiver before he heard the sound. At first he thought she was laughing, but her tears warmed his skin. "Alice . . ."

Her cheeks were streaked, and she traced the scar on his chest where he had taken the bullet in the Wilderness. "Amanda told me about the letter."

The letter. He suddenly comprehended the tension during supper. *Damn.* "What did she say?"

"That she never received it."

Because he had burned it.

"Wil, tell me that things would have been the same if she had."

Don't pull back. But he couldn't deny his single regret. He got up and started to dress.

"Wil?"

Finished dressing, Wil left the bedroom and went into the parlor. Except for a few sputtering embers in the fireplace, the house was dark. He wished Alice had remained in Fredericksburg. At least in his own home, he could wrestle with his inner demons in relative peace. Careful not to disturb the sleeping household, he stepped onto the porch and lit a cigar. From the direction of the former slave cabins in the walnut grove came a mournful harmonica tune.

"Wil . . ."

Surprised to find anyone awake at such a late hour, he took a drag on the cigar. "Amanda," he acknowledged. She edged in beside him. His blood simmered. "Why did you tell Alice about the letter?"

She lowered her head. "I hadn't meant to. Wil, I'm sorry, but we need to talk."

"Not now." He butted the cigar and moved toward the sound of the harmonica, leaving Amanda behind. On the front steps of the shack sat Jesse. As Wil approached, the young man stopped playing and stood at attention.

"Haven't you heard the war is over?"

"Is it?" The tone of Jesse's question warned Wil that he wasn't the only person on the farm who wrestled with demons. Jesse held up a flask. "Care to join me, sir?"

"If you agree to address me by my given name."

Pouring from the flask, Jesse handed him a tin cup, then raised the flask. "What shall we drink to, Wil?"

"Demons."

Jesse grinned, and the cup and flask clinked. Wil's throat burned as the whiskey went down. His tongue already loosened from the alcohol, Jesse spoke about endless marching with the Stonewall brigade. Wil gulped the remainder of the drink, and as Jesse poured more whiskey into the cup, he relayed his experience of being relieved of duty from the martyred general. When the flask was empty, Jesse retrieved a bottle from the shack. He settled back on the porch step.

"In Helmira," Jesse said, pouring more whiskey into the cup, "we used to bet on each day's body count. Should we drink to the glory of war?"

Wil raised the cup.

"Wil?"

He nearly tripped over his own feet when he turned to see Alice standing behind him.

"When you didn't return, I started to fret."

He took a swig from the cup. "We're celebrating old times."

Jesse pressed the whiskey bottle to his lips with a drunken snigger. Alice came closer, sniffed the contents of the tin cup, and wrinkled her nose. "You're drunk. Both of you."

"I reckon so." Wil draped his arm over Alice's shoulder. "Join us, Alice. You saw enough maimed men in the hospitals to enlighten us on war's glory."

In disgust, Alice flipped his arm off her and scurried toward the house. "On second thought, sleep with your horse tonight," she shouted over her shoulder.

With a frown, Jesse lowered the bottle. "It's my fault that she's mad at you."

Wil shrugged. "She won't stay that way for long."

"She's a lot like my ma."

Caroline. How many other lives had he ruined? "Tell me about your mother. Was she happy?"

Jesse nodded. "I think so."

"Then that's all that matters. And I'm the reason you can't return home?" Jesse merely lowered his head. *His son.* He had to stop denying the truth and come to terms with that fact. "Jesse, if I had known, nothing would have been different. I had already earned a trip to the Point because of gambling, horse racing, and . . ." A mulatto house servant by the name of Florence. "My father banished me from Charleston after my indiscretion with your mother. I suspect her family made certain that I never found out about you. It's doubtful that I would have done the honorable thing back then, but even if I had, Caroline would have never been happy in the role of a military wife."

"You believe me?"

"I do."

With the admission, Jesse's frown changed to a smile. "Then my mother is the reason why you haven't returned to South Carolina with your family?"

They understood each other better than he had expected. "I won't have Alice suffer any humiliation for things I have done."

"And that's why you shouldn't let her go off fuming. Unless, of course, you really like sleeping with your horse."

Wil laughed. Why was it that he never seemed to learn from his mistakes, yet a man barely out of his boyhood possessed so much wisdom? He bid Jesse goodnight and staggered slightly on the path to the house. The same mournful tune of the harmonica that had drawn him to the shack followed him.

Once inside the bedroom, he crept through the darkness. Near the bed he stumbled and banged his shin against the frame. He bit his tongue to keep a curse from flying. After undressing, he joined Alice in bed. Her back faced him. No doubt she was pretending to be asleep. He reached for her arm and felt the clingy warmth of her flannel nightdress.

She shook his hand from her arm. "I thought I told you to sleep in the barn."

"Alice, I won't beg for forgiveness. It's not my nature, but under the circumstances, I'm managing the best I can. I will apologize for letting you down, but the answer is that I don't know if things would have been different if Amanda had received the letter. I burned it. That should tell you something about the state of my mind at the time. I know I don't say it often, but I can openly admit that I love you. That should also tell *you* something."

With a growing smile, she rolled onto her back. Her arms went around his neck. "And tonight with Jesse. What was that about?"

"Not knowing who I am anymore."

"Wil, when are you going to learn that you don't need to carry the burden alone? I nearly lost you during the war. Sometimes I get the feeling you're sorry you survived. You have left all of our lives up in the air waiting for a pardon that may never come. What happens to Emma and me if the Yankees should decide to arrest you?"

"The pardon will come," he assured her.

"Sam's been promising you that for months. Even if it does come through, do you seriously think the Yankees will allow you to rejoin the military?"

"I have no false illusions about resuming my career." A grin formed on his mouth. "Although it could be a possibility if I become a Republican."

Alice whacked him over the head with her pillow. "One Republican Yankee in the family is quite enough, thank you." But she was laughing, and at that moment, it was all that mattered. As he grasped her hand and kissed it, she stopped laughing. "Wil, I do fret about you. I keep seeing moods that I thought were buried a long time ago. Then when the two of you were making light of war atrocities..."

"Nostalgia. It's not something veterans tend to talk about, except in the company of others who went through it. It'll pass in time."

She snuggled next to him and pressed a hand to his chest. "I know it's some manly reason why you think you can't talk about it, but I'm not a little wallflower that may wilt. As you astutely pointed out, I saw the hospitals. If I can help, let me."

Content just holding her, Wil tightened his grip. For now the melancholy was gone, but the fact that it had reappeared troubled him. Closing his eyes, he clutched Alice as if she could keep his mind from spiraling downward into the abyss.

There had been a brief respite in the weather, and Wil had been gone for nearly a week. Alice had difficulty imagining him in the role of drafting and surveying for the railroad, rather than commanding a brigade in Petersburg. But those days were gone. More of a concern now was if the winter became worse to the point that he would be unable to return home.

Her guardian spirit continued to elude her. Perched on the knoll, she let the sun warm her face. Wil had always envisioned her as an otter, but a line drawing was the closest she had ever been to the real animal. As she understood the philosophy, the guardian spirit must be an animal for which she felt kinship.

A doe entered the clearing to graze. A dawdling fawn mystified Alice. Deer didn't tend to have tiny young during winter. She sucked in her breath. The doe was the totem of Wil's first wife, Peopeo, and the fawn—their son. The deer flagged her tail for the fawn to follow. Curious, Alice trailed after them.

At the edge of the forest, two red-tailed hawks swirled in an acrobatic dance high in the sky. Their piercing cries echoed around the aerial display. A cold wind made her shiver, and the birds floated to another region of the sky. The doe and her fawn had also vanished. Was one of these animals her totem?

Disappointed the answer had eluded her yet again, Alice trudged back to the farmhouse. A freshly whitewashed picket fence surrounded the house. Jesse had recently reconstructed the fence that had been ripped apart by Yankees during the war, but when had he whitewashed it? "Amanda?"

"Miss Alice, you had best hurry."

Frieda? But the old Negro servant had died nearly two years before. Frieda's stooped form and wrinkled face came into view at the door. Fighting tears, Alice threw her arms around the blind woman's neck. "It's so good to see you, Frieda."

"You see me less than two minutes ago, girl," Frieda grumbled. "You had best get upstairs. Miss Amanda frettin' dat you don't make it in time for da weddin'."

"Wedding? But Frieda, you can't be here."

"Get." Frieda pointed her cherry walking stick to the top of the stairs.

She must be dreaming. Playing along, Alice dashed up the stairs. Inside the bedroom, Amanda sobbed in front of the mirror dressed in yards of white silk—a wedding dress. Mama patted her sister on the back.

"Mama, Amanda—what's going on?"

Mama scurried from the room. "I'll wait downstairs."

Alice remembered now—Amanda's wedding day to her first husband, John. Only seventeen at the time, her sister looked more like a girl. "Amanda, why are you crying? This should be the happiest day of your life—at least until you meet Sam."

"Sam? Who's Sam?"

"Never mind, you'll meet him later."

Amanda dried her tears with Mama's lace handkerchief. "You wouldn't understand, Alice. Mama wanted to let me know that a woman has certain responsibilities once married."

The talk—Mama's lecture on what a woman should expect in the marriage bed. Several years after the wedding, Amanda had confided that Mama had terrified her silly about a woman's obligation to satisfying her husband's physical needs. Alice fought the urge to giggle. "Amanda, don't let Mama frighten you. It's not an ordeal, but a perfectly pleasurable way to share your love."

"Alice! How would you know about such things? You're not married."

Not married? That's right, she had only been fourteen. Alice gazed into the mirror and saw herself, not some adolescent girl. Recalling the day, she smiled to herself. "Because the man I'm going to marry is downstairs, standing with John."

"Lieutenant Jackson. Alice, he hasn't behaved improperly, has he?"

Lieutenant... "No. I've barely met him, but I know it to be true." Even on this day, her heart had flip-flopped in that schoolgirl way. But Wil had ignored her because of her youth.

With trembling hands, Amanda stood. They hugged. Just as it had happened nearly thirteen years before, Alice led the way from the bedroom. At the bottom of the steps, she gave Amanda a reassuring squeeze. In the parlor, John stood next to the preacher, and beside him was Wil. For four long years, he had worn Confederate gray. She had almost forgotten that in the time before the war, he wore Federal blue.

His eyes met hers. Absent from them was their mischievous spark. Of course, hidden behind his stoic mask he buried the pain of the tragic loss of his Nez Percé wife only a few months before. Then he exchanged gazes with Amanda.

Alice spotted the looks of longing. *Even then, they had cared for each other.*

The house walls seemed to melt away, and Alice found herself sitting atop the knoll. Surrounded by blue sky, the hawks continued soaring and diving in their aerial display. A feather from one of the dancing birds swirled in the breeze and floated to the ground. She collected the bright red tail feather. Confused by the meaning, she decided she'd ask Wil when he returned home. Nonetheless, she had discovered what she set out to do. Her guardian spirit was the red-tailed hawk.

Chapter Eight

*T*HE RICKETY SHACK HAD SWELLED TO TEN STUDENTS, and most of them were reading and writing. Amanda placed her hand over Lily's to help her form letters. Once finished, Lily beamed at her.

Pleased the servant was once again taking pride in her work after her ordeal with Mr. Chandler, Amanda commended her. "I haven't seen my sister in nearly a fortnight. She left my house rather suddenly. I presume Wil has returned."

With difficulty, Lily wrote several more letters on her slate, forming the word "hawk." "Mr. Wil ain't back."

That was peculiar. Alice disliked being alone in the house in Fredericksburg when Wil was away. "Is she all right?"

"After findin' her spirit, she be fine."

Animal totems again. Sometimes Amanda felt like strangling Wil for filling Alice's head full of Indian legends. "I'll stop by and see her after school."

"Yes'm."

For the rest of the school day, Amanda fretted. As soon as she dismissed her eager pupils, she drove the buggy to the red brick house. She tethered the horse to the hitching rail and made her way to the door and knocked. A baby cried inside.

Rocking the baby in her arms, Alice answered the door. Emma continued to squall. "She's teething. I've rubbed some laudanum on her gums. Hopefully, she'll settle down soon."

"Here, let me take her." A lump formed in Amanda's throat as she gathered Emma in her arms. She hadn't held a baby since the loss of her own. Pale and haggard looking, Alice shoved stray hair from her face. For ten minutes, Amanda strode the floorboards and rocked before Emma stopped fussing and fell asleep.

Alice put Emma to bed upstairs, then sank into a chair across from Amanda, exhausted.

Concerned about her sister's well being, Amanda said, "You look like you've been up with her all night."

"Not really. She fusses more when Wil is away. There's no doubt that she's her papa's girl."

Amanda blew out a breath in relief. "You should have stayed at the farm while Wil is away. Mama and I would have helped you with Emma."

"I have Lily—at least on the days she doesn't attend school," Alice reminded her.

Something else was bothering her sister. "Alice, are you still fretting about finding your spirit guide?"

"I know what it is," Alice stated matter-of-factly. She lifted a red feather. "It's the hawk."

Amanda sucked in her breath—the same word Lily had written on her slate.

"Amanda, did you know the hawk can travel through time?"

"That's impossible," Amanda stated adamantly.

Alice's eyes grew fixed. "Is it? Then how can you explain the things I've seen?"

"I don't know. What sort of things did you see?"

"I saw Frieda . . ."

"Wishful thinking."

"No, I saw you before your marriage to John. Mama had just given you the talk about your wifely duties. You were crying."

A slight smile crept to Amanda's face. Mama had filled her with horror stories about the marriage bed. Before that moment, she hadn't realized what it meant to be married at all. But Alice already knew that. She had relayed the story to Alice when she got a little older. "What does any of this have to do with traveling through time?"

"Because I discovered that you loved him even then."

Amanda knew perfectly well that Alice wasn't speaking about John. Annoyed with her sister's persistence, she replied, "Alice, why do you insist upon pursuing this? I barely knew Wil when I married John. He was stationed in the Northwest when I first courted John, and I met him after we were betrothed." Why did she feel the need to defend herself? They had danced a few times but nothing had ever happened between them that would suggest any sort of intimacy. "Even then, Wil had the habit of gambling and drinking too much. He was so different from John that I didn't understand why they were friends."

"They were friends because John took demerits on Wil's behalf at West Point, otherwise he would have been dismissed the first year."

"I realize that. John told me after we were married. Alice, I don't wish to quarrel. Before the war, we only saw each other a few times. After John and I were married, Wil went to New Mexico, so I don't know when this supposed love could have ever developed."

Alice forced a smile. "I'm sorry, Amanda. I haven't been fair to you, or Wil. The dreams must have led me astray. I won't bring it up again."

Thankful that Alice had finally relented, Amanda patted her sister's hand. "I'm as much at fault for not explaining things to you before. Instead of fretting so much about the past, you need to take the time to rest, so you have some energy for that beautiful little daughter of yours." When Alice laughed, Amanda only hoped that her sister would finally let the entire subject rest.

By late November, except for several officers, most of Sam's men had been mustered out of the military and returned home, only to be replaced by a smaller group consisting of green troops. Although some of his more problematic men were gone, he had to occasionally deal with drunken soldiers harassing the citizens. The more common offenses were ad nauseam requests for townspeople to take the Oath or shearing off Confederate buttons when the former soldiers often had little else to wear. In spite of these difficulties, his new command had joined the war late and was less worn out, easing tension a little.

Sam raised a hand to signal the patrolling party to halt. He brought his own mount to a walk before stopping. His bug-eyed sergeant saluted. "Sir . . ."

"Let the boys rest."

Another salute. "Yes, sir."

He overheard Sergeant Riley bellow the order. These days the boys didn't need rest. Unlike during the war, they weren't marching or riding for hours or miles on end. Bored men with menial duties were more likely to get into trouble. Beyond drills and patrols, there was little else that he could find for them to do.

Sam leaned back in the saddle and surveyed the forest. Out of the corner of his eye, he thought he saw something dash through the woods. Most likely a deer. There it was again—running toward them. If it had been a deer, he would have spotted the flash of white beneath its tail. He motioned for the other men to take a look and pulled his field glasses from a leather case.

A sharp sting hit his shoulder. Sam reeled from the saddle and struck the ground. *Gunfire.* Knocked senseless, he saw the boys scramble for their horses. Shadowy figures bolted in several directions. He blinked and the image became clear.

A private loomed over him, holding out a hand. "Sir . . ."

Lightheaded, Sam waved him on. "Never mind me. Get whoever is responsible."

Pain spread throughout his arm. Amid the confusion, he heard shouts and hoofbeats.

"Sir . . ."

"I said . . ."

"Most of the boys have gone after 'em, but we're not leaving you behind. Sergeant Riley's orders, sir."

"Outranked by a sergeant," Sam grumbled. Wobbly on his feet, he attempted to stand.

"Sir . . ." The private caught him as he sank and gently helped him to the ground. "Sir, you've been hit. You're in no condition to be up and about. We'll see you back to town."

Sam finally looked. Blood spattered his left shoulder. He laughed slightly, then gritted his teeth in pain. "I thought the war was over."

The private wrapped Sam's arm in a cloth, making a sling. It quickly became saturated in crimson. "Some folks must not realize that."

The private's hands went under his arm and lifted him. Another private was on his left side. Together, they aided him onto his horse. One man climbed on behind him to help him stay on. The other private rode beside them.

A wave of dizziness washed over Sam. He nearly slipped from the saddle, but the men aiding him held him in place. His horse plodded on. Each step was agony. He recalled little else, and when they finally reached town, he collapsed from the pain, only to wake flat on his back in a dingy room with a single light. "Amanda . . ."

"We've sent for your wife, sir. The doctor is on his way."

Reassured, Sam closed his eyes until a bass voice boomed.

"Colonel . . ." A man with a gray beard and spectacles stood over him. With the private's help, they stripped away his wool jacket and shirt. The doctor examined the wound by inserting a probe. Sam screamed. The private held him down and kept his thrashing at bay.

Once he recovered, the private put a tin cup to his lips. Brandy trickled down his throat. "Thank you." His voice rasped, and he looked at the soldier. "Bowen—isn't it?"

"Yes, sir."

"I knew a Major Bowen in Libby."

"My cousin, sir."

Small world. "Did he . . ."

"He survived, sir."

That much was a relief. The major had fought over a rat, helping to create a distraction when he escaped from the hell hole. Sam glanced to the doctor. "How bad is it, Doc?" The doctor peered grimly over his spectacles but continued arranging his instruments beside the table. "Bowen, if he so much as tries to amputate, you have orders to shoot him."

The private arched an eyebrow. "Shoot him?"

"You heard me."

Bowen readied his pistol. "Yes, sir."

"Not to worry, Colonel," the doctor said, raising a hand. "I believe I can save the arm."

"You believe," Sam grumbled, detecting a Southern accent. "You're a Virginian."

"I'm a doctor first. Now let me do my job." As the doctor placed a cone over his face, Sam drifted into a world of darkness.

After receiving the message that Sam had been wounded, Amanda failed to trust her judgment driving the buggy. She left Rebecca in Mama's care and had Jesse guide the buggy to town. Barely had they arrived at headquarters, when she met Lieutenant Greer inside the door. Out of breath, she pressed a hand to her chest. "How is he?"

"The surgeon removed a bullet and bone fragments from the colonel's shoulder. There could be nerve damage, which might give him limited use of the arm. Otherwise, he's going to be mighty sore for a while, but the doctor thinks he'll pull through. Mrs. Prescott, we believe this was the work of Douglas Chandler. I found remnants of a Rebel flag near where the colonel was wounded. I assure you that we'll find him and bring him to justice."

Doug Chandler? How little any of them had known what lurked beneath his charming exterior when he had helped rescue Wil from the river. "I'd like to see my husband."

The lieutenant bowed. "Of course."

Before he took her to Sam, she met with Doctor Gordon. In greater detail he confirmed what the lieutenant had already informed her. Amanda grew impatient to see Sam. "Doctor, please."

"Right away. I have given him some laudanum to ease the pain." He led the way to the back.

Unlike during the war when Sam had been wounded, he had a cot. Upon seeing his pale face, she held her breath until spotting the irregular rise and fall of his chest. His left arm was swathed in bandages of a makeshift sling. She grasped his good hand. "Sam..."

His eyelids flickered open. A contented smile formed on his face. "I had a dream that you were standing over my grave."

"Hush now. You know I don't want to hear such words coming from your mouth." She sat on the bed beside him. "The doctor says there's a good chance for full recovery."

"I want to be buried in Maine."

"My distraction these past few months has caused you to think about such things, but I love you. I always have. Now concentrate on mending."

"I told you from the beginning that if you loved him, I would step aside."

First Alice, now Sam. Amanda successfully fought the tears. "You must be speaking through a laudanum haze. Your words are downright silly."

"Amanda, I know full well that you married me because..."

She pressed two fingers to his lips. "Because I love you. How many times do I have to tell you before you'll believe it?"

With her reassurance, he closed his eyes. She kissed him on the cheek and said a silent prayer. *Forgive me.* She had become so preoccupied by the loss of the baby that Sam had carried the burden. *Let him live, and I will make amends.*

A day later, Lieutenant Greer, Private Bowen, and Jesse had moved Sam to Alice's house. Although the trip was a short one, it was agonizingly bumpy. With each jolt of the wagon, Amanda coddled him like a mother hen. Alice graciously placed a straw mattress in the study, so that he wouldn't find it necessary to navigate the stairs. Over the next few days, he carried out his duties from his bedside to the best of his abilities.

Day and night, Amanda tended him. Caring for him seemed to give her a sense of purpose. Sam wished that she'd agree to having another baby. Although she treated his daughter as one of her own, she was meant to have her own child. Upon inspecting his wound, she beamed. "It looks better every day."

"Amanda, could you bring Rebecca by?"

"Of course. I'll have Jesse bring her on his next trip to town. Mama might decide to come with her though," she warned. "You know how she hates being alone on the farm with only Ezra there." She began wrapping his arm. "If you're feeling strong enough, Alice would like you to join us for supper. She's expecting Wil home."

He doubted that his former commander would appreciate that his home had been turned into Yankee headquarters.

As if reading his mind, Amanda spoke, "Alice promises to break it to him gently."

She finished wrapping his arm in a neat sling, then Sam held up his right hand. "I'm awkward using this hand."

"I'll help you, and you'll be in company who understands."

Fortunately, Amanda's mother didn't make the trip. Due to his Northern heritage, Jean had never cared for him, and it turned out to be a pleasant evening. The women outdid themselves preparing the meal—a simple fare of roast chicken, carrot and barley soup, potatoes, and wine. For a Southern family these days, the repast was a feast. Sam kept his mouth shut. Any offer of help from him would have offended his hosts.

Again, he felt a twinge of regret. After Wil had been gone for a month, Emma squealed in delight to see him. Even now, he couldn't pretend to have the same kind of relationship with Rebecca. But then, he had been stationed in New Mexico during her entire babyhood, and when she had been a toddler, the war kept him away most of the time. *Damn this job.* If he resigned, it would likely help Amanda, too.

While they ate, Amanda avoided eye contact and said only a couple of words to Wil during the entire meal. Sam suspected Alice also noticed the awkwardness between them, but he'd maintain silence in that regard too. He trusted Amanda.

When the women cleared the table, he retired to the threadbare sofa in the parlor. No matter how he held his arm, he couldn't get comfortable. Wil offered him a cigar. Sam muttered his thanks. "My humble apologies for not having any brandy," Wil said. A gleam entered his eyes. "But I do have some of Edmund Dawson's home brew."

Home brew? What the hell, it might help the pain in his arm. "Then I had best bypass the cigar." Sam held up his right arm. "I only have one good hand these days."

"And you're lucky you didn't lose the other." Wil produced a flask and poured an amber liquid into a glass.

After handing the glass to Sam, Wil sat across from him. For some reason when he was in Wil's company, he felt like a green lieutenant again. He fidgeted in his seat, which only succeeded in sending a sharp pain through his arm. "I let my guard down, Captain. I think I need more of your Indian-style training."

Wil laughed. "You survived the war. You'll survive this too."

Sam took a swig of corn whiskey, burning his throat as it went down. A moment passed before he was able to speak again. "But at what cost?"

"That I can't answer." Wil tapped his fingers on the flask. "Sam, I don't think Chandler shot you."

"Why not?"

"Chandler may be many things, but he's no coward. If he wanted you dead, he would have faced you."

"You're certain of that?"

Wil nodded and drank from the flask. "He wouldn't have missed, either."

Small comfort. Sam gulped the rest of the whiskey down. "What about those that ride with him?"

Wil poured more whiskey into his glass, then sat back as if contemplating his question. "A distinct possibility. I presume you have evidence they've returned to the area?"

At least the more whiskey he drank, the less his shoulder hurt. "Greer found remnants of a Reb—Confederate flag near where I was shot."

His slip hadn't gone unnoticed. Wil arched a brow. "A Confederate flag? What if I told you that I have one?"

"You son of a bitch. Don't even joke about such a thing."

Wil was laughing again.

"I'd have to arrest you, which would set Alice and Amanda to feuding." Sam held up his glass for more whiskey. "Wil, I need your help."

To this statement, Wil sobered and poured the whiskey. "I've already made it clear that I won't spy for you or anyone else."

"I'm not asking you to."

Wil took a gulp from the flask, then leaned back in the moth-eaten chair. "Then what?"

"I need to know if Chandler's band of horse thieves is back before someone takes a potshot at me again. Lieutenant Greer is a good soldier, but he's a green officer. And the rest of my boys these days are greener than he is."

Wil shook his head. "I don't like Greer. He fancies his job too much, and I'm likely to say something that will get me thrown in jail again."

Sam hesitated bringing up his next bargaining point. "I'll pay you what I would a scout."

"I'm no scout, and I can't slip in and out of places like Chandler."

"Maybe not, but I recall in New Mexico that you often used some rather unorthodox Indian methods. I also know you don't like me making my headquarters here. You've only remained quiet to keep the peace."

"I haven't said anything about you being here because I haven't had a chance to voice an opinion yet."

So much for thinking that Wil might have altruistic motives. "Will you help me?" Wil's emotionless face gave no hint as to what his answer would be. "You know," Sam continued, "I could just as easily change my mind and make this place my permanent head-quarters. Greer is itching for a promotion."

Wil held up a hand in surrender. "I'll do it, if you allow me to take Jesse and supply us with suitable horses that have no U.S. brands."

"Done." Sam came close to saluting. Instead, he held out his hand. Wil studied it a moment, then shook it. "Thank you, Captain."

"I'm not doing it for you, Prescott. I figure there will be hell to pay if you get your head blown off the next time. Greer might indeed get that promotion then."

Sam laughed but a spasm shot through his shoulder. He sucked in his breath and clutched his arm. At least now he was certain he would discover if Chandler was behind the recent happenings.

Chapter Nine

*T*HE NEXT DAY, GREER DELIVERED a pair of light-bodied bays in the murky dawn. While the lieutenant tethered the horses to the rail behind the house, Wil examined them. Fine looking horses, but he would have traded both of them if he could have a single sturdy warhorse like his Appaloosa cross, Poker Chip.

"Jackson, I'm opposed to this foolhardiness. I'm only here because of orders."

Wil glanced over at Greer. For a brief second, he spotted a wild look of fear in the lieutenant's eyes. "Why do I not find that surprising?"

"They'll be a hundred fifty dollars apiece if anything happens to them."

"If I had that much to spend on a horse, I certainly wouldn't buy one of your government-issued nags."

Greer's fingers twitched over his pistol. "One hundred fifty. Is that clear?"

The lieutenant wasn't merely green, but he was fear driven as well. A man like that was unpredictable in tense situations. Wil decided not to press him. "It is."

The lieutenant relaxed.

"Wil . . ." Alice stepped outside with Emma in her arms. "Can you take Emma a minute while I finish up in the kitchen? She keeps getting underfoot." She slipped Emma into his arms. "Good morning, Lieutenant."

"Ma'am..." Greer tipped his hat slightly and mounted his horse.

Alice retreated to the house, and Emma's green eyes widened. She pointed at Greer and laughed. The lieutenant's hands jerked on the reins.

"Relax, Greer," Wil said. "I don't make a habit of teaching infants how to shoot Yanks."

Greer scowled, and Wil watched him as he rode off. Satisfied the lieutenant was gone, he placed Emma on the back of the nearest horse, keeping his hands snugly around her waist so she wouldn't slip from the saddle. She pulled on the horse's mane and giggled.

"Wil," Alice said, rejoining him, "I wish you wouldn't do that. She'll learn all of my tomboy ways."

He took Emma from the saddle into his arms and turned to Alice. "Tomboy ways are bad?"

"They will be if she starts spitting and swearing."

A grin formed on his mouth. "But I like your swearing."

Alice snatched Emma from his arms. "You won't like your daughter using such language. After all, you know exactly what kind of men it will attract."

There was no hint of levity in her tone or on her features. "Alice..."

A small smile finally crossed her face, and she shifted her gaze from Emma to him. "I wish you weren't going. You've barely been home."

"This shouldn't take long, and I promise to try and find something closer come spring." He leaned down to kiss her, when he heard footsteps behind them.

Jesse shuffled his feet in the dirt. "I beg your pardon for intruding."

"Not at all." Wil motioned for him to join them, then returned his attention to Alice. "I need to be leaving now."

She handed him a bag containing rations. "Be careful."

With a promise that he would, he gave her a goodbye kiss and tied the bag to the saddle. He mounted up, and Jesse road abreast as they headed to the outskirts of Fredericksburg. In the eight months since the war's end, the buildings remained dreary. None of the houses in the burned section had been rebuilt, yet a few chimney stacks remained where grand houses once stood.

"Where are we headed, sir?" Jesse asked.

"You'll see."

At the edge of town, Frank Whyte's columned mansion appeared. Jesse's head snapped in Wil's direction. "You think Mrs. Whyte knows Chandler's whereabouts?"

A smile spread across Wil's face. "I'd be willing to bet on it."

For two days, they watched the Whyte mansion—sometimes in shifts—from the nearby woods. The wait reminded Wil of the restless boredom before a battle. He fingered the letter that had arrived earlier in the day from his sister, Sara, in Charleston.

"Sir." Jesse pointed in the direction of the Whyte mansion.

Unable to break Jesse of the habit of calling him sir, Wil watched as Frank Whyte went down the cascading steps. Holly clung to his arm, then threw her arms around him with a kiss. Whyte climbed into the carriage, shouting orders to the driver. As he leaned out to wave farewell, tears streaked Holly's cheeks. "She should have been an actress," Wil muttered under his breath.

Jesse arched an eyebrow. "Sir?"

Wil waved that his comment was unimportant and stuffed the letter in his waistcoat. "Fetch the horses. Mrs. Whyte will likely be taking a trip soon."

"But she just said goodbye to her husband."

Had he ever been that naive? It was probably for the best that Jesse hadn't grown up in his presence. "Trust me. I know what kind of woman she is."

Without further discussion, Jesse went after the horses. Within fifteen minutes of Whyte's leaving, a servant led a horse with a sidesaddle to the front of the Whyte mansion. Attired in a riding habit, Holly descended the steps, and headed out of town toward the Wilderness. If Wil had hunched a guess as to where Chandler might be hiding that would have been the one place he would have checked. But with Holly leading the way, it was unnecessary to rely on hunches.

Jesse looked straight ahead to the dirt road, and his brow furrowed in pain. "I was captured in the Wilderness."

Even now, Wil could hear the cannonfire—and the screams. He recalled the heat from the fires, and men burning alive. The smell of scorched flesh, then pain. The bullet had gone clean through his chest.

"I see you have your memories too," Jesse commented.

"I was wounded there."

"Mrs. Jackson mentioned it."

Wil glanced over at Jesse, but the boy continued staring at the road.

"She's a good woman. I hope I haven't disrupted things."

"You haven't. Jesse..." Jesse finally met his gaze, and Wil fell silent. There would be time enough later to read Sara's letter and discover the truth. *Fear.* It had been a long time since he had admitted to feeling such a thing to himself, and as long as he kept the letter in his pocket, he could continue to deny that Jesse might be his son. *Focus*, or Holly might slip from their grasp. He followed the tracks of her horse in the dirt.

Afternoon arrived before they reached the tangled, forbidding woods of the Wilderness. *Had it been nearly two years since he had lain here with a hole blown through his chest?* Tree trunks bore the scars from musket and artillery fire. Limbs had been shot off. Others were stripped of bark.

The screams grew louder, and Wil placed a hand to his temple. They forded a stream, and he thought he saw blood. *All of the rivulets were red.* Mounds of dirt had replaced the bodies. Most were buried in shallow, unmarked graves, leaving bony hands and feet to wash up during the spring rains.

Wil heard a Rebel yell. *Real or imagined?* Jesse showed no reaction. Once again, he needed to concentrate. At a crossroad, he glanced to the ground and discovered that Holly's trail had vanished. He brought his horse to a halt and dismounted, looking for broken branches or horse dung that might give a hint as to which way she had taken.

Leading his horse behind him, Wil retraced his steps and found the last set of tracks. He broke off a branch. After measuring the horse's stride with the branch, he notched the stick, while Jesse watched curiously. "An aid the Nez Percé taught me," Wil explained. With the stick, he swept the point in an arc, searching for clues.

Near the edge of the road, he spotted the layer of fall leaves covering the ground had been trampled. Holly had left the main road before reaching the crossroad. Back on her trail, they passed through a narrow woodland that changed to an equally narrow path of dry, brown winter grasses. A grinning skull sat atop a mound of dirt. The grassland continued for several hundred yards before Holly's trail disappeared yet again.

The area had been brushed clean of tracks. "Someone knows we're following," Wil said. On open ground, they were easy targets. "I suggest we retreat before . . ." *Damn.* "Mount up."

Once in the saddle, Wil cued the bay to a gallop. With the gelding's lightning fast response, dirt clods flew in the air. Jesse was soon beside him. Together, they neared the main road when two riders appeared in front of them. Wil veered to the right to avoid collision. A stone fence lay directly in their path. Unable to prepare for the jump in time, the horse swerved, but he sailed over the fence and hit the ground. Another horse leaped the fence. Jesse swung around to help, but Wil waved him on. Numb from the fall, he struggled to his feet.

The two riders reached the fence with pistols aimed at him. Wil recognized Chandler's men—Bruce and Leon. As they dismounted, he raised his hands.

"General," Bruce said cordially, "if you would be so kind as to hand me your gun belt." Wil complied, and the man continued, "Now if you would climb back over the fence . . ."

Still aching from the fall, Wil clambered over the fence with difficulty.

Bruce waved the pistol for him to turn around. When he failed to move fast enough, Bruce and Leon shoved him against the fence and began searching. Rough hands probed every pocket and fold of clothing until reaching his boot. They confiscated the knife he concealed there.

"Easy, boys." Chandler's voice came from behind. "After all, he was a brigadier for the Confederacy."

Allowed to move again, Wil turned around. Chandler trotted toward them, leading the bay gelding behind him. Beside Chandler rode Holly. They brought their horses to a halt.

"Wil, you never told me you can track," Holly said drolly.

Wil shrugged. "You never asked."

Chandler's eyes fixed on him. "General, I must ask why you have come here?"

"With recent happenings, I wondered if you had returned to the area."

A triumphant grin spread across Chandler's face. "Except for brief visits to my sister, I have never left."

All this time, Chandler had been hiding in the Wilderness—and most likely Holly's bed. "I had hoped we could resume our games of poker." Wil met Chandler's gaze. "It's rare for a player to come along that challenges me as you do."

Chandler laughed. "I think we understand one another, General. You task me, but you did serve the Confederacy. I have no intention of harming you." He glanced back at the bay gelding. "I will keep the horse, though. You may begin your walk back to town."

Holly smirked, but Wil made light of the situation. "Just like old times. I suspect I can maintain a brisk march."

"Do send Colonel Prescott my regards," Chandler added with a growing grin.

"I'll do that," Wil agreed.

Good to Chandler's word, no one harassed him as he set out on the return trip to town. Months had passed since he had taken up such a march. Wondering how far Jesse had got, he passed the skull before reaching the main road. He traveled a couple of miles before taking Sara's letter from his waistcoat. *Time to verify what he already knew.*

Wil tore open the envelope and began reading. *Caroline.* No wonder she had never told him about Jesse.

Against Amanda's wishes, Sam had returned to headquarters. On the doctor's advice, he had postponed venturing to the farm just yet with a promise to take it easy. So much for promises. He spent the first hour attempting to catch up on paperwork, which was

slow going at best without the use of his writing hand. After another hour, the writing on the papers started blurring.

He sought his cot, but his shoulder throbbed. Unable to get
comfortable, he returned to his feet and paced. Finally, he relented and gulped down some laudanum. Sinking into the cot, he
drifted.

"Sir . . ."

In a laudanum haze, Sam half-opened an eye to Lieutenant
Greer.

"Sorry to disturb you, sir, but Misters Jackson and Morgan are
here to see you."

"Jackson?"

"And Mr. Morgan, minus one of the horses we provided them,
I might add."

Horses? They had provided horses? "Send . . . send them in.
Also, get me a cup of coffee." Sam rubbed his eyes and climbed
from the cot. In spite of wobbly legs, he managed to locate his
desk and ease into his chair.

A few minutes later, Greer escorted Wil and Jesse in. The lieutenant placed a steaming cup of coffee on his desk. "Well . . . ,"
Sam said, waiting for someone to break the silence.

"You look like the devil, Sam."

He could always count on Wil to be straightforward. At least
his head was slowly clearing. "Thanks," Sam replied, taking a sip
from the tin cup. "I needed that. Greer reports that you're missing
a horse."

"I warned you that I wasn't a scout."

Greer glared at Wil. "That will be a hundred fifty dollars, *sir*."

"And I've already told you that I don't have it."

"One hundred . . ."

"Bill me."

"Enough!" Sam stood. "Lieutenant, dismissed."

"But sir, you're in no condition . . ."

"I don't expect to repeat myself, Lieutenant. Dismissed." The
lieutenant saluted and left the office. After Greer's exit, Sam returned to his chair. "What was that all about?"

Wil shrugged that it was unimportant.

"Then tell me what happened." Wil relayed his encounter with Chandler. "So Chandler is the one who shot me?"

Wil shook his head. "I didn't say that. He neither claimed nor denied that he had."

"In any case, I'm going to increase patrols."

"Sam, he will elude you until he is ready for a confrontation. I'm sure he knows that you have fewer men these days."

"I can vouch for what the general says, sir," Jesse piped in. "Chandler prides himself on his guerrilla activities during the war. A peace agreement hasn't changed his mind about the Cause. If necessary, he will fight for it."

"I see." Sam wished he could continue to rely on Wil and Jesse's help, but for them, the war was over. From now on, he'd have Greer keep an eye on Holly.

"Sir . . ."

Sam glanced up at Jesse.

The boy looked at Wil. Wil nodded, and Jesse swallowed hard. "I might be able to give you some leads to recover your wife's stallion."

The barn fire—so Jesse had known more than he originally let on. No wonder he was nervous. The revelation had been a great personal risk. "I won't have you arrested, if you cooperate."

"Thank you, sir."

"I'll check into it, Sam."

For a brief moment, Sam was pleased that he could count on Wil's continued support, then he realized the stallion belonged to Amanda.

Rumors of a Negro uprising during Christmas came to naught. Throughout most of the month, Sam had his men remain on the alert, but he didn't share the citizens' apprehensions. Although Amanda fretted over the fact that he had been wounded, she relished having him home more often. His arm was still in a sling, and he only went into headquarters every few days. Less than a week after the new year, Miss Sophia Hatch, a schoolteacher from Ohio, had arrived in Fredericksburg to educate the black children, and Sam had received notice that his troop numbers were to be reduced yet again.

On a frosty January morning, Amanda accompanied Sam to town. Patches of ice clung to the banks of the Rappahannock, but the ford to town, thankfully, remained passable. They halted the buggy out front of the new school building on Caroline Street. While the wood structure had been built hastily, it was far superior to the dismal log hut in the shanty village.

Inside, Sam waited by the entrance as Amanda approached the desk and held out her hand. "I'm Mrs. Samuel Prescott."

A woman in her mid-thirties with tightly pinned hair stood to greet her. "Miss Sophia Hatch," she replied, taking Amanda's hand. "It's a pleasure meeting you, Mrs. Prescott. Your students have told me good things about you. I'm looking forward to teaching here."

"They need a full-time teacher." Although she meant the words, Amanda was fully aware that her voice lacked conviction.

Miss Hatch looked at her quizzically. "I assure you that I'm a fully qualified teacher."

"I realize that. I'm . . ." Her voice wavered. "I'm just going to miss teaching the children."

Miss Hatch smiled in relief. "Most understandable. I can't thank you enough for sending the children my way. I'm an outsider here, and no one seems to trust too easily these days."

"Unfortunately, that's very true," Amanda agreed, recalling her first trip to the shanty village. "I'm glad that I could help bridge the gap." After the loss of her baby, helping others who were less fortunate had filled her with a sense of purpose. Overnight that purpose had vanished. "I wish you the best of luck with the school." As she left, Miss Hatch expressed her thanks. Sam remained by the door. "It's best for the children," she said to him.

"I worry about what's best for you."

"I'll be fine."

"Amanda . . ." He shook his head.

Several times, he had attempted to convince her to reconsider having another baby. She yearned for one, but fear of losing another was stronger.

He escorted her outside. A light snow had begun to fall. "With a bum arm, I won't be much use at headquarters for several weeks. Greer can report anything of consequence to me on the farm, so that I can make it my duty to take your mind off things for a while."

She couldn't help but laugh. "You're not serious."

"Why not? I have a perfectly valid reason for taking medical leave."

"Are you sure that's what you want to do?"

He leaned down to kiss her. She pressed closer, eagerly returning the kiss. "Most definitely."

For the first time in months, Amanda felt a glimmer of hope for the future.

Over the next month, Sam escorted Amanda on long buggy rides. As his shoulder healed, they behaved more like newlyweds by dancing well into the night, then retiring to their upstairs bedroom. Smiles had returned to Amanda's face.

On one sunny Saturday morning, with Amanda at his side, Sam guided the buggy down the lane past fallow fields. Spring planting would begin soon. "Amanda, I'm thinking of resigning my commission."

Amanda blinked, then stared at him in stunned silence.

"I thought you'd be happy."

Her eyelashes fluttered once more. "What would you do?"

"Farm. Jesse's been showing me what I need to know."

"Sam, it takes more than a month to learn how to run a farm."

"I'm aware of that, but I don't want us to be separated anymore."

She gripped his hand. "There's nothing I'd like more, but what will happen to the citizens of Fredericksburg if you should resign? Another commander may not care what happens to them. The friction between Northern soldiers and Southern citizens could be as great as anytime during the war. The troops are unlikely to be here forever. If you feel you should, then resign when they've all gone home."

Somehow when she stated things in a logical manner, they made sense. But it meant more time apart, and shouldn't they occasionally think about their own lives, rather than everyone elses? He guided the buggy around, back in the direction of the house. "I'll think it through before doing anything rash."

"Good." With a smile, she squeezed his hand.

When they neared the lane to the farm, a number of riders in blue headed his direction with Lieutenant Greer in the lead. "Sir . . ." He halted his horse beside the buggy and saluted. "The Johnsons report two horses were stolen."

Before asking, Sam knew he was going to regret his question. "Any suspects?"

"Chandler. A black thoroughbred fitting the description of the one he rides was seen less than a mile away."

Sam let out a frustrated breath. "Let me see my wife to the house."

"Yes, sir." Another salute.

With a click of his tongue, Sam turned the buggy into the lane, bringing it to a halt near the picket fence. After climbing down, he helped Amanda. "It's not too late to change your mind." He kissed her on the mouth.

"I know my duty as you do yours."

She was smiling, and that's all that mattered for the time being. "If you can ask Jesse to ready my horse, I'll fetch my gun."

"Of course."

He went up the walk to the house. In the kitchen Rebecca was helping Jean after collecting eggs from the hen house. With a hug, he gave his daughter a goodbye kiss on the forehead.

"Off again," Jean said critically.

It hadn't been a question. She knew. One of these days he hoped she'd be able to see past the blue uniform. After a round of goodbyes, he collected his gun.

Jesse had his horse waiting in the farmyard. Another kiss for Amanda, and he mounted up. She was still smiling, and he hoped her mourning for the baby had finally passed. He gave her one last look before setting off with his men.

After a brief ride, they forded the river and met a carriage, carrying a thin, elderly man and a woman. Like Amanda, the woman was blonde, and on her hands, she wore delicate lace gloves. Sam sucked in his breath. The woman who had attacked and accused him of killing her kin, but she held the same vacant expression he remembered before the assault.

The man tipped his hat in greeting, but the woman stared straight ahead, without noticing them, as if she were drugged. Maybe it was for the best. He had no desire to repeat their previous encounter.

Chapter Ten

$\mathcal{A}$LONG WITH HIS FEW REMAINING MEN, Sam had scoured the Wilderness for Douglas Chandler and his band to no avail. Within a couple of days he had returned to the farm, letting Lieutenant Greer oversee the search, while he continued to recuperate. In his presence, Amanda felt like a schoolgirl again. By the end of March, the weather was unusually warm for early spring, and Sam was well on the road to recovery, resulting in his absences becoming more frequent again. She had fallen into another melancholy mood, as in two days' time she would turn thirty.

Usually more prevalent during the summer months, typhoid fever had made an unwelcome appearance in the shanty village. Warm spring weather combined with the crowded conditions had paved the way for a handful of cases. Ready to aid those in need, Amanda journeyed to the area south of Fredericksburg only to discover Lily among the stricken. Inside Lily's makeshift cabin, Amanda placed a cool cloth to the mulatto's forehead.

"How is she, Amanda?" came Alice's voice from behind her.

"Thank goodness you're here, Alice. Lily's been calling for you."

Alice's gaze met hers. "Doctor Gordon won't come."

"Won't come?"

"He says he's too busy."

Amanda recognized the real reason. Doctor Gordon always seemed to be too busy when it came to treating patients in the shanty village. "Then we'll do the best we can."

Alice crossed the mud floor and grasped Lily's hand.

A feverish smile appeared on Lily's face. "I goin' to die, Miss Alice."

"We both thought we were going to die when we were splashing through the water of the bombproof in Petersburg. Remember the shells whistling overhead? You're going to survive this too."

Helpless, Amanda watched as Alice comforted Lily.

"Amanda, there's no reason for you to remain here. I live much closer. I can stay with Lily."

The shanty village was no place for a white woman at night. "But who will see you home?"

"Wil's home. He shall see that I make it back and forth safely. I'll send word if I need extra help."

Reluctantly, Amanda agreed and sent her well wishes to Lily. Outside the shack, Jesse waited for her. He helped her into the buggy. The rains had eased in the past couple of weeks, enabling more frequent trips to and from Fredericksburg. Saddened by Lily's illness, she didn't attempt to speak until they had traveled several miles. "We foolishly thought the suffering would end with the war."

"Yes, ma'am."

"Jesse, do you ever express an opinion?"

"It's not my place, Mrs. Prescott."

Amanda had hoped that as time went on, he would come to trust the family. Frustrated by their lack of progress, she sat back but looked up again when Jesse slowed the buggy. An uprooted tree blocked the road. He clambered down. "I'll see if I can move it, but it may be necessary to go around."

Before he reached the log, a horse snorted behind them. Jesse turned to the sound at the same time Amanda did. Three men on horseback had joined them. The lead man sat astride a black thoroughbred and wore a moustache—Douglas Chandler. Distressed by his sudden reappearance, Amanda struggled to remain calm. With a cordial smile, he tipped his hat. "Mrs. Prescott, are you in need of some help?"

She breathed out and relaxed slightly. "Thank you. I'm certain Jesse can use a hand."

He waved for his men to proceed.

"We haven't seen you in quite some time, Mr. Chandler."

The men grunted and snorted in an attempt to move the downed tree from the road. "I grew weary of being accused by *Yankees* for misconduct that I had no part in."

The way he had said Yankees made her uneasy. She shifted in the seat, hoping Jesse wouldn't be long in returning. "Then why did you run? My husband would have listened to you."

His eyes raged. The men groaned, and the log was heaved from the road. Amanda grasped the reins to move the buggy forward, but Mr. Chandler leaned forward and wrapped a hand around her wrist. "I rather doubt that."

"Chandler," Jesse shouted, "let her go!"

He glanced from her to Jesse, then back again. "I was only making polite conversation, and she hasn't thanked us properly."

Amanda forced a smile. "I'm most appreciative of your help."

"Well Jesse, what do you think?" Chandler asked with a thoughtful smile, then his tone turned biting, "Or have they turned you into a Yank too?"

"I think . . ." Jesse reached the buggy and disengaged Chandler's hand from Amanda's wrist. " . . . that you need to leave the lady alone."

Chandler straightened in the saddle as the other men surrounded Jesse.

"Jesse," Amanda said, swallowing hard, "I think it's best if we find out what they want and be moving on."

Twisting the hairs of his moustache between his fingers, Chandler gazed at her with that haunted frenzy of battle-weary soldiers. "A wise woman. Have you told her about your involvement with her missing horse? No, I see that you haven't. Step down from the buggy, Mrs. Prescott."

Before she could follow his order, Jesse placed himself between them. The man to his right cracked a gun butt on the back of Jesse's head. Amanda climbed from the buggy. Jesse lay sprawled in the dirt, and as she helped him sit up, Chandler's men unhitched the horse. Blood matted Jesse's hair. "Let me see how bad it is." Why had she never learned to carry a handkerchief? She tore a piece of cloth from her petticoat and dabbed at the blood. "I don't think it's serious."

The horse was free, and the men shoved the buggy over the side of the road. With a crash it flipped onto its side and smashed into a tree. Chandler aimed the revolver at Amanda. "Get rid of the hoops. You're riding with me."

Humiliated, Amanda stood. Chandler's piercing gaze warned her that he wasn't going to avert his eyes. She took a deep breath and raised her skirts.

"Pay close attention, Jesse. You might learn something about women."

The other men hooted. Determined not to let them see her fear, she fumbled with the crinoline. More catcalls. She fought the tears and dropped the crinoline to the ground.

None too gently, Chandler seized her forearm and lifted her onto his horse. His arm locked around her waist. "Jesse, you ride the buggy horse. Just remember, the boys won't hesitate to shoot if you try anything stupid." He spurred the black in the side, and they cantered off.

After a couple of miles, Chandler brought the horse to a trot, then a walk. Jesse halted the buggy horse beside them. His face paled, and he leaned against the horse's neck like he might faint.

"Please let me tend him," Amanda pleaded.

"Later."

Chandler kicked the black, and they were cantering again. The frantic pace continued for several miles until they arrived at a log cabin in the woods. Darkness had confused her sense of direction, but they hadn't crossed the river. They were likely somewhere in the Wilderness. She felt his hot breath on her neck. Too frightened to fight, Amanda sucked in her breath. He laughed, then flung her from the horse's back.

Exhausted, she fell to the dirt, but Chandler was beside her, twisting her arm and half-dragging her to the cabin. Lanterns flickered on. Chandler produced a flask from his waistcoat and passed it around. "We need your help, Mrs. Prescott."

"First, I'll tend to Jesse." Jesse clutched his head in pain on the dirt floor. Her heart beat a frantic rhythm. She took a deep breath and bent down to examine Jesse. "What sort of help, Mr. Chandler?"

Chandler swigged from the flask before passing it to the next man. "Hank's taken ill."

She wiped the blood from the back of Jesse's head as best as she could. "Send for a doctor."

"You know a doctor won't help us." Chandler sat on a cot, confiscating the flask from one of the other men.

The wretched lighting made cleaning the wound difficult, but Amanda finally spotted the source of Jesse's bleeding. The wound definitely was superficial, but his muscles tensed when she dabbed at the back of his head. Finished with the job, she stood. "Very well. Take me to Mr. Hank."

"Relax, Mrs. Prescott," Chandler said, rising with a reassuring smile. The other men bound and gagged Jesse. "We won't harm you."

So suave, but she recalled his rough treatment and prayed that he was telling the truth. He gripped her arm and drew her to the adjacent room. Even if she screamed, who would come to her aid? Unable to control her trembling, she accompanied him to the other room. Clad in nothing but underdrawers, a freckle-faced boy lay on the cot. Sweating in a delirium, he called for his mother. Amanda took a closer look. "Typhoid fever. He needs a doctor's help, not mine."

"I already explained to you that a doctor won't help the likes of us. Your husband has seen to that."

"If you didn't burn property and kill innocent people."

He seized her arms so suddenly that she let out an involuntary cry. His sky-blue eyes danced in a frantic rage, but they quickly softened. He released her arms. "I beg forgiveness, Mrs. Prescott. We killed a lot during the war. If your husband continues to press us we will fight again, but we haven't killed anyone since the surrender."

Uncertain whether to believe him, Amanda was unable to stop from shaking. "Tell that to the dead barmaid."

He had her by the arms again, gripping her so tight that his fingers dug into her skin. "I didn't kill Lora."

All fight vanished. "I'll do what I can for Mr. Hank if you let me go."

He did as she asked, and throughout the night, she sponged the boy's forehead and offered words of comfort. He wailed in pain, and like so many of the boys that she tended during the war, he called for home. She attempted to get some broth down him, and by morning, a little color had returned to his cheeks. In the afternoon, he struggled to his feet.

Amanda lent a helping hand. The other men cheered when Hank joined them in the main room.

"You've done well, Mrs. Prescott," Chandler said in approval.

"He was already well on his way to recovery. Now may Jesse and I leave? I've done everything you've asked."

"When Hank is well enough to travel. I can't have you returning to your husband and revealing our location before I'm ready to greet him."

She shivered. At some point, he had every intention of confronting Sam. "I won't tell him," Amanda insisted. "Besides, I *don't* know where I am."

Taking out his pocket watch, Chandler shook his head. "I can't take the risk. Sit down, Mrs. Prescott."

The chair swayed on uneven legs as she followed his instructions. The men resumed their drinking. Or perhaps they had been imbibing all night while she had tended Hank. One man, a skeleton-looking figure, leered at her. She shoved stray hair away from her face and glanced over at Jesse. He was no longer tied. She fretted about the meaning. "Mr. Chandler, if you don't mind, I must visit the necessary."

He regarded her skeptically, then replied, "Bruce, accompany the lady to keep her from getting any wayward notions in her head."

The bone-thin man escorted her from the cabin and to the back toward the outhouse. *Remain calm.* If she could distract Bruce in some way, she might be able to escape. She swung the door open.

"Hurry it up," Bruce grumbled.

"Some things can't be hurried, Mr. Bruce."

He glared. "If'n you don't hurry, I'll come in after you. Is that clear?"

She nodded weakly and stepped inside. After attending to necessities, she cracked the door wide enough to see where Bruce stood. He had moved from outside the door to the side, but within striking distance if she tried to make a run for it. She might not have another opportunity.

Carefully lifting her skirts, Amanda made a mad dash from the outhouse. Heavy footsteps charged after her. A hand seized her arm, while the other smashed into her nose. Wiping blood from her face, she staggered before falling. Her head spun, and she smelled whiskey-laden breath. She pummeled his face with her fists. "Let me go!"

In response, another fist struck her cheek.

"Bruce!" Chandler yanked the bony man away from her. "You're not to touch the colonel's wife." He tossed Bruce's hat after him, then helped Amanda to her feet. "My apologies, Mrs. Prescott. While you shouldn't have attempted to escape, Bruce had no cause to treat you in such a manner." Grasping her elbow, he guided her to the cabin.

Holly stood inside the door. Amanda's breath caught. She blinked, then again. "Holly?"

"Amanda..." A distinct waver registered in Holly's voice as if she had been equally surprised. Seemingly calm again, she asked, "Doug, what's she doing here?"

"Tending to Hank," Chandler responded. He showed Amanda to the chair. Glancing over at Holly once more, she obeyed his silent command. He drew her arms behind her back. Coarse rope bound her wrists. "I'm sorry that I have to resort to this, but you will leave when I say you can." With a laugh, he seized Holly's hand and led her to the adjacent room.

A few minutes later, guttural moans erupted. Holly let out brief, little shouts, which Amanda was uncertain were cries of pain or pleasure. Bruce was looking at her again. He chewed tobacco and blatantly stared at her breasts.

A red-bearded man, whom she had overheard the others call Leon, joined them. "He'll kill you if you touch her again."

"Don't mean I can't look." With a leer, Bruce began unbuttoning her bodice.

Amanda struggled against the ropes. "Please . . ."

"See—she's askin' . . ."

Jesse threw a crunching blow to Bruce's jaw. "Didn't you hear what Leon said? The lieutenant will kill you."

When Bruce rubbed his jaw and backed off, Amanda said a silent prayer.

Stunned, Holly lay spread eagle on the bed with a Confederate flag beneath her buttocks. Although Doug was often rough, he had never been brutal. Her entire body ached from his painful thrusts. She suspected he had been deliberately trying to break her bones or suffocate her. With that condescending grin of his, he took out a cigar. "I require that you return to town and fetch Colonel Prescott. Tell him to meet me here—alone."

Stiff and sore, Holly struggled to sit up. "You won't hurt Sam?"

Without lighting the cigar, he sniffed it and rolled it between his fingers. "Sam . . . how touching. Do you fall for every man who gives you a poke?"

"Sam and I never . . . Bastard." Holly swung at him, but he caught her hand and swiftly pinned her to the bed. His erect member pressed against her crotch. She smiled up at him. "Why Doug, I didn't know you were the jealous sort."

He forced her legs apart and impaled her in one powerful thrust. *God, if she survived.* Over the years, she'd had some eccentric bed partners, but Douglas Chandler was in a league all his own, which made him all the more beguiling. He frightened her, yet when in bed with him, her terror changed to excitement.

As he hammered her harder and faster, she beat the bed in a wild frenzy. Tears flowed down her cheeks, and when he gave her the final battering thrust, she sobbed and screamed. Nearly unconscious, she lay powerless on her back. She felt an involuntary smile creeping to her lips.

Doug rolled off her and tugged on his trousers. Through the stinging bruises, Holly reached for her own clothes.

"Not yet, my dear."

"What do you mean?" she asked in a euphoric fog.

"The other boys haven't had their turns."

With a shriek, she leaped for the derringer that she stashed in her bag. "I'm not some whore . . ."

"You will do as I say." He gripped her arm and twisted it behind her back. His weight pressed her face down on the bed to the point where she could barely breathe. He placed a pistol to her head. "You see, I can't let them have Mrs. Prescott. *Sam* would never forgive me, and my boys are spirited. They need a woman every now and again. I do expect them to be duly entertained. Is that clear?"

She heard the pistol cock and nodded her head.

"Good." He let her up slowly. "After the boys are finished, you are free to fetch the colonel." He gathered her clothes together. "These will be returned when Bruce and Leon say they have been satisfied."

Holly spat at him. The flat surface of his hand against the side of her face knocked her off balance. A gasp escaped her, and he hit her again.

Doug called for Bruce and Leon. Both men entered the room and ogled her naked body. "She's all yours, boys."

Bruce dropped his pants. Humiliated and ashamed, Holly closed her mind. If she didn't perform as Doug ordered, she had no doubt that he would kill her.

Early in the morning, pounding came to the door. To Wil's surprise, Holly stood before him with a smudged face, red eyes, and stray hair. The only time he had ever recalled her with a disheveled appearance was in bed. "Rough night, Mrs. Whyte?"

She twisted the handkerchief in her hands and stared at him, unblinking. "You can save your gloating for later, Wil. They have Amanda."

His amusement shifted to immediate concern. "Who has Amanda?"

She placed the handkerchief to her face as if ready to cry into it. Her sides heaved, but no sound came out.

He had never seen Holly shaken. Wil grasped her arm and led her to the sofa in the parlor. Holly glanced up with tears streaking her cheeks and looked beyond him. Alice had joined them. "Who has Amanda?" he repeated.

"Doug Chandler."

A hand flew to Alice's mouth in sheer terror.

Chandler again. "Where? And how many are with him?" Wil asked in an attempt to keep his voice even.

Holly wrung the handkerchief. "Three others and Jesse. They're in a cabin in the Wilderness—not far from the turnpike and Brock Road."

He was all too familiar with the area. Wasting no time, Wil collected his gun belt from the study.

"Wil, you can't go after him. He requested Sam—alone. I only came here because Sam wasn't at headquarters. He's been out all night searching for Amanda."

He strapped on the gun belt. "When is Sam due to return?"

"No one knows."

Wil tucked a knife into his boot. "What happens to Amanda in the meantime?"

Holly grasped a trembling hand to his forearm. "Doug won't give you any special treatment again. I had no idea what he was up to. I was aware that he had stolen a couple of horses, but I thought he got most of his money from gambling. And the night of the dance, you made it quite obvious that we once had been..." Apparently recalling Alice's presence, she twisted the handkerchief. "I'm sorry, Wil."

He nodded. "When Sam returns, inform him that I've gone ahead." He shoved his hat on his head.

"Wil..." By the door, Alice threw her arms around his neck and gave him a fretful farewell kiss. "I love you," she whispered, leaving the worst of her worries left unsaid.

In her silence she had become a true military wife. He assured her that he would be fine and went out to the stable. After saddling his horse and mounting, he pressed the gray for speed. As he headed in the direction of the Wilderness, thunder rumbled. Had the sound been real or was he hearing ghostly cannon fire from the depths of his mind again? Wil glanced to the sky. No clouds were building. War memories were creeping through once more.

Much of the day had passed and the sun was setting by the time he reached the Wilderness. The screams in his mind grew louder. His only link to sanity had been . . . Alice. But he had been thinking of Amanda, and he had to stop fooling himself. He had never stopped loving her.

Wil halted the lathered mare and tied her to the budding branches of a sycamore tree. Only then did he realize how cold the day was. Branches creaked in the blowing wind. Overgrown with brambles, the trail was barely more than a deer path. Nez Percé warriors had taught him to move swiftly and silently. After he traveled a few hundred yards, the tangled forest opened to a hollow. In the clearing stood a two-room cabin. Leon stood out front, shivering in the chill, and he heard laughter from inside. Men's voices.

For a moment, Wil fought the overwhelming urge to forge blindly ahead. If he wasn't careful, he could wind up getting Amanda killed. Four against one with Jesse an unknown factor. He circled around back where the horses were tethered to a rope between two trees. One by one, he released them, slapping the last one on the rear. The horses bolted.

As hooves pounded and kicked up clumps of frozen dirt, he retreated to the cover of the forest. Leon bounded into view, waving a fist and screaming obscenities at the horses. Bruce joined him, and both dashed off after the horses.

With the odds a little more even, Wil carefully negotiated his way over to the cabin. Crouched below a window, he overheard Amanda, crying softly. *Easy,* he reminded himself. He heard a smack, and a muffled cry from Amanda. His composure gave way. He drew his pistol and lunged through the door. Brittle wood splintered from the frame. Almost too late, he saw what he should have taken into account before making a move.

With an arrogant smile, Chandler pressed an arm against Amanda's throat and aimed a gun to her head. He was flanked by Jesse and another baby-faced man in his mid-twenties with a cowlick at the back of head, almost making him look comical. On the battlefield, Wil would have reprimanded any officer behaving in his own rash manner, but when he had thought Amanda was in danger . . .

"So pleased you could join the festivities, General," Chandler said in greeting.

Amanda's eyes were wide with fear.

"I was wrong about you, Chandler," Wil said. "I didn't think you were a coward. Must you hide behind a lady's skirt?"

The pistol wavered near Amanda's temple. "The way I see it, as long as I've got the lady, I hold the ace. Now drop your gun."

"Amanda?"

"I'm fine . . ."

Chandler pressed his arm against her throat, cutting off her breath. His eyes sparkled in a peculiar way. "You heard her. She's fine. Now drop the gun."

Wil had witnessed the same demented look on the battlefield. Yet Chandler was a gambler and capable of bluffing. Wil couldn't risk Amanda's life. Careful not to make any fast moves, he lowered his gun to the floor. Jesse and the man with the cowlick shoved him against the wall and searched him. Hands probed over him until Jesse reached his boot where he had hidden the knife. The young man's almond eyes met Wil's, but he continued on. "He's clean," Jesse announced.

"You disappoint me, General." Chandler lowered his pistol but kept a tight grip on Amanda's arm. "I told you that I wouldn't be so lenient the next time. How could you have signed the Yankees' Oath?"

"The war is over," Wil reminded him.

The gleam in Chandler's eyes returned. "Some of us won't stop fighting until the Confederacy resumes its former glory."

"There was never any glory—only death. Others of us want to get on with our lives."

"As an engineer?"

Engineer—Wil had already determined that he was unsuited for civilian life. "It was my training at West Point. Let the lady go, Chandler. I'll be your mediator when the colonel arrives."

Chandler's nostrils flared as the baby-faced man drew Wil's hands behind his back. A rope bound them. Amanda bit Chandler and screamed a warning. Then pain, and nothing.

Chapter Eleven

ONLY A SLIVER OF LIGHT SHONE THROUGH THE CRACK under the door. Bound like a trussed turkey with her back next to Wil's, Amanda ached. He was dead weight slumped against her and had yanked her shoulder and arms into painful positions. At first, she feared that he might not be alive, but she occasionally heard ragged breathing. She felt a tug on the ropes about her wrists. Thank goodness, he was coming around. "Wil?"

He groaned. "My head . . . feels like someone took a sledgehammer to it."

"A gun butt would be more accurate. You've been out cold for some time." He tested the ropes and tightened the ones around her wrists further. She let out a cry as the bindings bit into her flesh.

He quickly apologized. "Amanda, are you all right? Did they hurt you?"

Wil didn't normally hedge. "They didn't ravish me, if that's what you're asking." She thought she heard him breathe out in relief. "They're going to kill us, aren't they?"

"No." His voice had been firm.

"Stop protecting me. You know I don't like it when you do that."

"I'm not protecting you. They're not going to kill us—not if I can help it." He pulled on the ropes, and her shoulder bent at an awkward angle.

She yelped.

"Sorry, Amanda. I've got a knife in my boot if I can get to it. I'll see if I can loosen your ropes." The bulk of his weight leaned against her, and he struggled with the bindings.

As it had so many times in the past, her fear lessened when he was with her. "Wil, why were you afraid to mail the letter?"

His fingers continued working on the ropes. "That was a long time ago."

"Four years."

He stopped fighting the ropes. "Things have changed during that time. What happened to propriety, Amanda?"

"I keep wondering . . ."

His back straightened.

"So, you do too."

Without comment, he fumbled with the rope again. The bindings began to loosen around her wrists—not much, but enough so that she could wiggle her hands.

"Can you reach the knife?"

"No." She felt his hands on the ropes, returning to the task at hand. "Wil, I know why you risked your life in coming here. I don't expect you to openly admit it, but there's something you should know."

"Amanda, don't say it. That was another life. You'll regret it."

So why did she yearn for him to touch her? She felt ashamed. The rope loosened and her right hand was free. She twisted around but was nearly blind in the darkness. After some fumbling, she managed to release her other hand. She struggled with the knots binding Wil.

"Get the knife," he instructed.

After what she had been about to confess, Amanda was unable to face him, much less touch him. "I was about to say something very foolish."

"Fret about that later. For all we know, Chandler could be right outside the door."

His calm was what she needed to regain her poise. Her heart pounded, and she reached out a trembling hand and touched him on the thigh. Hesitant, she didn't need to be able to see to know that a wicked grin had spread across his face. "Wipe that smirk off your face, Wil Jackson, or I shall leave you tied."

"That could be entertaining."

"Damn you."

"And I have finally made you swear."

Refraining from giving him an angry retort, Amanda proceeded. She lifted his trouser leg and slipped the knife from his boot. "I don't think it's good that we know each other so well."

"Why? I made you forget the danger for a little while, didn't I?"

He had, and she should have guessed that Wil would resort to levity no matter how dire the circumstances. "I can't see to cut the ropes. The knife might slip."

"There's no time for caution. Just do it."

Amanda groped through the darkness and found the coarse rope binding Wil's hands. She positioned the knife and hesitated.

"Go ahead, Amanda."

She took a deep breath and sliced through the ropes. "Did I cut you?"

"I'm fine." As was his usual habit, he hadn't answered the question. Free of the wrist bindings, Wil appropriated the knife and quickly severed the ropes around their ankles. He gripped her arm and helped her stand.

She was in his arms. "And your head?"

"I'm fine, Amanda. We need to concentrate on getting you out of here."

Too late—footsteps trod outside the door. Wil shoved her behind him with his body forming a protective shield. She clutched his sack coat and bit her lip to keep from screaming. Although she had no doubt that he was unafraid, Wil couldn't stop Chandler and his men on his own. Hinges creaked, and she clenched his wool coat tighter. Ready to take action, his muscles tensed. Lantern light illuminated the room. Wil sprang toward the light, and the lantern crashed to the floor.

Smoke and screams filled the air, and the smell of burning flesh. Others were scuffling. In the flickering firelight, Amanda couldn't make out which man was which. Recalling that a blanket had rested on the cot, she coughed from the smoke and stumbled to the cot. She seized the blanket and threw it over the burning man. He rolled on the floor, wailing. She heard shattering glass when a vise-like hand grabbed her arm and shoved her through the window.

Jagged edges sliced into her arms and face. Nearly headfirst, she tumbled to the ground. Amanda paused to catch her breath. Someone followed her through the window. Soft moonlight filtered through the night sky, but she couldn't quite make out his features. Judging by his gangly form, he definitely wasn't Wil. She scrambled to her feet and dashed into the darkness. Naked tree branches clawed her arm, tearing her sleeve, but she kept running. A firm hand latched onto her arm. Her fists flew, but the dark figure caught her forearms. She fought against his grip but couldn't break his hold.

"Mrs. Prescott, I want to help you."

Jesse... "Please... Let me go."

He motioned for her to keep her voice down. "Please Mrs. Prescott, I want to help you," he repeated.

Help? She ceased her resistance, and he loosened his grip. "What about Wil?"

"I'll go back for him, but first, I must know that you're safe."

Should she trust him? "I'll hide in the woods and wait for you and Wil."

"Here." He placed Wil's knife into her palm and curled her fingers around it. "Use it, if necessary." As he turned, a daguerreotype tumbled from his pocket. Amanda retrieved it from the ground. *Jesse's family*... Smoke billowed from the cabin, and she stumbled deeper into the forest. Brambles cut into her hands. The sound of gunfire made her jump. *What if neither of them returned?*

She huddled among brambles, ignoring the pain of thorns poking into her skin. Footsteps crunched against dead fall leaves, and a man came to a halt almost next to her. She held her breath. He took a step away from her, and she breathed. As he moved off, she shifted position, snapping the winter-dried brambles. She covered her mouth to keep silent.

An arm thrust through the protective boundary of thorns and

seized her. Amanda screamed. More pounding footsteps... The hairy hand let her go, and knuckles crunched. A man yelped.

More scuffling, then Wil cursed a string of oaths that would have normally made her blush. Amanda had no recollection of moving, but found herself in his arms. Quickly catching herself, she stepped back. "Jesse went looking for you."

Out of breath, Wil shook his hand in pain. "He's coming. Amanda, are you all right?"

"Frightened, and a few cuts, but overall, I'm fine."

Wil grasped her elbow and led her further from the cabin. She overheard men's voices trailing after them. If it hadn't been for Wil's strong grip guiding the way, she would have bolted. Gunfire echoed through the darkness, and Jesse shrieked.

"Go ahead, Amanda." Wil turned back.

"I'm staying with you this time." Amanda clung to his sleeve until they reached a sprawled body face down in the dirt. "Jesse..." Instantly beside him, she checked for a pulse. "He's alive."

Wil was already helping Jesse to his feet. On the opposite side, Amanda drew Jesse's arm over her shoulder. The other men's shouts returned to the area of the burning cabin. Quickening their pace, they continued through the tangled woods. Jesse was barely able to move and more of his weight pressed upon her. She stumbled over a root and nearly fell.

With little moonlight to illuminate the way, Amanda could barely see the path. She let Wil lead the way. He was an engineer. He'd know how to use the moon as a source to guide them. Footsore and weary, they must have traveled over a mile before passing a tumbled-down house, long abandoned by war. "Wil, Jesse needs rest."

He agreed. The house had four rooms. Disposed of by passing armies, haversacks and coats of faded blue had crumbled to dust. A tattered quilt was about all that remained. Spreading the cover on the rotting wood floor, they attempted to make Jesse comfortable. Wil bent down and pressed a handkerchief to Jesse's back. Like the time she had sprained her ankle when smuggling supplies, he ministered aid with a surprising gentle touch.

"How is he?" she asked.

"He's lost a lot of blood."

"Wil, do you think you can fetch some water?" Amanda grasped his handkerchief and wiped the blood seeping from Jesse's back.

Wil found a tin container and left the house. Her heart thumped, and Amanda ripped her petticoat and dabbed away blood. The bullet had passed right under Jesse's shoulder blade. Keeping busy helped her not to fret too much. Like the many wounded that she had tended in the hospitals, Jesse was thirsty. Wil brought in a ladle with water. She helped the boy drink.

"I left my horse near the cabin. I can circle around and fetch her . . ."

"No."

"Amanda . . ."

"I said, no. You're not leaving us alone."

Wil nodded. "I'll keep watch by the door. If you need my help, call."

"Thank you, Wil." Her petticoat served as makeshift bandages. Finally, she was able to stop the bleeding. Then she tended to her own cuts. Instead of brooding on her thirtieth birthday, she was doing much as she had in the past four years—tending wounded. After nearly an hour, Jesse rested, and she placed the daguerreotype of his family beside him.

Amanda went to the door. Wil sat on the step out front, staring into the darkness. "He needs a doctor," she said.

"Then let's hope your husband finds us before Chandler does," he replied evenly.

"Wil . . ." She sat on the steps beside him. "I know you're worried about him."

"Amanda, " he said, without looking in her direction, "I know what you're thinking. I'm fond of Jesse because he's Caroline's son, but he's not mine."

"What about the letter from his mother?"

Wil sighed. "She never mailed it because she wanted Jesse to find it. I received word from my sister in Charleston. A month after I returned to the Point, Caroline was attacked." He clenched a hand. "While I wasn't exactly the ideal parent, I gathered that she took some comfort in telling Jesse that his father was a lieutenant in the army, not some goddamned rapist."

Amanda held sympathy for Caroline. Single and in a family way through no fault of her own. Could she blame her for using Wil's name? Even in her moments of need, she continually turned to him. Without thinking, she slipped her arm through his. "I blamed you for not mailing the letter."

He finally glanced at her. "You had every right to."

"No Wil, I was wrong. I needed someone to blame. First, I lost John at Manassas, then I thought you were dead after Sharpsburg. In my grief, I turned to Sam. I loved him, but I wasn't certain which of you . . ." She felt tears fighting their way to the surface. "Please don't hate me."

He placed a hand under her chin and kissed her full on the mouth. "I could never hate you. I thought you knew. I have always loved you."

No! After all this time, he had voiced it. "Wil, no. It's wrong for us . . ." He cut off her sentence by kissing her again. She recalled times past—the comfort of his arms, stolen kisses, and flirtatious adventures—all to lead to what might have been. Trembling with fear, she clung to him.

His hand lifted her skirt and traced the length of her inner thigh. In the near total darkness, his silhouette seemed like nothing more than a shadow gliding through the night. Douglas Chandler could still be searching for them, wanting both of them dead. She clenched Wil tighter.

He knelt before her and spread her legs. *Draw away.* Amanda immediately silenced the doubting voice. If only she could be rid of her shaking as easily. She felt his hands again, parting her drawers. His exploring fingertips revived a passion and compelled her to open her legs wider. For far too long, they had ignored a desperate need. Without further ceremony, he unbuttoned his trousers and was inside her.

To meet like this nearly fully dressed covered their shame. But she felt no shame, only exhilaration. Even while married to John, she had known of her love for Wil. But their love was forbidden.

His fingers dug into her skin as he frantically clutched her hips. She bit her lip to keep from crying out until she could no longer hold back. With a shudder, she wailed. *Oh God, what had they done?*

Wil held her and pressed his face against hers. Tears streaked her cheeks, and she draped an arm around his neck. For ages, she hung onto him tight and cried. He whispered that it would be all right.

Amanda brushed away her tears and pounded a fist to his chest. "You were supposed to be dead. Why did you have to return?"

"Sorry to disappoint you." He stood and fastened his trousers. "You seemed to have been enjoying my company a few minutes ago."

"Wil . . ." She said his name as if it were a curse and lowered her skirt. "What about . . ." *Sam and Alice.* She choked back another sob. *How could she have betrayed her own sister like this?* "I had best check on Jesse."

She scrambled to her feet, but Wil caught her arm. He placed his hands on each side of her face and kissed her. At first, she resisted, but her lips parted. She gave him her tongue, and her yearning renewed. She shoved away from him and returned to the house.

Jesse quietly rested on the tattered blanket where she had left him. His forehead was feverish. With her back against a wall, Amanda tucked her knees to her body. Exhausted, she drifted, only to wake to someone gently shaking her and to Wil's coal-black eyes in the morning dawn. Maybe the previous night had been nothing more than a dream.

"We may need to move quickly," he said in his usual, calm manner.

"Wil . . ."

He waved at her to keep quiet. As he checked the door, she heard hoofbeats. Amanda fought the urge to flee and hunkered down beside Jesse. The boy scrunched his face in pain, but nodded that he was holding his own.

"It's all right." Wil extended a hand. "It's your husband."

Refusing the offer of his hand, she stood and met Wil's gaze. The look in his eyes—the silent longing. Throughout the years, she had pretended that having his love didn't matter. Under the darkness of night, the forbidden had come to fruition. Unable to pretend any longer, she stroked his hand.

"Amanda . . . ," came Sam's voice.

Wil grasped her arm and delivered her to Sam waiting beside the door. "She's still shaken."

In relief, Sam hugged her and kissed her. Without really hearing his questions, she felt numb. Wil returned to help Jesse. Her knees buckled. Sam caught her to prevent her from hitting the floor as darkness engulfed her.

Chandler and his band had left Hank behind. Not only had the boy been burned in the fire, he hadn't fully recovered from his bout with typhoid. The soldiers had little trouble capturing him, but after finding Amanda in the abandoned building with Wil and the wounded Jesse, Sam had left Greer in charge of hunting down the remaining guerrillas.

On the trip to the farm, Amanda appeared to have slipped into a stupor. Upon arrival, she nearly swooned again, and he carried her up to the house. Once inside, he gently set her on the sofa and rubbed her hand. "Amanda . . ."

With a concerned expression, her mother brought a damp cloth. "Will some tea help?"

"It's worth a try, Jean. Amanda . . ." He continued to pat her hand.

Rebecca brought Amanda her rag doll, and Amanda dissolved into tears.

"I'm going to take your mama upstairs, Rebecca. She needs rest." Sam aided Amanda up the stairs and to their bedroom. At least she was walking under her own power, but she stared straight ahead as if in a daze. He helped her out of her dirty and torn dress and change into her nightdress. Besides the bruises on her face, more welts and cuts covered her arms and legs. He held back the

urge to hunt the bastards down himself. Greer was a capable officer. Amanda needed him now.

Jean brought some tea and toast. She helped him dab the cuts
with a cloth. Amanda nibbled on the toast until she dozed off.
With his arms around her, Sam stayed by her side. After what
had happened to Lily and the barmaid, he should have been fore-
warned that something like this might happen. But how did he
capture someone who knew the countryside like the back of his
hand and could slip in and out of places like a ghost? *Damn*—for
Amanda's sake, he had to find a way.

By late afternoon, Amanda awoke. Her emerald eyes still
seemed empty, but they were more alert. Jean brought in more
tea with a bowl of broth. Famished, Amanda spooned the broth
to her mouth.

At least that much was good. She was eating. "Care to tell me
what happened?" Sam asked.

Avoiding eye contact, she shook her head. "I can't."

"Amanda, did they . . ."

Amanda shoved the tea and broth aside. The teacup tottered
and crashed to the floor, shattering into many pieces. "No!" She
crumpled into a heap on the bed and began sobbing.

Sam climbed in next to her and held her. He brushed the hair
from her face.

"Sam, I love you. I thought I'd never see you again."

He hushed her and continued holding her. Beside the bed,
Jean cleaned the shards from the floor. After an hour, Amanda fell
into another fitful sleep. His arm and back ached from remaining in the same position for too long. He got up and stretched. He
had spent nearly two days searching for her, overwrought the entire time whether he'd find her alive. Now that he had . . . *What if
she didn't come out of it?*

Amanda's mother met him outside the door. "Is she going to
be all right?"

He shook his head. "I don't know. I'll stay with her tonight, but
if she's not any better in the morning, we need to fetch the doctor."

Jean merely nodded and squeezed his hand. "We normally
don't see eye to eye, but I know we both want to see Amanda well."

That was probably the closest concession he'd ever receive from Jean. "On that point, we are in full agreement." Running a hand through his hair, Sam returned to the bedroom. Without bothering to change, he joined Amanda on the bed. At least she was now beside him. He wrapped his arm around her as if that would protect her. His energy drained, he fell asleep.

Sam woke to the gray light of dawn. Amanda had already risen. Worried that she might be stumbling around the house in a muddle, he called for her. Sam raced down the stairs only to find her in the kitchen, serving breakfast. "Amanda . . ."

"I'm fine, Sam." She poured a cup of coffee. "Mama's already taken Rebecca outside. Please, sit down and eat."

Unconvinced, he obeyed. She hadn't made eye contact. "I still think it might be worth fetching a doctor."

"Nonsense."

As if to prove her point, she waited on him hand and foot. The meal consisted of a stack of flapjacks with sausage and a mound of butter—his favorite breakfast. "If you don't mind, I'll stay around a couple of days."

"That would be silly. You have your duty." She sat across from him and smiled.

Although she struggled to keep her face even, he could easily see the smile was forced. "My duty can wait. Greer is looking for Chandler. Amanda . . ." He reached across the table and grasped her hand. "You've been through an ordeal."

Glancing to the table, she withdrew her hand. "They wanted me to care for Hank." With those words, she opened up and began to speak about the terrifying experience that Chandler had put her through. Occasionally, her voice wavered, and when she made eye contact, she would immediately look away.

"We should thank Wil for going after you."

Amanda jumped up to fetch the coffeepot. "After I've had a chance to recover some, I'll invite him and Alice over to supper."

As she poured, he leaned back in the pole-backed chair. "It won't do any good. He'll be in Petersburg within the next day or two."

She set the coffeepot on the table and pressed a hand to her chest, taking a deep breath. Rebecca came charging through the door with Jean on her heels. He tugged the laughing and squirming Rebecca onto his lap. "There are Yankees outside," Jean announced.

"Probably Greer." Sam set Rebecca down and got to his feet. By the time he reached the front steps, Greer stood at the bottom with his hat in his hand. "How's the missus, sir?"

"Better."

"We got Leon, sir. Found him holing up in a nearby barn."

That much was good news—only two at large. "Chandler?"

Greer shook his head. "We would cover more ground with a few more experienced men in the field."

His lieutenant was being polite. The only other experienced man available was himself. "I can't leave now."

Amanda stepped onto the porch. "There's no reason for you to sit home and nursemaid me. I'll be fine."

He drew her inside the door, so they might speak in private. "I said that I'd stay with you for the next couple of days. I meant it."

"Don't be foolish. Your men need you." She lowered her voice. "Sam, I'd like to see Doug Chandler brought to justice, not for what he did to me, but he'll continue hurting others unless he's captured. What if he kills someone the next time?"

It was just like Amanda to be thinking of others. Sam placed his arms around her. He heard her sniffle and thought she might be crying again, but her eyes remained dry. "I'll do as you ask as long as you promise to take care of yourself."

"I shall." Another sniffle.

He sought her mouth, but she withdrew from his embrace. *Too soon.* "I'll inform Greer, then get my things."

"Please be careful."

"I will," he promised. "I love you."

The tears she had been fighting suddenly streaked her cheeks. "And I, you." Amanda dashed up the stairs. How could he leave her in such a state?

Finished bandaging Jesse's wound, Alice lowered his shirt.

"Thank you, Mi—, Alice."

"You're welcome." Between the trips to the shanty village tending Lily and now Jesse, she was worn to a frazzle. They had brought Jesse to the study where Amanda had tended Sam. Fortunately, once Jesse was strong enough, he'd be moved to the farm for Amanda to care for. Alice felt she should make the trip to the farm to see how Amanda had fared, but Wil assured her that her sister would be fine.

"Would you mind telling the general that I'd like to see him? It's in regard to the letter."

The letter from Wil's sister, revealing Jesse's true parentage—he had shown it to her after his return with a wounded Jesse. "Of course. Jesse. I know that he's still fond of you."

On her way out of the room, he muttered his thanks. She closed the door behind her and shoved stray hair from her face. Thankfully, Wil had been helpful in minding Emma while she tended to the extra chores. With Lily still sick, she couldn't fathom how she would manage once he left for Petersburg the following day. She went into the parlor. "Jesse's resting, but he'd like to see you when you get the chance."

"So is Emma." Sound asleep and sucking her thumb, Emma was curled in Wil's arms.

"You've been playing rough-and-tumble games again. No wonder she never sleeps when you're away."

"I'll take her upstairs."

Exhausted, Alice sank to the sofa and kicked off her worn-out shoes. She leaned back and closed her eyes. Soon she drifted, only to wake to the soothing touch of someone kneading her tense shoulders.

"Alice, I've been thinking—come to Petersburg with me."

She cracked one eye open. "Tomorrow?"

Wil sat beside her.

"What about Jesse?" Wide awake, she shook her head. "I don't see how it's possible."

"Obviously, I haven't thought the notion through," he responded with disappointment lingering in his voice.

"Mama would never forgive us if we gave up the house."

"Then why isn't she living here?"

Why? He *knew* very well why. Amanda could better afford to care for her. "You said you would try and find something closer to home."

"And do what? Become a shopkeeper?" Frustration had changed to anger. "Never mind that I brought it up. It seems there's not much difference between war and peacetime. I'm still away from my family for months on end."

"At least no one is shooting at you anymore."

"No, they save that for when I'm home."

Alice slid her arm through his. "You haven't said much about what happened."

He stood. "There's nothing to say."

Something *had* happened. During the war, he had withdrawn from her in the same manner. "We'll talk about Emma and me moving to Petersburg on your next trip home. Jesse will be gone then, and Lily will be well on the road to recovery."

He nodded but added nothing. "I'll go see Jesse now."

As he strode from the room, nausea spread through the pit of her stomach. Every morning in Petersburg, she had the ritual of running for the chamber pot to retch after he left. Nearly a year had passed since the shells had stopped screaming over the city. The feeling now was rawer—much deeper, but what could it mean?

She dashed upstairs. The hawk feather lay atop the dresser. Alice studied it. After Amanda's visit, she hadn't touched it. Her sister doubted her, but she *had* traveled to the past. In her mind, she heard Frieda's voice. "Pick it up, girl."

Alice clutched the feather to her bosom. "Frieda, what shall I do?"

The sightless servant appeared before her, holding her cherry walking stick. "You got to be careful, Miss Alice." Frieda jabbed a bony finger in her direction. "If you ain't, you lose both of dem."

A hand went to her mouth. "Wil and Emma?"

"*She* bring da fever."

Frieda faded from her view, and Alice found herself standing alone in front of the dresser. Even the red tail feather remained untouched. Everything else had been nothing more than a dream—no, a vision. While Frieda was in the past, she had always possessed the ability to foretell the future. But had she really seen the old servant?

Lily had typhoid. Was that what she had meant by her warning? Alice picked up the hawk feather. No matter how hard she concentrated, she couldn't bring Frieda back.

In the study, Jesse lay on a straw mattress—same as Sam had when he had been wounded. *Sam*... The most difficult thing Wil had ever done was hand Amanda over to him. "Alice said that you wanted to see me."

"I've read the letter," Jesse said.

"I'm sorry I had to bring you that news."

"Are you? It probably came as a relief."

"I would have never wished such a thing for Caroline." And how many other lives had he ruined? He wanted to see Amanda before he left but fought the urge. The sooner he was away from Fredericksburg, the better for all concerned. Wil rubbed his forehead. "But I thought you should know."

"Of course. Sir, if it had been true?"

"I had already accepted you as my son, so nothing would have changed."

"And now?"

"You're still Caroline's son."

Jesse extended his hand, and Wil took it, sealing a bond between them.

Thank God her monthly had started. For three days, Amanda had traveled more floorboards than she cared to think about. With safety in numbers, she vowed never to be alone with Wil again. After pacing the length of the study for nearly two hours, she decided to write a letter and explain the situation to him. *Explain what?* That due to the unique set of circumstances she had broken her wedding vows?

Taking the seat behind the desk, she scrambled to locate some paper and dipped a pen in ink. Words failed her. She recalled being in Wil's arms. She *wanted* to see him again. With a groan, she shoved the pen and paper to the floor.

"Amanda..."

Fighting tears, she blinked. "Sam... I didn't know you were home."

He reached down, returning the supplies to the desktop. "I wanted to let you know that we've captured Bruce."

Bruce—not Douglas Chandler. "I'm pleased. Let me start supper."

As she passed him on her way to the kitchen, he drew her into his arms and kissed her. She closed her eyes. "I know you're still upset by all that's happened, but you needn't play the doting wife every time I appear."

Doting? She waited on him hand and foot to cover her shame. "I need to keep busy. It occupies my mind."

He let her go and nodded. "I understand."

She'd rather that he screamed at her in a fit of rage. But how could he know the depth of her guilt? The man that she loved and how she had failed him. She imagined the pain on his face if he ever found out. "I'll start supper."

"Amanda..." He grasped her hand. "A warrant has been issued that anyone caught harboring Chandler will be arrested. The move won't be a popular one, but I'm certain that's how he's been eluding us."

"What will happen to Hank?"

His brows narrowed in confusion, then he hesitated a moment as if deciding what to tell her. "All of Chandler's men, along with Chandler once he's found, will likely be tried and hanged."

"Then I tended him for..." With a sudden sick feeling, she pressed a hand to her stomach. "How is this any different from the war? I patch you up, only to send you out again to God knows what, and I tend others only to watch them die at a later date."

His arms went around her once more, and she sobbed on his shoulder. Sam withdrew a handkerchief from his pocket.

Amanda dabbed her eyes. "Even after all of these years, I've never learned to carry a handkerchief."

He smiled, and his blue eyes flickered at her in a familiar way. *Lord forgive her*, she had mistaken him for Wil. After John's death, Wil had been the one to comfort her and say that she'd eventually learn to carry a handkerchief.

Chapter Twelve

*D*URING THE FINAL WEEK OF APRIL, the trial had begun for Douglas Chandler's men, making Sam's visitations to the farm even less frequent. Some folks in town protested the proceedings, while others welcomed them. Amanda feared that she might eventually need to testify, but Sam assured her they would only call on her as a last resort.

After tucking Rebecca in bed with a goodnight kiss, she wandered out to the walnut grove to check on Jesse. The boy remained in considerable pain but was regaining his strength. He had already returned to the duties of light farm work.

On the moonlit night, Amanda strolled across the farmyard when she heard hoofbeats in the lane. *Sam . . .* But it was Wil. Behind his own horse, he led a stallion. *Her stallion*—the one that had been missing since the fire. Wil brought his mare to a halt by the hitching post.

"Red!" She rushed over and threw her arms around the horse's neck. Red nickered in response.

Wil dismounted and tied his mare.

She rubbed the stallion's neck. "Wil, where on earth did you find Red?"

With a smile, he lowered his hat. "Jesse gave me a few leads, and it just so happened the new owner lived near Petersburg. Sam said he'd see the charges against Jesse were dropped if he paid folks back."

"I see," she responded, avoiding his gaze, "but how could you have afforded buying him back for me? I know Jesse hasn't made that kind of money yet."

Silence.

Being the proud sort, he wouldn't easily admit that he had been short on cash. "Wil, I know you couldn't have come by Red cheaply."

"I pawned my watch," he finally admitted.

"Then I shall buy you a new one." Only with her words did she realize that she had been caught up in the moment. She was alone with Wil.

He fidgeted with his hat. "Amanda, I'm sorry if I have ruined our friendship."

She finally met his gaze. "You didn't ruin..." She swallowed hard. "But it can't be that way between us—not again. Too many would be hurt if they ever found out."

He replaced his hat to his head. "Rather than cause you further discomfort, I shall say farewell. I'm off in a couple of days to Petersburg for four to six weeks."

At least another month. Why did the thought of not seeing him make her heart ache?

"Amanda...," came Mama's voice from the house. Mama's frail frame lugged Amanda's rifle down the brick walk.

"Everything is all right, Mama. It's only Wil. He's returned Red."

Relief spread across Mama's wrinkled face. She passed the rifle to Amanda and slipped her arm through Wil's. "Where are your manners, Amanda? Invite Wil in for some tea. Have the servant see to the horses."

As they went up the walk, Amanda overheard Mama ask Wil about Alice and Emma. He responded in a composed manner. A lump formed in her throat. Could he truly love both of them, and when the time came, how would she ever face Alice?

Mindlessly, Amanda prepared the tea while Mama chatted with Wil in the parlor. When she brought in the teapot and platter, he stood to assist her. "I don't know which is worse," Mama continued, "the guerrillas or the Yankee despots."

"Mama, that's not fair. Sam is doing the best he can under difficult circumstances."

"And where is he now? The war is over. If he hadn't fought for the Yankees, he would be home with his wife and daughter."

"Yes, Mama." It was no use. Mama had never liked Sam, and nothing she said would ever change the crotchety woman's mind, even though Wil spent just as much time away. Amanda quietly served the tea, then made herself comfortable on the tapestry sofa, while Wil recounted his tale of tracking down Red.

When he glanced in her direction, Amanda looked away. Suddenly cold, she rubbed her arms. But it wasn't the chill that bothered her. She wanted Wil to take notice. She always had. Now that he was here, she felt no shame. As if he had read her innermost feelings, a smile spread across his face.

After nearly an hour, Wil readied to leave. "I'll see Wil to the door," Amanda said. Mama said her goodbyes and began clearing dishes away, while Amanda escorted Wil to the foyer.

With a bow, he kissed the back of her hand. His touch made her shiver. *All a pretense for anyone who might be watching.* "Do you want me to leave, Amanda?" he whispered so Mama wouldn't overhear. His dark eyes met hers.

Yes! "No." Her heart had ruled. "Mama will retire in about half an hour. I'll meet you outside the kitchen door."

He grinned in confirmation. "Good evening, Amanda."

Unable to continue with the sham, Amanda closed the door behind him and slumped against it. She caught her breath and wandered to the kitchen where Mama washed the teapot in the basin. "Why don't you go on up to bed, Mama. I can take care of the washing up."

"I'm perfectly capable of tending to a few chores."

"I realize that. Thank you, Mama."

The old woman smiled, but Amanda's nerves buzzed like angry bees. She glanced to the door. *What had she been thinking?* Resolved that she wouldn't set foot from the kitchen, Amanda busied herself tidying the room. Finally, Mama finished washing up and bid her goodnight. Amanda lowered the lamp to a flicker.

By now Wil was most certainly outside the door, waiting for

Mama's light to go out upstairs. How long would he linger before he realized that she had changed her mind? Already, she tugged with indecision. Her heart pounded, and her palms grew sweaty. But she kept her resolve and slumped into a chair near the table.

In the early days of the war, she recalled her grief after losing John. Wil had been there to comfort her. With his fondness for chasing the ladies, she hadn't taken his sympathy seriously—at least not until she had learned that his Indian wife had been captured for stealing supplies. *"They left her for me to cut down."* Even now, his words haunted her. Only then had she believed his sincerity, but she already carried Sam's child.

A gate creaked outside. *He was leaving.* Amanda rushed to the door and called his name into the darkness. She wrung her hands and tried again. "Wil?" She hurtled down the steps, caught her foot in her skirt, and tumbled to the bottom. "Wil, don't go." With a cry of anguish, she pounded a fist to the ground.

"I'm here, Amanda."

Thank God. She breathed out in relief. She couldn't bear the thought of losing him again.

Wil stepped out of the darkness and helped her to her feet. "Are you all right?"

In response, her arms went around his neck, and she kissed him on the mouth. "Promise me that you won't leave me. Not now."

"I promise." Taking her in his arms, he carried her up the steps. Once inside the door, he headed down the hall toward the back bedroom.

Like a small child, she felt awkward. Why had she been so weak and unable to send him away?

After reaching the bedroom, he set her upon the bed and helped her with her bodice buttons. "I want to see you." He lit a lamp.

The darkness surrounding their previous encounter had provided her with a perfect denial to the actual events. Amanda snapped her eyes shut, but he pushed a stray lock from her cheek and kissed her. He eased her bodice from her shoulders and dropped it to the floor, then unhooked her corset. Unable to contain herself any longer, she unfastened the buttons of his jacket.

They were kissing again, while undressing each other. As layers of clothing were peeled away, Wil took the sight of her in. At first, she was afraid to return the look, but he smiled in that persuasive way of his, putting her more at ease. The cool, spring air nipped at her bare skin, and she had never thought that she could be so content in her nakedness.

No longer was he a shadow in the night, but real flesh and blood in the way she had imagined. Around his neck, he wore the symbol of his guardian spirit—the mountain lion. The angles of his chest were lean but finely muscled. Only a pale scar marred the near-perfect symmetry in a graphic reminder of the bullet that had nearly claimed his life in the Wilderness.

Hesitant to look further, Amanda trailed a finger across his chest. Decisive and confident in his abilities to pleasure a woman, he was more adventuresome than Sam by first touching her breast, then her nipple. Intent on her reaction, he watched her before applying his tongue, subtly, yet adeptly.

Her reluctance faded, and she took a long, slow look at him. Her gaze lingered, then she traced her hand lower with her fingers curling around his hard member. His lips moved with increasing passion from her breasts to her belly until her skin tingled beneath his touch. She ran a finger along the length of his back to the curve of his posterior.

Wil reached the triangular patch between her legs. She stroked through his thick, black hair, squeezed his shoulder muscles, and gasped. He teased her by withdrawing his tongue ever so slightly, then he was touching her again—more forcefully than before until she drew him to her. Once he was atop her, she gripped him, and his erection pressed against her sent another delightful swell coursing throughout her.

Amanda parted her legs wider, and he slid inside her and settled into a steady rhythm. Her back arched from the bed as a torrent surged over her. She clutched him so tightly that she could barely breathe and panted for air. Then like a candle, the flicker gently sank lower and lower until burning itself out.

Wil gave her a broad, satisfied smile before kissing her. She couldn't love him, yet she did. The country might have been re-united, but her heart was more divided than ever.

It was nearly dawn. Amanda nestled in the bend of Wil's arm and traced the scar on his chest. Although his hunger was satiated for the time being, she was an addiction, and he would continue to crave her.

"Wil, we can't continue to meet like this."

He laughed. "Why not?"

Her hand formed a fist. "Damn you. I thought you had changed." She swung.

A grin tugged at the corners of his mouth as he dodged her fist. "And I have made you swear again. Amanda, I meant no disrespect. Many Indian tribes would never expect people to make a choice if they cared for each other."

She touched the medicine pouch. "All this time, I thought I knew you, but I never really have—until now." She shook her head. "I wasn't raised in an Indian lifestyle. I can't think that way. In my mind what we're doing is wrong."

"Then make a choice," he demanded. "As I recall, you did once before. If you are satisfied with the decision, I'll leave, and we can continue to pretend that it doesn't matter."

"But it does matter." Amanda stroked her fingers through his beard. "You promised that you wouldn't leave."

He grasped her hand and kissed it. "You can't have it both ways, Amanda."

"Wil . . ." Her voice wavered. "I don't want to lose you again, but I . . ."

His fingertips brushed against her cheek. "I'm sorry for causing you this anguish. I'll leave."

As he got up, Amanda caught his elbow. "I love you, Wil. No matter what happens, nothing can ever change that fact. You may think I've only recently realized it, but I think I knew when we first met."

When they first met. After the loss of Peopeo, he had vowed to never love again. That promise had only lasted a short while, when his West Point friend, John Graham, had introduced him to his fiancée, Amanda McGuire. Even after John died, he couldn't bring himself to love her in the way she deserved. *He had been afraid, and now everyone paid the price.* Wil rejoined her in bed. "I don't have any answers."

Her hand stroked his bare chest. "I suppose we'll just have to wait for time to sort things out. You will stay for breakfast?"

"Won't that prove a little awkward?"

"Only if Mama notices that my bed hasn't been slept in."

Lies. His own lies were one matter. Besides, Alice was used to him being gone for lengthy periods of time, without serious questioning. Now, he was forcing Amanda to resort to them as well. The contour of her breast pressed against him, and her light lavender scent intoxicated him. "I once knew a navy man who brought a book from the Orient. It had at least a hundred pictures of different positions."

"Positions?" When she realized what he was talking about, her eyes widened. "Is that possible?"

"I'm not sure, but it could be fun finding out."

She whacked him with a pillow across the arm. "Wil!" She dropped the pillow to the bed. "I don't think I'm as adventuresome as you, and please don't enlighten me on how many *positions* you've had personal experience with. I don't want to know."

With a laugh, he pulled her atop him and tasted her mouth. "Then we'll forego such experiments until another time."

"Another time," she whispered, returning his kiss. Then tears entered her eyes, and she rolled to his side. "So now we return to pretending."

"If you prefer, we can announce our *affaire de coeur* to the world."

A wild gleam entered her green eyes, and she thumped him with a pillow again. "You know that's not what I meant."

Although she laughed, the worry lines on her face revealed a deep-seated fear. *What had he done to her?* But she was an intense hunger that he couldn't live without. The blanket had fallen from her breast, and he responded by suckling her nipple.

"It'll be light soon," she reminded him, drawing away.

A young girl's voice called for Amanda from the parlor. "Mama."

Amanda leaped to her feet and pulled a chemise over head. Her breasts vanished from his view. "Wait here at least fifteen minutes after I leave before coming out to the kitchen for breakfast."

He nodded that he'd oblige. Underdrawers went over the spread of her hips. Stockings. Corset. She flushed slightly when she realized that he was watching, but she finished dressing. Over by the mirror, she twisted her blonde hair into a knot and pinned it. A few stray hairs lingered, but Amanda dashed into the hall, barely taking the time to close the door behind her.

He overheard Rebecca whine that she was hungry, and Amanda reassured the girl that breakfast would soon be ready. Extremely relaxed, he drifted. When he woke, sunlight beamed through the window.

Wil hurriedly dressed, then went into the hall. In the kitchen, Amanda's mother and Rebecca were already seated at the table. A round of "good mornings" greeted him. Amanda set a platter of bacon on the table. "I told Mama about how you decided to spend the night rather than heading back to Fredericksburg in the dark after visiting with Jesse."

Well, that was partly true. He had visited Jesse to see how he was faring. And Amanda had avoided making eye contact. He withdrew a chair for Amanda and waited for her to be seated before joining the family at the table. If only he hadn't been afraid, this could have been *his* family. Rebecca pretended to feed her rag doll the bacon off her plate. Unless she turned out to be a tomboy like her mother, Emma would be playing similar games soon. He washed down the bacon and eggs with a cup of coffee, while Jean asked when Alice and Emma would be stopping by for a visit.

"Most likely after I leave for Petersburg." He glanced over at Amanda. Picking at her food, she continued to refrain from looking at him.

"Except for Christmas, we haven't seen hide nor hair of them in several months," Jean said with disappointment.

Amanda tossed her fork to the table with a loud clang. She looked over at him but quickly averted her eyes. There was more friction between her and Alice than he had been aware of, and he highly suspected that he was the cause. "I'll remind Alice to visit soon." Wil stood. "I need to be leaving."

Amanda jumped to her feet. "Mama, if you can help clear the dishes away, I'll see Wil to the door." She motioned in the direction of the parlor and hooked her arm through his. Once they were on the porch, her arms went around him. "Will I see you before you leave for Petersburg?"

"I'll meet you when you visit the shanty village." This response seemed to satisfy her.

He gave her an intimate, farewell kiss. "Bye, Amanda."

Her eyes widened, and she stiffened from sheer terror. "Never say goodbye unless you mean it."

Early in the war, Wil had made a pact to never say goodbye. "The war is over."

"Not in our hearts."

He nodded that he understood. "Then I shall see you at a later time," he replied, careful to use his exact wording from that earlier time. He gave Amanda another kiss before a rattle came from someone turning the door knob. Withdrawing from her arms, Wil went to the lean-to where the horses were stalled and began to saddle his horse. Straw rustled, and a pistol barrel jabbed him in the back.

"I need your help," came Chandler's voice.

"A gun to the back is a poor way of asking." The gun was removed from Wil's back and promptly uncocked. He turned slowly. Chandler had several days of beard growth and circles under his eyes. "Why should I help you?"

Chandler straightened. "Justice. My men have been unfairly accused. We may be gamblers and horse thieves, but we didn't start the fire, shoot the colonel, or kill Lora."

"You kidnapped Mrs. Prescott and shot Jesse."

"Hank was sick. The doctor wouldn't help us. Mrs. Prescott nursed in the hospitals during the war. I felt she was the sort of woman who wouldn't turn us away. She would have been released, unharmed. As for Jesse, that was an accident. If you hadn't interfered, he wouldn't have been wounded."

Undecided whether to believe him or not, Wil asked, "Let's say for argument's sake that I believe you about Jesse. Why didn't you simply tell Mrs. Prescott why you wanted her to accompany you?"

"I didn't think she'd believe me."

"I can't say I do either."

Chandler's eyes revealed no fear, but there was intense wariness in them. "General, I need your help. Unless I head for the mountains, it's only a matter of time before the Yanks nab me."

"Then head for the mountains. Stealing horses is a hangable offense."

"I can't leave. Estelle would have no one if I left."

Estelle? His sister. Chandler had mentioned her on a couple of occasions during poker games. "Take her with you."

Chandler shook his head. "I can't. Since the Yanks burned our home, she's suffered from hysteria. You got Jesse off, and I helped drag you out of the river. The way I see it, you owe me the courtesy of listening to what I have to say."

He did owe Chandler that much. "Say your piece."

"We're being set up."

"By whom?"

"A Yank most likely. None of them like us."

"Can't say that I blame them." Wil grabbed the gray's saddle from a fence rail and placed it on her back. "I also don't deal in conjecture."

"Sir, it wasn't us. My boys will be hanged for crimes they didn't commit. I will surrender for things I am guilty of, but I would be in your debt if you could help me find out who is responsible for the other crimes."

"I'm due in Petersburg in a couple of days." Wil cinched the girth.

"So you're saying you won't help. You're an officer of the Confederacy, not some goddamned engineer."

Wil faced Chandler once more and laughed. "How old are you, Chandler?"

"How . . ." Puzzlement entered Chandler's blue eyes. "Twenty-four, sir."

Only slightly older than he had been during the war with the Mexicans, and after Peopeo's death, he had almost drifted through a similar abyss. "You remind me of myself at your age. I'll speak to the colonel on your behalf, but I want one thing understood. You don't go near Mrs. Prescott or my family again, and if I discover that you're lying, I'll hunt you down myself. Is that clear?"

"It is. Sir, there is something else."

Wil waited for him to continue, and Chandler handed him a pair of saddlebags. Inside was a bullet-ridden Confederate battle flag.

"I can't surrender it to the Yanks. If they try to take it, there will be bloodshed. I'd like for it to remain in Southern hands."

With a nod, Wil fingered the tattered flag. *All that was left of a foolish promise. More needn't die unnecessarily.* "I'll see that it doesn't fall into enemy hands."

Chandler saluted.

"Wil?"

Amanda—she wouldn't understand. Wil threw the saddlebags across the mare's rump and tied them to the saddle. She gripped the rifle and aimed it at Chandler. "Amanda, there's no need to get involved."

"I am already involved, or have you forgotten Mr. Chandler's hospitality?"

"Ma'am," Chandler said, raising his hands, "I truly apologize. I never meant to frighten you."

"You've always been a sweet talker, Mr. Chandler. Reminds me of someone else I know." She glanced in Wil's direction. "Isn't that correct, Mr. Jackson?"

Wil stepped between them, and she lowered the rifle. "He's willing to turn himself in, but not die for crimes that he didn't commit."

Fire blazed in her green eyes. "Which offenses did he not commit? I saw what was in the saddlebag."

If she revealed the flag's existence to Sam, then Chandler wouldn't be the only one arrested. Wil grasped the rifle, and Amanda relinquished it to him. "It's a small price to pay to keep men from dying senselessly."

As if a sudden chill had overcome her, she crossed her arms over her breasts. "What do you intend on doing with it?"

"I gave my word to preserve it."

Her eyes narrowed in annoyance. "And you would foolishly die, defending it."

Damn, she was beautiful when she was angry. "I almost did."

She opened her mouth to say something, but closed it again.

"Lieutenant Chandler and I have concluded our business, so I really must be returning to town. Tell Sam about the flag. It wouldn't be the first time your husband and I were at odds."

She glanced from him to Chandler, then back again. "You know I won't tell Sam."

It was obvious that she wanted to say more, but she remained silent. Wil nodded that he understood. Resisting the temptation to give her a goodbye kiss, he returned her rifle, then finished saddling his mare. He mounted up, and Chandler joined him.

At least with Chandler beside him, Wil could rest easy that he couldn't harm Amanda.

After returning to the house, Amanda busied herself with morning chores. In the back bedroom, she stripped the bed of linens, hoping no sign existed that she had spent the night with Wil. Although shamed by her weakness, she no longer vowed not to see him. She traced a hand along the mattress where they had lain together. When she thought he had died at Sharpsburg, only Sam's love had helped her keep her sanity. Then at the war's end, Wil's aide had erroneously reported his death. She had nearly died inside herself, but she managed to keep a brave face for Alice's sake. *How could anyone ever forgive her?* All this time, she had been jealous of her own sister.

"Amanda . . ."

At the sound of the voice in the hall, she blinked. "Yes, Mama."

"There's someone to see you."

If Wil had returned, Mama would have said so. She went into the hall, and Mama gestured to the parlor where Holly waited. Amanda swallowed hard. "Holly, what brings you here?"

"Amanda, may I speak with you in private?" Holly glanced in Mama's direction.

Had she seen Wil leaving? Holly would most certainly use that fact against her. "Of course," she replied, attempting to keep her voice even. She showed Holly to the study and closed the door behind her.

Holly pursed her lips and fidgeted with her handkerchief. "Amanda . . ." She cleared her throat. "I was hoping that you might be able to help. I'm . . . in a family way, and it most certainly isn't Frank's."

Family way? Had she heard correctly? Holly was pregnant? "How . . . how can I help?"

"You're known throughout the county for your medicinal knowledge."

Shocked by the request, Amanda shook her head. "That was my servant, Frieda. I know some of her medicine, but ridding a body of a baby is dangerous. It could kill you as well."

"Frank will kill me if he learns about a baby that isn't his. Amanda, you were there that night. You know I'm not responsible."

Only after the death of Holly's first husband had Amanda ever felt sorry for her. "I can't, Holly. It would be too risky."

Holly placed the handkerchief to her eyes and dabbed them. "Then maybe I should ask, what would you do if it were you?"

"I wouldn't . . ."

"Wouldn't what?" With a growing grin, Holly met her gaze. "Purposely miscarry a child, even if it wasn't Sam's?"

What did Holly know? "I have no idea what you're talking about."

Her grin faded. "Then let me spell it out. I went to Doug about my little problem before seeing you. We both saw Wil leave here."

Amanda tried to remain calm. "And there's a simple reason. He returned my horse, the one that Mr. Chandler stole from me several months ago."

With a wave Holly dismissed the explanation. "You were in his arms and sharing more than a friendly kiss. Amanda, I don't give a hoot if you're diddling Wil. Heaven knows, he's been brooding over you for quite some time. I just never thought pure-as-gold Amanda would ever reciprocate."

She couldn't come out and make an admission. That would only delight Holly to no end. "What is it you want, Holly?"

"I've already told you. I need to take care of my problem— simple as that."

"If I help you?"

"Then I promise not to tell Sam about seeing you in Wil's arms."

Could she trust Holly? She had no choice. "There's a woman in the shanty village who can see to your problem." Amanda went over to the desk and wrote the woman's name on a slip of paper, then handed it to Holly.

"And you would trust this woman if you were in my place?"

Amanda shook her head. "I don't think I could do what you're intending."

"Even if it were Wil's?"

"Holly, I'll have you know, nothing improper has happened be- tween us." Amanda took a deep breath. The lie had been easier to utter than she thought possible.

"Whatever you say. In any case, I'll keep my promise when I see Sam. But I will be reporting the fact that Doug was here. I hope to see that bastard hang."

Before Amanda could respond, Holly slipped out the door. *What was she going to do?* Pace more floorboards until she was certain that she *wasn't* carrying Wil's child.

Chapter Thirteen

SAM STOOD AS LIEUTENANT GREER ESCORTED HOLLY into headquarters. He motioned for her to have a seat. "What's so urgent?" he inquired.

Failing to rush, Holly spread her skirts and settled on the chair opposite him. "I have some information that I thought you might be interested in and wondered what it is worth to you."

Already he didn't like the direction of the conversation. "What kind of information?"

"The whereabouts of Douglas Chandler."

He leaned back in his chair. "I'm listening."

"You didn't say what the information is worth."

Her eyes glistened. Sam had the feeling that no matter how he responded, he wasn't going to like the answer. "Holly, I'm not in the mood to play your games. If you have knowledge of Chandler, I can't imagine why you would want to help him after the way he treated you."

"Very true." A condescending grin appeared on her face. "But my information may prove to be very embarrassing for someone dear to me."

He didn't believe for a minute that she cared about anyone's feelings. "Who?"

"You."

Now he knew she was joking. "Since when have I been dear to you?"

"Sam, don't be so skeptical. After all, you *are* the brother of my late first husband."

Her words said one thing and her actions another. As if bored or toying with him, Holly studied her fingernails. Obviously, she wasn't going to say anything until he prodded her further. "How will your information be embarrassing for me?"

"Because Douglas Chandler was on *your* farm in deep conversation with Wil Jackson."

Jackson and Chandler? On his farm? "Did you overhear what they were saying?"

The grin returned to her face. "A little."

He motioned for her to continue.

"How's Amanda?"

Amanda? Why did Holly constantly resort to riddles? "She's been melancholy since her ordeal with Chandler, but that's not uncommon for women to feel that way. Get to the point."

Holly's grin widened. "It appears that she's less melancholy when you're not around."

Don't react. She was trying to divert his attention from Chandler. "What has this got to do with Chandler?"

"Because Wil and Doug were on your farm."

God, he hated this job. Holly and her gossip failed to help matters. He couldn't allow himself to get distracted. "Holly," Sam said, taking a deep breath, "I can't go charging after Jackson on the basis of innuendos, but if you definitely saw Chandler with him, I have good cause to question him."

"I know Doug Chandler, and he was speaking to Wil Jackson less than twelve hours ago on your farm."

"All right. I'll question Jackson. Thank you, Holly."

Delighted, she sent him a victorious grin, which made him nervous. He called for Greer to ready his horse. Ten minutes later, he had a couple of his boys accompany him and rode over to meet with Wil.

Officially, the house still belonged to Amanda's mother. As a former Confederate general, Wil had been stripped of his citizenship and wasn't allowed to own property. Yet he struggled to pay the back taxes on the house. Through Amanda, Sam had offered to help with the taxes but had run up against that stubborn Southern pride.

With his sword clanking at his side, Sam trudged up the steps and wondered how he might feel under similar circumstances. Wil would most likely give just about anything in order to resume his military career. He, on the other hand, was growing weary of it. But what else would he do? Now he had some idea why Wil was finding the transition so difficult. He lowered his hat and knocked on the door.

The door opened. "Sam . . ." Alice sent him a welcoming smile and waved for him to come inside.

"Alice, this isn't a social call."

"It rarely is." Her smile vanished. "Every time you visit, I fret."

"I don't have any warrants, so remain calm, but I do need to speak with Wil."

"Make yourself at home in the study. I'll fetch him."

Fidgeting with his hat, Sam went into the study. The desk wasn't much larger than a camp desk, but it served its purpose. Was that the problem? He continued to question the reason behind what he was doing. He understood the necessity of some organization to rebuild the South, but to deprive citizens of their rights seemed inhuman. Hadn't they suffered enough? Was it any wonder that some took the law into their own hands?

"Sam."

He hadn't heard Wil enter the study. "Wil," he acknowledged.

Wil motioned for him to have a seat. "What can I do for you?"

Sam remained standing as Wil made himself comfortable behind the desk. Holly's chatter ran through his head. *Don't get sidetracked.* While he wouldn't necessarily trust Wil in that regard, he had faith in Amanda. "Have you been out to the farm?"

"Yes. I returned your stallion."

Definitely a logical reason for Wil's presence on the farm. Sam relaxed slightly. "Red?"

Wil nodded. "As a matter of fact, I was going to stop by your office in the morning. I ran into Doug Chandler while I was there."

At least Wil wasn't trying to hide his meeting with Chandler, but he was too good a poker player for Sam not to remain suspicious. "Go on."

"He admits to stealing horses, but nothing else that he's been accused of."

"Do you believe him?"

Wil leaned back in his chair and steepled his fingers. "I'm not certain, but if you're going to hang a man, shouldn't you be sure? He's willing to make restitution for the horses."

"He's in no position to bargain."

"But you are. He's only requesting fairness in the justice system. Is that too much to ask of the Yankee courts these days?"

Sam finally sat. "No. I'll see what I can do, but I can't make any promises. How am I to make contact with him?"

"I presume he will get in touch with us."

"Then you don't know where he is?"

Suddenly wary, Wil straightened. "Should I?"

"At ease, Captain. I'm only attempting to find out the details." With his assurance, Wil relaxed. Holly's words went through his mind one more time, and he chided himself for even listening to her gossip. Still, Amanda had always cared for Jackson, and if she hadn't got with child, he doubted that she would have ever married him.

"Was there anything else, Sam?"

"Yes, expect to receive a summons to appear in court against Chandler's men."

"And how am I to do that dividing my time between here and Petersburg?"

"I don't know, Wil. But it's either you or calling Amanda to the stand." Sam thought this reasoning would satisfy him.

Instead, Wil's gaze grew fixed. "If you have me testify against Chandler's men, you'll lose any bargaining power that I might have had to bring him in without bloodshed."

"I can't put Amanda through the stress of a trial. She's been through enough already."

"Of course."

Sam replaced his hat on his head. He needed to make more time for Amanda. Wasn't just being there for her part of his duty as a husband? And he had been fooling himself that being stationed so close to home would allow him the luxury to be at her side constantly. He resolved to make the trip to the farm on this night.

Amanda felt the bed shift, and stretched. She blinked sleepy eyes and nearly murmured Wil's name. Sam's face hovered over her in the flickering light. "Sam, I wasn't expecting you home for another couple of days."

"I needed to see you, Amanda." He undressed and climbed in next to her.

As he took her in his arms, she closed her eyes. They hadn't had relations since she had been with Wil. Sam had dismissed her initial melancholy state to the fact that she was in shock from her ordeal. He kissed her and touched her in a familiar pattern. She went through the motions. After all of the nights waiting and fretting about whether he would return alive, why couldn't she feel now?

She had given him her vows. His face blurred as he rose above her. She was guilty, and like in *The Scarlet Letter*, she should be branded with a red "A" on her forehead. But she loved him. Both of them. She felt as if she were being torn in half. A part of both, yet neither. How could she live this way?

Things were more carefree when she was with Wil. Amanda imagined the warmth of his caresses on her skin and hungered for more. Engulfed in Sam's scent, she wanted to make the vow to never see Wil again. To see him would only continue severing her heart into little pieces. But how could she avoid him when she so desired his company?

To satisfy Sam, Amanda resorted to something she had never done before and pretended to climax. She fought the tears as he held her and kissed her. After he fell asleep, she could no longer keep the tears at bay. She tossed and turned throughout the night and rose early to prepare breakfast. Ezra carried wood in for the fire, and she added a slab of bacon to the griddle. When Sam was home, she always made certain to serve some meat.

Just like any other morning, Mama joined her, soon followed by Sam and Rebecca. But it wasn't like other mornings. She was personally responsible for tearing her family apart.

"I'll escort you into town," Sam said over his morning coffee. "Until Chandler is apprehended, I don't want you going alone. I'll have one of the boys accompany you back."

"That won't be necessary," Amanda insisted.

"Amanda . . ."

"I'll carry a pistol. Will that satisfy you?"

He nodded and stood. "I'll get the buggy ready."

After Sam left the kitchen, Amanda finished her morning chores. She went outside where Sam had the buggy with her stallion hitched to it and his horse tied behind. She rubbed Red's nose. The horse nickered. "It's good to have you back, Red."

Sam helped her into the buggy, and he climbed in on the opposite side. After traveling several miles, he asked, "What's wrong, Amanda?"

Unable to meet his gaze, she glanced at the dry, weedy fields. With no seed to plant, most of them would likely remain fallow for sometime to come. "I'm feeling poorly." Not entirely a lie, she did have a headache and her muscles ached.

"And last night?"

"What about it?"

"You seemed . . . distant."

"You know I don't want any more babies. I thought we had agreed to take precautions."

"I'll remember next time."

Now she was making Sam take the blame for her shame. She finally met his gaze. "Sam, I love you."

"Do you? Sometimes I wonder."

With the same tenderness as on the day they were married, she gripped his hand. "I could never stop."

"But . . ."

Did he suspect something amiss? "But what?"

He shook his head. "Nothing."

For the remainder of the trip, silence hung between them. Sam dropped her off at the shanty village. With so many sick with typhoid fever, she saw to the new cases before looking in on Lily. Alice was tending the servant.

Amanda held her breath. She hadn't seen Alice in several weeks—not since before... Her sister gave her a hug. "Amanda..."

Covering her mouth, Amanda dashed for the door and went outside to retch.

"Amanda..." Alice patted her on the back. "Typhoid doesn't usually cause retching in the beginning."

"I do have a headache." *From guilt.*

Alice pressed a hand to Amanda's forehead. "You feel a little warm. If it's the fever coming on, you should be resting."

Amanda quickly changed the topic. "How's Lily?"

"She's going to be fine, but it's going to be a while before she's up and about again." Alice studied her. "I think you need to scoot on back home. If you're not feeling well, I can get Wil to accompany you."

"No!"

"All right. I'm merely trying to help."

"I know. I'm sorry Alice." Her own sister—she had betrayed her own sister. Would she ever be able to look Alice in the eye again? "Perhaps you're right. I think I'll head home."

"That's wise. I'll stop by to see you in a couple of days."

When Wil was in Petersburg. At least he'd be at a safe distance. "Thank you, Alice." Amanda said her goodbyes and drove the buggy from town. She heard hoofbeats. Without looking around, she knew who was trailing her. He had promised to meet her before he left. She tapped the whip to Red's rump, and he picked up a trot.

The hoofbeats got closer, and a gray pulled even. She waved the whip at Wil. "Go away!"

He brought the gray to a halt. Amanda slowed the buggy. A mistake—she peered around. Sad-faced and forlorn looking, he sat upright in the saddle, watching her.

She reined Red in and waited for Wil to catch up. "I can't live this way, Wil. I've lied to both of them."

He dismounted and lowered his hat. "I'll be leaving tomorrow," he reminded her.

"And if I agree to see you, we'll only delay what must happen in another month."

"Let's delay it then. The thought of not enjoying your company before I go, Amanda, wrenches my heart."

His black hair ruffled in the breeze and with his hat in hand, he looked more like a lovesick schoolboy than a veteran soldier. She had never thought of Wil Jackson in that light and couldn't help but giggle. Confusion spread across his features. "You remind me of a schoolboy, rather than a grown man."

He placed his hat over his heart. "I'm wounded. Is that what you thought of me the other night?"

She only giggled harder.

He tied his mare to the back of the buggy and climbed in beside her. Without a word, he took the reins from her and clicked his tongue for Red to resume a trot.

"I've packed a picnic lunch," she said, breaking the silence.

His eyes met hers. "I thought you couldn't live this way."

"What way? I merely mentioned that I have brought lunch." The buggy swerved to the edge of the road. "Wil, you need to watch where you're guiding Red, or we'll wind up in the ditch. We just got the buggy fixed from when Mr. Chandler dumped it over the side."

He shifted his gaze to the road ahead.

"We have ruined our friendship. Wasn't that worth something?"

A suggestive smile crossed his face. "We've enhanced our friendship."

"But we can't change how things turned out. I've already told you that I don't blame you anymore. Both of us were too stubborn when it counted."

"It counts now, Amanda." A couple of miles later, Wil brought the buggy to a halt near a grove of trees with blackened branches from the fires during the war. "I think I'm hungry for that picnic lunch."

And likely more. Amanda fiddled with the gold ring on her left hand and slipped it in her bag. After climbing from the buggy, Wil helped her down. He secured Red, and they spread the blanket under an oak near a pond. He stretched out his long legs. To ease her discomfort while they ate, she prattled on about the new typhoid cases.

"Amanda, you don't need to be nervous—not around me."

Her heart pounded, and she shoved the sandwich that she had been pretending to eat back into the basket. "Is it that obvious?"

"You get *chatty* when you're uneasy."

She should have known that she couldn't fool Wil.

"I meant it when I said I wanted to enjoy your company before I leave." He grasped her hand and kissed it. "I'm doing so."

With the touch of his lips, she trembled. She knew him equally well. "You needn't lie, Wil. After all these years, I know what's on your mind."

His eyes glistened. "But I *am* enjoying your company."

Amanda withdrew her hand from his grip. "That doesn't change what you've been thinking."

That condescending, know-it-all grin of his returned. "Am I the only one? I see that you have removed your wedding band."

"Wil . . . ," she said between gritted teeth. "I'm not proud of the fact that I'm living my life full of lies and deceit, but when you're around . . ." She clenched a hand. "If only I had told you how I felt, you might have mailed the letter."

"As you have already stated, we can't change how things turned out, but even if it's fleeting, we're together now."

She wished she could look at things so simply, yet she couldn't deny her love. Without thinking, she was in his arms, kissing him. As he unhooked her bodice, he nibbled her earlobe. Her headache grew worse. Suddenly hot, she drew away. "Wil, I'm not feeling too well."

"You look a little flushed. The last time I saw you like this you were . . ."

"I'm not with child," Amanda snapped.

"Whatever you say."

"Wil . . ." She felt dizzy and sank to the blanket.

Wil pressed a hand to her forehead. "I think you've got the fever." He tugged on her arm and helped her to her feet. Her knees buckled, and he gathered her in his arms. Once in the buggy, she clutched his arm. Her head was spinning, and she barely noticed as they pulled up the tree-lined lane to home. Thankful for his aid, Amanda climbed the stairs to bed, while Wil looked on in worry.

She grasped his hand. "I've never seen you fret before."

He squeezed her hand and whispered his love.

Uncertain how much time had passed, Amanda tossed the linens from the bed. Blue eyes replaced the dark ones. "Where's Wil?" The eyes narrowed as if in pain. She latched onto his arm. "I don't deserve to live."

Sam held her and hushed her. Covered in sweat, she rocked into a twitching sleep.

Chapter Fourteen

*D*URING THE NIGHT, AMANDA'S FEVER HAD SPIKED. Alice had finally convinced Sam to get some rest. Wil had delayed his departure to Petersburg and had gone to fetch Doctor Gordon. When he left the farmhouse, she saw it in his eyes: he was fretting about Amanda.

As she had done for Lily, Alice wrung a cloth in a basin and placed it to Amanda's forehead, then continued on, washing her sister's feverish body to help cool her.

Amanda's eyes fluttered open. "Wil . . ."

Her heart sank. Her sister kept calling for Wil, not Sam. She gripped Amanda's hand. "Wil is fetching the doctor. You're mighty sick."

"No," Amanda howled. She gripped the blanket in her hands until her knuckles turned white. "Let me die."

"Don't speak such nonsense." Alice placed her hands on Amanda's shoulders and struggled to get her to lie back.

"It was my fault."

"Things always seem worse in the middle of the night or when you're sick. Now rest."

Finally relenting, Amanda leaned back to the feather pillow. "Where's Wil?"

Why did she keep asking for Wil? Although his conduct had become more erratic than usual of late, Alice had attributed it to her tending Lily's bedside. But if Amanda was calling for him . . . She chastised herself for even considering such a preposterous thought. Wil had been a friend of the family for years, yet her vision had warned her of their love on Amanda's wedding day to John. Was this what Frieda had meant when she had said that *she* would bring the fever? She could lose both of them. Wil and Emma? Or had she meant Wil and Amanda? "I've already told you that Wil went to fetch the doctor. He'll be back soon."

"He'll come to see me then?"

Alice sucked in her breath. Maybe her imagination wasn't running wild after all. The fever—Alice reminded herself once more, but the nagging doubts refused to be held at bay. "Amanda, why is it so important to see Wil?"

In a feverish state, Amanda responded, "Because we love each other."

Not I, but we. Stunned by the admission, Alice sank to the edge of the bed. "How do you know that he loves you?"

A glimmer appeared in Amanda's green eyes. "He told me."

Before *she* had courted Wil, Alice told herself. Her sister was confused and had no sense of time. So why did she have such a sick feeling? Alice pressed a hand to her stomach. Both Wil and Amanda had been avoiding her of late. When had the behavior begun? She couldn't think straight. Right after Amanda had been abducted by Doug Chandler. Coincidence? Her eyes swam. Hadn't she told Amanda to face the truth? And she was the one who had ignored the facts staring her in the face.

Uncertain whether to scream or cry, she stared at the blank wall. A rap came at the door. Another knock, a little louder this time. She blinked when a gray-haired man entered the room. "I knocked, but no one answered."

If Doctor Gordon was here, that meant Wil had returned. Alice dashed from the room. She nearly stumbled down the stairs but caught the rail to keep from falling. She entered the parlor. Without any sign of guilt or remorse, Wil stood before her. Tempted to fetch the shotgun, she looked up. "Has everything between us been a lie?"

"A lie?"

"I know, Wil. About you and my sister."

As usual, his demeanor was calm. "What did she tell you?"

She made a fist. "You kept saying that she was only a friend. Look me in the eye and tell me that."

He met her gaze. "She's a friend and your sister."

He had chosen his words too carefully. "Then you haven't bed her?"

Silence. His features remained an impossible to read poker face.

"Say something."

He sank into the wingback chair. "If it's a confession you're looking for, I'll supply it, but I don't think that's what you want to hear."

She had hoped for his denial, or that he would beg for forgiveness. Their life could have returned to normal. But nothing had ever been ordinary between them, and it wasn't Wil's way. Painfully aware that he had always loved Amanda, Alice choked back a sob. "Goddamn you, Wil! Get out! Go to Petersburg and don't bother coming back."

He stood and stared at her a moment. "I never lied to you."

Alice pointed an index finger in the direction of the door. As he turned to leave, she moaned. After all they had been through, she still loved him, but she couldn't find it within her heart to call him back.

A distant voice whispered, "You're alone now, Amanda."

"Mama?" Where was she? Amanda glanced about the room but couldn't find her.

A cool cloth went to her forehead, and someone helped her lay back. "I might have expected something like this from Alice," Mama continued, "but I thought you were smarter. You should have remembered that it's in men's nature to stray. While you've been lying in bed near death, he's vanished. You meant nothing to him, and now your husband has left you penniless."

"No!" Amanda bolted upright.

"Amanda . . ."

Alice, not Mama. She sank to the pillow and fought the tears. "Alice, I'm so sorry."

Alice hushed her. "Here, take some broth. You need to regain your strength."

Had she been dreaming? Trembling, Amanda sat up and took the tray from Alice's outstretched arms. "Why are you sitting with me?"

Her sister pulled the rocking chair next to the edge of the bed. "I'd be lying if I said that I hadn't cried my share of tears. The first thing I did was cry my eyes out to Mama, but when I saw you hovering so near death . . . Amanda, you're my sister. I don't want you to die."

Amanda spooned some broth to her mouth. "Sisters don't behave the way I have."

Alice laughed slightly. "It happens more often than some people care to admit, and I was quite aware when I married Wil that something had happened that neither of you cared to talk about, then on the day that you told me . . ."

No longer hungry, Amanda shoved the broth aside. "Alice, I don't want forgiveness. I don't deserve it."

"I haven't forgiven—not yet," Alice admitted. "I haven't told Sam. He may suspect, but I don't think he knows for sure."

Then Mama's reprimand had been a dream. Embarrassed, Amanda still couldn't look her sister in the eye. She mumbled her thanks.

"I presume you're afraid to ask the next obvious question. The Yankees issued a subpoena for Wil to appear in court. He testified, then returned to Petersburg and has been there for nearly three weeks. I think it's best if he stays there a while longer."

She had been sick for three weeks? "And you should join him," Amanda said. "Even during the war you were often at his side. I can mind Emma."

"I appreciate what you're trying to do. Wil had suggested the same thing back in March. Now I understand why, but the hurt doesn't get repaired quite that easily. Besides, you're not well enough to look after Rebecca, let alone watching Emma too."

"Alice, I can't be the cause of tearing you and Wil apart."

"You should have thought of that before things went too far."

Alice's voice was laced with bitterness, and Amanda swallowed hard. "You're right of course." Yet, if she were faced with the same set of circumstances, she knew in her heart that nothing would have changed.

With Amanda's recovery, Alice had returned to the house in Fredericksburg. At the onset of June, the days were growing warmer, and there had been so little rain that farmers were already complaining. By the middle of the month, Wil had been away for six weeks. Secretly, she had hoped that he would ask to come home. His stubbornness would prevail, and she would likely need to make the first gesture. She wasn't quite ready to forgive him with open arms, so she channeled her frustration and anger into her work. While Douglas Chandler continued to elude the Yankees, his men had been sentenced to die.

Because of the upcoming hanging, she had numerous orders for new dresses. Due to continuing shortages, she was unable to acquire the necessary materials and sew enough. As a result, she had been forced to turn customers away. A knock at the door distracted her from cutting fabric.

Wil stood outside with his hat in his hand. She swallowed hard. "Wil?"

"If you want me to leave, I'll do so, but I didn't have time to send this." He pressed some bills into her hand—at least a couple hundred dollars.

She closed her hand around the money and stuffed it in her pocket. "No, come in—please. Emma would like to see you."

Once in the parlor, Emma danced on her toes upon seeing him. He tossed the little girl in the air and caught her in his arms, only making her shriek with delight.

Alice cleared her throat. "How long are you going to be home?"

He launched Emma toward the ceiling once more. "Several days."

Maybe she should take Amanda up on her offer and return to Petersburg with him to get her marriage back on track. "I missed you."

He stopped tossing Emma and met her gaze. "I won't make excuses. It happened."

His mind worked in a black-and-white world. Why hadn't she realized it before now? "Do you still love me?"

"I already told you that I never lied to you."

"No, Wil. I want to hear you say it. At this moment in time, do you love me or do you no longer care?"

"Alice . . ." He glanced at Emma, then back again. "I've never stopped loving you."

"Then we can talk." She took Emma from his arms. "I'll put her down for her nap." Alice rushed Emma to her room. The toddler kept dancing in her crib and calling for Papa. "You can play with Papa later. Right now, I need to talk with him." Several minutes passed before she was able to quiet Emma enough to take a nap. When Alice returned to the parlor, Wil sat on the sofa. He stood when she entered.

His face remained that impenetrable stoic mask. She hated it when she couldn't read him. "Wil, I won't lie. I've been hurting something fierce, but it was my anger speaking when I told you to not come back. I'm glad you're home. Mama says that I should look the other way, but if that's what you want from a wife while you visit other women's beds, then you might as well divorce me."

"And if I refuse to grant one?"

Disappointed with his response, she sank to the sofa. "We'll remain married in name only."

His gaze softened, and he sat across from her. "I have always valued your opinion."

Alice blew out a breath in relief. "Then what do we do to make things right again? I'll return to Petersburg with you if that will help."

"I'm not certain there is anything *we* can do to make things right."

She fought the tears. "I don't understand. Life seemed to be returning to normal."

He arched a brow. "Normal? Alice, we were married during wartime. What exactly is normal about that?"

"And you thought that you'd never survive." She grasped his hand. "Together, we *can* make things work."

He shook his head and stood. "Haven't I given you enough grief? If you want a divorce, I'll grant it."

Stunned, Alice slumped on the sofa. Suddenly determined not to give in so easily, she cursed. "Damn it to hell, Wil! Is a divorce what you really want?"

"No," he admitted softly.

"Then let's talk about what's important." He reseated himself across from her, and she continued, "Is it over between you and Amanda, or did you stop by and see her before coming home?"

"I haven't seen her."

That fact was good, but she could see it in his eyes. He refrained from asking about Amanda's health. Alice resisted the temptation to hurl biting accusations. "But that doesn't mean you're ready to give her up." Unable to hold the tears at bay any longer, she lowered her head to her hands. "And I promised myself that I wouldn't do this."

"Alice . . ." Wil grasped her hands and withdrew them from her face. "I won't see her. I'll stay in Petersburg for the summer. We can decide what to do after that."

His words gave her new hope. "Mama won't like it, but we can give up the house here. I'll join you in Petersburg just as soon as you find suitable accommodations for Emma and me."

"I'll see to the arrangements when I return."

She clutched his hands with tenderness. "I love you, and I don't want to lose you."

"Sometimes, I wonder why."

"Because I like a man who doesn't mind if a lady swears."

He laughed and kissed her hand. Time was her friend, and she was confident that her broken heart would eventually heal.

Chandler's men were scheduled to die at dusk. Because Sam had managed to keep her off the witness stand, Amanda had agreed to cook their final meals. A somber thought—preparing the last meals that three men would eat. As she guided the buggy through the late afternoon streets, crowds were gathering around the taverns and shops. Once she arrived at the jailhouse, the guard escorted her to Sam's office. Outside the door, she overheard heated words and Wil's voice coming from within. If she had realized that Wil was back in Fredericksburg, she would have sent Jesse with the food.

Taking a deep breath, Amanda knocked and made certain not to look in Wil's direction. "I hope I'm not interrupting anything important," she said, entering.

Sam stood to greet her. "Not at all. I was just going to have Lieutenant Greer escort Wil out."

"Amanda, I'm pleased to see that you have recovered from your illness."

She heard a teasing tone in Wil's voice. Still, she didn't look at him. "Thank you. Sam, I have the meals in the buggy."

"I'll get one of the boys to help you." He pointed to Wil. "Out, Jackson. I can't do anything to stop the hangings. Chandler never even kept his word to meet with me."

"I warned you what would happen if you had me testify."

"There's no sense in discussing it further. What's done is done."

Sam escorted her to the outer office and called for one of his men. Amanda saw Wil's back as he was leaving. Thankful that she had successfully avoided him, she went outside with the private.

Wil waited beside the buggy. He lowered his hat as she approached. "You needn't worry, Mrs. Prescott. I'll be leaving Fredericksburg tomorrow—most likely for good."

She should be jumping for joy, so why did his news make her ache? She showed the private to the back of the buggy. He lifted a basket out and carried it to the jailhouse. As soon as he was out of sight, Amanda asked, "And Alice?"

"She'll be coming with me as soon I can make the arrangements."

Thankful that she hadn't destroyed her sister's marriage, she continued, "I'm sorry for revealing things that I shouldn't have to Alice. I didn't know what I was saying at the time."

"I understand, Amanda."

There it was again. The way Wil said her name, her cheek felt as if it had been lightly caressed. They were in too public of a place to share anything more than a passing glance. They stared at one another a moment.

He grasped her hand, took note of the gold band on her finger, and kissed her knuckles. "Bye, Amanda."

Forever. "Wil," she said, in a hurried rush, "I need to see you before you leave."

He finally let go of her hand. "I don't think it's a wise idea. I'm already breaking my promise by accidentally running into you this afternoon."

His words were like a knife plunged into her heart. Short of breath, Amanda clasped her hands together. "Please, Wil, I want to see you."

He let out a deep breath. "Are you going straight home?"

She nodded. "Sam didn't want me to remain in town during the execution."

"Then I'll meet you at the old Taylor place. I don't need to be present at the hanging. I've watched enough men die to last a lifetime."

"In an hour?"

"I'll think of nothing else." He flashed a smile that sent shivers down her spine. With a bow, he kissed her hand once more.

She refrained from touching him. He placed his hat on his head, then vanished in a group of people. *What had she done?*

"Ma'am . . ." A lanky private with carrot-colored hair stood before her, tipping his hat. "The colonel ordered me to escort you home."

She couldn't come out and say that she would be meeting Wil. "That won't be necessary, I don't need an escort."

"Sorry, ma'am. Colonel's orders."

Left with no choice, she agreed for him to accompany her. "Very well, then." The private helped her into the buggy, and he rode alongside her as they headed out of town. She would need to think of a way of diverting his attention before reaching the Taylor place. "What's your name, Private?"

"Anderson. Jake Anderson, ma'am."

"And you're from Pennsylvania?"

"That's right." Relaxed in her company, he started to tell her about home and his sweetheart. She spotted the longing in his eyes. The war was over, so why couldn't he go home?

Near a grove of trees, Amanda drew back on the reins and brought Red to a halt. *It had almost worked before.* An unsuspecting private should be easier to fool.

"Why are we stopping?"

"I need to attend to necessities. I shall only be a moment." Amanda scrambled from the buggy before the private could help her. As she entered the forest, Jake politely turned his back. Once out of his sight, she dropped her crinoline to the ground in order to move more freely. Raising her skirts, she scurried along an animal path. The trail progressed deeper into the woods. She left it, scrambling through brambles until she had circled to a few feet of where she had entered. Shielded by the foliage, she kept a clear view of the private and Red. Thorns dug into her arms as she crouched and waited.

Five minutes passed. Jake began to shift uneasily on his feet. Ten minutes. "Mrs. Prescott?" He turned to the spot where she had entered the grove. "Mrs. Prescott, are you all right, ma'am?" Another five minutes, and Jake marched into the forest, calling for her.

Amanda waited until he was deep within the woods before approaching Red. She tied Jake's horse to the back of the buggy, then climbed in. She gave Red a tap of the whip to his rump and flicked the reins. The stallion took off at a canter, and the private shouted after her.

Chapter Fifteen

*A*CCOMPANIED BY LIEUTENANT GREER, Sam stepped into the courtyard. In the fading daylight, crowds were already forming and chanting. Relieved that Amanda was safely away from town, he inspected the scaffold. *Innocent men.* He reminded himself they had abducted Amanda. *But that's not why these men had been sentenced to die.*

"Sir," Greer said, "I think we should station guards outside the courtyard. Chandler might show up."

One man against a garrison. Chandler wasn't coming now, but the suggestion was a necessary precaution. "Post the guards, and keep the crowds back."

Greer saluted. In spite of the outbreak of typhoid throughout the county, about thirty or forty men stood in the courtyard—the privileged upper echelon of the town—bankers, newspapermen, mostly carpetbaggers. Holly's husband—the balding Frank Whyte—was among them. No wonder the natives got riled. Even though the war was over, Southern boys still died. He had hoped that Jackson would remain for the execution, but after forcing him to take the witness stand, Sam doubted that even Wil would be able to bridge the gap between factions.

The crowds stood on roof tops and clambered into trees, hooting and catcalling. Sam faced the scaffold. The hammering and pounding of its construction had taken place the day before.

Out of breath, a red-haired private with freckles bridging his nose dashed over to him and saluted.

"You were assigned to escort my wife home, Anderson."

"And that's . . ." He gasped for breath. ". . . what I attempted to do, sir. Mrs. Prescott said she didn't need an escort."

"Have you decided that taking orders from my wife is more appropriate?"

Breathing easier, the private continued, "No, sir. I explained to her that you had given me orders to accompany her home. She agreed to let me escort her. When we got to the suburbs, she said that she needed to tend to necessities. While pretending to do so, she gave me the slip, sir."

"Gave you the . . ." Sometimes, Amanda was too stubborn for her own good, and with her experience at smuggling supplies during the war, finding a way for escape was a trivial matter for her. *What did it all mean?* Ever since Chandler had kidnapped her, she had been behaving oddly. He recalled Holly's words about Amanda being less melancholy when he was away. Amanda had got flighty upon seeing Wil, and Wil had rescued her from Chandler, as well as having been present on the farm for Holly to see.

Sam's mind ran wild. Amanda wasn't the sort to carry on an illicit affair. *But Jackson?* No wonder he hadn't stayed for the execution. His hands bunched to fists. For the moment, his duty required his presence, then he'd hunt the bastard down. "Return to your normal duties, Private."

"Yes, sir," the private replied with a salute.

Sam had difficulty concentrating. His heart ached. To accuse Amanda of what he was thinking, he needed proof. Solid proof— like finding the two of them together indulging in their betrayal.

"Sir . . ." Lieutenant Greer returned to his side. "It's time."

With a nod, Sam climbed the scaffold's thirteen steps. The commanding general was to have presided over the executions, but had passed that duty onto his shoulders. The soldiers lined at the top of the scaffold remained at full attention.

Greer handed him a paper listing the charges. Sam abhorred the pleasure the lieutenant took in his duties. The crowd hushed as the three prisoners were lead out and went up the scaffold's steps. Sam read the charges—arson, kidnapping, wounding a Federal officer, and accomplices to the murder of a local woman. "Any final words?"

"If you're going to hang us, do so with charges that we're guilty of. We didn't burn anything or kill anyone."

The three ranged from early to mid twenties—younger than himself. Amanda had nursed the one to health, only to die here. Would his duty have been easier if they hadn't been healthy and in their prime? "The court has decided otherwise."

"A Yankee court."

Sam heard a hiss from someone in the courtyard, then silence. Not even a whisper. He gave the signal to the line of soldiers and the nooses were adjusted and white hoods slipped over the prisoners' heads. One of the prisoners began singing "Dixie" beneath the hood. The others joined in.

Bile rose in the back of Sam's throat, but he managed to keep a passive soldier's stance. Taking a deep breath, he gave the signal, and his soldiers shoved the front part of the platform from beneath the prisoners' feet. The singing stopped as the bodies fell several feet before being jerked to a sudden halt. The prisoner on his right, the lucky one, did not struggle. The others thrashed. Minutes ticked by—one, two. After four minutes, the writhing on his left stopped. Another agonizing minute passed before the final body was still.

Sam said a silent prayer that he would never need to preside over such a grisly event again. Resignation was preferable, and as each day passed, it seemed the only way out.

Not only had Wil made a vow to Alice, he had promised himself that he wouldn't see Amanda again. Yet, he would meet her. He had never been able to refuse anything she asked of him. When the crowd hushed, he had known the deed was done and mounted his gray mare, reining her to the edge of town. He envisioned Peopeo perched on a spotted horse with a rope around her neck. She had bravely recited a prayer in her native Nez Percé tongue. He had tried to reach her. *Then thrashing . . .* Strange—he hadn't thought of his first wife in a long time.

Soon after Peopeo's death, he had met Amanda, but she had already been betrothed to his West Point friend, John Graham. Before reaching the old Taylor place, he nearly reined the mare around. So why, when he finally had the chance to win Amanda's love, had he burned the letter? Until he discovered the answer, he would continue to doubt his own actions.

At the end of the lane, he dismounted. Overgrown with shrubs and brambles, the path to the house was barely larger than an animal trail. Long abandoned by war, the tumbled-down cottage with sagging shutters came into view. A red stallion was tied out front.

As he tethered the mare, Amanda came onto the steps. The gold ring was missing from her finger. "I didn't think you were coming."

He lowered his hat. "I almost didn't."

"Wil . . ." Her arms went around his neck. "I couldn't bear the thought of not seeing you again."

In her arms, it would be so easy to let go, but he forced himself to withdraw from her embrace. "Amanda, I've come to say goodbye."

"Goodbye?" There was a soft, choking sound at the back of her throat. "I thought you loved me."

"I do, but I'm not the one that you want."

Her eyes brimmed with tears. "Shouldn't I be the one to decide?"

"Think about it. We become close during crises."

She brushed the tears away. "I admit, you've been there for me during some rough times, but I have always cared for you." Her arms went around his waist. "You were the one afraid to commit. Yes, Wil, I said afraid, and for some reason, you're feeling it now. Stop being afraid."

Laughing slightly, Wil resisted the temptation to touch her. "I thought I was the one who usually told you to not fear the unknown."

Her hands went under his jacket and traced along his back. His tension slowly gave way. She grasped his hand and drew him inside the cottage. Straw had been spread across the floor with a blanket covering it. A single candle flickered in the window.

"Amanda, the longer we're together, the more difficult it will be to say goodbye."

"Goodbye?"

He heard that soft, choking sound again. "No matter what happens here, I will be leaving tomorrow."

Amanda intertwined her fingers with his. "Even if it's fleeting, we're together now."

His own words. Unable to endure her presence any longer without tasting her mouth, Wil kissed her. "If we go any further, I won't be able to say goodbye."

"Then don't."

"If I don't, we'll return to lives filled with lies and half-truths. I can't put you through that again."

She swallowed hard. "When I had the fever and discovered you were gone, I wanted to curl up and die."

What had he done? He tightened his grip on her hand. She had once been a strong and determined woman. Both of them were mere shadows of their former selves. If only he could go back and mail the goddamned letter. But he *had* been afraid—truly afraid to love her. "Amanda, I'm sorry."

"For what? For the way things turned out? I told you that I was equally to blame." In her arms, his resistance weakened. She laughed slightly. "You taught me that sharing intimacies can be fun-loving. I missed you, Wil."

Six weeks away had been sheer agony—not knowing whether she had lived or died. But he had made a promise to Alice. As Amanda stroked and soothed, he couldn't think straight. The war might be over, but promises were just as fleeting. "Amanda, I burned the letter because I couldn't give myself to you in the way you wanted."

"What?" She stepped away from their embrace. "You said you loved me."

"I do, and if we had met in a different time or place, things might have worked."

She frowned. "So you *were* afraid because of the war. Why did you marry Alice?"

"Because a good friend reminded me that war or not, life is too short to go on living as I had been."

Amanda pointed to herself. "We *have* ruined our friendship."

If he drew her in his arms, and pretended the conversation hadn't taken place, she'd relent. It was time to face the truth that he had known in his heart. There was only one way to prove his love. "I reckon so, but it may not be too late to salvage the rest of our lives. I'll see that you get home safely."

With some hesitation, Amanda returned the gold band to her finger. "After that, will I ever see you again?"

"I don't know." He took her hand, and together they stepped outside into the cool evening. For a brief instant, regret tugged at Wil once more. But there was nothing left for them—only to part.

As the buggy neared the farm, Amanda drew closer and hooked her arm through Wil's. His muscles tensed. With a few token kisses, he would change his mind about leaving. She now understood what Alice had meant by letting him go. "What now?"

"Cherish our memories." He had that stoic look that she remembered so well from the past.

"Damn you, Wil."

A small smile crossed his lips. "See the bad influence I am. I'd make you into a habitual swearer if I stayed around."

"Please don't joke."

He briefly glanced in her direction before shifting his gaze back to the lane. "My humble apologies, Amanda."

She heard it again—the way he said her name. It reminded her of his caresses—to never be touched again. She fought the tears. "Wil . . ." There was no sense in saying anything. They had been foolish for giving no thought to tomorrow.

The buggy turned into the lane, and his eyes met hers. "I feel it too."

"Then maybe we can think of another way."

He brought the buggy to a halt out front. "You know there isn't." He reached a hand to her face and stroked it. "I never meant to hurt you, but all I have ever brought is grief."

"That's not true."

Wil climbed from the buggy and came around to her side to help her. For one last time, she was in his arms. She thought he'd give her a farewell kiss, but he stepped away from their embrace. "As usual, you're being polite, Mrs. Prescott."

The formality made their parting final. He bent at the waist and kissed her hand.

"Jackson! You son of a bitch!"

Sam... He wasn't supposed to be home until tomorrow. Red-faced, he hauled along the rifle from over the mantel and charged down the front steps toward Wil. *She couldn't be the cause.* Amanda placed herself between them, but Wil shoved her aside, and she went tumbling. He braced himself for the impact. Before she could regain her feet, she heard the rifle butt crack against Wil's skull. He sprawled on the ground, groaning. Sam raised the rifle to strike him again.

Amanda regained her feet. "No, Sam!"

Another blow crunched down. Sam aimed the rifle to Wil's head. With a blood-splattered face, Wil drew his pistol on Sam.

"No! Both of you—stop it! How do you think I'd feel if one of you died because of me?"

Sam's finger hovered over the trigger. "Right now, I don't give a damn, Amanda."

"Wil, lower the gun. Please..." She grasped Sam's arm and tugged. He failed to budge. "All right, kill one another. It's certainly a manly way of settling things."

The blind fury faded from Sam's face. He lowered the rifle. "Get out of here, Jackson. If I ever see you around here again, I'll kill you." He grasped her arm and hauled her in the direction of the house.

Out of the corner of her eye, she saw Wil struggle to his feet. He clutched his side in pain. She fought Sam's hold, only causing him to tighten his grip. Once inside the parlor, while he paced the floor, she sat in the wing-backed chair. Through the window, she could see that Wil had managed to mount his horse. He slumped in the saddle and rode away. She fretted over how badly he might have been hurt and whispered goodbye.

Sam stood over her. "Amanda..."

She had imagined the hurt on his face a thousand times with her crying remorseful tears. Now that her guilt had been exposed, she felt nothing.

His voice was forced but calm when he spoke. "Before we got married I asked you if you loved him."

Should she make a denial or lame excuse? "That's just it, Sam. I have always loved both of you. During the war, it was easy to pretend otherwise, but after the loss of the baby . . ." She clenched her hands together. "Wil was there for me."

As if acknowledging the truth in his heart, Sam blew out a breath and nodded. "I don't mean to sound indelicate, but whose baby was it?"

"Oh Sam . . ." Her throat tightened, temporarily cutting off her breathing. Amanda gasped for breath. "He was your son. We've buried two on the hill. I never thought I'd feel anything again after losing two children."

He smacked a fist into his palm, cracking it next to her ear. "I presume Jackson helped you feel again."

Still no tears, but she hung her head. "He's gone. You needn't fret that he'll interfere again."

"What do you mean gone?"

"He only agreed to see me to say goodbye."

Sam's eyes widened. During the war, they had made a similar pact of never saying goodbye unless it was forever.

"He's leaving for Petersburg and not returning."

"How long have I been living like a fool?"

Her throat closed off again. "Never. I've been the silly fool. I loved you both even though I knew it was wrong to do so."

Tears brimmed in his eyes, and he sank to the sofa. "And now? What do we do now?"

Suddenly cold, Amanda crossed her arms. "Give me whatever punishment you feel I deserve. I never stopped loving you, but I acted impulsively and don't blame you if you despise me for it."

"Despise you? Amanda, I could never despise you, but I need to know what to do to make it right. I thought once the war was over . . . That's the problem, isn't it? I still haven't been here when you needed me."

She reached out and gripped his hand. "Sam, you can't blame yourself for what I've done."

"But you still love him?"

Hope reflected in his eyes that she might deny her love for Wil. Even now, she couldn't bring herself to do so.

Every step the mare took was sheer agony. On the outskirts of Fredericksburg, Wil brought her to a halt outside the columned mansion and slumped over the gray's neck. A black servant shrieked, and excited voices rushed toward him.

"Rough night, Mr. Jackson?" came Holly's droll voice.

"Laugh, if you wish."

"What *are* you doing here?"

A sharp pain shot through his head and side as he attempted to dismount. He slid from the saddle and fell to the ground. "Nowhere else to go."

"Try home?"

He laughed but sucked in his breath. The servant grasped his arm and attempted to help him up.

"Leave him be, Sally."

"Yes'm." Sally let go of his arm.

"Get back to the kitchen to your work." With a curtsy, Sally dashed in the direction of the mansion. Attired in a silk dress, Holly loomed over him. "Now Wil, I require an explanation if you expect me to help you."

Wil clutched his side and struggled to his feet. "Your compassion never ceases to amaze me."

"Was this Doug Chandler's doing?"

"I fell off my horse."

"You may get by with lying to others... Someone has obviously beat the tar out of you. I'll have Sally fetch Sam."

"That wouldn't be a good idea."

The corners of her mouth tipped up into a knowing grin. "I see. Really, Wil, you need to learn that discretion is the better part of valor when it comes to extramarital affairs."

"You should know." The flat of her hand connected with the side of his face and nearly sent him reeling. He placed a hand to his throbbing cheek. Fortunately, she hadn't struck the same side as Prescott.

Holly inspected his face. "Sam really did this? He has more gumption than I had him pegged for. I hope Amanda was worth it."

"And how did you find out, Mrs. Whyte?"

Her grin widened. "A little bird. The only thing that surprised me is how long it took for you to finally bed her. You're definitely losing your touch, Wil."

"Holly . . ."

"Oh, all right. Do come in. I'll have you cleaned up in no time." She hooked her arm through his, bumping his injured side. He sucked in his breath. "It appears that Sam got you good. You could have broken ribs as well."

"They're not broken."

She arched a brow. "Voice of experience, I take it? It truly amazes me that you survived four years of war in one piece."

"I almost didn't," Wil reminded her.

She led him to the back of the house to an adjacent building. Savory smells drifted through a window, reminding him of how long it had been since he had last eaten. They entered the kitchen, where Sally was preparing the midday meal.

"That smells mighty good."

"Feed him," Holly ordered the servant. "Should I send Sally for Alice?"

"And tell her what?"

Holly laughed and motioned for him to have a seat at the table. "That you fell from your horse, of course."

Wil eased himself into a chair. "What would that cost me?" He shook his head. "I won't lie. Alice is too smart for that anyway."

Sally set a bowl of stew in front of him, while Holly collected a porcelain basin and filled it with water from a pitcher. She ordered the servant to fetch Alice. Another dutiful curtsy, and Sally hurried from the kitchen. "Damn you, Wil. Why did you have to come here?"

Famished, Wil gulped down the stew. "You were the closest."

Holly sat across from him. "That's not what I meant, and you know it." She dabbed a cool cloth near his right eye. He winced. "I know it hurts."

"Compassion, Mrs. Whyte?"

Her eyes narrowed in annoyance. "Stop it, Wil. Or I'll leave you to fend for yourself."

"You have my apology."

She continued daubing. "I warned you that our kind wasn't meant to love."

A sorry mess indeed, but he couldn't make such an admission to Holly.

"Even when we were together," said Holly, "I was quite aware that you loved *her*."

"So? It's not like we shared anything beyond the sack."

"You're doing it again. What are you so afraid of?"

Everyone saw it. Why did he continue denying it? "I fully expected not to survive." *The reason he had burned the letter hadn't been due to fear alone.*

"And now that you have . . ."

He had been dragging Alice into his personal hell. The cloth in Holly's hand turned red as she scrubbed away caked blood. The blood of all of those he had killed. *Why had he been spared?*

Twenty minutes later, Alice appeared and called to him. "Wil?"

Upon Alice's entrance, Holly lowered the cloth to the bowl and vacated the kitchen. Alice was out of breath as if she had run the distance from their house to Holly's, and her eyes were puffy and red as if she had been crying.

"You have no cause to believe me, but I told Amanda goodbye. It was a pact we made during the war that we'd only say 'goodbye' if it was for good. I'll be on the train this afternoon as planned. If you have no desire to accompany me at a later date, I understand."

"Are you suggesting that I shouldn't join you in Petersburg for my well-being? The Yankees are no longer laying siege to the city."

Her voice held a slight tremor, but otherwise, it had been firm in conviction. "Alice . . ." His voice broke. He should have known that she would follow him anywhere.

A slight smile crossed her face. "It seems I have made you speechless again." She picked up the cloth and dabbed it to his battered face. *She* had been the reason why he had survived.

Chapter Sixteen

A FORTNIGHT LATER, ALICE still hadn't received a letter from Wil that he had found suitable accommodations for Emma and her in Petersburg. During those two weeks, she had passed the time by visiting the shanty village every few days. With the days growing hot in the July heat, the number of typhoid cases was spreading. Anticipating that Wil's letter would arrive any day, she packed her trunk. Ever since the Yankees had looted Fredericksburg, there had been few furnishings. She was going to miss the house. Mama and she had moved to town after Papa had died, while Amanda stayed to manage the farm.

A floorboard in the hall creaked. Emma must have climbed out of her crib again. Alice sighed and went into the hallway, nearly running headlong into a man. With a scream, she ran the way she had come. Strong hands latched onto her arms.

"Mrs. Jackson."

Doug Chandler. Terrified, she struggled against his grip. "What do you want, Mr. Chandler?"

"If you do as I say, I won't hurt you."

She continued fighting. "Let me go!"

He shoved her against the wall, pinning her so that she could barely breathe. She felt his breath on her neck. "I said I won't hurt you, and considering how your husband might as well have put the nooses around my boys' necks himself, I'm granting you a lot of respect." He loosened his hold just enough so that she could face him. Sweat beaded on his forehead and his face was flushed.

Like so many in the shanty village, he had the fever. "I need your help."

"Then fetch a doctor. First you abduct my sister, and now you attack me. Why?"

"It's not for me, but my sister."

His sister? "How can I possibly help your sister?"

He released her left arm and wiped the sweat from his brow. "You helped wounded soldiers and won't refuse when someone is in need."

She plunged a fist into his face. Struggling against his grip, she ripped a button from his coat. A vise-like hand caught her wrist.

"You can come along peaceably, or I'll take you from here kicking and screaming if necessary. As I recall you have a daughter."

"No!" *Not Emma.*

With the brunt of his weight, he pinned her against the wall. "I won't repeat myself. Get your daughter, and we'll be leaving."

He maintained a secure grip on her arm, and Alice's breath caught in her throat. "Miss Emma..." Her voice wavered. Together, they went into Emma's room. The toddler sat up in her crib and rubbed sleepy eyes. "We're going on a little trip."

Emma brightened with a smile. "Papa."

Keep a brave front for Emma's sake. "We'll see Papa in a few days, but right now, Mr. Chandler is taking us to see his sister. He tells me that she's a real nice lady." The mindless chatter helped settle her nerves. She wrapped Emma in a light blanket and gathered her in her arms. Chandler led them down the stairs to the kitchen and out the back door where a black thoroughbred and a bay gelding waited. *Stolen horses most likely.*

Run. Her legs refused to obey. Chandler might shoot her and take Emma with him anyway. "I'll take the child, so you don't get any ideas."

"She doesn't like strangers," Alice lied about Emma's outgoing personality.

But Chandler swept Emma from her arms. Not a cry or a peep. He mounted the thoroughbred, and Emma gripped the pommel. *Damn Wil for introducing her to horses already.* "Mrs. Jackson." He motioned for her to mount the bay. Alice obeyed.

Chandler led them through the dark streets of Fredericksburg. Up ahead, she heard a clatter of hooves. A Yankee patrol crossed the intersection in front of them. Her heart thumped wildly, and she straightened in the saddle.

"Don't even think about calling for help." Chandler drew his pistol. "Or this little girl might get caught in the crossfire."

Alice slumped as the patrol continued on down the road without spotting them. As they made their way out of town, the moon rose, casting a dreary hue to the war-torn buildings. The lights of Fredericksburg faded. After a couple of miles, Emma began to squall. "Please let me take her. I promise that I'll do as you say."

Silence.

"Mr. Chandler . . ."

"I heard you. The girl stays with me."

Her hands trembled, and the gelding snorted from her nervousness. He was going to continue to use Emma so that she would cooperate. They rode a few more miles before arriving at a farmhouse. Unlike many of the farms in the area, the house had only suffered from neglect rather than damage related directly to the war.

Still holding Emma, Chandler dismounted. He motioned for her to do the same. Once on the ground, he placed the wailing Emma in her arms. Relieved to be holding her again, Alice rocked the toddler and hushed her until she quieted.

Chandler grasped her arm and led her to the house. Once inside, he collapsed into a chair. Sweat rolled down his face. Footsteps thumped upstairs. A thin, elderly man charged down the stairs with a shotgun, and he nearly stumbled on the final step. "Doug . . ."

"I've brought help for Estelle."

"Won't the Yanks be lookin' for her?"

He shook his head. "Not for several days. Her old man is out of town, and her servant has Sunday off, then goes to school on Monday. I'll move Estelle if need be, but I think we'll be fine for a while."

"No." Her voice was weak, but Alice managed to utter it again. "You won't get by with this."

Chandler wiped the sweat from his brow and leaned back in the chair, closing his eyes. "George, take her to Estelle's room."

The elderly man grasped her elbow and guided her to the stairs. At least they hadn't taken Emma from her again. The steps creaked under their weight as they went up. At the top, a darkened hallway loomed. George steered her toward the room on the left. Even before entering, she smelled sickness. Alice debated whether to leave Emma behind but decided her daughter was safer at her side than anywhere near Chandler.

Inside the room, a woman with blonde hair in a cotton nightdress lay in the bed. Her forehead was covered with sweat, and a stench permeated the room. Estelle had the fever too. Alice approached the bed. Even though Estelle wore a plain nightdress, her hands were covered by delicate, lace gloves. "Hello, Estelle. I'm Alice." She placed Emma on the floor. "I need some fresh water and a clean nightdress," she said to the old man.

"I'll see what I can do."

She turned back the sheets, and the rank odor of urine and human waste assaulted her nostrils. "Some clean linens as well." Alice removed a lace glove. Glistening white skin stretched a thick band across a disfigured hand, lending an image of webbing. Chandler appeared in the doorway with the requested items in his arms. "I could use your help, Mr. Chandler. Your sister is very sick."

Chandler came closer. "She was burned when the Yankees set fire to our home." His gaze grew fixed. "Faith was about the same age as your daughter. Estelle tried to put the fire out with her bare hands."

Alice shuddered and removed the other lace glove before stripping the soiled nightdress from Estelle's body. "Please, Mr. Chandler, I could use your help."

He blinked, and with his aid, she changed the linens. With a surprisingly delicate touch, he helped wash Estelle. In gentle, wide circles, he sponged his sister's neck and arms. An affectionate smile crossed his lips, and he continued sponging—carefully and quietly. He reached her breasts and obeyed the brotherly taboo by letting Alice finish. After drying and changing Estelle into a clean nightdress, he kissed her on the forehead.

"You're very fond of her."

His blue eyes sparkled, but not in that haunting way that had troubled her so much in the past. "We only have each other."

For a moment, Alice felt sympathy. "I'll do the best I can, but I can't make any promises that she'll survive. She needs a doctor."

The twinkle in his eyes vanished. "If you wish to leave here with your precious little girl, you had best make certain that Estelle lives." He stormed from the room, slamming the door on his way out.

For two days, Estelle hovered between life and death. When Chandler periodically checked on her, kindness returned to his mannerisms, and he made certain they were properly fed. Exhausted from the ordeal, Alice curled into a rocking chair with Emma.

On the following morning, Estelle's fever finally broke. Alice helped her sit up and fed her some broth. "Estelle, could you speak to your brother about letting us go? You're getting well now."

Estelle smiled but said nothing. Emma climbed onto the bed, and Estelle's smile widened to a grin. She drew Emma into her arms. "My Faith is a lot like your little girl."

Present tense. Estelle was hysterical. Alice stepped over to the window. An oak tree grew beside it. If she grabbed Emma, she might be able to put her tomboy skills to some use and clamber down the tree. *Wait—until nightfall.* She now knew that Doug Chandler never had any intention of letting either of them go.

Shrieking wildly, Lily burst into Sam's office and waved a letter in his face. "Miss Alice is gone."

"Gone?" He glanced at the letter and recognized Jackson's handwriting. He shoved it aside for more important matters. "I'd hardly say that moving to Petersburg is gone."

Her voice only climbed higher and more frantic. "You don't understand. She don't join Mr. Wil. Dis is his letter tellin' her dat he make da arrangements for her to come to Petersburg, an' it only arrive today."

Today? "What makes you think that Alice is gone?"

"Da house be empty for several days by da look of it."

Alice was likely as distressed by recent events as much as he had been. "Are you certain? Could she be visiting a neighbor?"

"I check. She ain't."

Ever since discovering the truth about Amanda and Jackson, he had been avoiding going home. Funny—wasn't that partly what had caused the problem in the first place? "Could Alice have gone to Amanda's?"

Lily shook her head furiously. "She'd tell me if she was goin' to see Miss Amanda. Her trunk was packed. Miss Emma gone too."

Her trunk packed, but she hadn't taken it with her? Something *might* have happened to Alice and Emma. Sam stood. "I'll check into it. Lily, would you like to accompany me to the house? Greer, round up several of the boys."

The lieutenant poked his head in the door. "Sir?"

"Have my horse saddled and waiting."

"Yes, sir." Greer saluted and vanished.

Sam buckled on his weapons belt. On his way out the door, he grabbed his hat. Once outside, his horse stood ready and was flanked by three of his boys. After mounting up, he pulled Lily on behind him and rode over to Alice's house.

As they neared the brick house, nothing appeared out of the ordinary. Sam went up the porch steps and raised his hand to knock. With the slightest touch the door creaked open. "You found it unlocked?" he asked, turning to Lily.

"I did. Miss Alice always lock da door dese days."

"Of course." It wouldn't be safe for a woman alone to have done otherwise. Sam stepped inside and motioned for his boys to follow. "Alice?"

No response.

The study and parlor appeared normal. None of the pots and pans were out of place in the kitchen. Sam wiped the sweat from his brow. If Alice had been home recently, the windows would have been open in the sweltering heat. As he put a foot on the stairs, a sense of dread filled him. Upstairs, the windows were open with curtains made from rags blowing in the light breeze.

As Lily had stated, a half-packed trunk sat in the bedroom. He picked up a hawk's tail feather from the dresser, then moved onto Emma's room. Clothes were spread out as if waiting for the girl to fill them. Wherever Alice went, she left in a mighty big hurry. But where could she have gone?

"Sir." Private Bowen entered the room and handed him a button. "I found this in the hall."

CSA was inscribed on the button. Sam showed it to Lily.

"Mr. Wil ain't got nothin' Confederate dese days, 'ceptin' . . ."

"Except what?"

"Nothin'. It don't belong to Mr. Wil."

Which could only mean Chandler. *God*, how was he going to track him down? Even if the locals didn't aid Chandler, he had so few men left, and they had no desire to learn what was necessary to get the job done. Sam entertained the idea of contacting Jackson. Under the circumstances, he had no doubt his former commander would help. Even if Sam buried his wounded pride, Wil would be unable to return to Fredericksburg in time. Alice's life might be at stake. He'd recruit Jesse.

Chandler had obstructed Alice's plan. As if detecting what she had in mind, he made certain that Emma was out of her reach, unless he was physically present to watch her. With each passing day, Estelle continued to regain her strength.

A pounding headache, hovering between chills and fever—damn, she had typhoid too. Short on energy, Alice struggled to speak. "Please talk to your brother about letting us go."

Estelle merely smiled. "I'll care for you the way you did me. Your darling daughter is such a joy."

Suddenly lightheaded, Alice needed to sit before she fell, while Estelle cooed to Emma.

"Alice, you're looking mighty pale."

Emma giggled, and Alice thought she overheard Estelle call her Faith. "Emma," she corrected. Determined to stand, she got to her feet. A bit wobbly, she took a few steps and stumbled. "Estelle, you need to speak with your brother."

Estelle grasped her arm and helped her to bed. "Alice, you need rest."

"But Wil's expecting me, and Emma misses her papa."

"My husband died during the war," Estelle replied.

Alice felt a cool, comforting hand on her forehead.

"Here, let me write to Wil. I'll let him know that you've taken ill. I'll take care of you and little Faith."

Faith . . . Alice drifted in and out of her fever. *How long had she been lying here?* She thought she heard Emma cry and got up. As soon as she arrived by the door, the crying stopped. She meandered over to the dresser. On top was the bright red tail feather of the hawk.

Alice clutched it to her body and returned to bed. As if on a raft floating along the Rappahannock River, her body swayed through the current. Overhead, two hawks soared in their ritualistic mating dance. Then came the clip-clop of hooves and a bouncing rhythm. The carriage bumped along a tree-lined lane. Instead of a feather, she clenched a letter in her hand. Upon examination, she recognized Wil's handwriting. The letter was addressed to Amanda. For some reason, she felt nothing—no anger nor jealousy.

The carriage halted outside Amanda's farmhouse. Sam hobbled up the steps, and her sister came to greet the carriage. A Negro helped her from the carriage. "Dan?" The servant had run off when the Yankees had camped along the river during the war.

"Alice," Amanda said, greeting her with a smile.

"Amanda, has Sam been injured?"

"How do you know Sam?"

"You've only been . . ." Alice caught her breath. She wore her striped dress with pagoda sleeves and frilly trim current to the latest fashion. A past event. Amanda had risked her life to save Sam after he had been wounded in the leg. When her sister had missed visiting her and Mama in town, Alice had called to make certain that Amanda was all right. If she went up the steps, she would find Sam in the back bedroom. It was also the day that she had given Amanda the report that Wil was missing after the battle at Sharpsburg.

The letter... Alice's heart pounded like a beating drum. It was the letter that Wil had burned.

"Is that for me?" asked Amanda.

Alice recalled her words from four years before. "There's been a terrible battle in Sharpsburg, Maryland. Colonel Jackson's regiment was heavily involved. He's been listed as missing."

A groan escaped Amanda's lips. She grabbed hold of Alice's arm to keep from falling. "Not Wil, too."

"Missing doesn't mean dead. In fact, in all of the confusion of battle, men easily get dazed and lost. I'm certain that he's on his way back now."

Steadying herself, Amanda straightened. "You're right. One shouldn't always assume the worst, but these days it's difficult to think otherwise."

Alice's hand trembled as she extended her arm holding the letter. "Here... he sent you this."

"Wil sent me a letter?" Amanda grasped it and studied the handwriting. A smile spread across her face. "It's definitely from Wil."

"Why don't you open it?" Alice held her breath while Amanda unfolded the letter. Her sister's eyes brightened with apparent delight. Suddenly impatient, Alice said, "Well, what does he say?"

"Wil, he..."

"Amanda, please."

Amanda's face reddened, and Alice snatched the letter from her sister's hand. "Alice, that's private."

Alice easily recognized Wil's writing style. He only rambled when talking about deep emotions. Similar to letters that she had received, he wrote about a hard march and that he'd be facing battle soon. He hinted at a romantic rendezvous with Amanda when he returned. For Wil, it was definitely a love letter. Then what she read next. She choked out the words, "He wants to marry you."

"Who would have thought? Wil Jackson wanting to marry anyone... What should I do, Alice? He may not even be alive."

"I think—I think..."

"Alice?"

A breeze swept through, whisking the red feather into the wind. "Marry him, Amanda. He's alive."

Alice felt herself floating toward the sky with the feather, then rough hands lifting her, helping her up. She heard a woman's voice cooing to a baby, clapping hands, and repeating the name Faith. The coarse hands carried her outside until she felt the bouncing rhythm of a wagonbed beneath her. Then she heard the sound of rushing water—the Rappahannock River.

Now she knew what Frieda had meant by her warning. Estelle would bring *her* the fever, and she would lose Wil and Emma.

For two days, they had searched for Alice and Emma in the broiling July heat. If only it would rain, the days might cool off some. Sam took a swig from his canteen and swallowed dust. He spat the grit out of his mouth. Jesse extended an arm, offering his canteen.

Sam thanked him and swallowed the thirst-quenching water. Jesse had supplied numerous leads, all of which had turned up empty. Even with Jesse's presence, none of the residents claimed knowing Chandler. Once more, he motioned for his men to move forward to cover more ground.

As they neared the river, they halted on a slope. Sam took his field glasses from their leather case and scanned the area. Due to lack of rain, even the river was getting low.

"Colonel . . ." Jesse pointed to their right.

Sam nearly dropped the field glasses. On the road ahead, a woman walked toward them. "Alice?" He handed the field glasses to Jesse and kicked his mount in the woman's direction. Arriving by her side, he vaulted from his horse. "Alice. Where's Emma?"

In a daze, she blinked. "Emma. She was right . . ." She glanced around. "Sam?"

Her dress was soiled, and sweat trickled down the sides of her face. In her hands, she held a hawk's feather—the same one he had found on the dresser. *How could that be?* "Alice, you're sick. I need to get you help." He helped her on his horse and climbed on behind her. He spurred his horse to a gallop. Had they found Alice in time? And what of Emma?

* * *

"Alice, come out of it." Amanda sponged a cool cloth on Alice's forehead. Thank God, Sam and his men had found her. But there was still no trace of Emma. When Alice refused to let go of the hawk's feather, Amanda decided to let her keep it. What harm could come from it? Lily had given her the letter from Wil, and she handed it to her sister.

"What's this?" Alice asked.

"Wil wants you to join him in Petersburg. He misses you and sends his love."

Alice frowned. "It was meant for you."

"No. Alice . . ." Amanda pressed her hand to Alice's forehead. She was burning up. "It's for you."

"He wants to marry you."

Amanda wished she had never discovered the existence of the letter that Wil had burned. She unfolded the letter. "See Alice, it's addressed to you. He can't wait for you to join him. Read it. It's for you, not me."

"He loves me?" A smile spread across Alice's face. "Read it to me, Amanda."

"I can't." Amanda forced a smile. "You know your husband. He often has a flare for the over melodramatic. He's included some personal things that I think you'd rather I not read aloud."

Alice clutched the hawk feather to her breast, and the letter floated to the floor.

Sam wasn't going to like it, but Wil needed to return to Fredericksburg. She would attempt to wire an urgent message and hoped all of the necessary telegraph lines had been restored. She prayed that Wil would make it back in time. "Alice, don't you dare do this."

With a beaded brow, Alice smiled a euphoric grin. "It's better this way. Take care of him, Amanda."

"Noooo!" *What had she done?* Determined not to let her little sister die, Amanda vowed to nurse her day and night until she was better.

* * *

As long as something belonging to the hawk was near, Alice had discovered that she could travel to past events just as easily as getting into a carriage and visiting friends. Only some events had changed drastically from the recollection of her memory. It was her chance to right an unnecessary wrong. She clutched the red-tail feather.

Amanda stood in front of the mirror in a blue silk dress, waiting for the back to be buttoned. Alice forced a smile and fastened the dress.

"I can't believe he's going through with it. Wil has never struck me as the marrying kind." Amanda held up a trembling hand. "Now, if I could only make my hand stop shaking."

"Relax, Amanda. You needn't fret. Mama's happy—not like when you seriously considered marrying that . . ." *Yankee? What of Sam?*

"What's wrong, Alice?"

"Nothing," she said, shrugging away the intrusive thought. "You and Wil shall be very happy." She hugged Amanda.

Stepping back, Amanda grasped the chicory bouquet from the dresser. "I'm ready," she announced.

As Alice led the way from the bedroom, her stomach churned. *Was this really the way things were supposed to be?* Dreams had been ruined by . . . *What?* She couldn't finish the thought.

At the bottom of the stairs, Amanda took a deep breath. Alice gave her a reassuring squeeze and took her place beside Mama. Wil stood beside the preacher. Cleanshaven except for his moustache, he looked particularly handsome in his gray jacket with shiny brass buttons and gold embroidery on the sleeves. And so typical of Wil, he failed to show any trace of nerves. His eyes sparkled when Amanda approached, but for a brief moment, Alice thought he glanced in her direction.

When the preacher began to speak, Alice's whole body ached. In a fog, she listened to the couple recite their vows, and Wil slipped a gold band on Amanda's finger. The wrong had finally been made right. Her sister *was* Mrs. Brigadier William Jackson.

Chapter Seventeen

NIGHTFALL HAD ARRIVED BY THE TIME WIL reined the gray mare up the lane. Sam was the first to greet him as he dismounted. "I'm sorry for behaving rashly the last time you were here."

Relieved that Sam wouldn't pose a threat, Wil replied, "You're not sorry, but I accept the truce. Where's Alice?"

"Inside. Amanda has been tending her. The doctor is uncertain if she'll make it. Between the fever and not having found Emma..."

His entire family—he felt powerless to keep it from happening again.

Sam led the way along the brick walk. He halted near the steps and met Wil's gaze. "Need I remind you that if she dies, you're free?"

Wil barely managed to remain calm. "I'll pretend I didn't hear that. Now if you don't mind, I'd like to see Alice."

"Of course, but I do have to ask one question, Jackson. What *will* you do if she dies?"

Drift through the abyss of madness... "Sam, I don't expect any open welcomes, but please take me to her."

"You are worried. I thought... Never mind, it wasn't important." Sam's blue eyes briefly flickered in a respectful way.

Wil almost expected to be addressed as captain, but there was no returning to long ago days of New Mexico.

"No matter what's gone between us, I shouldn't have said that."

Wil nodded that he accepted the apology, and Sam showed him to the back bedroom. Amanda rose from the rocking chair beside the bed and left the room without making eye contact or acknowledging him. He approached the bed. "Alice . . ."

Like a ghostly form, she lay deathly still. Even her breathing seemed non-existent. *Too late—she was already gone.* He pressed his fingers to her neck and felt an irregular pulse. He let out a breath, only then realizing he had been holding it, and called her name again.

Her eyelids fluttered open. "Wil . . ."

Her voice was barely above a whisper. He sat on the edge of the bed beside her. "You scared me half to death."

She forced a small smile. "Nothing frightens you."

"Right now, you're scaring the hell out of me." When he reached for her hand, a red feather fell to the quilt. *The hawk.*

Her smile widened. "I'm not afraid."

"Alice . . ." His voice broke. "I'm sorry for the pain I've caused you, but you can't die. What would become of Emma and me?"

"You've found Emma? Let me hold her."

"Not yet, but I will," he promised. He untied the medicine pouch from around his neck and folded her fingers around it. Without bothering to remove his boots, he climbed in next to her and wrapped his arms protectively around her.

For nearly a week, Amanda had Lily tend Alice. In that time, Wil never left Alice's side. The trays she sent in usually returned with the food left untouched. It was almost as if he had decided that if Alice died, so would he.

Lily set the tray on the kitchen table and furrowed her brows in worry. "I sorry, Miss Amanda. I get more down Miss Alice, an' dat ain't much. Maybe you can talk some sense into Mr. Wil."

See Wil? "I can't go in there. It wouldn't be right."

"Ain't no sense in frettin' 'bout what's right when what you say can make a difference."

"You don't understand, Lily. This is my fault."

"Dat Miss Alice got da fever?" Lily shook her head.

"No, that Alice doesn't care if she lives."

"She does care, Miss Amanda, or she wouldn't last dis long. She live in hope dat Miss Emma be found."

Emma... Sam and his men continued their search, but with each passing day... "Lily..." Amanda squeezed the servant's hand. "I don't know how much Alice has told you..."

"Enough."

Lily's emphasis on the word warned Amanda that Alice had confided in her. "Then you should understand why I can't go in there."

"I don't understand nothin'."

The servant's voice edged on insubordination, reminding her of Frieda. "Maybe Alice hasn't told you as much as you think."

Lily raised a hand in frustration, then pressed it to her chest. "I know 'bout you an' Mr. Wil. I also know you ain't da sort of woman who do such a thing if you don't care. He need you now as much as Miss Alice."

Amanda closed her eyes and said a silent prayer. With renewed strength, she took a deep breath, picked up the tray, and carried it to the back bedroom. She hesitated. Another deep breath. She knocked and went inside. "Wil Jackson," she said, setting the tray on the dresser, "I've about lost my patience with you. I spend all of my time cooking, then sending Lily in, but you don't touch anything. If you have complaints about what I prepare, I expect you to take it up with me, not disregard what I fix."

While Amanda poured a cup of tea, she looked in the mirror. Wil rose from the bed. The same one they had... A shiver ran down her. Finished pouring, she finally faced him. His hair and shirt were rumpled, and deep circles under his eyes suggested that he had slept as little the past few days as he had eaten. She handed him the teacup.

He took a sip, then finally met her gaze. "Any word on Emma?"

She shook her head.

He let out a deep breath. "If the truth be known, Amanda, I prefer coffee."

"I shall send some in next time. Now eat, and I'll check on Alice. Just don't complain the food is cold. You only have yourself to blame for that." Satisfied that her message was received, Amanda approached the bed.

Barely clinging to life, Alice looked so pale. A smile formed on her face. "Thank you, Amanda," she whispered.

Amanda glanced over her shoulder. Wil was eating. That's what Alice had meant by taking care of him. She grasped her sister's hand. In it was the medicine pouch. "If I knew my animal guide, I'd send it to help too."

"Surely you know."

"How would I?"

"With some people their guardian spirit is obvious. Sam used to whittle carvings."

Until he had been captured and sent to Libby. After the prison experience, he had stopped whittling. "He used to make carvings of Red. The horse is my totem?" Amanda brushed sweaty strands of hair from Alice's face. "What does a horse guardian mean?"

"Beauty and strength."

"Then I shall fetch one of the carvings." Relieved to be away from the sickroom, Amanda dashed to her bedroom. She opened a dresser drawer and withdrew a wood carving in the shape of a horse.

"Amanda . . ."

"Sam," she said, facing him. She opened her hand to reveal the carving.

He took the horse figurine from her palm and studied it. "Where did you get it?"

"Wil gave it to me after visiting you in Libby. I was taking it to Alice. She said that my animal spirit is the horse."

He nodded and returned the carving to her. "I never realized how much all of our lives were intertwined."

His eyes flickered in a familiar way, and she thought he would take her into his arms. But his arms remained at his side. It would take longer, if ever, for him to forgive her.

Alice clutched the medicine pouch and absorbed the warmth of the mountain lion. Wil rested beside her, silently watching her.

She reached a hand to his bearded face. All thoughts of anger and blame vanished. "I'm feeling better."

He stroked her cheek. "You still feel warm."

"I tell you that I'm feeling better." Alice shoved herself to a sitting position. "I'm hungry."

"I'll have Lily bring something."

As he rose from the bed, she grasped his wrist. "Wil, don't leave me."

"Then I'll call Lily."

She nodded that his suggestion met with her approval. Before long, Lily brought in a tray with a bowl of broth. Alice hungrily spooned the broth to her mouth, while Wil looked on. "Are you still not convinced?" she said with a giggle.

Silence.

She shivered. "Wil, stop it. You're frightening me." Worried that he might have contracted the fever, she traced her trembling fingers across his face. Thankfully, his skin was cool to her touch.

"I had typhoid long ago if that's what you're thinking."

"Then make love to me."

"Alice, I don't deserve your forgiveness."

But she saw a glimmer in his dark eyes—something else holding him back. "Is it because you still love her?" He snapped his eyes shut and shook his head. "Then what?"

Tears were in his eyes when he reopened them. She had never seen her stoic warrior cry. "Because I never stopped loving you."

"I realize that now." She unfastened his shirt and traced a hand over his chest, lingering over the scar near his heart. She kissed him there, then let her fingers trail lower. She reached for the buttons of his trousers and stroked him, suddenly realizing what he already knew. "Be with me, Wil."

Something changed in his face—not the familiar emotionless mask that detached him from everything else during the war, but he was in control again. She helped him undress.

Alice giggled. "The first time we were intimate I knew nothing of what I was doing."

"You learned quickly," he said, smiling in fond remembrance.

"And you tarnished my reputation in the process."

"As I recall, *you* asked me."

She giggled again. "Which doesn't change the fact that I was ruined after that night."

"You didn't act ruined," he responded with a slightly wicked grin. "Alice..."

She kissed him on the mouth before he could say anything further. Her kisses went to his neck, then to his chest, traveling the length of his body and absorbing his scent and the coarseness of his skin. Already nearly sapped of her strength, Alice lay back, bringing him with her. He tossed her nightdress to the side, and as she clung to him, his lips and hands caressed her.

This was where she belonged—happy and carefree in his arms. She drifted higher and higher among the layers of sensations until her arms grew light and formed wings. Soaring through the sky, she uttered the cry of the hawk. The breeze on her face was frosty and invigorating. From her newfound vantage, keen eyesight allowed her to visualize everything. Past and present were tightly woven. He could never have loved her without Amanda chipping through his detached exterior, only to reveal an already broken heart. *But what of the future?*

She suddenly understood the true power of the hawk. The acute vision could only reveal glimpses into the past, a little at a time. She hadn't continued far enough, and saw Amanda dressed in black, bent over Wil's grave. The letter *had* been meant for her, not Amanda.

"Wil, I..." He pressed his fingertips to her lips. She held out the red-tail feather. "When she's old enough... Give it to Emma."

Papa waved at her to join him. Beside him stood her childhood friend, Timmy Mullen, and Frieda. The withered servant's wrinkles had faded, and she could see again. Alice gasped for breath and reached for Wil's hand. Their fingertips nearly touched, but missed. She whispered her love in his ear. Except to mate, the mountain lion was a solitary hunter, and the hawk floated through the clouds toward the light.

The corners of Alice's mouth were tipped up in a contented smile. Wil traced a finger over them. Her sweet face was euphoric as though she were in a tranquil slumber. With loving care, he washed her—slowly and gently from her long, slender neck down to her toes. Rose-colored spots covered her abdomen. Wishing he had something more proper, he dressed her in her nightgown. No sense fretting. Lily would see to her attire in the morning. In the flickering lamplight, he combed through her reddish-brown hair, twisting a few strands between his fingertips.

He carefully arranged her hair and dabbed a bit of perfume to her wrists. She always loved the scent of lilac, and the stench of sickness faded from the room. Her flesh was growing cold. He kissed her dead lips and studied her for a moment. *Peaceful.* He had best tell the rest of the household and snuffed the lamp.

Wil halted by the door and clenched his hands. *How often had he cheated death and narrowly escaped its grip?* With a scream, he bolted across the room and shoved the porcelain pitcher and basin from the dresser. Glass shattered. In a violent rage, he tossed the lamp. More shattering. He hurled the mirror to the floor.

Surrendering to his grief, he sank to the floor covered in broken glass. He poised a shard over his wrist, then clutched it. Blood dripped from his hand.

"Wil, be kinder to yourself."

It was *her* voice. He lowered his head and wept.

Two days later, they lowered the pine box into the red earth behind the farmhouse. Beneath the expansive limbs of the old oak was the McGuires' final resting place. Even Amanda's first husband, John, had wished to be buried in the family plot. As a career military officer, the rich farmland was the only place he had truly known as home. When her firstborn son, Benjamin, had died, she had been unable to cry. For weeks, she had lived in a stupor and might have died right alongside him if Alice hadn't been there for her. Now her sister was gone.

Quietly sobbing, Amanda dabbed Sam's handkerchief to her eyes. Mama stood beside Wil, tightly gripping his arm with tears unashamedly streaking her face. Wil failed to show any emotion, but the white bandage wrapped around his right hand revealed the fury that lurked underneath. The injury had taken three stitches. After she had viewed Alice's ghostly form lying on the bed, her hand had been less than steady while performing the task. And their unspoken fear of what might have happened to Emma still pervaded their thoughts.

Sam grasped her elbow and guided her down the hill to the farmhouse. Amanda glanced over her shoulder. Wil had always been a strong shoulder when she required his help. He needed someone right now.

"Don't go to him, Amanda. I'll lose you for good, if you do."

"Sam," Amanda chided. "How can you say that? My sister's barely in her grave. We've both suffered a loss." Her tears returned, and she touched the handkerchief to her eyes.

"And now . . ." Sam shook his head.

Inside the house, the neighbors had sent food. They had little to give, but their thoughtful gifts were much appreciated. Lily served the guests that had come to pay their final respects. Finally, Mama and Wil arrived. He escorted Mama to the wing-backed chair, where she kept dabbing her eyes.

Amanda resisted the temptation to hug them. *They had already been punished enough for their transgressions.* Wil's dark gaze met hers. Absent from them was their familiar mischievous spark. She was vaguely aware of Sam leaving the room. By the time she glanced over her shoulder, he was gone.

"Sam . . . ," she said, running after him. Outside the house, she finally caught up with him at the end of the brick walk. "Sam, where are you going?"

"I thought I'd return to the search for Emma, where I can be of some use."

"I need you here."

"It didn't look that way to me." He started across the farmyard.

"Please, Sam. I've lost my sister, and I want you to stay." He came to a halt, and she moved next to him and grasped his hand. "I can't undo what's been said and done, but I've never stopped loving you."

"Forgive me for being petty about my own feelings, Amanda. I recall what it was like when Charles died." For the first time in weeks, he draped his arm around her shoulders. "I've just been so afraid of losing you."

"You won't lose me. I promise." She went up the steps, when Wil stepped onto the porch. She made certain not to meet his gaze while passing him. "Wil . . ." She cleared her throat. "Are you returning to Petersburg?"

Without turning, he answered from the bottom of the steps. "Not until Emma is found."

"My boys," Sam said, "found the house where Chandler had taken them."

Wil met Sam's gaze. "Why wasn't I informed?"

"You had other things on your mind," Sam replied softly. "And I didn't want you getting any notion about going after him yourself. Let my boys handle it. Agreed?"

"Agreed."

Amanda spotted it. Wil's words said one thing, but his eyes revealed another. She wondered if she should warn Sam. Wil continued down the walk and mounted his horse. Overhead, Amanda spotted a hawk in the sky. Alice wanted them to cooperate. "Sam, he's lying. He's going after Doug Chandler himself." Her knees weakened, and she dashed inside, collapsing to the floor. The tears returned. She hugged her knees to her chin.

A small hand touched her arm. "Mama, please don't cry."

She drew Rebecca into her arms, and a strong hand gripped her shoulder. Sam . . . She had been reckless and nearly destroyed her marriage. To her relief, he bent down and held them both.

Day and night blended, and Wil had difficulty keeping track of which was which. Like a dutiful servant, Lily reminded him when he should eat and sleep. Not that he was succeeding at much of either, but the servant tended to his needs upon his return to the house in Fredericksburg. Short of cash, he had little to pay her with and wondered why she stayed. Pacing the length of the study, he stopped and examined the map of the surrounding counties. Even with Jesse's help, Chandler could be most anywhere. He had difficulty concentrating and rubbed his eyes.

"Mr. Wil . . ." A rap came at the door, and Lily poked her head in. "Mrs. Whyte is here to see you."

What could Holly want? "Send her in."

Attired in a flowery dress and a fashionable hat with a feather, Holly entered the study.

"What are you doing here?" he asked.

She approached the desk. "Wil, I came to pay my respects. I didn't think I'd be welcome at the funeral."

In spite of his disbelief, he motioned for her to have a seat. "And?"

"Why do you always think I have ulterior motives?" she asked, smoothing out her skirt.

"Because you usually do," he grumbled. He sat in the chair behind the desk and glanced at the map.

"Are you going after Doug?"

He met Holly's gaze. "If I were, why would I tell you?"

"Then don't, but I know if Sam is too inept to catch him, you'll do what's necessary, especially in light of what's happened." Wil shook his head, denying it, and she continued, "Then why are you studying maps?"

He stared at her with a cold fixation. "Because I'm a god-damned engineer. I study maps and drawings for a living."

"I'm only asking because if you are going after Doug, I want to be involved. You *do* recall what he did to me?"

"I do." Wil thought it over. She might be of some benefit, but how could he be certain that she hadn't gone right back to Chandler? He nearly asked her if she could add to the potential locations of Chandler's whereabouts that Jesse had provided him with. Instead, he asked, "Why did you really come here?"

Holly pressed a hand to her chest and flickered her eyelashes.

"Dispose of the routines, Holly. Even you have admitted that we know each other too well."

"I'll forgive your rudeness. I remember what it was like after I lost Charles."

His mind was sinking. Without Alice, there was no one to reel him back to the surface. "I'm sure you shed many tears over Charles's death."

"Wil, please. I truly came here to see how you're faring. After all, we are *old* friends."

Still skeptical, he leaned back in the chair. "Who sent you?"

"No one sent me," she insisted. "I came because I wanted to."

For once, he believed her.

"Is there anything you need?"

He shook his head.

"I mean *anything*."

Her tone had turned suggestive. "I have no money, Holly," he said, breathing out in disgust. "If I don't return to Petersburg soon, I'll lose the house to your carpetbagger friends. Not that it makes any difference. As a former Confederate brigadier, I'm not allowed to own property anyway. And without an officer's rank I can't fathom what you could possibly want."

"Wil . . ." Holly wrapped her arms around his neck and wriggled into his lap. "I don't need money or titles."

"Like hell." He stood, sending her sprawling to the floor. "Mr. Whyte must not be keeping you suitably entertained."

She cursed, but he helped her to her feet. Smoothing her skirts, she cursed again. "I thought you might be able to use some solace."

"From you?"

Holly straightened her hat. "Don't sound so surprised. It's not like we haven't comforted each other before."

"I'd hardly call anything you ever provided comfort."

Suddenly miffed, she placed her hands on her hips. "I give up."

"Then go. I didn't invite you in the first place." With a scowl, she hustled from the study. Wil reseated himself and stared at the maps once more. His vision blurred. Another knock. Expecting Holly, he shouted, "I told you to get the hell out."

"Sir?"

"Sorry, Jesse."

Jesse nodded and approached the desk. "I spoke with a number of the Yankees, and I finally found one willing to talk after a few beers and for a couple of greenbacks." He pointed to the map. "Chandler took Alice and Emma here."

Not in the Wilderness this time, but clear across the county in the opposite direction. The details weren't much, but they were a place to start. Finally, he'd be able to keep the vow he had made to Alice. He would find Emma or die trying.

At headquarters, Sam leaned back in his chair as Lieutenant Greer read his report. "Mrs. Whyte left Jackson's house at approximately three o'clock. About five minutes later, Jesse Morgan entered the premises."

Straightening, Sam checked his pocket watch. Jesse had been at Wil's less than half an hour ago. "Lieutenant, continue watching Mrs. Whyte."

"Sir, do you really think she'll lead us to Chandler?"

"With Mrs. Whyte you never know. She has the propensity for seeking adventure in some rather peculiar places—if you know what I mean."

"I do, sir." Greer arched a brow but saluted. "Your orders will be carried out, sir."

"Dismissed." On his way out, Sam collected his gun belt and hat. If he had any scrap of honor left, he'd arrest Wil for his own damned good. Four years of war and the bitterness between sides following it had changed him. He hated to admit it—even to himself, but he was counting on Wil and Jesse to lead him to Chandler.

Whether they found Emma alive or not, he fully expected Chandler to die. Not that he could blame Wil. If Rebecca had been the missing child, he would have been ready to choke the life out of Chandler with his bare hands.

Outside in the relentless July heat, one of Sam's men accompanied him to Jackson's house, where they met with two other privates. "Jackson and Morgan left about ten minutes ago, sir," Private Anderson reported.

"Anderson, follow them and report back to me periodically. We'll be coming up from behind."

The private saluted. What he wouldn't give for a decent scout. Of the remaining boys, Anderson was better than most, but he was green. By the time the private gained the expertise necessary, the army in its infinite wisdom would certainly muster him out of the service.

By an act of Providence or sheer bad luck, he had been forced to resort to tactics similar to those of the guerrillas. Sam sucked in his breath at the implication. Why else would he be using Jackson's proficiency without his knowledge? He tried to dismiss it by rationalizing it would increase the likelihood of finding Emma alive. But he wanted blood—Chandler's blood.

Chapter Eighteen

A SINGLE LAMP BLAZED inside the farmhouse. Wil dismounted. As he tied his mare to the rail, Jesse joined him. "An old man lives here—definitely one who helped hide Chandler in the past. Let me see if I can get any information from him."

To this, Wil agreed. Jesse knocked. The door cracked open and a shotgun barrel greeted them.

"George, it's me—Jesse Morgan."

The shotgun lowered. "Jesse?"

The door opened, and Wil resisted the urge to charge in and beat the information from the old man. *Remain calm*, and let Jesse do the talking.

"Jesse, I haven't seen you in quite some time. The Yankees hanged the boys." The old man was nearly in tears. "Only Doug escaped. A couple of times the Yanks almost found him, but he managed to stay one step ahead. Then when he got the fever—he holed up in a cave along the river. When Estelle got sick, he started taking risks that he shouldn't have."

"I know, George. In fact, I'm looking for Lieutenant Chandler. Do you have any idea where he might be these days?"

The old man rubbed his chin and eyed Wil suspiciously. "Who's your friend?"

Wil held out a hand. "Captain John Cole, formerly of the First South Carolina," he responded, using the same alias he had when helping Sam break out of Libby.

George shook Wil's hand, then shrugged. "I haven't seen Doug in several weeks. Both him and Estelle were mighty sick with the fever. A woman from town helped Estelle. Nursed her upstairs."

Wil tried to channel his impatience. No use. Things were moving too slowly to suit him. "She had a child with her."

"That's right." George arched a brow. "How would you know that 'less..."

"George," Jesse interrupted, "Where did Doug go?"

"Reckon I don't know," George answered with a shrug. "Doug never keeps me apprised of his whereabouts."

"Does he visit any of his old haunts?"

The old man's eyes narrowed. "Why did you say you were lookin' for Doug?"

The endless line of questioning was going nowhere. "Enough!" Wil aimed his pistol at George. The old man shrieked before raising his hands. "Because the goddamned bastard took my wife and daughter, and I'm going to kill him when I find him."

"Wil..." Jesse stepped between them. "You don't want to kill an old man and become like Chandler. Let me talk to George—alone. Why don't you go upstairs and see if there are any clues?"

Clues—for what? That Alice may have left behind. Wil shoved the pistol in its holster. After more than a month, there would unlikely be any evidence, but he agreed. *Let Jesse help.* He went upstairs. A lingering staleness guided him to the bedroom on the left. Lighting a candle, he had no doubt this was the room where Alice had nursed Chandler's sister.

On the floor, he found a tiny shoe—Emma's. He picked it up and could almost hear her excited squeals. He really *had* lost everything. Voices downstairs drifted his way—not heated, but calm in discussion. He returned his attention to the room. There might be something of Alice's as well.

A hair brush sat on the dresser. Blonde hair rested among the bristles, definitely not Alice.

"Wil..." He turned to Jesse standing in the doorway. "George knows of a couple of places where Chandler may have taken his sister. Estelle suffers from hysteria from the time the Yankees burned their home to the ground. What I didn't know was that she lost a child in the fire."

A madwoman had Emma.

"George says we can use this room for the night and start fresh in the morning."

"Can we trust him?"

"I think so. He didn't know what had happened to . . . Alice."

Why couldn't he think straight? "I can't rest."

Jesse remained calm and collected. "If we cross Chandler's path, I think it best that we do so refreshed and during the daylight."

Command decisions used to come easily, but now they eluded him. *Take someone's advice for a change, and listen to Jesse.* In spite of his youth, he had a good head on his shoulders. With the boy's help, he would reach his objective. Wil merely nodded.

"I'll see to the horses and take the first watch."

When Jesse vanished from the room, Wil realized that he should have offered to care for the horses. Each day was a haze since Alice had died. How long had it been? Days? Weeks? He couldn't lose sight of his vow and held up the tiny shoe.

He *would* find Emma in the morning. If not tomorrow, then the day after. For several minutes, he paced the floor before finally settling into the rocking chair beside the bed. Fear had possessed the hawk. This was where she had got sick, and he hadn't been here to help calm her concern. *Would it have made a difference?*

The candlelight fluttered and snuffed out. Instead of relighting it, he remained in the dark. If he could touch the hawk's spirit, he might be able to see her again. Nothing. As usual, he was alone. Sometimes, he felt the mountain lion guiding him was a curse.

"Wil . . ."

Jesse lit the candle, and Wil blinked. *How long had he been sitting in the dark?* "I warned you that I can't rest. I haven't since . . ."

Jesse nodded that he understood. "Would some laudanum help? I brought some just in case . . ."

Just in case if he had the urge to kill himself again. "That's Amanda's doing."

"I didn't tell her where I was going," Jesse said, holding up a hand in protest.

"You didn't need to. She knows." He only hoped that she had maintained silence with Sam. "Let me take this watch." Without waiting for a response from Jesse, Wil made his way down the stairs to the darkened rooms. The old man must have gone to bed. Continuing on, he went outside to check on the horses. Jesse had stabled and fed them. On a nearby rail rested his saddle. He retrieved his saddlebags. Inside was the Confederate flag Chandler had given him and the hawk feather. He placed Emma's shoe alongside the flag and took out the feather.

The hawk would give him the power to see Alice. He held the tail feather next to him and heard the haunting cry of the screech owl. A fox yipped from deep within the forest. Night sounds— nothing from a day spirit like the hawk.

Wil stepped outside the barn and stood at his post. He rolled the feather between his fingertips. Perhaps she didn't respond because she knew what was in his heart. He had loved them both. A man who prided himself on remaining detached had fallen for not one, but two sisters.

Several hours later, Wil heard the door to the house open and footsteps on the stairs. A dark figure strode toward him. He recognized the light tread as belonging to Jesse.

"Wil, I think you should try and get some rest."

He shook his head. "I can't."

"Are you certain you won't try the laudanum?"

For a minute, Wil entertained the notion. If he took enough laudanum, then he could kill the pain, but he mustn't lose his focus on what he had set out to do. "Not now."

"I thought you might say that. I brought some coffee."

Wil muttered his thanks. The hot drink kept him alert, and by morning, he was already saddling the horses when Jesse joined him. The young man offered him a biscuit, but he declined. They mounted up and headed for the first farm that George had suggested. As they rode up the lane, Wil recognized the Wallace cabin. The elderly Mrs. Wallace had labeled him a traitor and nearly shot Sam. At the time, a younger woman had also been present—a blonde one in her early twenties, and in a hysterical state, she had accused Sam of killing her daughter. Blonde hairs had been in the brush at George's. Chandler's sister—Estelle. If he had only known then what he did now.

As they neared the cabin, a hunched woman stepped onto the porch. Wil lowered his hat. "Mrs. Wallace."

"Mr. Jackson," she acknowledged. Shielding her eyes, she peered to the lane. "I don't see any Yankees. Have you remembered your true calling, or are they lying in wait to ambush an old woman?"

Wil dismounted. Almost instantly, Jesse was by his side, ready to intercept him if he tried anything similar to what he had with George. "I'm looking for Doug Chandler."

"I have already informed you that I've never made the gentleman's acquaintance."

"You have," Wil replied, careful not to take a step toward her. "And you've harbored his sister, Estelle."

"Sorry, you're confusing me for someone else. I don't know her either. Now if you don't mind, I have chores to tend to." She turned.

"Mrs. Wallace. My wife is dead, and Estelle has my daughter."

She faced them once more. "You have my condolences, but you must be mistaken. Estelle wouldn't hurt anyone. She's grieving. First, she lost her husband in the war, then her daughter, Faith, died in a fire, when the Yankees burned her home."

Faith—an ironic name. At least, he had made progress. The woman admitted to knowing Estelle. "I reckon I know how she feels right now, but she has *my* daughter. Emma is all that I have left."

Her wrinkled face remained stern. Jesse tugged on his arm. "We might as well be leaving. We're not going to get any help here."

Wil nodded and placed his hat on his head.

"Brigadier Jackson . . ."

His title. Out of respect, he removed his hat.

The lines on her face were etched in sorrow. "I haven't seen Estelle since you happened by those odd months ago. Doug used to bring her frequently, but after that incident, he was afraid the Yanks would find out."

"Find out what?"

"That she had been married to my grandson. Doug feared they would use Estelle and me to get to him. Most likely, he was right. I tried to convince him to leave Estelle with me and head west. A boy like him will never change, but he wouldn't have any of it. He feels responsible for Estelle. I guess she's all that he has. Anyways, he tends to be particular who he leaves her with. After all, not many are willing to look after a woman not right in her head, but he has a few friends. I'll give you the names I know, but knowing Doug, he's got others looking out for her that he's never told me about."

"Much obliged, ma'am."

"Will you do me a courtesy for supplying you with the names?"

"If I can."

"When the Yankees finally catch up with Doug, see that Estelle is brought here. She'll need someone to care for her."

Wil agreed to her terms. Between Jesse's familiarity of Chandler's movements and their new leads, he came to the conclusion that Chandler's network must span at least three counties. If necessary, he would search them all. After leaving the Wallace farm, they crossed a stream. Wil heard hoofbeats on the trail behind them. He glanced over his shoulder. No one.

By late afternoon, they arrived at the Rapidan river. While letting the horses drink, Wil spotted a Yankee soldier further downstream. Someone *had* been trailing them, but he had been too slow-thinking to take action. "Yanks are following us."

"Colonel Prescott?"

"I'd be willing to bet that he's responsible."

With a casual glance over his shoulder, Jesse nodded that he saw the man in blue.

"If this is the best Prescott has these days, he shouldn't be difficult to shake. I think it might be best if we split up. He can't follow both of us." Wil unfolded the map from his saddlebags and pointed to a ford in the western portion of the county. "I'll meet you here in two hours. Fire a warning shot if you get into any trouble."

"Yes, sir."

"Jesse... he's most likely the lead scout. You needn't go through with this."

"I want to," Jesse responded, without hesitation.

So little feeling lately, but Wil felt kinship to Caroline's son. "I would have been proud, if you had been my son."

"Thank you, Wil."

As Wil tucked the map into his saddlebags, Jesse mounted his horse. He touched the hawk feather. Still, nothing. *She was really gone.* After the way he had behaved, he supposed he couldn't blame her. *Why did he always learn lessons the hard way?*

"Wil..."

With a nod to Jesse, he blinked and climbed aboard his mare. Jesse squeezed his horse to a trot and guided it along the riverbank. In full view, the Yankee hadn't moved from his post. Wil waved at the soldier, then reined the gray in the direction of the tree line. With a little luck, the scout would track him and not Jesse. Nearly a mile passed before he heard a gunshot. Behind him. He reined the mare around and cued her to a gallop. By the time he arrived at the river's edge, he found the Yank on his knees. Tears streamed down the boy's face, and he pleaded for his life, while Jesse kept a trained eye and a pistol on him.

Wil joined Jesse. "It appears you have the situation in hand."

"He thinks I'm going to kill him." Jesse lowered his voice to a whisper, so only Wil would hear. "What *should* I do with him?"

"Jackson! Morgan!"

"I think the matter has already been decided." Wil glanced around as Sam rode into the open, flanked by two of his men with their rifles aimed at them.

"Jesse put the gun down," Sam ordered. Jesse lowered the pistol. "Anderson, are you all right?"

The scout got to his feet and dusted himself off. "I'm fine, sir."

Sam dismounted. "I could have ordered both of you shot."

"You didn't," Wil replied, "so there must be a reason."

"Wil, I know what you're trying to do. If I were in your place, I'd be on the same mission. I want Chandler too. You can talk to people around here who treat me with suspicion. We have a common cause. Help me find him... Captain."

Captain. Wil had never expected to hear the honorary title again. "How can I refuse when you give a speech like that?"

"Thank you," Sam replied, taking a breath in relief, "and I promise that he'll pay for what he's done."

Small comfort. As Wil reached in his saddlebag for Emma's shoe, Sam stood beside him. *The flag*—he had forgotten about the flag, and Sam immediately cast his gaze in the direction of his men. "I'll surrender it."

Sam replied, low enough so his men wouldn't overhear, "You won't be of much use to me sitting in jail, Jackson. Besides, the only thing I saw was a child's shoe. Emma's, I presume?"

"It is," Wil admitted. He heard a familiar cry in the sky and looked up. A red-tailed hawk soared in the wind. She had wanted him to renew his alliance with Sam. He gripped Emma's shoe next to him. For the first time since setting out, he held hope they might find his daughter alive.

Two days later, and after traveling at least fifty hot and dusty miles, Wil accompanied Jesse as they approached yet another farmhouse. With the ground they had covered, they had checked more than twenty houses. *Nothing.* He hadn't given up hope. On several occasions, he had spotted the hawk floating through the sky. With her keen eyesight, she was guiding him to Emma.

In a garden to the side of the house, a woman with streaks of gray running through her hair hoed the weeds. The presence of a woman made the house a distinct possibility. One thing Wil had learned about Chandler was that he only rarely took his sister to places where a woman wasn't present, which was why he had needed Alice's help when Estelle had taken sick with the fever.

As they dismounted in the farmyard, the woman dropped her hoe and came to greet them. "Ma'am," Wil said, lowering his hat. "We've had a mighty hard ride and were hoping we might be able to fill our canteens at your well."

She brushed the dirt from her hands onto her apron. "From the look of things, you've been in the saddle for days."

"We have been," Wil agreed. "Yanks have been chasing us."

Examining them from head-to-toe, she regarded them quizzically. "For what?"

Would she show sympathy or run for a shotgun as others had done? Wil lifted the flap to his saddlebags, exposing the tattered Confederate flag. "For this."

She fidgeted but smiled, gesturing to the opposite side of the house. "Help yourselves to the well."

"Much obliged, ma'am." Wil and Jesse led their horses around to the side.

While Wil busied with the canteens, Jesse peered inside a window. He shook his head and went to the next one. "I'll check around back." Before rounding the corner, Jesse ducked back. "Wil . . ." Jesse waved for him to follow.

Around back, a blonde-haired woman, wearing lace gloves, hummed as she cut black-eyed Susans. *Estelle* . . . He scanned the yard for Emma. *Where was she?* In spite of Mrs. Wallace's words, he recalled the fury Estelle harbored from her attack on Sam, and right now, she held pruning shears.

Satisfied that Emma wasn't present, Wil started forward. Jesse shoved out an arm to block him. "She knows me. Fetch Colonel Prescott."

"I can't leave—not now."

"Then keep watch for Chandler." As Jesse strode forward, Wil lowered his hat over his eyes and kept his hand poised on his pistol. "Estelle . . ."

The woman glanced up and shielded her eyes from the sun. "Jesse?"

"This is my friend, Captain Cole."

Her eyes narrowed. "Don't I know you?"

"I don't think so." Wil scanned the outbuildings and the windows of the house. No sign of Chandler or unusual movement.

"Estelle," Jesse continued, "I'm looking for Doug."

She finally glanced from Wil to Jesse and shook her head. "He's not here."

Wil let out a breath. At least if Emma were here, then she wouldn't be caught in any crossfire. "The child? Where is she?" he asked impatiently.

"Faith?"

Convinced they had found Emma, Wil raised his voice. "Her name is Emma. Where is she?"

Estelle began to cry. "Jesse, I don't think I like your friend."

Enough. "Emma!" Wil charged into the cabin.

The middle-aged woman greeted him at the door with a rifle. "Is this how you repay my kindness?"

"I'm intent on fetching my daughter." He gestured to the gun. "The only way you're going to stop me is by using that."

"Your daughter?" The rifle lowered slightly.

No sign of Emma. In the middle of the room, stairs led to a loft. Wil shoved past the woman and moved toward the stairs.

"Noooo!" With pruning shears poised in the air like a dagger, Estelle lunged into the room. Jesse seized her arms and pinned her against the wall until she dropped the shears. "He's going to take Faith! Stop him!"

A whimper came from the loft. Wil followed the sound and continued up the steps. "Emma?" Still screaming, Estelle shook a fist, but the other woman had lowered the rifle. He reached the loft. On a straw mattress, a toddler, clad in a dirty nightdress, stirred and cried. Like him, her skin was coppery and her hair, black. "Emma," he whispered. He collapsed to his knees beside the mattress and pulled her to him. Tiny hands gripped his jacket. Her cries escalated until she shrieked. He hushed her and rocked her. "It's all right, Emma. Papa's here."

Sniffling her tears, she clung to him. He sat hunched with his arms around her until she was still. She drew away slightly. Tears streaked her cheeks, and she stared at him with green saucer-like eyes. She blinked and tugged on his moustache. "Papa."

Footsteps rattled on the stairs. Overcome by emotion, Wil fought the tears. Nothing could make him move. He only clutched Emma tighter.

"Is she all right?"

Without looking around to locate Sam, Wil weakly nodded his head. He had kept his promise. The hawk was finally at peace.

* * *

With the end of the war, Amanda thought her days of senseless waiting had ceased. During the day, she had busied herself with chores, and it kept her from thinking about the worst. A couple of days had passed since her last word from Sam. Even that message had been scrawled in haste and only to let her know that he was all right, but they'd had no success in locating Emma.

As the sun sank lower in the sky, she made the trek to the family graveyard on the hill, where Mama and Rebecca stood over Alice's grave. Mama dabbed her eyes with a black handkerchief. "I miss her too, Mama, but it's past Rebecca's bedtime."

She grasped Rebecca's hand and returned to the house. Even though the windows were opened wide, not a breeze stirred. The upstairs bedrooms sweltered in the July heat. She should move Mama and Rebecca to the room downstairs where it was cooler, but she had been unable to enter the room since Alice had died. After changing Rebecca into a nightdress and tucking her in bed with a goodnight kiss, Amanda wandered to the porch in the fading sunlight.

Mama rocked. "She forgave you."

Amanda sank into the chair beside her. "I didn't want her forgiveness. What I did was wrong."

"It was," Mama agreed, "but it didn't cause her death."

"Mama . . ."

"No, Amanda, hear me out." The handkerchief went to Mama's eyes. "Alice was usually the impetuous one, but you've got to stop blaming yourself. Typhoid killed her. You did all you could to save her, but the decision rested in the good Lord's hands. She forgave you, so you need to work on forgiving yourself."

Amanda chewed on her lower lip. "How can I? I've hurt all of those close to me."

"Hurt mends with time, and I fret that I have made things worse."

Mama had never been the comforting sort. Alice's death had affected her more than anyone could have fathomed. "How so, Mama?"

More dabbing of the handkerchief. "By not accepting your Yankee husband. Sam is a good man, and I'll tell him so when he returns."

The confession choked off Amanda's breath. *If* he returns. If he thought she still loved Wil, he might do something foolish that would get himself killed. She grasped Mama's hand and squeezed it, when she heard trotting hoofbeats enter the bottom of the lane. "Mama, get the rifle."

Mama nodded and vanished into the house. A flickering lamp from inside cast broken light on the yard, but the horse's gray hairs stood out. *Wil*, and he had . . . "Emma. Mama, come quick!" Amanda rushed down the steps to greet them. "Wil, where did you find her?"

He dismounted carefully, so as not to drop Emma, and she swept the toddler in her arms. "Chandler's sister had her."

Just like Wil to not really answer the question. "Is she all right? Here, let me get her into the light where I can see her."

"As near as I can tell, she's fine." They stared at one another in awkward silence for a minute. "Take care of her, Amanda."

"Take care of her? Wil . . ."

"I'll see that she gets settled in, then I must be leaving."

"Leaving? But you just got here."

"It's the way things must be."

Mama met them on the brick walk. Thrilled to see Wil and Emma, she hugged the toddler to her breast.

"Have either of you eaten?" Amanda asked.

"I don't know whether Emma's been fed," Wil answered. "I suspect so. She hasn't been fussy."

And he hadn't answered about himself. "We'll make certain. Wil, we have some leftovers from supper if you care to join Emma." Amanda led the way inside and to the kitchen. Dust covered Wil. He must have been in the saddle for days searching for Emma.

While Mama fed Emma, Amanda served a cold platter of fried chicken and blackberry pie. Wil had a detached expression that she found difficult to read. He picked up the knife and fork but failed to eat. He might be a master at masking his emotions, but she sensed that he hurt. She resisted the urge to grasp his hand.

"Mama . . ." Rebecca stood in the doorway, clutching her rag doll.

"Rebecca, what are you doing up?"

Mama stood. "I'll put the girls to bed."

"Thank you, Mama."

As she passed, Wil took Emma's hand and held it a moment.

"On second thought, Mama, I'll bring Emma up."

Wil drew Emma into his arms, and Mama left the kitchen with Rebecca in tow. Emma's eyelids nearly closed. Struggling to stay awake, she flickered them open again. "I should be leaving," Wil finally said.

Amanda took Emma from him, and she swallowed hard. "I'll take good care of her."

"I know you will." His gaze finally met hers. "Your husband sends his regards. I'm sure he would have said more, but he's not likely to trust me with anything else. In fact, when it comes to you, I'm sure he has little confidence in me at all."

At least she knew that Sam was safe—for now. "Wil . . ."

"I meant it when I said goodbye. Circumstances beyond my control have forced me to return." He hesitated as if deciding whether he should say more, then he strode across the room. She heard his footsteps in the other room, and the door close as he left.

"Goodbye," she whispered.

Emma pointed in the direction Wil had gone. "Papa."

The child she longed for was in her arms. Now she had a child from each of the men she loved. Emma looked so much like Wil that every time she saw the toddler, she would be reminded of him and ache. And how could she ever explain to Emma why her papa wasn't coming back?

Remaining behind at the cabin, Sam had sent the women to town accompanied by a couple of his boys. After the middle-aged woman had discovered the truth about Chandler and Estelle, she cooperated. To his surprise, Chandler's sister had only given mild resistance about leaving, and she had protested less than Wil. He had managed to convince his former captain that Emma would be more comforted in her father's presence than anyone else's. He only hoped that he had done the right thing by sending Wil to Amanda.

For some reason, he was suddenly homesick for Maine. He wiped the sweat from his brow. It would certainly be a lot cooler this time of year than in Virginia. Maybe after Chandler was captured, he'd take a long overdue visit. He had never been to his brother's or his first wife's grave.

"Chandler ain't comin', sir."

Anderson's complaint brought Sam back to reality. "He will. It may take days, but one thing we've learned about Chandler is that he's dedicated to his sister." His boys would be sending reinforcements, but that would take time. Unless Chandler had recruited new boys to his cause, Sam had no doubt the three of them could bring him into custody. For now, they waited.

"A lot like goin' into battle." Anderson stood and fidgeted on his feet. "I gotta visit the privy."

"Use the pot, Anderson. I don't want anyone outside alone."

"Yes, sir." Anderson shuffled to the far side of the room and muttered, "Never thought I'd see the day receiving an order on where I should take a piss."

"I don't think I quite heard what you said, Private."

In a louder voice, Anderson responded, "Nothin', sir."

Jesse snickered, and Sam sent him a hard look. "Jesse, take watch from the loft."

The grin vanished from Jesse's face. "Is that an order?"

The young man still lacked trust in Yankees. "I can't order you to do anything, but I thought since you were helping Wil, you would help me as well." Jesse got to his feet and headed for the stairs. "Thank you, Jesse."

For hours, Sam watched from the windows for any sign that Chandler might be approaching. *What if Chandler did take days to return?* He only hoped his boys hightailed it back from town, so they could rotate watches.

At nightfall, he turned on lamps, making the house appear lived in. Chandler would grow suspicious if anything varied from the normal routine. Shortly after midnight, he thought he heard footsteps on the back porch and went to investigate. Taking a deep breath, he raised his pistol and cautiously opened the door.

The eerie call of the screech owl greeted him. "Wil?" Wil stepped into the light. Sam lowered the pistol. "I'm relieved you're here. We can use the extra manpower right now."

Wil merely nodded and came inside.

His muscles tensed. Sam thought of Amanda with her legs spread for Wil. He fought the urge to pummel Wil, and wondered if he would ever come to terms with the vision. "How was Emma?"

"She was in Amanda's arms when I left."

And Amanda would have her child—like Rebecca—not in the way she had planned. "I'm relieved that she's settled in." Sam hesitated with his next question. "And Amanda, was she . . ."

Wil let out a weary breath. "She was seeing to the needs of the children."

"I didn't mean . . ."

Wil's gaze met his. "You did, but I can assure you that we barely had time to exchange a couple of words, much less anything else."

Sam held up a hand in a truce. "The only time that I've known you to lie is when I ordered you not to go after Chandler. We're allies again for that reason." To this, Wil agreed. "I'd also like to know, when was the last time you had any sleep?" No response. "As I thought. Get some rest, Captain." Wil opened his mouth to protest. "I'm in charge here, and if you don't follow orders, I may just have to take another look in your saddlebags."

"Prescott, for being the supposed ethical one, you're mighty good at resorting to blackmail."

Sam laughed. "I had a good teacher."

"Fair enough. I'll try to follow orders."

Relenting, Wil eased into a chair and pulled his hat over his eyes, while Sam returned to his vigil. As the night wore on, his eyelids nearly fell shut.

"I think you're the one who could use some sleep."

Wil again. Annoyed, Sam said, "I thought I told you . . ."

"You did, but I can't rest."

Although Wil attempted to keep his expression that of an emotionless soldier's mask, Sam spotted confusion, defeat, and—

grief. Instead of jealousy, he felt sorrow. Wil *had* loved Alice, and most likely, Amanda too. And now he had nothing. No longer homesick for Maine, Sam had a sudden craving for Mexican food. "Do you remember the *cantina?*"

Wil's eyes remained dull, but he snorted. "Which part—the tequila or the *señoritas?*"

"Neither. The beans and tacos."

"Always thinking of your stomach, Prescott. If you knew what they had used for meat . . ."

"Don't spoil it. I don't want to know." They *were* more alike than different. Even before he had been shipped off to the New Mexico territory, he had cared for Amanda—while she was still married to John Graham. It was so easy to fall in love. No one could ever control the timing. So was it really all that surprising Wil might have felt the same way? A gun butt thumped from the loft, bringing him out of his thoughts.

Jesse poked his head over the edge. "A rider coming. Can't tell whether it's Chandler."

"Thank you, Jesse," Sam responded. "Let's see if he'll come to us."

Without being told, Wil crouched beside a window. Sam heard hoofbeats outside, coming toward the house. In the flickering lamplight, a man halted his horse by the rail, but the darkness prevented Sam from discerning his features. The horse spun around and shot off at a gallop. Wil stormed out the door. "Anderson, accompany him," Sam ordered.

Gunfire echoed outside, then silence. Sam had always hated the quiet before a battle and took a deep breath. "Jesse . . ."

Glass shattered. *Chandler.* Sam raced up the steps toward the sound. Chandler had Jesse pinned to the floor. Between them, they fought for a pistol. Sam aimed his gun. Unable to separate the mass of arms and legs for a clear shot, he held his fire. He jumped into the fray and seized Chandler's arm. The pistol went off, and both men lay unmoving. "Jesse?"

Jesse groaned but climbed from beneath Chandler. A little unsteady, Jesse stood. "Is he dead?"

For so long, Sam had wanted Chandler's blood. Now that he

had it, he felt empty. He knelt down and rolled Chandler to his back. A crimson patch spread across his chest, but the blue eyes flickered open. "You're dying, Chandler."

Chandler coughed, spitting up blood. "Estelle?"

"She's being cared for by townswomen. Wil tells me that Mrs. Wallace will see to her needs on a more permanent basis."

Satisfied, Chandler nodded and gasped for breath. "Colonel..." With a bloody hand, he gripped Sam's jacket. "We didn't... start the fire or murder..." He coughed—more blood. "Colonel..."

Even on his deathbed, he denied the charges. *Why?* "Chandler..."

Wil and Anderson joined them. The private gripped a bloody arm. "He got me, sir."

At a glance, the wound didn't look serious. "We'll get you to town and cleaned up."

"Yes, sir."

A tremor racked through Chandler's body, then he lay still. The war had made him, and over a year after its end, he was a casualty. Some glory.

Chapter Nineteen

*W*HEN AMANDA HEARD HORSES in the farmyard, she stepped onto the porch. Sam, Wil, and Jesse—all alive and fit. She bolted down the steps to greet them.

Sam swept her into his arms and kissed her. "Chandler's dead. The nightmare is finally over, Amanda."

"Thank heaven." She spotted blood on Sam's uniform. *Don't ask.* He'd tell her about it in his own time, and he was kissing and holding her again. She resisted the urge to hug Wil and Jesse. "You must be famished. Come up to the house, and I'll fix something to eat."

"I appreciate the gracious offer," Wil replied, "but I'm aware that my presence isn't welcome around here. If you would show me where Emma's things are, I'll collect her and leave."

"I'll see to the horses," Jesse said, leading his and Sam's horse away.

Emma? Wil wasn't the sort of man to look after a toddler. "But you said 'take care of her.' "

"I thought you realized it was until I returned."

"No. I thought you meant . . ." Amanda shook her head. "You can't take Emma."

Distinctly harsh, Wil's eyes narrowed. "Why not? She *is* my daughter."

Not another child. "Because Alice wanted me to care for her."

"As I recall, Alice is buried on the hill and not in a position to state her feelings."

Amanda choked on her breath. "Wil, you don't seem to understand. A girl needs a woman's guidance."

"I have a female servant."

"That's not the same," Amanda demanded. "A servant won't advise her in the way a mother can. And once Emma becomes a woman, she'll need to discuss certain topics in a frank manner that wouldn't be proper coming from you."

His eyes only grew harsher. "What sort of impropriety do you think I'm going to take with my own daughter?" he asked with growing impatience. "Amanda, I thought you knew me better than that. Or am I supposed to pretend that I never had a second family as well?"

Sam stepped between them and squeezed her hand. "Emma will be all right."

"But . . ."

His grip tightened. "She'll be fine."

Amanda swallowed hard and reluctantly nodded. "I'll fetch her things." Tears formed in her eyes. Not only had she lost her sister, but she was losing her niece as well. She went up the steps, making certain not to meet Wil's gaze while passing him. Unable to make the tears stop, she trudged up to the second story bedroom where Rebecca and Emma played. Taking a deep breath and brushing back the tears, she gathered Emma's clothes together and placed them in a canvas bag. Rebecca raced over and stuffed her rag doll inside. "That's very kind of you, Rebecca."

"Papa." Emma squealed with delight when Wil appeared in the door frame. His face remained an emotionless mask, but Amanda detected his deliberate care and gentleness when he picked up the little girl.

"Wil . . ." She handed him the bag and cleared her throat. "Are you returning to Petersburg?"

"Soon."

"Do you mind if I come visit her before you leave?"

For the first time in her life, his face was totally unreadable. He finally nodded. "You're always welcome, Amanda." He turned.

"Wil, take care of yourself."

Without responding, he continued through the doorway. She heard his footsteps on the stairs and lifted the lace curtain on the window. Outside, Jesse waited beside Wil's horse. Wil tied Emma's bag to the saddle, then Jesse held Emma while he mounted. He grasped the little girl about the waist and held her snugly in the saddle. Dear Lord, her niece was going to be a tomboy, just like Alice.

As they rode off, Amanda's knees weakened, and she collapsed to the floor. The tears returned, but Sam appeared beside her and took her in his arms. "You knew about this, didn't you?"

He brushed the tears from her cheeks. "Not until we were heading back. It is his right."

"I realize that, but how will he care for her?"

"He's pretty resourceful. He'll find a way. I thought you knew that."

She had. Perhaps there was hope. Without Alice, Wil needed Emma. She had been wrong in trying to keep them apart.

Bored with the likes of Lawrence Greer, Holly stifled a yawn. After only two tumbles in bed, his energy was spent. "Lawrence, you appear distracted."

His russet-colored eyes blazed. "They brought Chandler in this morning."

Shocked by the news, Holly sat up. "Colonel Prescott has finally captured Doug Chandler?"

He shook his head. "Chandler's dead. Apparently Jesse Morgan shot him."

Doug dead? Not only had he made her suffer through the humiliation of servicing Bruce and Leon, she had needed to rid herself of an unwanted child as a result. Delighted that Doug had been brought to a just end, she felt a grin form on her mouth. "That's good news, isn't it?"

"It would be, but the colonel didn't bring in the flag."

"What flag?" she asked, suddenly confused.

"The Reb flag that Chandler used to carry around. I overheard one of the boys say that Jackson has it now. Did you know the colonel served with him before the war? Now, he's protecting the Rebel bastard."

Doug had always treated the flag like some sacred object. *Wil had it now?* Holly stroked Greer's chest. "No, I hadn't realized they once served together," she deliberately lied. "But you shouldn't fret about such things, Lawrence. Colonel Prescott would haul Wi—Mr. Jackson in, if he indeed possesses a Confederate flag."

Greer pounded a fist into his open hand. "Even after I shot him, what did he do? Hire the goddamned Reb to track down Chandler." He snorted. "Why would a wolf turn in his own kind?"

Holly paled. "You shot the colonel? I thought Doug..."

His eyes danced, and he traced his fingertips over her lips. "You're so beautiful. If you weren't married to that old man..."

Full and intimate, he kissed her on the mouth. "Lawrence," she said, shoving away from his embrace, "you flatter me, but are you telling me that *you* shot Colonel Prescott?"

"Why would you find that so surprising? I tried to bring the unrepentant Rebs to justice, but each time, the colonel let them go until he had no choice left."

Even on the scaffold, Chandler's group had denied most of the charges, except for stealing horses. Holly pasted on her most provocative smile and massaged Lawrence's shoulders. "I had no idea you were such a strong, decisive man," she purred.

His hands slid over her naked skin, caressing and fondling as they went. Good, he was taking the bait.

For over a year, Wil had waited for a pardon. Alice had worried that it might never arrive, and now that he held the official paper in his hands, she was gone. Crumpling the paper, he went into the study and tossed it in the bin. The sooner he returned to Petersburg, the better. The house had too many memories of courting Alice, then returning with her as his bride. He poured a drink.

"Mr. Wil!" Lily squealed from outside the door. Waving a letter in her hand, she dashed into the study and jumped up and down. "My Nathan, he alive. He in a hospital in Maryland. Had amnesia, but now he gonna come back to me."

So Lily was leaving him too. A man without a wife—what had he been thinking that he could raise a child on his own? He pulled several bills from his pocket. "It's all I have."

Lily stopped dancing. "I find a nanny to mind Miss Emma afore I leave."

"That won't be necessary. I should have left her with Amanda."

"Wil . . ."

His gaze went beyond Lily to Holly standing in the doorway.

Out of breath, Holly approached the desk. "I knocked, but no one answered."

"Back to check on me, Mrs. Whyte?"

"No, Wil." Holly cast a glance in Lily's direction. "Please, it's important that I speak with you—alone."

He waved Lily a dismissal. After the servant left the room, he said, "There's no need to fret about my well being. I'll return Emma to Amanda, so she won't grow up in a house full of impropriety. Mr. Whyte can foreclose on the house, and everyone shall be relieved that I leave Fredericksburg, once and for all."

"I know you'd rather wallow in self-pity, but Lawrence Greer shot Sam."

Had he heard correctly? "As in Lieutenant Greer, the young and promising Yankee officer?"

She nodded. "The one and the same. He also started the barn fire and strangled the barmaid. Even I thought Doug was lying about his boys being involved until now."

Suspect of her motives, Wil eased into the chair behind the desk. "If this is true, why aren't you telling Sam, instead of me?"

She licked her lips and shot a glance over her shoulder before answering. "Lawrence would have become suspicious if I had gone to headquarters. As an alibi, I told him that I'd find out if you have the Confederate flag. Someone needs to warn Sam before Lawrence decides to take the law into his own hands again."

Could he trust Holly? Before his death, Chandler had come to him for help. His mind—still clouded and slow to think—he doubted his own judgment, especially when it came to Holly. She could be luring him into Greer's hands. "I'll surrender the flag."

"Dammit Wil, have you been listening to anything I've said? I don't give a whit about any flag, but Lawrence does. He thinks Sam has been shirking his responsibilities. Doug's death isn't enough for him. Once he realizes that you definitely have the flag, then he'll come after you too."

Wil leaned back in the chair. "Let him come."

"He'll use an indirect route, so Sam will be forced to take action against you."

A man driven by fear would strike a weaker opponent. *Amanda*... "Can you watch Emma for me?"

"Of course."

He grabbed his gunbelt and hat, and sprinted for the door.

"Wil," Holly shouted after him, "don't do anything stupid—like get yourself killed."

Once in the stable, he replaced the mare's halter with a bridle. Without bothering to saddle the gray, he climbed aboard and took off at a gallop. Neither Sam nor Greer was at headquarters. *Amanda's farm.* After a couple of miles, the mare was already heavily lathered. He brought her down to a trot but continued to press her.

A red-tailed hawk floated overhead. *She was with him.* His decision to listen to Holly had been the correct one. "Be careful, Wil." It had been *her* voice. The hawk vanished in the sky.

He urged the mare for more speed. As he traveled toward the Wilderness, screams echoed in his mind. Not today. *Focus.* He tuned out the death cries and concentrated on the sound of rushing water. With the continued drought, the Rappahannock was barely more than a trickle. He stopped long enough to allow the mare to drink.

Water splashed as they forded across the river and up the bank to dry ground. He cued the mare to a canter. Hooves pounded against the sunbaked road until they turned up the tree-lined lane and charged into the farmyard. Wil slid from the mare's back and nearly fell to his knees. Between the heat and frantic ride, his head spun. Sweat poured from his body, and he staggered up the brick walk. Out of breath and ready to succumb to the heat, he made it to the steps. Almost there, but he had to sit before he collapsed. "Amanda!"

"Wil?"

Thank God, she was all right. Seeing his need, she brought him a metal dipper. Cool water at last—he emptied the dipper.

"Wil, has something happened to Emma?"

He shook his head. "Greer . . ." His throat scratched, and he could barely speak.

Amanda retreated to the house and brought him another dipper full of water. She sat beside him on the steps as he drank his fill. "What about Lieutenant Greer?"

"He shot Sam."

Her mouth dropped open. "Sam? Are you certain?"

Before he could respond, three horses trotted into the farmyard. Flanked by Greer and Private Anderson, Sam dismounted and tied his horse to the rail. Holly *had* fed him false information.

"Jackson," Sam said evenly as he approached, "I think you know why we're here."

Still wobbly, Wil stood. "I have a fair idea."

Greer and Anderson shoved him against a tree and began searching him. They confiscated his pistol.

From behind him, Amanda said, "Sam, is this really necessary?"

"He's in possession of Chandler's flag."

"I know," Amanda responded. "I was there when Mr. Chandler gave it to him. Arrest me too."

When they were satisfied that he carried no other weapons, Wil was allowed to turn around. Greer had a smug grin on his face as they clamped shackles around his wrists.

"Sam! Do something!"

"It's out of my hands, Amanda. Jackson, if you'll cooperate . . ."

Their rivalry for the love of a woman had made them enemies—something fighting a war on opposite sides couldn't do. "I won't give you any trouble. You already know that."

Stern and unbending, Sam asked, "Where's the flag?"

"Back at the house. It's in the study. You won't have any difficulty finding it."

"Greer, fetch it. Anderson and I will see to the prisoner."

The lieutenant saluted. "Yes, sir." He strode to his horse.

Amanda stepped between them. "Sam, I can't believe you're arresting Wil."

Wil shot her a glance. "Please don't get involved, Amanda."

Her hands went to her hips. "I'm already involved. Sam . . ."

Sam glanced over his shoulder. Greer was astride his horse and squeezed it to a trot. "Amanda, go inside." In a lower voice, he warned, "Shut the door and make certain everyone is down."

She knitted her brows together in confusion. "Down?"

"Just do as I say—now, and hopefully no one will get hurt." This time, Amanda obeyed and went up the steps to the house. Sam unlocked the chains around Wil's wrists. "Holly came to me first," he explained.

"Then you know about Greer?"

The chains clanked to the ground. "I do, but besides Holly's word, I have no proof. After I thought about her allegations, Chandler's dying words finally made sense. I thank you for trying to warn me, but if my lieutenant plays true to form, we're all in serious danger. Anderson, return the general's side arm, then go inside and keep watch over my family."

The private handed Wil his pistol, then went inside.

"Now what?" Wil asked, rehosltering his pistol.

"As you might have guessed, Greer has no love for Southerners, or someone like me, who believes the citizens should be treated with respect, rather than punished. If you're willing to help me, I think we can draw Greer out."

"You have my cooperation."

"I was reasonably certain you would help." Sam's blue eyes flickered thoughtfully. "Captain, if anything should happen . . ."

"Don't say it."

Sam held up a hand. "You know it needs to be. Take care of her in the way she deserves."

Wil had been wrong. Even their rivalry for Amanda hadn't made them enemies. "That won't be necessary . . ."

"Spare me. You've been a soldier most of your life. You know exactly what it's like to get that feeling of your own death."

All too well. "I also know those feelings have yet to become fact."

With a punch to Wil's arm, Sam laughed. "Let's flush out a wayward lieutenant." They traveled the brick walk to their waiting horses. "Need a saddle, Jackson?"

Wil grasped the mare's mane and climbed aboard. "It's the way I learned to ride. Unlike you Yanks that couldn't even tell which end was which at West Point." Sam winced, and as Wil reined the gray around, he saw a curtain flutter in the house. Amanda stood at the window, watching them. She was the reason he had learned to open his heart—brief though that time had been. A debt that he could repay in only one way.

Alongside Sam, Wil cued his mare to a trot down the lane. Like all too many times before a battle, the road was quiet. Not even a bird sang in the summer heat. After a couple of miles, they brought their horses to a walk. Wil had that gnawing feeling in his gut the enemy was near. He traded glances with Sam. No words were necessary. Also a seasoned veteran, he felt it too.

As he surveyed the row of trees beside the road, Wil drew his pistol. Yellow jackets buzzed and cicadas echoed a chorus. The only other sound was their ragged breathing.

"I almost expect to hear that godawful Rebel yell," Sam muttered under his breath.

"I can try to accommodate."

"Jackson . . . ," Sam scoffed. He was silent a minute before continuing, "I wanted to kill you."

The admission only revived the memory of sitting on the steps, beside Amanda when she had uttered those fateful words. "*Touché*, how do you think I felt when I discovered that she carried your child?"

Sam met his gaze, but only momentarily before scanning the forest again. "Yet you helped her get a message across the lines to me with the news."

"I would have challenged you to a duel to protect her honor if you hadn't married her."

"It seems we have both put on a pretty poor show," Sam said with regret.

"And if we don't clear our heads for the task ahead, we'll both wind up dead." The mare sensed Wil's tension and pranced nervously on her feet. "Sam, I wish to be buried in Virginia—next to Alice."

"Now, who's talking nonsense?"

"You know it's the way things are meant to be." Wil heard a horse nicker from the woods.

"Captain..."

Wil waved for silence. Sam nodded that he had heard it too. They brought their horses to a halt, and Sam withdrew his rifle. Wil checked to his left, then his right. The forest could easily provide cover for a man and horse. Another nicker. *Behind them.*

Without thinking his action through, Wil launched himself across Sam's horse, sending both of them flying. Gunfire, then pain.

Another shot responded. *He needed her help.* Private Anderson had refused to disobey orders and leave the house, forcing Amanda to enlist Jesse's aid. She had insisted on bringing the wagon, and as they rounded the bend, her heart nearly stopped. Lieutenant Greer sprawled near the edge of the road with unseeing eyes staring up at the sky. The front of Sam's uniform was covered in blood. Briefly, she thought he had been wounded, then realized he was bent over a prone form.

"Wil!" She scrambled from the wagon.

Sam looked up as she ran in his direction. "The bullet was meant for me, Amanda."

"For you?" During the Mexican War, Wil had taken a bullet for her first husband and nearly died. Her legs sagged, and she dropped to the ground beside him. He was face down in the dirt with Sam pressing a crimson cloth to his back. Her heart fluttered. "He's alive?"

"Barely."

"Jesse..."

But Jesse was already bringing the blanket from the wagon. The men lifted Wil onto the blanket and hoisted it to the wagon bed. Amanda climbed in beside him. Axles groaned as Sam flicked the reins to the team. The wagon bumped along, and Amanda tore her petticoat and pressed the clean cloth to Wil's back. The bleeding slowed, and she said a thankful prayer. Helpless to do more, she wondered if this was how Alice had felt after he had been pulled from the river.

She grasped his hand. A light squeeze returned, but it had definitely been there. "I'm here, Wil."

The wagon hit a rut, and Wil groaned. He spoke, but his voice was so soft she couldn't make out his words. She leaned closer to hear him better. "Coward's way."

His meaning was clear. Soldiers considered a bullet in the back a coward's death. "I don't want to hear such words coming from your mouth. You saved Sam's life."

A slight smile appeared on his lips. "Didn't know . . . if I was . . . in time."

Tears streaked her cheeks. She brushed them away, and like so many times in the hospitals during the war, she held his hand and whispered words of comfort. Unlike the hospitals, her patient wasn't a stranger, and she feared that Wil had chosen death over life. Each jolt in the road made him writhe. She wished the wagon could go faster. He might not last the trip into town.

Wil's eyes rolled up in his head, and his muscles began to quiver violently. *A death spasm.* "Wil, I'll not have you die in front of me."

His shaking stopped, and he gasped for breath. Bleeding from the wound increased, and she placed a fresh cloth to it. His eyes closed, then flickered open again. A euphoric grin crossed his face. "I saw Alice."

"If you saw her, she's telling you to stay here. Emma needs you."

Finally, the wagon grated to a halt outside Doctor Gordon's office. A man with a gray beard and spectacles motioned for the men to carry Wil inside. In a back room, they put Wil on a surgical table. The doctor began to examine him. "Mrs. Prescott, as I recall you assisted in the hospitals. I'd like for you to assist me now."

Amanda pressed a hand to her chest. "Assist you?"

"I require assistance." Doctor Gordon laid out his surgical instruments beside the table, then began peeling away Wil's sack coat and shirt.

Sam grasped her arm. "I'll help, Amanda."

She took a deep breath. "No, I'll assist. You wait outside." Anticipating before the order came, Amanda found the brandy and poured a glass. Over by the table, she lifted Wil's head and helped him drink. The Nez Percé medicine pouch tied around his neck caught her eye. For strength—she hoped the mountain lion's influence was stronger than the hawk had been for Alice.

The doctor showed her how to hold the cloth cone over Wil's nose and mouth. During the war, assistant surgeons had taken on the responsibility. Her hands trembled as Doctor Gordon poured the chloroform into the cone. Some men went half-crazed when the chloroform was administered, others muttered obscenities. Except for muscles relaxing, Wil had no reaction. *He was dead.*

As if reading her thoughts, the doctor checked Wil's pulse. "He's still with us." The doctor turned Wil onto his stomach and took a probe to the wound in his back. His hands worked quickly and efficiently. He called for her to sponge blood away. Blood spurted. He tied the bleeding off, then with a clank, he dropped a lead bullet into a pan. She swabbed more blood away, and Doctor Gordon continued sewing and tying. He closed the wound. "If you would be so kind as to fetch your husband, we'll take him into the other room, and I'll watch him while he recovers."

"Of course, doctor."

Amanda went into the outer office where Sam and Jesse waited. Upon hearing the instructions, they vanished to aid the doctor. Exhausted physically and mentally, Amanda sank into a leather chair. When Sam returned, he was still covered in Wil's blood. He sat beside her and grasped her hand. "Amanda, if he lives, I'll stand aside."

She gave his hand a reassuring squeeze. "I gave you a promise. I meant it."

"I don't want to hold you to it, if you prefer..." His voice cracked.

Turning to him, she gripped both of his hands in hers. "I love you. I always have."

"You love him too."

But the division of her heart had nearly destroyed all of them. It's what Alice had meant by letting Wil go. "Sam, he didn't do this for me, but *us*. And now *we* need to convince him that he has a reason to live."

"How?"

"There's someone else that he still cares about—Emma. If you don't mind, I'll run and fetch her."

"I'll help you."

She tightened the grip on his hand. For so long, the truth had eluded her. They were stronger—together.

A hawk floated overhead. All sensation in his hands was gone, and his feet were numb. Wil's mind drifted, and he thought of *her*. The hawk lifted him toward the sky. Once he was airborne, the passage of time had little meaning. Voices whispered in the wind, and he heard someone call his name while he soared with the hawk.

"Wil . . ." It was *her*, and she sounded frantic. "Wil, please answer."

"Alice?"

Her auburn hair was pulled away from her face, and her smile—radiant. She wrapped her cloak around him and cradled him in her arms. "Sam's gone for help. Everything shall be all right now."

"Alice, how can you be here?"

She hushed him. "Save your strength."

The Rappahannock waters had nearly drowned him. Yet, this wasn't the way things had happened. He stroked her cheek. "I must be dead."

"Remember the power of the hawk," she whispered.

The past. She had come to him in the only way possible, and he had been ready to die before she had pulled him from the river muck. "I want to join you."

With his admission, she frowned. "Wil, what glory comes from war?"

Confused, he repeated the question before answering, "There is no glory—only death."

Her fingers stroked through his hair. She hugged him tighter. "That's where you're wrong. If it hadn't been for the war, our paths wouldn't have crossed so frequently. We would have never had Emma. You promised that you would cherish her."

"I do, but she's better off with Amanda."

"She needs her papa's love." Alice's words sounded as if they had been sent on the wind. She no longer held him, but was beside him. Glistening in the light, her fingers stretched toward him. Wil reached out to her. She whispered her love. Their fingertips nearly touched, but the shimmering changed to a feathered wing. With a cry, the hawk spread her wings and took to the sky, and his hand closed over emptiness. A red tail feather glided to the ground.

Wil let out an anguished groan. It wasn't *her,* but . . ."Amanda." He no longer regretted burning the letter. In his hand was the feather from the hawk. His midsection was swathed in bandages, and beside him sat Amanda.

"Wil, what was this foolish notion you got in your head about taking a bullet intended for Sam?"

He grieved for the hawk. "I owed it to you to make things right."

She gripped his hand. "The only regret I have is the pain we caused others."

His gaze met hers. Her green eyes reminded him of Alice. He *had* loved them both. "Amanda . . ."

"I've brought Emma."

"Emma?" He had ruined so many lives, and he had nearly followed the same course with his own daughter. "You were right. She needs a woman's guidance."

"I was wrong." Wil opened his mouth to object, but Amanda continued, "Yes, I said wrong. I shouldn't have tried to keep you apart. I can see how much she loves you. Without her mama, she *needs* her papa."

The same words Alice had whispered. Unconvinced, Wil reminded Amanda, "You wanted a child, and you're better able to care for her."

She shook her head. "Don't get me wrong—I love Emma, but I want a child of my own. You're Emma's papa. She's your responsibility. Sam . . ."

Sam entered the room, holding Emma. His daughter gave an excited shriek upon seeing him. Wil attempted to rise, but pain forced him to fall back to the cot.

"I want to thank you for what you did, Captain," Sam said, bringing Emma over to him, "but you shouldn't have taken a risk like that." He placed the toddler in Wil's arms and saluted, then clasped Amanda's hand.

Overcome by the moment, Wil swallowed hard. If Alice had been present, she would have joked about making him speechless. Although Emma's hair was black like his and her skin had the same coppery cast, her eyes were green like her mother's. Born in the midst of a siege on a sleeting wintery night, she was the force that had kept him going after Alice's death. And he had made Alice a promise. With a new resolve to raise his daughter on his own, he thought he heard the cry of the hawk.

Epilogue

July 1881

*H*IGHLY CRITICAL OF HER REFLECTION, Amanda twisted and turned in front of the mirror. The red-satin dress had a wide belt with a sash bow at the back. Streaks of gray lined her hair. She sighed. Nothing could turn back the clock and magically make her thirty again.

"Mama." With a shy smile, Rebecca poked her head in. "How do I look?" Attired in a plain wrapper to try to conceal the fact that she was in a family way, her daughter stepped into the room.

"You look lovely, Rebecca," Amanda said.

"I only wish Jonathan were here." Married for a year, Rebecca suffered the pangs of her first separation while her husband was away on a business trip to Richmond.

"I remember the feeling all too well." Only her separations had been due to the war, and now . . .

As if reading her face, Rebecca whispered, "I miss Papa too."

Nearly three years before, Sam had succumbed to a bout with pneumonia. Amanda had buried her grief and loneliness in her children and to running the farm. "This is supposed to be a happy occasion. He's here in spirit."

Trotting hooves entered the lane, and Rebecca parted the lace curtain. "They're here!"

If it hadn't been for the fact that Rebecca was heavy with child, Amanda swore to herself that her dark-haired daughter would have jumped up and down. Even then, Rebecca dashed from the bedroom swifter than she would have thought possible.

Ten years had passed since Wil had taken Emma from Virginia and followed the railroad west. Sporadically throughout the years, she had received Emma's drawings and paintings, depicting a vanishing way of life—the Indians. As the girl grew, her artistry became more sophisticated.

But what of Wil? After Sam's death, she had expected to hear from Wil—something, anything, even if it was nothing more than his condolences. If it hadn't been for Emma's communications, she would have never known that *he* was still alive. Then, earlier in the week from what seemed out of nowhere a wire had arrived, stating that he and Emma would be in Virginia.

After one quick last glimpse in the mirror, Amanda headed for the stairs. Even though the July heat was stifling, she broke into a cold sweat. How should she greet Wil? Uncertain whether to be elated or vexed by his visit, she would raise her hand but would decide at a moment's notice whether it was for him to kiss or for slapping his cheek.

Once she reached the front door, she saw Rebecca near the rose-covered trellis at the end of the brick walk. A carriage halted by the gate. Her heart pounded, but Amanda maintained a steady pace in an attempt to not appear overeager. A young lady with her long black hair pulled away from her face leaned out the window and waved.

"Emma?" The driver helped her from the carriage, and Amanda blinked in disbelief. The girl had grown into a woman. At sixteen, her niece was of a slender build like Alice, but she had the prominent cheekbones from Wil's Cherokee heritage. Expecting Wil to be right behind her, Amanda craned her neck in anticipation, while Rebecca greeted Emma. When her turn came, she gave Emma a bear hug. "You've grown into a fine woman, Miss Emma, but where's your papa?"

"He'll be along. I want to visit my mama's grave," she replied.

So Wil hadn't changed. To her knowledge, he had never visited the grave since the day Alice was buried. She suspected that it was due to fear that he might reveal emotions he didn't care to let anyone else see. "I'll take you there, but I'm sure you've had an exhausting trip. Rebecca has made some lemonade."

"Thank you, Aunt Amanda, but I'm not tired."

Emma's carefree enthusiasm reminded her of Alice. Amanda grasped her niece's hand. Rebecca joined them as they made the trek to the knoll behind the house to the family graveyard. As they reached the top of the hill, Emma looked strangely out of place. Her dress was of the current fashion with a sheer overskirt and bustle, but intertwined in her hair was a red-tail feather that blew in the gentle summer breeze.

Rebecca stopped briefly beside Sam's grave and bowed her head. His final wish had been to be buried in Virginia—his adopted home. So many loved ones—gone. Even after three years, she still expected Sam to come riding up the lane. Emma stared pensively at Alice's grave. Amanda cleared her throat. "I know you never really knew her . . ."

A smile spread across Emma's face. "But I do know her. Papa tells me stories, and she speaks to me frequently." She placed a hand over her heart. "In here."

The sun sank in the sky, cooling off the day a little. Together the three of them retraced their steps down the hill. At the bottom stood a man holding the reins of a spotted horse. Wil must have brought the Appaloosa from the west. Upon first sight, Amanda had to blink away a vision of him dressed in Confederate gray. A neatly trimmed moustache lined his upper lip, and the waves in his hair matched the black depths of a gleam in his eyes. Tufts of gray had formed near his temple and the lines around his eyes were a little deeper than she remembered, but he remained delightfully handsome.

Who had she been fooling? She had *wanted* to see him, or she wouldn't have chosen the red dress. The fact that he had remained silent for so long after Sam's death had only deepened the hurt of her loss.

With a smile, Wil lowered his hat. Amusement danced in his eyes. "Amanda, I apologize for arriving late. I trust that I haven't missed supper."

"Wil, you rascal. You've been gone for ten years, and all you can think of is your stomach." Ready to slap his cheek, she raised her hand. With a slight bow, he grinned as if he had read her thoughts. He took her hand in his and kissed it. Suddenly, her heart was no longer pounding, but fluttering. *Careful.* It had been too long, and their feelings had likely changed. She motioned to Rebecca. "You remember Rebecca?"

He took Rebecca's hand. "This beautiful young woman is Rebecca?"

Always the charmer—he definitely hadn't changed.

"Come," Amanda said. "I'll take you to see Jesse. I'm sure Emma has told you that he married a local girl, Eliza, and they have two boys and a girl."

After making the rounds of reacquainting with old friends and meeting new ones, they feasted. Jesse had roasted a pig over an open fire, and Amanda's son, Charles, played the fiddle. At thirteen, he was at that tall, gawky stage that adolescent boys went through, but he had already become an accomplished fiddler. Jesse's eldest, James, accompanied Charles, strumming the banjo.

Music and laughter made Amanda yearn for absent loved ones and friends.

"Amanda . . ." Even after all these years away from South Carolina, Wil had retained his Charleston accent. "You have a handsome son."

Delighted with his company, she felt her melancholy fading. They retreated to the chairs on the porch. With an ale in hand, Wil listened while she told him stories of Jesse teaching Sam how to run a farm after he had resigned his commission. Upon Ezra's death, the former slave cabins were demolished, and Jesse had built a house for his family in the walnut grove. And as he had already likely noticed, Rebecca was about to make her a grandma. "Wil, I have something for you."

He arched a curious brow.

"Wait here." Amanda retreated to the study. From a desk drawer, she retrieved the Confederate battle flag, folded to prominently display three stars. She returned to the porch and handed it to Wil. "It's from Sam."

For a moment, Wil clutched the flag and stared at it in silence. He swallowed hard, then he became uncharacteristically talkative, entertaining her with tales of the West and Indians. He went on to tell her about strong-willed Emma, and the danger she encountered with her boastful pride in her Cherokee heritage.

Amanda couldn't help, but laugh. "Like father, like daughter."

"I've never relayed that fact to anyone but those I could trust. Killing Indians is somewhat of a fashion of late."

In reality, she had known the killing and bloodshed hadn't ended with the war, but Wil's words reminded her of that fact. Such a terrible, tragic waste. Amanda glanced up. The music had stopped, and everyone had disappeared, including Emma. "It seems we're the only ones left at the party."

Wil checked his pocket watch and stood. "It's after midnight. Amanda, I apologize for keeping you up so late."

Sad the evening had to end, Amanda said, "I'll fetch Emma. I presume she went inside with Rebecca."

Wil merely shrugged. "She has a habit of vanishing when I'm in the company of a beautiful woman."

Warmth rose in her cheeks. After all these years, he could still make her blush, and for the first time since he had nearly died in Doctor Gordon's office, she was alone with Wil. "Old and fat is more like it," she lamented.

A suggestive grin spread across his face. "A few gray hairs—perhaps, but you are not old or fat, Amanda."

There it was—the way he said her name was reminiscent of earlier times. "You can't just return after all these years and expect our feelings to remain unchanged."

"I meant no offense. Thank you for a pleasant evening. Now, I really should be returning to town." As he went down the steps, she envisioned spurs jingling and a sword at his side, clanking. "If you don't mind, I think Emma might like to spend another couple of days here."

She blinked away the image. "Of course. Then where are you off to?"

"Colorado or Dakota."

The gate creaked. *He was leaving,* and she was letting him pass from her life yet again. Hadn't they learned any lessons? She ran after him. "Wil, why didn't you ever contact me after Sam died?"

He lowered his hat once more and shifted on his feet. "It wouldn't have been proper."

"Proper? From the man who scorns propriety?"

"Amanda, I was over two thousand miles away when I received the news. What could I have done? If I had returned, I would have only confused you as I had before. I vowed to myself to never put you through that again."

"But Sam's been gone for three years."

"And how long does it take for a broken heart to mend?"

Definitely not the sort of response that she had expected from Wil. "You know what it's like—the tears, the ache, and feeling so alone. After a while, a sense of purpose returns, and fond memories emerge. I still miss him, but you were my friend long before he was my husband."

"Then I apologize for having let you down, but my memories of our friendship are of a different nature."

His heart, not hers. "So why did you decide to visit now?"

"My daughter wished to visit her mother's grave." His black eyes grew piercing, but he bowed and kissed her hand. "It has been a most delightful evening. I bid you goodnight."

The tickle of his moustache made her shiver. She withdrew her hand from his grip. "And you're still afraid."

He straightened. "Of what?"

"Of loving someone—the way you did Peopeo—or Alice." Too many years had passed, and she feared she had said too much, too soon.

"Amanda," Wil said, taking a deep breath, "I'm still uncomfortable talking about Peopeo. I reckon I always will be, but I've seen what the army has done to her people. The Nez Percé will likely never see the Wallowa Valley again. For Emma's sake, I have learned to speak about Alice with little effort, but I should have known the hawk would force me to confront the past. What was it you said? If we didn't resolve issues during the war, we're left facing them now."

She recalled the words—after she had lost her second son. "Wil..."

He held up a hand to let him finish. "When I learned that Sam had died, I knew you'd expect to hear from me. Forgive my weakness, but I couldn't be the friend that you needed, any more than you could have consoled me after Alice's death. My motives would have been suspect, and with good reason."

He still loved her. "Then instead of rushing off to distant areas of the country, pretending nothing has ever happened, why don't we take the time to get to know one another again? It's been a long time since I've been courted."

His gaze shifted to the ground. She *had* said too much. Finally, he looked up and said, "Just as long as you don't expect me to wait too long before I whisk you off your feet again."

Amanda couldn't help but laugh. "I fancy at our age that would be quite a sight." Her arms went about his waist, and he leaned down and sought her mouth. When their kiss ended, she saw a flicker of light from the front window and a face peering out. Emma had a satisfied smile on her face. Through the power of the hawk, Amanda had the distinct feeling that the mountain lion would no longer be solitary.

Historical Note

Beyond the political aspect, very little has been written about Reconstruction. Even the Historical Society of Virginia has a small exhibit devoted to the era. Complicating matters even further, many of the diaries dating from the Civil War ceased abruptly at the war's end. The South was beaten, and many diary writers were too despondent or fearful to continue their journals.

After President Lincoln's assassination, what weighed on most Southerners' minds was the fear of the unknown. Few modern readers realize that the former Confederate states did not automatically reenter the Union. At the outset of Reconstruction, they were unrecognized states under military rule. While Virginia had fewer violent uprisings than some Southern states, due to the fact that more than fifty percent of the battles were fought on her soil, the state faced devastation on enormous scale.

As in the aftermath of any war, returning soldiers were in need of employment, but with an equally ruined economy, little money was available to pay wages. Buildings were damaged or destroyed, and shortages abounded—food, clothing, farm implements, and livestock. Famine was a serious threat. The military government distributed rations to fend off starvation, but the effort was disorganized and incomplete.

Taxes skyrocketed and inflation was rampant. Some texts claim that carpetbaggers appeared around 1867. My research suggests they descended upon the South at the close of the war. In fact, sutlers that had traveled with the Union armies were among the first to take advantage of the war-torn regions. Tourists also came in hoards.

Southern people resented Northern occupation, and Northern soldiers merely wished to return home, which combined to set off a variety of conflicts. Former Confederate politicians and officers—colonels and above, and former West Point officers—were reduced to non-citizen status. Many fled the country, fearful of eventually being tried for treason. Wil's experience of waiting more than a year for a pardon is realistic.

The shanty village is fictional, but is based on the facts from the era. Many former slaves took refuge near Northern soldiers' encampments or formed villages near cities. Sophia Hatch is the lone historical character in *Glory & Promise*. She came to Fredericksburg to educate the former slaves, where a school was eventually named in her honor. In reality, though, she moved to the area at the war's end, rather than several months later as portrayed here.

During the first years following the war, there was much confusion in the judicial system. Local courts were quickly reinstated, and these ruled on petty crimes. More serious violations were often juggled between local and military courts until a legal system was firmly reestablished. A military court would have ruled in a case similar to the events portrayed in *Glory & Promise*. However, capital hearings were held in Richmond and usually dragged on for many months, so in that sense, my account is fictional.

Throughout several counties in central Virginia an outbreak of typhoid actually occurred, and the lack of rain as depicted in the story was the beginning of a three-year drought. Both, of course, added to the already harsh living conditions. In true Southern spirit, parties by the citizens continued in an attempt to return to a normal life. While fraternization between citizens and Northern soldiers was socially frowned upon, it did occur and with nature taking its course, it sometimes led to love and marriage.

As in my previous books, I try to make no statement about Reconstruction itself. It is a dark, often overlooked era in U.S. history, and I have merely attempted to portray the people who lived through it.

Best regards,
Kim Murphy

Acknowledgements

My deepest appreciation goes to John Douglas Smith, author of a Ph.D. dissertation entitled "Virginia during Reconstruction, 1865-1870: A Political, Economic and Social Study." Without this dusty tome buried deep within the bowels of the University of Virginia Library, I would have overlooked many key period sources. Dr. Smith's invaluable research was by far the most comprehensive piece that I was able to uncover focusing specifically on Virginia and her people of the era.

A special thank you goes to my editors, K.A. Corlett, Catherine Karp, and Susan Lupsha, my cover designer, Mayapriya Long, and Doug and Kate Moore for providing a photograph for the cover art. As usual, I mostly wish to thank my family: my son, Bryan, and especially my husband, Pat; both of whom are often wondering if I will ever rejoin the twenty-first century.